The three stories in this volume feature many of J.T. Edson's most popular and best loved characters – DUSTY FOG, MARK COUNTER, THE YSABEL KID, and other well loved figures from the world of J.T. Edson.

But above all they recount the exploits of WACO, young, wild, courageous, and rapidly earning his place as one of the most valuable members of The Floating Outfit.

Also available from Corgi Books:

J.T. EDSON OMNIBUS VOLUME 1
J.T. EDSON OMNIBUS VOLUME 2
J.T. EDSON OMNIBUS VOLUME 3

*Title awaiting publication

J.T. EDSON OMNIBUS
Volume 4

TRIGGER FAST
THE MAKING OF A LAWMAN
WACO'S DEBT

CORGI BOOKS

J.T. EDSON Omnibus Volume 4

A CORGI BOOK o 552 13605 o

TRIGGER FAST and WACO'S DEBT originally published in Great Britain by Brown Watson Ltd.

PRINTING HISTORY – TRIGGER FAST

Brown Watson edition published 1964
Corgi edition published 1969
Corgi edition reprinted 1972
Corgi edition reprinted 1976

PRINTING HISTORY – THE MAKING OF A LAWMAN

Corgi edition published 1968
Corgi edition reissued 1973
Corgi edition reprinted 1978

PRINTING HISTORY – WACO'S DEBT

Corgi edition published 1968
Corgi edition reprinted 1969
Corgi edition reprinted 1972
Corgi edition reprinted 1976

Corgi Omnibus edition published 1990

This book is set in Plantin and Baskerville

Corgi Books are published by Transworld Publishers Ltd., 61–63 Uxbridge Road, Ealing, London W5 5SA, in Australia by Transworld Publishers (Australia) Pty. Ltd., 15–23 Helles Avenue, Moorebank, NSW 2170, and in New Zealand by Transworld Publishers (N.Z.) Ltd., Cnr. Moselle and Waipareira Avenues, Henderson, Auckland.

Printed and bound in Great Britain by
Cox & Wyman Ltd., Reading, Berks.

Trigger Fast

CHAPTER ONE

The Rosemary-Jo Lament

STANDING waist deep in the cool clear water of the swimming hole Freda Lasalle rubbed soap over her slender, naked young body. Overhead the sun, not yet at noonday height, gave forth enough warmth to make this outdoor bathing both pleasant and possible.

Only rarely these days did Freda, daughter of the ranch's owner and sole woman of the house since the death of her mother, have a chance to bathe and swim in such complete freedom. The two cowhands her father hired were poor spirited men who would be only too willing to hide and watch her bathe, drooling over the sight of her naked beauty. However, her father took the two men to town with him earlier that morning and she had the ranch to herself.

Freda did not intend to miss such a chance. She had cleaned out the kitchen stove as her first chore after breakfast and wanted to wash the soot and grime from her body. Until her father returned from Barlock with supplies she could do nothing about making a meal so she took the time to bathe, stripping off her clothes in the house and running naked to the water, then plunging in to splash happily around.

The girl made an attractive picture as she stood working the soap lather into her short brown hair, although the only witness appeared to be the redbone hound which lay on the bank and watched her. She stood almost five foot six, a slim, willowy girl in her late teens, blossoming forth into full womanhood. Her face had charm, without being out and out beautiful. It was a warm, friendly face, one a man would not easily forget. Given another couple of years her figure would fully ripen and as yet the Texas Panhandle weather had not

1

made her skin coarse or harshened the texture of her hair.

She looked at the small frame house with some pride, then ducked her head under the water to rinse the soap from her hair. The house might be small, but she kept it spotlessly clean and neat. Between the stream and the house stood a small pole corral, empty now, but large enough to hold the small remuda and harness horses they owned. To one side of the house stood a barn, stable and a couple more small wooden buildings, to the rear was a chicken pen and beyond that a backhouse.

On the side of the river away from her home a bank rose fairly steep in most places, but sloping down more gently to a ford below the swimming hole. Beyond the bank, a mile away, lay the two mile wide strip along which, by convention, the cattle herds stuck as they trailed north by the Lasalle place to the Kansas railheads. The passing herds caused little trouble and, as yet, the first of the new season had not come up from southern Texas.

Ever since her father came home from a Yankee prisoner-of-war camp, a sick man whose doctor warned he must get out into the dry plains country or die, this small ranch had been Freda's home. In the early days their neighbours helped them build the house, showed Lasalle much he needed to know, joined in with such communal tasks as gathering the free-grazing herds of cattle and cutting out each other's stock. The great trail drives wending their way north proved to be a boon to the small ranchers in this section. To the trail bosses they sold their surplus stocks, thus saving the expense of shipping the cattle north to market. True they might have made more money in Kansas, but the long drive north would eat that same money up, even if a small outfit handling maybe a couple of hundred head could have got through alone. Often too the trail bosses would turn over unwanted calves born on the way north and in that way helped bring new blood to the range.

In many ways it had been a lonely life for Freda, especially since her mother died. She grew up in healthy surroundings, free as a bird. Before her mother died she rode the range like a man, she could handle a horse, use a shotgun well enough and also could cook, mend or make clothes, do the chores a woman in a lonely ranch was expected to do.

Now she wondered how long the happy life might continue. To the north and west ran the great Double K ranch, the Lindon Land Grant, one of the huge open-range outfits for which

Texas had long been famous. When Lindon owned and ran it the Double K took its share in the local round-ups, helping out the smaller and less fortunate folk. Then old man Lindon died and his sole kin, back east, sold out the holding to an Englishman called Sir James Keller. At least so rumour had it for nobody had seen the mysterious new owner.

They felt his presence though. Two days before Brent Mallick, the local Land Agent and attorney for the Double K, paid a visit to Lasalle's and offered to buy them out. Freda remembered how Mallick smiled when her father refused the offer. There had been neither amusement nor friendship in the smile, nor on the faces of the two tough looking men who accompanied Mallick. She shuddered as she thought of Mallick's smile, with its implied threat—

"A Yankee rode into West Texas,
A mean kind of cuss and real sly,
He fell in love with sweet Rosemary-Jo,
Then turned and told her goodbye."

The redbone hound came to his feet even before Freda heard the pleasant tenor voice singing an old cowhand song. She threw a startled glance to where the bank of the stream hid the singer from view. From the sound of his voice he must be coming straight towards the house.

"So Rosemary-Jo told her tough pappy,
Who said, 'Why *hombre* that's bad,
In tears you done left my Rosemary-Jo,
No Yankee can make my gal sad.' "

The second verse of the Rosemary-Jo Lament came as Freda hurriedly waded out of the water. She grabbed up the towel from the shore and then ran for the house, the redbone following and helping scatter the chickens which scratched and pecked before the house.

"He whipped out his two trusty hawg-legs,
At which he warn't never slow,
When that Yankee done saw them a-spitting,
He said, 'It is time for to go!' "

* * *

Even as Freda reached the house and dashed inside, slamming the door behind her, she heard another verse of the song. The windows of the room stood open and as she could hear the singer clearly, she knew he must be close. She could hear the sound of more than one horse's hooves.

> "He jumped on his fast running pinto,
> Lit out like hell for the west,
> When Rosemary-Jo got her a fortune,
> He come back and said, 'I love you best.' "

Still drying herself Freda went to where she could peer out of a window and see the top of the river bank. Three riders came into sight, halting their horses at the head of the slope. Three cowhands from their dress, each astride a big, fine looking horse. The singer led a packpony which looked to be carrying their warbags and bed-rolls.

> " 'No no' cried she in a minute,
> 'I love me a Texan so sweet,
> And I'm going down to San Antone town,
> My sweet, loving Texan to meet.' "

The singer lounged in his saddle at the left of the party. Sitting his huge white stallion with easy grace, there appeared to be something wild, almost alien about him. His black, low-crowned, wide-brimmed Stetson hat thrust back from curly hair so black it almost shone blue in the light and the face it framed looked to be Indian dark, very handsome, babyishly innocent and young. From hat, down through tight rolled bandana, shirt, gunbelt, levis trousers, to boots he wore but one colour, black. The blackness was relieved only by the white, ivory she guessed, hilt of the bowie knife at his left side and the walnut grips of the old Colt Dragoon revolver hanging at his right.

The young rider's white horse moved restlessly, allowing her to see the low horned, double girthed Texas rig. That went without saying, a man who dressed in such a manner would use that kind of saddle. She also saw the butt of a rifle under the rider's left leg.

* * *

"So the Yankee went to the back country,
He met an old pal, Bandy Parr,
Who captained the Davis' State Police,
And a meeting they held in the bar."

They did not appear to be in any hurry, she thought, finishing drying herself and grabbing up clothing. The rider at the right side took her attention next for she could never recollect seeing a finer figure of a man. He towered over the other two, three inches at least over the six-foot level. For all his great size, the width of his shoulders, the tapering to a slim waist, he sat his seventeen hand bloodbay stallion with easy grace. He looked to be a light rider, the sort of man who took less out of his mount than a smaller, though less skillful person.

His costly white Stetson carried a silver concha decorated band, was on the same pattern as the other two's. It set on a head of golden blond hair, shading a face which had a classic, handsome cast of feature like those of a Greek god of old. His tan shirt had clearly been made to his measure, the bandana around his throat looked to be pure silk. In his dress he seemed to be something of a dandy, yet he also looked remarkably competent and those matched, ivory butted Army Colts in his holsters did not look like decorations, but hung just right for fast withdrawal.

"Rosemary-Jo got word to her pappy,
He fogged on his strawberry roan,
And said, 'From that ornery critter,
I'll save Rosemary who's my own.' "

By now Freda was struggling into her dress. Her head popped out of the neck like a squirrel peeping from its den-hole in a sycamore tree. She looked at the center man of the trio. She gave him barely more than a glance for, compared with his friends, he faded into nothing.

He didn't look tall like the other two, being at least six inches under the wiry six-foot length of the black-dressed, baby-faced boy. If his clothes were of as good quality as those worn by the others he did not have the flair to show them off so well. A costly black Stetson sat on his dusty blond hair. The face under the hat seemed to be handsome, though not as eye-

catching as that of either of his friends. His shoulders had a
width and appeared to be sturdy enough, but he faded into
nothing compared with the giant build of the big blond. Even
the brace of white handled 1860 Army Colts which rode butt
forwards in his holsters did nothing to make him more
noticeable. Freda smiled as she glanced at the gunbelt. The
small, insignificant cowhand must badly want everyone to
think of him as a real hard *hombre* and tried to improve the
impression by going armed in the same manner as his friend.

> "Now the Yankee went down to San Antone,
> Met the Texas boy out on the square,
> But his draw was too slow, and as far as I know,
> That Yankee's still lying out there."

With the final verse of the song ended the three men rode
slowly down the slope. At that moment, for the first time,
Freda realized her position, alone in the house and far from
any help. Three strangers, gun-hung and handy looking, came
riding down towards her. They could be hired hard-cases from
Double K for by now all the old cowhands of the spread were
gone, being replaced by men whose ability with guns exceeded
their skill with cattle.

Freda turned from the window and headed to collect the
shotgun which hung with a Le Mat carbine, over the fireplace.
She took down the ten gauge, two barrelled gun, checked the
percussion caps sat on their nipples and then stood uncertain
as to what her next move should be.

"Hello the house!" called a voice from outside. "Can we
ride through the water?"

Which did not seem like the action of a hard-case bunch
coming to scare her father into selling the ranch. The girl
realized she might be doing her callers less than justice with
her suspicions. She crossed the room, leaned the shotgun by
the door, opened it and stepped on to the small porch.

"Come ahead," she called.

The Lasalle family might be poor, but they still offered
hospitality to any passing stranger.

Slowly the big paint stallion, ridden by the smallest man,
moved into the water, followed by the white, bloodbay and
pack horse. Freda studied the horse, seeing it to be as fine
looking and sizeable as either of his friends' mounts. It didn't

look like the kind of horse one would expect so small and insignificant a man to be afork. Probably it belonged to that handsome blond giant and he allowed the small cowhand to ride it. Yet at that the small man must be better than fair with horses for the paint stallion did not look like the kind of animal to accept a man on it unless the man be its master.

Just as the men came ashore Freda felt something was wrong. Then she realized what. She had not fastened her dress up the back! The men were ashore now and she needed to think fast, to gain time to make the necessary adjustments. A flash of inspiration came to her.

"Take the horses around back," she told the three men. "Let them graze while you come in for a meal."

Not until the three men rode around the house and out of sight did Freda move. Then she stepped back into the house and began to fumble with the dress fastenings. At the same moment she realized that apart from a few eggs the ranch could offer its guests nothing by way of food.

The front of the house consisted of one big room, serving as both dining and sitting room. The kitchen and three small bedrooms all opened off the front room, a handy arrangement from the girl's point of view. She entered the kitchen, saw the coffeepot stood ready and looked to her skillet ready to fry eggs. Through the window she saw her guests removing the saddles from their horses.

Freda opened the kitchen door and stepped out, getting her first close-up look of the three men. The blond giant looked even more handsome close up and Freda wished she had donned her best dress instead of this old working gingham. She hardly gave the small man a glance, although his face did seem older and more mature. The dark boy seemed even younger now he was in close. His face looked innocent—until one looked at the eyes. They were red hazel in colour, wild, reckless, savage eyes. They were not the eyes for such an innocent face. If the youngster was, as she had thought at first glance, only sixteen they had been sixteen dangerous and hard-living years to give him such eyes.

"Howdy ma'am," greeted the small man, removing his hat as he saw her and showing he had some strength in his small frame for he held the heavy double girthed saddle in his left hand. "Thank you kindly for the offer."

"Sure is kind, ma'am," agreed the giant, his voice also a

Texas drawl, but deep and cultured. "Our cooking's not what it used to be."

"And never has been," grinned the dark boy, looking even younger and more innocent as he swept off the Stetson hat.

Watching the men walk towards her Freda wished she had taken time out to put on a pair of shoes and tidy her hair which still fluffed out and showed signs of washing. Yet there had been time for none of it and she must make do as she was.

Each man laid his saddle carefully on its side clear of the door, by the wall of the house. No cowhand worth his salt ever rested his saddle on its skirts, or placed it where clumsy feet might step on it. A cowhand took care of his saddle for without it he could not work.

"Go on through and sit a spell," she told them, indicating the door into the front room. "I'll fetch in the coffee."

By the time Freda arrived with the coffee she found her guests sitting at the table, their hats hanging by the storm straps on the back of the chairs. Her eyes studied them, knowing them to be strangers to this part of the range.

"You're from down south, aren't you?" she asked, pouring the coffee into cups.

Under the rules of rangeland etiquette the host could ask that much without giving offence. It left the guests free to tell as much or as little as they wished.

"I didn't think it showed," drawled the dark boy.

"You aren't looking for work hereabouts?" she went on, hoping they were not. Such men would stiffen any fighting force and they would be powerful backing if they aimed to ride for Double K.

"Work, ma'am?" asked the blond giant. "The word near on scares us off our food."

"I tell you, ma'am," the small man went on. "In all the years I've known this pair I haven't once got them to do a hand-stroke of work."

Freda could hardly restrain a smile as she noted the way the small man spoke. He really must be wanting to impress her, make her believe he gave the other two orders, or was in a position to have to put them to work. Then she thought of the big paint stallion, a real valuable animal. The small man must be the son of a rich ranch owner and the other two hired to be his bodyguard. Yet neither of the tall men looked like the sort to take pay for being a wet-nurse.

The small man's eyes flickered around the room. It looked
neat, clean, tidy without being so fussy a man wouldn't dare
breathe in case he messed something up. None of the furniture
looked new, but it had been well kept and expensive when
new. The drapes at the window were clean and colourful, and
enlivened the atmosphere. Over the fireplace hung a Le Mat
carbine, one of the old type known as the "grapeshot gun".
The upper of the twin, superposed barrels took the nine .42
balls in the chamber. The lower barrel had no rifling and
threw out either a .50 calibre grapeshot, or a charge of buckshot when needed.

Despite its brilliant conception the Le Mat was a weapon
long out of date, yet the house showed no more modern weapons—except for the shotgun leaning by the door.

Following the small man's gaze, Freda gulped as she saw the
gun. Nobody would keep a shotgun in such a position as a
normal thing. Her eyes went back to the small man once more.

"Menfolks not at home?" he asked.

"Not just now," she replied, then went on hurriedly.
"They'll be back any time now."

"Huh huh!"

He left it at that. The girl shut her mouth, holding down a
remark about the men her father hired, one much more com-
plimentary than they deserved. Some instinct told Freda she
need not fear her guests even though she was alone.

The small man's eyes were on her face; they were grey eyes
and met a gaze without flinching. Nor was there any of the
slobbering stare of her father's hands in the way he looked at
her. His eyes did not try to strip her clothes away and feast on
her young body. He looked like a man with close women kin.
He also looked in a manner which told Freda her last words
had not fooled him one little bit.

Suddenly she became aware of the strength in the small
man's face. She knew her first impression could have been
wrong; there might be much more than was at first apparent
about this small South Texas man. Her eyes dropped to his
gunbelt, seeing the fine workmanship in it—and how well
worn and cared-for it looked. He had none of the habits of a
show-off, nor did he in any way, by voice or gesture, call
attention to the fact that he wore two guns like a real bad
hombre.

"I'm afraid we're clean out of everything but eggs," she

said, wanting to prevent her confusion showing.

"Lon," drawled the big blond, "you've got a head like a hollow tree. What about those pronghorn steaks in the pack?"

"Ain't your fault we done got 'em, any old ways," replied the dark boy who then turned to Freda. "There I was, ma'am, trying to sneak up on that lil ole rascal. Then this pair comes—"

"How about you-all sneaking through the door, sneaking to the pack, sneaking out the steaks, then sneaking back and giving them to the lady," put in the small man. "You being so sneaky and all."

Freda noticed the way the small man addressed his friend. He spoke like a man long used to giving orders and having them obeyed. The black dressed boy came to his feet and performed the remarkable feat of draining his coffee cup while bowing gracefully to her.

"Reckon I'll have to apologize for this pair, ma'am," he said. "I can't take them no place twice. Folks won't even have them back to apologize for the first time."

He replaced the cup on the saucer and headed out through the kitchen. Freda fóllowed and in a few minutes he returned carrying a burlap sack and several thick antelope steaks wrapped Indian-style in leaves.

"You-all take the thickest for yourself, ma'am," he told her. "We're riding greasy-sack, so take whatever you need out of the bag."

The girl understood his meaning. To ride greasy-sack meant that they had no chuckwagon along and so carried their food in a burlap bag. She opened the bag to find it contained potatoes, carrots, onions and a few cans of tomatoes, corn and peaches.

Since the arrival of the three men Bugle, the redbone hound, had stuck pretty close to his mistress, showing no sign of friendship, following her into the kitchen. Now his tail wagged as he caught the scent of fresh meat.

"You come friendly all of a sudden," drawled the dark boy. "Is it me or this here meat you're in love with?"

"I can't take your food!" Freda gasped.

"Don't let that worry you, ma'am," he replied, tossing a two pound steak to the waiting jaws of the redbone. "Too much food makes Mark 'n' Dusty get all mean and ornery. Only with Dusty, him being the boss, you can't most times tell no difference. Say, was it all right for me to feed your dawg, ma'am?''

Freda nodded. She thought she had the three men sorted out now. The dark boy's name appeared to be Lon and from what he just said about Dusty being the boss it ought to make the small man's name Mark, for he was not likely to be the other two's employer.

At that moment the small man came to the kitchen door.

"Whatever Lon's telling you, ma'am," he said, "it's likely to be all lies."

"Just telling the lady what a sweet, kind 'n' loving nature you-all got, Dusty," Lon replied. "Course, like you said, it's all lies.''

The words puzzled Freda more than ever. The small man's name appeared to be Dusty and that made him the boss. Then she thought she had the solution, Dusty was their boss' son and they treated him in such a manner as a result of it.

"You wouldn't be looking for the Double K, would you?" she asked.

"Double K?" Dusty replied. "That's the old Lindon Land Grant, isn't it?''

"It was. Lindon died and an Englishman bought it."

"We've never been this way before, have we, Lon?" drawled the small man. "I run my herds over the eastern trails, it's better for us that way.''

Once more Freda noticed how he spoke; as if he was the trail boss when his ranch sent a herd to market. Yet he did not seem to speak in a boasting manner, or to be trying to impress her.

Through her cooking and the meal which followed Freda tried to understand the man called Dusty. The other two regarded him as their boss. Yet, from the banter which flowed between them, they were also good friends with much in common.

"You mean you came along the stream?"

The words came in a gasp from Freda as the import of something Mark just said sank into her puzzled head. A blush came to her cheeks for if they had been riding the bank of the stream they must have seen her bathing.

"Why else do you reckon we'd put up with Lon's caterwauling?" asked Dusty, a smile on his lips. It was a friendly smile, not the leer of a venal sneak who would sit watching a nude girl in the privacy of her bathing.

Then Freda understood and the blush died away. The three men must have spotted her from a fair way back down the river. To avoid causing her any embarrassment they swung from the bank edge and rode parallel to it but well clear, with Lon singing to warn her of their presence. They also took their time, allowing her a chance to get to the house and dress before riding in.

Tactfully, and in a diplomatic manner, Dusty swung the conversation away from the subject. Then Lon started her laughing with an exaggerated story of how he hunted and shot the pronghorn, which had tasted so delicious, despite having his two friends along.

The meal had ended but Freda wanted her guests to stay on and talk. She felt starved for company and good conversation and for the first time realized how lonely her life was.

Suddenly Bugle raised his head, looking across the room from where he had laid since finishing his steak. At the same moment Lon's youth and levity fell from him like a discarded cloak. He looked older, more alert—and deadly dangerous.

"Your pappy run seven—eight men, Miss Freda?" he asked.

"No, why?"

"There's that many coming up right now."

Then the others heard the sound of approaching hooves, coming at a good pace towards the river bank, down it and through the water. This had a special significance. The stream marked the boundary of the ranch house and nobody but the owners and their hired help had the right to cross without first calling for permission to do so.

Freda rose to her feet and darted to the door, opening it and stepping out. Eight men came across the stream, riding towards the house and halting their horses in a rough half-circle. They looked a hard bunch, with guns hanging low at their sides. She only knew one of the eight but could guess at the purpose of their visit.

The man she knew was called Preacher Tring—he'd been at Mallick's left hand when the Land Agent offered to buy them out. Now it looked as if Tring had returned to make sure the Lasalle family did sell out.

CHAPTER TWO

The Name's Dusty Fog

FREDA stepped across the porch and halted at the edge of it looking towards the eight men, not liking what she read in their eyes. They, with one exception, were men in the thirties or early forties, and with one exception wore cowhand dress—but they weren't cowhands.

Preacher Tring sat in the center of the group. A big blocky man with heavy rounded shoulders and a nose hooked like a buzzard's beak. He wore a round topped hat of the style circuit-riding preachers favored. His white shirt looked dirty, the black tie crooked. His sober black suit also looked stained and rumpled as if he'd worked hard in it that day. Around his waist hung a gunbelt, a brace of Navy Colts riding the fast draw holsters. Slouching in the saddle of a fine black horse Preacher Tring looked like a particularly evil buzzard perched ready to slash the eyes out of a corpse.

"What do you want?" Freda asked.

"We've come to move you folks on," answered Tring, his voice a harsh croak which was well suited to his looks. "Boss made you a good offer for this place. Now he allows you've had time to think about it. Price still goes, even after the place gets wrecked."

"How do you mean, wrecked?"

"Going to wreck the place, gal," Tring answered, waving a hand towards the buildings, then down to the corral. "Then happen your father doesn't sell out it won't just be the place we wreck."

Freda grabbed Bugle's collar as the dog stood by her side, his back hair rising and a low growl rumbling from his throat. She knew the men would shoot down her dog without a second

13

thought and did not want that to happen.

"You wouldn't dare!" she gasped.

Without even troubling to reply Tring turned his horse and rode towards the corral. He unshipped the rope from his saddlehorn, tossed the noose over the right side gate post and secured the other end to the horn. Turning his horse he rode forward slowly until the rope drew taut. The big black threw its weight forward to try and drag whatever lay behind it.

Laughing and making coarse comments the men sat their horses and watched Tring. They did not trouble to look at the house, knowing the quality of Lasalle's hired hands and expecting no opposition except maybe from the rancher himself. Only Lasalle could not be at home or he would be outside and facing them.

"Go on, Preacher!" yelled the youngest of the bunch, a brash, tall youngster in his late teens and who clearly considered himself the hardest rock ever quarried. "Get off and push!"

This brought a roar of laughter from the others and a snarled curse from Tring. He often boasted of his horse's strength and pulling power, so did not intend to allow the animal to make him a liar.

Tring spurred his horse cruelly. Steel shod hooves churned up dirt as it threw weight against the taut rope, trying to tear the corral's post from the earth. The man cursed savagely as the post held firm. He raked his struggling horse from neck to rump with sharp-rowelled petmakers, but to no avail.

From behind Freda came the crash of a shot. The rope split and the horse, suddenly relieved of the strain, stumbled forwards, throwing its rider over its head. Tring's companions turned to see who dared interfere with the Double K.

The small Texan stood in the doorway of the house, smoke rising lazily from the barrel of the Army Colt in his right hand. He looked at the hostile group of eight hard-case riders.

"I'm taking cards," he said. "The name's Dusty Fog."

With that the sleek Colt pinwheeled on his finger and went back to the holster at the left side of his body. He stepped forward, passing the girl, to halt between her and the men.

Only it was not a small, insignificant cowhand who passed her. Now he seemed to have put on inches, and to exude a deadly menace. Never again would Freda think of him as being small.

He faced the men, hands thumb-hooked into his belt, eyes watching them, daring any of them to make a move.

Snarling out incoherent curses Preacher Tring sat up. He had lost his hat and his head was completely bald, which added to his general air of evil. He forced himself to his feet and looked at the small Texan. From the expression on Tring's face, Freda thought he would grab out his gun and shoot down this impudent stranger who came between him and his desires. In the heat of the moment Freda clean forgot about the other two men and did not wonder why they failed to stand alongside their boss at such a moment.

"Easy Preacher!" a man spoke hurriedly, urgently. "He's speaking true. That there's Dusty Fog all right. I saw him when he brought the Rocking H herd to Dodge against Wyatt Earp's word."*

Not until then did Freda fully realize who her small guest really was. She could hardly believe her eyes or ears as she looked at the small Texan called Dusty Fog.

She'd heard the name often enough, but never pictured the famous Dusty Fog as anything but a handsome giant, a hero of the same kind she read about in books. In the War Between The States she, and almost every other southern girl, dreamed of Dusty Fog as their knight in armor. He had been the boy-wonder, the Confederate Cavalry captain who, at seventeen, made the Yankees wish they'd stayed at home and who carried a fighting cavalryman's reputation as high as that of Turner Ashby or John Singleton Mosby.

Since the War his name rose high as a cowhand, a trail boss who ranked with Charlie Goodnight, Oliver Loving, Stone Hart, the pick of the trail bosses. It had been Dusty Fog and his friends who tamed the bad Montana mining city called Quiet Town,† after three lesser men died in the trying. He was the segundo of the great OD Connected ranch in the Rio Hondo country. He had ambidextrous prowess with his matched bone handled guns. His speed of drawing those same guns and his accuracy in shooting were all legends. Now he

* Told in TRAIL BOSS
† Told in QUIET TOWN

stood before Freda Lasalle, a man of five foot six at most, a man she had dismissed as nobody and hardly spared a second glance.

Tring also thought of all he had heard of Dusty Fog and liked none of it. The small Texan stood alone, facing eight of them—or did he stand alone—where he was two other men were likely to be.

The tall, handsome blond stood at the corner of the house. He stood with empty hands but that meant little for rumour had it that Mark Counter could draw and throw lead almost as fast as Dusty Fog. In his own right that handsome blond giant had a name himself.

If anything Mark's reputation as a cowhand stood higher than Dusty's. He had a name for being somewhat of a range country Beau Brummel who helped set cowhand fashions now as he had once done amongst the bloods of the Southern army. A rich man in his own right, son of a prosperous Big Bend rancher, Mark still rode as a hand for the OD Connected, working as a member of the floating outfit and siding Dusty in any trouble to come along. His strength was a legend, his skill in a rough-house brawl spoken of with awe and admiration wherever it was seen. How fast he could handle his gun was not so well known. He rode in the shadow of the Rio Hondo gun wizard for all that he stood a good six feet three inches tall.

Small wonder the hired guns from Double K looked uneasy when they saw Mark Counter all set to back his *amigo* against them.

Slowly Tring lowered the hands which had hung like curved talons over the butts of his Navy Colts. He'd been set to chance taking Dusty Fog with odds of eight to one in his favor. Eight to two were far from being bad odds, even eight to those two—then the odds dropped to a level where Tring did not intend bucking against them.

A sinister double click announced another man stood at the side of the house opposite Mark Counter. Not one of the assembled gunhands thought it to be a trick of their ears, or imagination. That showed in the way they looked towards the dark boy, noting the twin barrel ten gauge in his hands.

Freda also looked and felt surprise. This was not the innocent looking boy who talked and joked with her inside the house. The clothes might be the same, but the face was a mean, cold, slit-eyed Comanche Dog Soldier's mask, alert, wolf-cautious and watching every move.

They called him Loncey Dalton Ysabel, the Ysabel Kid, *Cabrito* depending on how well folks knew him. Three names, but they all added up to one thing—a real dangerous *man*. His father had been a wild Irish-Kentuckian border smuggler, his mother the daughter of Chief Long Walker of the Comanche and his French-Creole squaw. That marriage brought a mixing of bloods which produced a deadly efficient fighting man with an innocent face and a power of danger inside him. He had the sighting eye of a backwoodsman of the legendary past and the same ability to handle a rifle. He could use his Dragoon Colt well enough when needed. From his French-Creole strain he gained an inborn love of cold steel as a weapon and an ability to use that James Black bowie knife which would not have shamed old Jim Bowie himself. Tied in with that came the skill of a Comanche Dog Soldier at riding anything with hair, ability to follow tracks where a buck Apache might falter and the keen eyes which came in so useful when riding scout. He could move through thick brush as silent as a shadow, speak seven languages and fluent Spanish. All in all it made the Kid a real good friend—or right bad enemy.

From the way he stood and watched the Double K men he was no friend.

"Don't see how all this comes to be your concern, Cap'n Fog," Tring said, in a much milder tone than he usually adopted. "These here nesters—"

"Stop handing us that bull-droppings, *hombre*!" growled Mark Counter, moving forward to flank Dusty and face the men. "These folk don't plough. They run a brand and keep cattle. That makes them ranch folks."

The youngster in Tring's bunch thought he was real fast with a gun. He had come through a couple of cowhand backing-down sessions and didn't reckon this trio would prove harder to handle than the others.

He swung down from his saddle to step by Tring and face the two Texans in his toughest and most belligerent manner, even though he wasn't showing good sense.

"Who asked you to bill in?" he asked in a tough voice.

"We're in, boy," Dusty answered, sparing him hardly a glance. "You, *hombre*, get afork your hoss and take your pards off with you."

Tring wasn't fixing to argue. He bent and took up his hat, placing it on the bald head. Tomorrow would be another day. The Texans would be riding on soon and he would return. Freda Lasalle was going to wish he had not when he came back. Or maybe Lasalle would pull out in a hurry when he heard what had happened—or what might have happened had not those three interfering Texans been on hand.

So Tring turned to collect his horse. His backers did not want trouble, he could read that on their faces. Only the fool kid wanted to make fuss, bring off a grandstand play.

Full of brash conceit and over-confident both in himself and the ability of the others to back him, the young hard-case took a pace forward.

"Listen, you!" he said to Dusty. "Our boss sent us to do a job, and we aim to do it, so you can smoke off afore you get hurt."

Dusty did not even look at the young man, but threw a glance at Tring as the bald man mounted his horse.

"Call him off, *hombre*," Dusty said gently, "or lose him."

Tring made no reply. He watched the young gun-hand, wondering if he might be lucky and give the rest of them a chance to cut in.

"Listen, you short-growed ru—!" began the youngster.

He stopped faster than he started, and without finishing his speech, for a very good reason. Dusty Fog glided forward a step. His right fist drove out and sank with the power of a mule-kick into the youngster's stomach. The young gunny's hand started moving towards the butt of his Army Colt as Dusty stepped forward. He failed to make it. The hand which he meant to fetch out the Colt clutched instead at his middle as he doubled over croaking in agony.

Instantly Dusty threw up his fist-knotted left hand, smashing it full under the youngster's jaw, lifting him erect and throwing him backwards into the horses. Then the gunny slid down into a sitting position. Through the spinning pain mists and bright lights which popped before his eyes he saw Dusty standing before him and again tried to get out his gun. Dusty jumped forward, foot lashing out in a kick which ripped skin from the gun-hand, brought a howl of pain from the youngster and sent the Colt flying.

Bending forward Dusty took a double handful of the youngster's shirt and hauled him erect, shook him savagely, then let him go. The youngster's legs were buckling under him as Dusty's right fist lashed up at his jaw. Mark Counter winced in sympathy as the blow landed. The youngster went over backwards, crashing down and made no attempt to rise.

Dusty looked at Tring, his eyes cold and hard.

"You always let a boy do your fighting?" he asked.

"Boy played it on his own," snarled Tring, hating backing down but not having the guts to take Dusty up on it. "We ain't after fuss with you."

"Fussing with a gal'd be more your game," drawled Mark. "Wouldn't it?"

Never the most amiable of men, Tring still managed to hold down his anger and resentment at Mark's words.

"The boss made these folks a fair offer for their place," he said. "He wants more land to build up his holding. We just figured to toss a scare into the girl and her pappy. Didn't mean her no real harm."

Freda watched everything, still holding Bugle's collar. She wanted to say something, take a part in the drama being played out before her. Dusty did not give her a chance for he clearly aimed to handle the entire affair his own way. She went back to shove Bugle into the house then came towards Dusty.

"We aren't selling," she said.

"You hear that?" asked Dusty.

"I heard it!" Tring replied.

"We'll be going up the trail today. But we'll be coming back this way and if these folks aren't here and unharmed, *hombre*, you'd best be long gone or I'll nail your hide to the door. Understand?"

"I understand, Cap'n Fog."

"Then get that kid on his horse and ride out of here."

A growled order from Tring brought two men from their horses to help the groaning youngster to his feet then into his saddle. Freda watched them, seeing the conspicuous way they kept their hands clear of the guns at all times. This puzzled her for, from what she had heard, Double K hired tough hard-cases.

Under the right circumstances Tring's bunch might have been hard and tough. Yet every last one of the seven who were capable of thought knew they faced three men who were with but few peers in salty toughness and were more than capable of handling a fight with guns or bare hands.

So the Double K's hard-case bunch got their horses turned and headed off, leaving behind an undamaged house and a Colt Army revolver lying where the youngster let it fall.

Among the other men, thinking himself either hidden from view or unsuspected of being able to do any harm, the youngster leaned forward over the saddlehorn. The way he hung forward he looked like he was still too groggy to do anything, but his left hand drew the rifle from his saddleboot. They passed through the river and rode up the slope. This was his chance. Thirty yards or more separated him from the three Texans and the girl. It was a good range for rifle work and not one at which a man might make an easy hit with a fast drawn Colt. He could turn, make a fast shot at that small bond runt who whipped him. Then he and the rest of the boys could make a stand on the rim and cut the other two down.

The horse was almost at the top of the slope when he wheeled it around in a tight, fast turn and started to throw up the rifle. The move came as a surprise to the other Double K riders. It did not appear to be so much of a surprise to the people against which the move had been directed. The youngster saw that almost as soon as he turned the horse.

Always cautious, more so at such a moment, the Kid stayed right where he had been all the time and did not join Mark and Dusty before the house. After watching Dusty hand the hardcase youngster his needings, the Kid rested the barrels of the ten gauge on his shoulder although his right hand still gripped the butt, forefinger ready on the trigger and hammers still pulled back.

From his place the Kid saw the leaning over and might have passed it off as a dizzy spell caused by the whipping Dusty had handed out. Then the Kid noticed the stealthy withdrawal of a rifle and he waited for the next move.

"Dusty!" the Kid snapped, even as the youngster swung his horse around.

With men like the three Texans to see was to act. Neither Dusty nor Mark had seen the rifle drawn, but they were watching for the first treacherous move, ready to copper any bet the other men made.

At the Kid's word Dusty went sideways, knocking Freda from her feet, bringing her to the ground. She gave a startled yell, muffled for he stayed on top of her, shielding her with his body. The girl heard that flat slap of a bullet passing overhead, but the crack of the shot was drowned by the closer at hand roar of the shotgun.

Even as he yelled his warning the Kid brought the shotgun from his shoulder. Its foregrip slapped into his waiting left hand, the butt settled against his shoulder and he aimed, then touched off first the right, then left barrel. He expected the charge to spread at thirty yards and was not disappointed in it. He did feel disappointed when the men let out howls, including the youngster who jerked up in his saddle, screamed in pain, turned the horse and headed after his bunch as they shot over the bank top and went from sight, although their horses could be heard galloping off beyond the rim.

Freda managed to lift her face from the dirt and peer out by Dusty. She saw Mark kneeling at one side, holding his right hand Colt at arm's length, resting his wrist on his left palm and his left elbow on his raised left knee. Her eyes went to the other side of the stream. She could see no bodies, nor any sign of Tring and his men.

Holstering his gun Mark walked to her side, she saw him towering above her. He bent down, gripped Dusty by the waistbelt, and with no more apparent effort than if lifting a baby hoisted him clear of the girl. Then in the same casual manner Mark turned and tossed Dusty at the Kid who came forward muttering something under his breath and too low for Freda to catch—which in all probability was just as well. Ignoring the choice and lurid remarks made about himself, his morals, descendants and ancestors by his friends, Mark bent and held a hand toward Freda.

"If you throw me I'll scream," she warned.

"Ma'am," Mark replied, gallantly taking the hand and

helping her rise. "I never throw a real good looking young lady away."

By the time Freda stood up again she found the Kid and Dusty had untangled themselves and the Kid came forward bearing the ten gauge and showing a look of prime disgust at such an ineffective weapon.

"What the hell have you got in this fool gun?" he growled. "I reckon to be bettern't that with a scatter."

"I charged it with birdshot. There's been a chicken-hawk after the hens and so I—"

"BIRDSHOT!" the Kid's voice rose a few shades. "No wonder I didn't bust their hides. Landsakes, gal, whyn't you pour in nine buckshot?"

"Because I didn't think I'd need it!" she answered hotly, the reaction at her narrow escape almost bringing tears.

"Easy gal, easy," said Dusty gently. "Lon's only joshing you. It's just his mean old Comanche way. They've gone and they won't be back."

"Not today," she agreed bitterly, thinking of the morrow and the visit it would surely bring.

"Nor any other day," Dusty promised. "We'll call in at the Double K and lay it plain before the new boss. If he makes fuss for you we'll make it for him on our way down trail."

CHAPTER THREE

Wire Across The Trail

IT took Freda a couple of minutes to catch control of her nerves again. She made it in the end, helped by the thought of how lucky she had been. Tring and his men might have done much worse than wreck the buildings and rip down the corral on finding her alone at the house. She thought thankfully of the unfastened dress, it caused her to request the three Texans take their horses around back and then come in for a meal. That gave her a chance to fasten the dress. It also kept the horses out of sight. Had Tring and his men seen three fine looking animals such as Dusty, Mark and the Kid's mounts out front they might have waited in the background until the visitors departed.

"Whyn't you call in the local law?" Mark asked.

"In Barlock?" she replied. "There'd be more chance of help in a ghost town."

"Well," Dusty drawled, "We'll ride in and see their boss. It might do some good for you."

"Riders coming in, Dusty," remarked the Kid, walking towards the side of the house with his hand hanging by the butt of the old Dragoon and the despised shotgun trailing at the other side. "Three of them, coming from back there a piece."

Freda ran towards the Kid, sudden fear in her heart. She reached the corner of the house at the same time he did, staring across the range to where three men rode towards them, following the wagon trail into town. She clutched at the Kid's right arm, holding it tight.

"Don't shoot, Lon," she gasped. "It's my father!"

"Wasn't fixing to shoot, so let off crushing my dainty lil

23

arm," he replied. "You-all near on as jumpy as those other pair."

"Something's wrong. I'm sure something's wrong," she went on.

"Won't get any righter until we know what it is," Dusty answered, coming to the girl's side.

None of the approaching trio rode real good horses. Two were youngish, cowhands; although not such cowhands as the OD Connected would hire. The third looked in his late forties, sat his horse with something of a cavalryman's stiff-backed grace. It showed even slumped up and dejected as he looked. His clothes were not new, but they were clean and neat—and he didn't wear a gun. The three Texans saw this latter point even before they noticed the rest. A man without a gun was something of a rarity anywhere west of the Mississippi and east of the Pacific Ocean.

Nearer the house the three men split up, the hands making for the door which led into the room they used as living quarters. The older man rode forward, halted his horse and swung down from his saddle. His face bore a strong family resemblance to Freda, now it was lined and looked exhausted, beaten, like the face of a man who has taken all he can and wants to call it quits.

He came forward, hardly looking at the three Texans, laid his hand on his daughter's arm and shook his head gently.

"We're licked, Freda," he said. "Mallick has taken over the two stores and won't let any of us small ranchers buy supplies unless we pay cash."

"But Matt Roylan has always known our credit is good," she answered.

"Yes, but the Double K has taken over Matt and Pop Billings' notes at the bank and will foreclose if they sell. I saw Mallick, he said we could have all the supplies needed and he'd take it out of the price he offered for our place."

"He can't pull a game like that!" Dusty said quietly stepping forward.

"He's done it," George Lasalle answered.

"And the local law stands for it?" Mark asked.

"Elben, he's town marshal, takes orders from the Double K and has men supplied to back him."

Never had Freda felt so completely helpless and so near to

tears. They must have supplies, food at least, to tide them over until the first drive came up trail and they could sell cattle to the trail boss. Then they would have enough money to straighten their account, as they had in previous years.

"Sloane sold out," her father went on. "I saw his wagon before Billings' store, taking on supplies. Mrs. Sloane was crying something awful."

Then for the first time he seemed to become aware that there were strangers, guests most likely, present. Instantly he shook the lethargy from him and became a courteous host.

"I'm sorry, gentleman," he said. "I shouldn't be troubling you with our worries. Have you fed our guests, Freda?"

"We had a good meal, sir," Dusty replied. "Your daughter's a fine cook."

At that moment the two hired hands emerged from their room carrying what looked like all their gear. Without a word they swung afork their horses and rode away, not even giving a backwards glance. Dusty watched them, thinking how he would not take their kind as cook's louse even, but most likely they were the best hands Lasalle could afford to hire. Now it looked like they were riding out.

"Where're they going, papa?" Freda asked.

"They quit. A couple of Double K men saw them in town and told them to get out while they could. I told them I couldn't afford to pay them but they said they were going anyway."

"But we can't manage the place without their help," Freda gasped. "You can't gather and hold the shipping cattle alone and we have to get a herd to sell so we can buy supplies."

"Never knew that ole hoss of mine so leg-weary as now, Dusty," Mark remarked in a casual tone.

"Ole Blackie's a mite settled down and ain't willing to go no place at all," drawled the Kid. "And it looks like this gent needs him a couple or so hands for a spell."

Lasalle and his daughter exchanged glances. He did not know who these three young men might be, but he knew full well what they were. They looked like tophands in any man's outfit, seventy-five-dollar-a-month men at least and he could not afford to pay for such talented workers.

"Happen Mr. Lasalle here can let us stay on a spell we'll have to get word up to Bent's Ford and warn Cousin Red not to wait his herd for us," Dusty remarked more to himself than the others. He turned to Lasalle. "Take it kind if you'd let us stay on and rest our horses. We'll work for our food and bed."

A gasp left Freda's lips. She could hardly believe her ears and felt like singing aloud in joy. After seeing the way Dusty, Mark and the Kid handled the eight Double K hard-cases and made them back off, she did not doubt but that the ranch would be safe in their hands.

"We haven't much food," she said, "but the way you told it none of you do much work either."

From the grins on three faces Freda knew she had said the right thing. Her reply showed them she had the right spirit and knew cowhand feelings. Her father did not take the same lighthearted view.

"Just a moment, Freda," he put in. "These gentlemen are welcome to stay over and rest their horses, but we won't expect them to work for their food."

"Why not?" asked Dusty. "The way this pair eat they need work, or they'll run to hawg-fat and be good for nothing when I get them back to home."

"But—but—!"

"Shucks, give it a whirl, sir," interrupted Dusty. "Mark here's good for heavy lifting which don't call for brains. Lon might not know a buffalo bull from a muley steer, but he's better than fair at toting wood for the cook."

"And how about you?" asked Freda. "What do you do?"

"As little as he can get away with," Mark answered.

The girl laughed and turned to her father. "Papa, this is Captain Dusty Fog, Mark Counter and the Ysabel Kid."

It took Lasalle a full minute to reconcile Dusty's appearance with his Civil War record, or his peacetime prominence. Then Lasalle saw the latent power of the small man, recognized it as an old soldier could always recognize a born leader of men. His daughter was not a victim of cowhand humor. This small man was really Dusty Fog. He still did not know what he could say or do for the best.

Then his daughter took the matter out of his hands, made a decision of her own and showed him that she was a child no more.

"I'll show you where the hands bunked," she said. "You

can move your gear in and then I'll find you some work."

"I'm beginning not to like this here job already," the Kid told Dusty in an audible whisper. "This gal sounds too much like you and I'm all for a day's work—providing it's spread out over three days."

With that the three cowhands started to follow Freda, leaving her father with his mouth hanging open, not knowing how things came to happen. Then he recalled a piece of news overheard in town, something which might interest the three cowhands.

"Mallick's started wiring off their range. He's already fenced off the narrows all the way along their two mile length from the badlands down to where they open out on to his range again. He doesn't allow any trail herds to cross the Double K."

"He's done what?"

Lasalle took a pace backwards before the concentrated fury in Dusty's Fog's voice as the small Texan turned back towards him. Mark and the Kid had turned also and they no longer smiled or looked friendly.

"Put wire across the trail, clear across the narrows. Says any trail herd which wants to make the market has to swing one way or the other round his range."

The girl looked from her father to the three cowhands. She knew cowhands hated barbed wire and fences of any kind. She knew all the range arguments about wire; that cattle ripped themselves open on the spikes; that a man might ride into such a fence during the night hours and not see it until too late. She also knew the hate went deeper than that. From the Mississippi to the Pacific a man could move or let his cattle graze without being fenced in. He could ride where he wished and had no need to fear crossing another man's land as long as he obeyed the unwritten rules of the range. Through all that expanse of land there were few if any fences and the free-roaming cowhands wanted to see it stay that way.

"How about the herds already moving north?" Mark asked quietly. "This's the trail Stone Hart uses and he's already on his way."

"I think we'd all better go into the house and talk this out," Lasalle replied, but some of the tired sag had left his shoulders now and he seemed to be in full command of himself.

He led the way around the house side and in through the front door. The Kid collected the fallen Army Colt, although Lasalle paid no attention to it, or to the shotgun which the Kid leaned against the door on entering. He waved his guests into chairs and rooted through the side-piece drawers to find a pencil and paper. With these he joined the others at the table and started to make a sketch map of the outline of the Double K. It looked like a rough square, except that up at the north-eastern corner the narrows thrust out to where it joined the badlands. All in all Lasalle drew quite a fair map, showing his own place, the other small ranches and the general lay of the land.

"Did some map-making with the Field Engineers during the War," he remarked. "This's the shape of the Lindon Land Grant. We ranch here. This was the Doane place, but they've sold out. This's the Jones place and the last one here is owned by Bill Gibbs. The town's back here, out beyond the Double K's south line. If the new owner can buy us out it will make his spread cover a full oblong instead of having the narrows up here."

Taking the pencil Dusty marked the line taken by the north-bound trail herds. He tapped the narrows with the pencil tip. Freda noticed that he handled the pencil with his left hand, yet he drew his Colt with his right. He must be truly ambidextrous, she thought.

"And he's run wire down this way," Dusty said. "From the badlands up that way, right down to where the river starts to curve around and down to form his south line."

"So I've heard. I haven't been out that way."

"Which means any drive that comes up is going to have to swing to the west," Mark drawled. "Or go east and try to run the badlands."

Lasalle nodded. "Mallick claims the trail herds won't cross Double K."

"Which'd mean the drive would have to circle right around their range to the west, lose maybe a week, maybe more's drive, or cut east and face bad water, poor graze, worse country and the chance of losing half the herd," said Mark quietly. "I can't see any trail boss worth his salt doing that."

"Me neither," agreed the Kid. "What do we do about it, Dusty?"

"Wait until the Wedge comes up and see what Stone allows to do."

"Huh!" grunted the Kid, for once not in agreement with Dusty's reply. "I say let's head up there to the narrows and haul down that fence."

"The Double K have twenty men at least on the spread," Lasalle put in. "They have such law as exists in this neck of the woods. Elben has eight men backing him in Barlock, all being paid by the Double K."

"Which sounds like a powerful piece of muscle for a man just aiming to run a peaceful cow outfit," drawled Dusty. "Have you seen this new owner?"

"Nobody has yet, apart from the hard-cases stopping folks crossing their range. They say the new owner hasn't arrived yet, that he bought the place without even seeing it."

"So we don't know if he is behind this wiring the range or not."

"No, Captain, we don't. Only it's not likely Mallick would be doing all this off his own shoulders is it? It'd take nearly four mile of barbed wire to make a double fence along the narrows and that runs to money."

Changing hands Dusty started to doodle idly on the paper. This ambidextrous prowess was something he had taught himself as a child, mainly to take attention from his lack of inches. He thought of Englishmen he had known, a few of them and not enough to form any opinion of such men as a whole. Yet none of those he had known ever struck him as being the sort to make trouble for folks who couldn't fight back.

"We ought to head over and see if this English *hombre's* to home, Dusty," growled the Kid, sounding Comanche-mean.

"It'll wait until we've a few more men," Dusty replied.

"Hell, after they come here today—"

Lasalle stared at the Kid. This had been the first time Tring's visit received a mention. Freda hurriedly told of the arrival of the Double K men, their threat to the property and their departure. The rancher's face lost some of its colour, then set in grim lines as he thought of what might have happened had Dusty, Mark and the Kid not been on hand. His attempts to thank the three young Texans met with no success for they laughed it off and, the way they told it, Freda did the running off wielding a broom to good effect on the hard-case crew.

All in all Dusty seemed far more interested in the closing of the trail than in being thanked for a very necessary piece of work.

"Lon," he said. "Reckon you could find Bent's Ford, happen you was looking for it?"

"Likely, but I'm not looking."

"You are. Just as soon as you've thrown a saddle on that white goat out back."

"Be late tonight when I get there," drawled the Kid.

"Happen that fool Blackie hoss makes it," grinned Mark.

"Ole Blackie'll run hide 'n' tallow off that brown wreck you ride," scoffed the Kid. "I'll make Bent's tonight all right, only I might find the hard boys have been here and took off with your guns."

"I'm here to protect them, Lon," Freda put in.

"Sure, with birdshot in both barrels. Say, reckon you can throw up a bite of food to eat on the way, something I can carry easy."

She sniffed. "I'll flavor it with birdshot. Just remember that I've nothing in the house, except for what's in your greasysack."

"Do what you can," Dusty suggested. "Then Mark and I'll take you into town and buy supplies."

"Mallick won't let us buy anything on credit," Lasalle pointed out.

"We never said anything about credit."

An indignant flush came to Lasalle's cheeks as he caught the meaning of Dusty's words. He thrust back his chair and came to his feet, facing the small Texan across the table.

"I can't accept charity—"

"And none's being offered. Man, you're the touchiest gent I've come across in many a year. This's a loan until Stone Hart arrives and you can sell some stock."

"And any way you look at it Dusty and I'm going to eat our fair share of that same food."

Freda stepped to her father's side and laid a hand on his sleeve, her fingers biting into the bicep.

"We accept," she said and her voice once more warned her

father not to argue. "Thank you all for helping."

"There's another thing though," Lasalle said, surrendering the field to his daughter. "Mallick has told the storekeepers they won't serve any small ranch folk unless they bring a note from him. He keeps a deputy in each store to make sure the owner obeys."

"Well now," drawled Mark idly, "reckon we could do something about that, don't you, Dusty?"

While agreeing with this big *amigo* on the point that they could do something about it, Dusty did not want to make war in Barlock until he had a fighting force at his back. While he and Mark could likely go into town and make Elben's deputies sing low, they might also have to do it to the tune of roaring guns and that could blow things apart at the seams. Dusty wished to avoid starting hostilities if he possibly could. It was not fear of odds which worried Dusty, odds could be whittled down and hired gunmen did not fight when the going got too stiff. With the Wedge at his elbow Dusty could make the hired hard-cases of Double K think the going had got too stiff, then likely put its new owner where he must make his peace.

Every instinct warned Dusty that more than lust for land lay behind this business. The Lindon Land Grant spread wide and large enough to satisfy a man, especially a man new to the cattle business. The entire area was well watered, that could not be the cause fo the trouble. So he must look deeper for the reason and when he found it would best know how to avert trouble.

Dusty wanted to meet the English owner if he could, Mallick certainly, to get the measure of his enemies, if enemies they should be. It might be that both were new to the west and did not know the cattleman's hatred of barbed wire, or the full implication of Lindon's Grant. If so, and they listened, he might be able to steer them in the right direction.

"What do you want me to do at Bent's, Dusty?" asked the Kid, breaking in on his pard's thought train.

"Leave word for Cousin Red to carry on up trail without us. I don't want him waiting at Bent's, or coming back to help us. That herd has to make the market. And don't spread the word about this wire trouble. I don't want this section swarming with hot-headed fools all looking for trouble."

"They'd likely be down here and rip down that fence," drawled the Kid. "Which same could sure show the Double K bunch how folks feel."

"And might start lead flying." Dusty answered.

He looked beyond the mere basic events. If Keller or Mallick aimed to keep the fence they had trained fighting men to help them. No matter what public opinion might think about the fences Keller had the law behind him in his right to erect one.

Before any more could be said Freda came in and announced she had food ready for the Kid's departure. So setting his black Stetson at the right "jack-deuce" angle over his off eye, the Kid headed out back to saddle his white stallion.

The girl followed him and watched the big white horse come to his whistle. She had the westerner's love of a good horse and that seventeen hand white stallion sure was a fine animal.

"Isn't he a beauty?" she said, stepping forward. "Can I stroke him?"

"Why sure," grinned the Kid, "happen you don't want to keep both hands. See, old Blackie here's mammy done got scared with a snapping turtle just afore he was born and he don't know whether he's hoss or alligator."

Freda studied the horse and decided that, despite the light way he spoke, the Kid called it right when he told of the dangerous nature of his horse. That seventeen-hand white devil looked as wild and mean as its master. So she refrained from either touching or approaching the horse. This was a real smart move for Blackie would accept the touch of few people, in fact only the Kid could handle his horse with impunity, it merely tolerated the other members of the floating outfit when circumstances forced them to handle it.

With his horse saddled ready to ride the Kid went astride in a lithe, Indian-like bound. He looked down at Freda and grinned, the grin made him look very young and innocent again. Removing his hat he gave her an elaborately graceful flourish with it, then replaced it.

"You get some buckshot in that gun, gal," he said, "and afore I get back here. *Birdshot*, huh!"

Before she could think up a suitable reply he turned the horse, rode around the side of the building, through the water and up the slope. He turned, waved a cheery hand, then went from sight.

Only then did she realize that he had not asked for directions to Bent's Ford. A momentary suspicion came to her for Dusty claimed they had never travelled this way before. Then the thought left her and she felt just a little ashamed of herself at having it. The Ysabel Kid needed no spoken directions to help him find his way across country. Out there, although the first drive of the year had not yet passed, he would find enough sign to aim him north and all the trails converged at Bent's Ford in the Indian Nations.

"Lon gone?" Dusty asked, coming to the front door as the girl returned to the house.

"No. He's sat on the roof, playing a guitar."

Somehow Freda felt in a mad gay mood, far happier than she had done for a long time. She gave a guilty start, realizing it must be the excitement of the day and the pleasure at having company which made her act in such a manner.

CHAPTER FOUR

A Pair of Drunken Irresponsible Cowhands

"ABOUT these supplies?" Mark Counter asked as Dusty and Freda entered the room from seeing the Kid on his way to Bent's Ford.

"I've told, Mark," Lasalle replied. "Mallick won't let us buy any unless we sell out to him."

"Looks like we'll just have to go in and see Mr. Mallick," drawled Dusty.

"Poor Mallick," Freda remarked, the gay mood still on her.

Her father watched her and for the first time realized how lonely she must be out here miles from town. He wondered if they might be better to take Mallick's offer, leave the ranch and make a fresh home in a town where she could have friends of her own age.

Then he thought of the strength Mallick had in Barlock. With Elben, the town marshal, backed by eight gun-wise hard-case deputies, Dusty and Mark would be hopelessly out-numbered. They stood a better than fair chance of leaving town headed in a pinewood box for the boothill.

"It's risky—!" he began.

"Could be, happen we rode on in and started to shoot up the main drag," Dusty agreed. "Only we don't aim to. We'll just ride on in peaceable and ask him to act a mite more sociable and neighborly."

"And if he doesn't want to act more sociable and neigh-borly?" Freda asked.

"Don't reckon there's much we can do at all," drawled Mark, sounding mild but there was no mildness in his eyes.

" 'Cepting maybe try moral suasion," Dusty went on, just as mild sounding.

"Ole Dusty's real good at that, too," Mark said. "Yep. I can't think of a better moral suader than him. Excepting maybe his Uncle Devil and his cousin Betty."

"And what if Mallick doesn't fall for this moral suasion—whatever that might be?"

"Tell you, gal," Mark answered. "We'll likely hide behind you."

They left it at that, although Freda wondered what moral suasion might be. Her father was smiling now, looking more confident in himself all the time, more like the man she always remembered. Freda saw for the first time the strain he had been under for the past few years since her mother died. Now he looked better, ready to take on the world and its problems.

"Where at's your hosses, gal?" Mark asked, taking up his hat.

"Out back, grazing, I'll show you."

"I've seen a couple of hosses afore, gal, can likely tell them from a cow, happen the cow's not a muley. I'll hitch a hoss to your buggy for you."

Freda smiled. "I'll come along, there's a muley cow or two out back and I wouldn't want to drive into town behind it."

"Pick a couple of saddle horses out for us, Mark," Dusty put in. "No sense in going in there shouting who we are."

"Yo!"

With the old cavalry reply Mark turned and left the room with Freda on his heels. Lasalle watched her go, then turned to Dusty with a worried look in his eyes.

"I've never seen Freda act that way," he said. "It's—well—."

"Yeah, I know," grinned Dusty. "I've seen girls get that way around Mark afore. Don't worry, it won't get serious and you can trust Mark." He nodded to the old Le Mat carbine on the wall. "Does that relic work?"

Indignant at the slur on his prized Le Mat, Lasalle forgot his daughter's infatuation for Mark Counter and headed to the wall. He lifted down the Le Mat and walked to the table.

"Work!" he snorted. "I'll say it works. And I'll show Tring just how well if he comes back today."

Dusty grinned. "Way him and his bunch took off," he

drawled, "they were toting birdshot and they won't feel like riding anyplace today."

With that he took up the young gunhand's discarded Army Colt. He turned the weapon in his hands, checking its chamber was full loaded and that the weapon worked. It had some dirt in it, but the Colt 1860 Army revolver was a sturdy weapon and took more than a bit of dirt to put it out of working condition. He rubbed the dirt off the revolver, set the hammer at half cock and turned the chamber, making sure it would rotate properly.

"Here, let me handle that," Lasalle said. "You said the Kid used the shotgun on Double K?"

"Both barrels and a good ounce of birdshot, way they took to hollering when it sprayed out," Dusty answered. "So shove in some powder and pour a load of buckshot on top this time. It doesn't fan out but it's a mite more potent close up."

Outside Mark caught the best two of the ranch's small bunch of saddle stock and led them back to the house. He slung his saddle blanket on one horse, then the double girthed range rig while Freda watched. He felt her eyes on him and hoped she wasn't going to get involved in romance that could have no successful end.

Mark did not mind a mild flirtation but he made a rule never to become involved with a sweet, innocent and naïve girl like Freda. In his travellings around the west he had seen, and known intimately, a number of women who were either famous already, or would be one day. They were all mature women who knew what time of day it was and knew better than to expect anything permanent to come of romance with a man like him.

For all his worries Mark did the girl less than justice. Freda did not think of herself as being halfway towards marrying him. Some woman's instinct warned her it would be no use falling in love with a man like Mark. Yet she wanted to be near him, to see how he walked and talked, so that she might know the feeling again if it came with a more marriageable man's presence.

She pointed out the harness horse and helped Mark hitch it to the small buckboard wagon. Then they walked back to the house to find her father sitting at the sitting-room table with a formidable collection of weapons before him.

"We're ready to go, Dusty," she said.

"Reckon you can hold down the house while we're gone, George?" Dusty asked her father.

"Can I?" growled Lasalle. "I reckon with old Bugle here to give warning and all this artillery I just might be able to."

"Keep the shotgun handy then. It's got buckshot down the barrels—I saw to that."

Freda poked her tongue out at Dusty and headed for the door. He grinned, took up his hat and followed her out. Lasalle came to the kitchen door, the Le Mat carbine resting on his arm and the Army Colt thrust into his waistband. Freda could see the change in her father now. He looked almost as young and happy as he had on his leaves during the war, before being taken prisoner and sent to a Yankee hell-hole prisoner-of-war camp.

At first Freda kept up a light-hearted flow of banter with the two men as they rode by her on borrowed horses. They kept to the wheel-rut track the buckboard carved into the ground on many trips to Barlock, travelling across good range country with water, grass and a good few head of long-horn cattle grazing in sight of them. Freda saw the way Dusty and Mark watched the range, studying it with keen and careful eyes, watching for some sign of approaching danger, even while they laughed and joked with her.

Not until they were halfway to town did Freda mention the trouble.

"Why did you stay on to help us, Dusty?" she asked.

"It could be because I like you folks and don't take to Double K shoving you around," he replied.

"It wouldn't be because of that fence, too?"

"That's part of it," Dusty agreed. "The range has always been open and I'd hate to see it fenced. There's no need. A man's cattle can roam, feed anywhere the graze is good and not cut the grass down to its roots because they're hemmed in by a fence. Down home in the Rio Hondo our round-ups take a month and cover maybe three hundred square miles. We work with the other outfits, share the profits, take our cut. Any stock from out of our area is held until it's spread's rep. comes for it and we send men to collect ours."

"The fence blocks a cattle trail, Freda," Mark went on soberly. "Which makes it a whole lot worse. You didn't see

Texas right after the war. Not the way I saw it when I came
though with Bushrod Sheldon on our way to join Maximillian.
There were cattle every place a man looked and no market for
them. Then we found a market up north and men started to
move their herds up towards Kansas. It was the trail herd
which saw this area opened up, the Indian moved on out. Men
died on those early drives, more than do these days. They were
learning the lessons we know now and a lot of times a man
didn't get a chance to profit from a mistake. A code grew up,
gal. The code of the trail boss, the way he and his crew lived
on the trail. One thing no trail boss will do is risk losing his
herd and that's what it'd mean to push 'round here.''

The girl watched Mark, surprised at the sincere and sober
way he spoke. She began to get an inkling of the way the
cowhands felt about that fence across the narrows of the
Double K.

"You know how Lindon got that Land Grant?" Mark went
on.

"I'm not sure," she admitted.

"On the agreement that he kept the trail open, never closed
it down. That was why he got the narrows, it's good winter
graze and it lets the herd run through good food without being
on his main grant land too long. Now the trail's closed there
can only be the one answer—war.''

"Would it come to that?"

"Likely," Dusty answered. "Stone Hart's coming north, be
along most any day now. He's a good man—and a damned
good trail boss. He won't waste time going all that way around
when he's got clear right to cross. So Wedge'll fight, and if he
can't force through the men following him north'll fight. Most
of that fighting'll be done over your land, not on the Double
K. At the end, no matter who gets their way, no matter who
wins, you small folks lose out.''

"How do you mean?"

"You make a living here, not much more. You need to sell
your stock to make enough to carry you through," Dusty explained. "There'll be none of that. And once the shooting
starts you'll be in the middle, stock'll go, maybe folks be
killed. You'll be the ones who go under and that's what I'm
trying to prevent. That's why I'm waiting for the Wedge to
come.''

"But would your friend allow that to happen?"

"Stone makes his living running contract herds for small ranch owners like your pappy. He'll have around three thousand head along with him, six or eight spreads shipping herds. Those folks are relying on Stone, just as you are on selling your stock. He never yet let his folks down and I don't figure he aims to make a start at it now."

"Won't there be trouble when he comes anyway?" she asked, watching Dusty's face and wondering how she ever thought of him as being small.

"Maybe," replied Dusty. "Maybe not. Only I've never yet seen the hired gun who would face real opposition and we'll have that behind us with the Wedge. If we can get through, talk this out with Keller, or whatever you called him, we might show him how wrong he is."

"Never knowed a gal like you for asking questions," Mark drawled in a tone which warned her the subject must be dropped.

"And I'd bet you've known some girls," she answered.

"Couple here, couple there."

"When did you first get interested in girls, Mark?"

He grinned at her. "The day I found out they wasn't boys."

Once more the conversation took on a lighter note and continued that way until they came towards the town of Barlock, buckboard and horses making for the main street.

Barlock was neither large nor impressive. Like most towns in Texas it existed to supply the needs of the cattle industry, growing, like the State itself, out of hide and horn, beef fattened on the rolling range land. The surrounding ranches supplied year-long custom for the cowhands had no closer place in which to spend their monthly payroll. During the trail drive season added wealth could be garnered from passing herds, their crews taking a chance of a quick celebration before leaving Texas.

All this did not mean that Barlock grew larger than any other weather-washed township out on the rolling plains. There were some fifteen business premises, two stores, two saloons, the inevitable Wells Fargo office with its telegraph wires and its barns and stables, a livery barn, a small house in back of town which showed its purpose with a small, discreet, red lantern. The rest were just like any other small town might offer, being neither more nor less grand.

Mark and Dusty now rode at one side of the wagon and the girl was surprised to see how they no longer kept protectively close to it. They passed into town, going by a blacksmith's forge, then the barber's shop.

"That's the Land Office," she said, indicating the next single floor, small wooden building.

"Saloon, ma'am," Dusty replied in a louder tone than necessary. "Why thank you kindly for pointing it out."

On the porch before the Land Office lounged two tough-looking men with prominent guns and deputy marshal badges. They appeared to be loafing, yet clearly stood guard to prevent anybody entering and bothering whatever might be in the office. Neither spoke, nor did they move, but studied the passing party with cold, hard, unfriendly eyes.

"Thanks for showing us the way in ma'am," Mark went on, also speaking in a far louder tone than necessary. "Let's find us a drink, *amigo*."

"Been eating trail dust for so long I need one," Dusty replied, then in a lower voice, for they had passed the Land Agent's office. "Where at's the jail gal. Tell, don't point."

Freda's finger had started to make an instinctive point but she held it down and answered, "At the other end of town, beyond the Jackieboy Saloon."

"We're going in this place here," Dusty said. "Wait out here for us. What's in that shop opposite?"

"Dresses."

"Couldn't be better. See you soon."

They swung their horses from her side and rode to the hitching rail outside the smaller of Barlock's saloons. Freda swung her own horse towards the other side of the street and jumped down. She crossed to the window of the dress shop and stood looking in the window, admiring a dress which would cost more than she could possibly afford.

Time dragged slowly. She wondered what might be keeping Dusty and Mark for there was no sign of either man. How soon would one of Elben's deputies get suspicious and come to ask her why she waited before the saloon? For five minutes she pretended to be examining the horse's hooves and the set of its harness, then leaned by the side of the wagon looking along the street.

The tall shape of Mark Counter loomed at the batwing doors. Freda heaved a sigh of relief. Then her smile of welcome died on her face as she watched the way her two friends came into sight.

For a moment Mark and Dusty stood on the sidewalk before the saloon. Then they started to walk towards the Land Agent's office without showing a sign that either of them had ever seen her before. Their hats were thrust back and they went on unsteady legs in a manner she knew all too well. They seemed to have spent their time in the saloon gathering a fair quantity of liquid refreshment. In fact they both looked to be well on their way to rolling drunk.

Hot and angry Freda stamped her way across the street on to the sidewalk behind them. She aimed to give them a piece of her mind when she caught up with them and to hell with the consequences. They had come into town to help her and the moment they hit the main street they took off for the saloon to become a pair of drunken irresponsible cowhands. She would never have expected it of either of them, yet the evidence stood plain before her eyes.

"Yippee ti-yi-ki-yo!" Dusty whooped, sounding real drunk. "Ain't no Yankee can throw me."

"Le's find another saloon 'n' likker up good," suggested Mark Counter, making a grab at the hitching rail on the end of the Land Agent's office and holding it to get his balance, allowing Dusty to go ahead. "Another lil drink sure won't do us any harm."

From his tone and attitude he already carried enough bottled brave-maker in him to settle him down. Freda came forward, her cheeks burned hot with both shame and rage. She saw the two deputies looking towards her friends and felt the anger grow even more. Dusty and Mark were headed for trouble, she hoped they got it.

"They sure didn't waste any time," said one deputy.

"Never knowed a cowhand who did," replied the other. "Nor could handle his likker once he took it."

"That big feller looks like he might have money. Let's tell them we'll jail 'em unless they pay out a fine."

"Sure. They'll be easy enough."

Dusty Fog looked owlishly towards the two men who blocked the sidewalk ahead of him.

"Ain't no Yankee can throw me!" he stated again, belligerently.

"You pair's headed for jail," answered the taller deputy. "Come on quiet, or we'll take you with a broke head."

"Jail!" yelped Dusty, fumbling in his pants pocket. "You can't do that to us. I got money—look."

He held out a twenty dollar gold piece before the men. Two hands shot out greedily towards the coin, both deputies eager to get hold of it. By an accident it seeemed Dusty let the gold piece fall from his fingers. It rang on the sidewalk and both deputies bent forward, reaching down to grab it.

Dusty's hands shot out fast, closed on the bending deputies' shirt collars and heaved. They shot by on either side of him, caught off balance and taken unprepared by the strength in the small Texan's body.

Out of control, the two men went forward into Mark's waiting hands which clamped on the outside of each head. Mark brought his hands together, crashing two heads into each other with a most satisfying thud. Both deputies went limp as if they'd been suddenly boned. They would have fallen to the ground only Mark gripped their collars again and held them up, leaning them against the office wall and jamming them there as if standing talking to them.

Turning fast, hands ready to grab at the butts of his Colts, Dusty looked along the street. Nobody appeared to have seen them for the street remained empty except for the girl. A girl whose face seemed to be twisting into a variety of different expressions. Relief, amazement, anger, amusement, they all warred for prominence on Freda's face.

Then Dusty was grinning, not the slobbering leering grin of a drunk, but the grin she had seen before, when he talked with her before leaving for Barlock.

"Lordy me, gal," he said, taking her arm and leading her to the Land Agent's door. "I'll never forget your face when we came out of that saloon."

CHAPTER FIVE

Moral Suasion

BEFORE any of the thoughts buzzing around in Freda's head could be put to words, before she had hardly time to collect her thoughts even, she saw Dusty Fog open the door of the Land Agent's office. Freda suddenly realized the reason for the piece of play-acting. By pretending to be drunk and incapable Dusty and Mark put the watching deputies off guard and enabled the two Texans to handle the matter without fuss or disturbance.

Wondering what would come next Freda followed Dusty through the open office door, into the hallowed and protected halls of Karl Mallick, Land Agent.

The office was designed for privacy, so that the occupants could talk their business undisturbed. There was but one large room, Mallick living in Barlock's best, in fact only, hotel. All the windows had been painted black for the lower half of their length and could only have been looked through by a person standing on tiptoes and peering over the black portion. The two deputies on watch outside whenever the office was in use prevented such liberties being taken.

It was a room without fancy furnishings. Nothing more or less than a set of filing cabinets in a corner, a stout safe in another, a few chairs, a range saddle with rifle and rope in a third. In the center of the room stood a large desk and at the desk, head bent forward as he wrote rapidly on a sheet of paper, sat Karl Mallick, Land Agent and attorney for the Double K.

Mallick had much on his mind as he wrote a letter. He set down the pen and began toying with the branding iron which lay on his desk top. He heard the door open and scowled. Only one man in town should be able to enter without knocking and he would be hardly likely to come around in plain daylight, not to the front door, unless something had gone bad wrong in their plans.

Raising his head, so his black bearded face looked towards the door, Mallick found he had visitors.

"What the—!" he began, coming to his feet as he stared at the small man and the girl who entered.

"Just sit again, mister," Dusty answered.

Behind him Mark entered, still supporting the two deputies, and dumped them in a heap on the floor. Mallick sat, but his right hand shot down to pull at the drawer of his desk, getting it open and exposing an Adams revolver which lay inside ready for use in such emergencies.

Whatever use Mallick intended to put the gun to never came off. Dusty let Freda's arm free and he lunged forward fast. His right hand trapped Mallick's left wrist as it lay on the desk top. With his left hand, gripping it between his second and third fingers, Dusty caught up the pen Mallick had laid aside. Moving faster than Mallick had ever seen, Dusty inserted the pen between the bearded man's two middle fingers. Then Dusty closed his hand, gripping down hard. With his hand scant inches from the butt of the Adams revolver Mallick stopped as if he'd run against an invisible wall. Pain, numbing, savage, agonizing pain rammed through his trapped hand. He could not cry out. All he could do was claw the right hand from the desk drawer and reach towards Dusty's trapping fingers.

Dusty released the hold before Mallick's hand reached his. He stepped around the desk, took out the Adams and thrust it into his waist band. Then he moved back and took his first look at the Land Agent.

Although he was tall and bulky Mallick did not give the impression of being a really hard man. He wore a good eastern style suit, white shirt and a neck-tie of sober hue. His face, what showed of it from behind the black beard, looked like the face of a man who spent some of his time out under the sun, which might be expected in his job. The eyes were light blue, cold and at the moment filled with hate as he studied his visitors.

He did not have the look of a western man.

Slowly his hand dropped towards the branding iron.

Having closed the door Mark Counter stepped forward and took up the heavy iron, handling it like a child's toy. He looked down at Mallick as he stepped back holding the iron between his hands, left below the handle, right at the head.

"Lead us not into temptation," Mark drawled, "just like the good book says. Feller tried to hit me with one of these things, one time when he got riled."

"What do you pair want here?" Mallick snarled, his accent sounding eastern. New York most likely from the way he spoke. "This's private property. You could be jailed for attacking those deputies and coming in here."

"Why *hombre*," replied Mark calmly. "We found these two gents all a-swooning away in the heat and hauled them in."

"And it's a trio, not us pair," Dusty went on. "You likely know Miss Lasalle. Her pappy came in to see you this morning. Allows anybody wants to trade at the store has to come and get a note from you."

"Where'd you hear a fool tale like that?" growled Mallick.

"I just told you *hombre*," Dusty answered, his nostrils quivering as he sniffed the air suspiciously. He threw a glance first at Mark, then at Freda. "Whooee! I thought that bay rum you used was strong, Mark."

"That's not mine," replied Mark, also sniffing.

"Don't look at me either," Freda gasped, also sniffing the sickly sweet aroma which aroused Dusty's interest. She was both surprised and puzzled by it and laid the blame on some lady visitor to Mallick, only if she used that kind of perfume she was not likely to be a lady.

"Smells like a Dodge City blacksmith's," drawled Mark.

"You ought to know," Freda answered, then blushed. A young lady should be unaware of the fact that a blacksmith, used in the way Mark spoke, had nothing to do with shoeing horses, but rather as acting as a pimp for ladies of easy virtue.

"I've better things to do than listen to you lot jawing," snarled Mallick, wanting the subject changed, although not for the obvious reason.

"That's where you're wrong, mister," Dusty drawled quietly. "You never had anything so important as seeing that we get the note to the store. See, old Mark here's an easy-going boy when he's fed. Trouble being we're staying out at Freda's place and they're short on food. And when Mark gets hungry he gets mean and riled."

"Which same I'm getting hunger on me right now."

Saying this Mark raised the branding iron before him and tightened his grip. At first none of the others could see any sign, except in the way Mark's face became set and grim. Then slowly, before the surprised eyes of Mallick and Freda, the stout iron bar began to bend. Freda saw the strain on Mark's face, saw the way his shirt sleeves, roomy as they were, went taut against the swell of his biceps as they rose and writhed under the pressure he put on. The bar began to bend, take the shape of a C, then an O. Not until it bent around in a full circle did Mark stop his pressure and toss the branding iron down before Mallick.

"Yes, sir," he said. "I can feel the hunger coming on right now."

Mallick made no reply. He stared down at the branding iron and the pallor which came to his face showed he appreciated the situation in full. Through all the Panhandle country he doubted if more than one man could equal the display of strength he just witnessed.

Footsteps sounded outside the building, and over the blackened lower part of the window showed a familiar hat's top. Mallick recognized it and so did Freda but she kept quiet. She did not need to speak, the flicker of relief which passed across Mallick's face warned Dusty and Mark, told them all they needed to know. The footsteps came to a halt before the door and a knock sounded.

"Mr. Mallick!" called a voice. "You all right, the boys aren't out here."

Even as Mallick started to rise, opening his mouth to utter a yell to the man outside, his plan failed. Dusty's left hand flipped across his body, the white handled Army Colt left his holster, its seven and a half inch barrel thrusting up to poke a yawning muzzle under Mallick's chin, at the same instant the hammer clicked back under Dusty's thumb.

"Get rid of him!" Dusty warned in a savage whisper, "or you'll be talking without a top to your head."

Mallick hired paid killers, men who sold their gun-skill to the highest bidders. He knew such men would never hesitate to carry out such a threat as Dusty made. Nor, looking at the small Texan's grim face, did he doubt but that his slightest hesitation would see a bullet crashing in his head. Mallick slumped back into his chair, sweat pouring down his face as he opened his mouth. He tried to keep his voice normal, and yet still convey a warning that things were wrong to the man outside. He hoped that for once in his life Elben the town marshal might show some sign of sense.

"It's all right, marshal," he called. "I told them to go along to the saloon."

Much to Mallick's relief the words prevented Elben from entering the room. He hoped the marshal might be following his usual practice of spending the afternoon in the saloon and would miss the two men, then mention the fact to the boss who would form his own conclusions and have a party down this way fast.

In this Mallick was to be disappointed. Elben shrugged, knowing no important business to be taking place inside. He strolled on, passing around the end of the building and heading down to the small house with the red light, having some civic duty to attend to, the collection of his weekly contribution from the madame to what they referred as election campaign expenses. From the house he returned, after a time to the jail.

While Elben attended to his self-appointed duties Mallick, one of the men who employed him, sat in the Land Agent's office hoping against hope that help would come.

"Write!" Dusty snapped, pointing to the pen and paper. "Make it *pronto*!"

Mallick did not argue. He had worked himself up the path to defiance when he saw Elben's hat passing the window. Only Dusty had pricked the balloon before it could be used and Mallick had nothing left with which to be defiant. He threw a glance to where Mark Counter took the rope from his own saddle, went towards the moaning deputies and began making a good fastening job on them. Then he took up the pen and began to write.

Having watched everything with puzzled, then smiling interest, Freda turned to Dusty and asked:

"Is that what you call moral suasion?"

"Rio Hondo style," Dusty agreed, taking the paper Mallick

wrote out and the letter, comparing the signatures on them. "It'll do. Hawg-tie him, Mark."

"Like a hawg," Mark agreed, gagging the deputies with their own bandanas. "I picked up your double eagle, out there, Dusty, want it back?"

"My need's greater than your'n," Dusty answered. "But keep it to send a telegraph message to Uncle Devil for me after we leave here."

With hands long skilled in securely tying things, Mark flipped the rope around Mallick's shoulders. Dusty sat on the edge of the desk and watched the hog-tying process, he also started to question Mallick.

"Like to see your boss," he began.

"He's not here yet," Mallick replied.

"When'd he be coming out here?"

"I don't know."

"Who ordered the fence built?" Dusty asked.

"Keller did!"

"You said he wasn't here," Freda pointed out.

"He sent a telegraph message. Told me to buy you folks out and fence his property."

"How long have you been out west, *hombre*?" Mark asked, quickly securing the man's wrists together.

"Long enough."

"You know how us folks feel about wire?" Dusty went on.

"Yeah. But Keller ordered me to lay it."

"He doesn't know how much land he's got then?" Mark said, thinking how much wiring a vast spread like the Double K would cost.

Mallick surged against the ropes and the expression which flickered across his face at the words surprised Dusty. Although he did not know what might have caused it the words had hit Mallick hard. Dusty could read facial expressions and knew fear when he saw it. He saw it this time in the bearded face of the Land Agent. Mallick threw a look at the waste-paper basket, then jerked his eyes away once more. Yet he left it too late. Dusty followed the direction of the other man's gaze. The basket contained only a small pile of pieces of paper as if a man idly ripped up something and tossed it in. Only an idle action and odd scraps of paper would not bring the fear and desperation to Mallick's face.

Bending down Dusty scooped the paper from the basket. Mallick gave a snarl of rage and struggled impotently against the securing ropes, but Mark held him down and Freda jumped forward with her own handkerchief to gag him. Once more the girl proved herself capable of cool and fast thought for neither Dusty nor Mark gave her any sign of needing help.

"What is it?" she asked.

Dusty spread open the crumpled torn pile of paper and looked down at it.

"A map of some kind. It'll take time to fit all this together right and we don't have time to spare, gal. I'll take it with me."

Fear, hate and worse showed in Mallick's eyes as he struggled impotently against the taut ropes which held him fast. He felt himself lifted to his feet, hauled into a corner where he could not be seen from the windows, then sat with his back against the wall while Mark lashed his ankles together. Mark knew his business, knew the discovery of Mallick and his crowd might mean death for the girl, Dusty and himself. So Mark aimed to see discovery was less likely. He dragged the now conscious and groaning deputies to where Mallick sat, propped them against the wall and used the last of the Agent's rope to secure their feet together. They now sat tied in line and it would be unlikely, if not impossible, that they could manage to roll, wriggle or crawl out into view, or even to where by kicking or stamping against the walls they might attract attention.

Freda crossed the room and looked down at the three bound men.

"We won't be selling, Mr. Mallick," she said.

"Let's go, gal," Dusty drawled, watching Mark lock and bolt the rear door.

Cautiously Freda started to open the front door, meaning to peer out and make sure their departure would be undetected. This action did not meet with Dusty's approval.

"Go on straight out, gal," he ordered. "Act like you've been to see Mallick on business, not like you're robbing the bank."

Holding down the comment which bubbled at her lips Freda stepped through the door. She had no sooner got outside than a hand caught her arm and turned her. She gave a muffled squeak, felt herself scooped up into Mark's arms. His face came down, lips crushing her own in a kiss. The girl struggled, her little hands hitting Mark on the shoulders. Then he released her and she staggered back a pace. Her right hand came around in a slap which jerked his head aside.

"Just because I talk friendly—" she began hotly.

"When you pair of love-birds have done," Dusty put in. "I've locked the door and we can move off."

Freda's angry outburst faded, contrition came to her face. Then she flushed red and glared at the two men. Mark put a hand to his cheek and grinned.

"That's a mean right hand you've got, gal."

"I'm sorry," she replied. "But you might have warned me. I've heard about you."

"Yeah," grinned Mark. "I could feel it. Anyway it spoils things when the gal knows what she's going to get. I'll see to getting word to Ole Devil and you take care of Russian Olga here, Dusty."

"Who's Russian Olga?" Freda asked, watching Mark walk along the sidewalk making for the Wells Fargo office, while Dusty headed her across the street towards the waiting buckboard.

"She's a gal we saw one time,"* Dusty replied. "Claims to be the female fist fighting champion of the world, only she got licked that time."

"Girls fist f— You're jobbing me!"

"Nope. There's a few of them about. Get the buckboard and head for the store and when we get inside don't be surprised at how I act. I don't want anybody thinking we're friends."

"Scared I might ruin you socially?" she asked with a smile.

"Call it that," grinned Dusty in reply. "That slap you gave Mark'd've helped if anybody was watching, wouldn't make you look real friendly with us. Only we had to stop anybody seeing me lock the door and Mark reckoned kissing you'd be as good a way of hiding me as any."

"And I slapped his face, poor Mark."

"He'll live."

Freda remembered where Mark was headed and a thought struck her.

* Told of in QUIET TOWN

"Won't your Uncle Devil object to your neglecting your work?"

"He'll turn the air blue and blister my hide, but he'll be behind me all the way and if this thing blows too too big he'll get help here, happen we send for it. Now get in the buggy—and remember, gal, you've just been made to sell your home. Act like it, don't look so all-fired pleased with yourself."

When Freda entered Roylan's store she looked dejected almost on the verge of tears. Matt Roylan, sleeved rolled up to expose his muscular arms, leaned his big bulky, powerful frame on the counter and looked across the room towards the door. The lean, gun-hung hard-case with the deputy's badge also looked. He leaned by the cracker barrel into which he dipped his hand at regular intervals. His eyes studied the girl, then went to Dusty who followed on her heels.

"Supply her," Dusty ordered as they reached the counter.

"Says which?" asked the gunman.

"You want to see the paper?"

Dusty made his reply with a cold smile flickering on his lips. The lanky gunman studied Dusty, reading the signs in the matched guns, in those well-made holsters and the workmanship of the gunbelt. He knew quality when he saw it—and he saw it in the small Texan. Without knowing who Dusty was, the gunman knew what he was. Dusty belonged to the real fast guns, one of the magic handed group who could draw and shoot in less than half a second.

For his part Dusty tried to give the impression of being a typical hired hard-case, a man who used a brace of real fast guns to off-set his lack of inches. From the looks on the gunman and Roylan's faces Dusty had made his point, they took him at face value.

"You one of the boys from the spread?" asked the gunman, meaning to be sociable. "Mallick hire you?"

"Go ask him," Dusty answered in an uncompromising tone.

Watching from the corner of her eye Freda felt amazed at the change in Dusty. He seemed to be able to turn himself from an insignificant cowhand to any part he wanted to play. Right now, happen she didn't know him, she would have taken him for a brash, cocky and tough hired gunhand who knew he had the other man over a barrel in more ways than one. She saw that neither Roylan nor the deputy doubted that Dusty brought her from Mallick's office after forcing her father to sell out.

"You and your father are leaving after all, Freda," Roylan said, a touch of sadness in his voice as he looked at the note Dusty tossed in a contemptuous manner before him. His voice held such genuine sadness that Freda felt guilty at having to deceive him, yet she knew she did not dare take a chance on letting hint of her true position slip out.

"She's leaving, *hombre*," answered Dusty, saving Freda from needing to lie. "So shake the bull-droppings from your socks and make with some service."

In his own right Matt Roylan could be a tough, hard man. However he knew the futility of tangling with Double K in what now amounted to their town. He might jump the two hired hard-cases, lick them, although the small one looked fast enough to throw lead into him before he could bat an eye. Even if he did manage to lick the two men and throw them out, the Double K held his bank-note and would foreclose on him.

So Roylan stared to collect the order Freda gave him. Yet somehow, as he worked, Roylan got the feeling that Freda was not quite so grief-stricken as she tried to appear. The girl could not act well enough to continue her pose, at least not well enough to fool an old friend like Roylan. The storekeeper noticed this and felt puzzled by it. He threw a glance at Dusty who sat by the counter and dipped a hand into the candy jar to take one out. Roylan couldn't think how, but somehow Freda had gathered the note from Mallick, the girl was all right and things not so black as they looked. That would be impossible—unless the small Texan was not what he seemed. Yet he had the mannerisms of a tough hard-case hired gun.

One thing Roylan knew for sure, with the note from Mallick and the presence of one of the Double K's toughs, he stood in the clear. If it came out later that Freda managed to trick the paper from Mallick in some way all the blame could be laid on the deputy who accepted the note as genuine.

"How long've you been with Double K?" asked the gun-hand, giving Dusty a long and curious stare.

"Not long," Dusty answered truthfully. "You always this nosey?"

The gunman grunted and relapsed into silence once more, except for the crunching of the cracker he took out of the barrel. He did not know all the men out at the Double K but knew Mallick hired efficient men when he could find them, and this small Texan looked and acted efficient. One thing the deputy knew for sure. The Texan wouldn't take to having his word doubted and could likely deal harshly with any man who doubted it.

Freda felt tension rising inside her with every minute. She watched Roylan collecting the goods from the shelves. He seemed to be taking his time and she wanted to beg him to hurry. At any moment Mallick would be found and the alarm given. Then Dusty and Mark would need to face a hostile town, or at least such a part of the town as felt under obligation to Double K.

At last the order had been gathered and she paid for it. Then Roylan began to box it and carry it to her buckboard. Dusty watched this. The load did not look much after seeing the OD Connected's cook collect a chuckwagon full at a time, but the Lasalle family did not need such quantities of food and what they now had would be the difference between survival and being driven out.

Freda left the store, wanting to be outside so that she might see what happened around town. The gathering of supplies had taken some time and she thought Mark might be making his way towards her, but at first she saw no sign. Then Mark and another man left the Jackieboy Saloon. She saw Elben the town marshal and others she recognized as his deputies surround the pair in a menacing half-circle. A pair of riders came slowly along the street into town, beyond the Jackieboy Saloon but Freda gave them no second glance. She stared at the men before the saloon for another moment. Then she turned and darted back into the store.

"Dusty!" she gasped. "Mark's in trouble."

CHAPTER SIX

The Ysabel Kid Meets A Lady

HOLDING his big white stallion to a mile devouring trot the Ysabel Kid rode north. He found and now followed the signs of last year's drives with no difficulty for the sign lay plain for a man to see.

Ahead lay the fence. The Kid saw it and a frown came to his brow. Like Dusty and Mark he hated fences of any kind, probably more so than his friends for they would grudgingly admit some fences had their uses. To the Kid any kind of fence was an anathema. The free-ranging blood of his forefathers, all breeds which never took to being fettered and walled in, revolted against the sight of anything which might bring an end to the open range.

Touching the white's flanks the Kid swung to one side, heading down the stream which marked the boundary of Double K and which carried the barbed wire on the bank he rode along. Likely Double K had men watching the fence and he did not want to be delayed in obeying Dusty's orders while he made war.

The wire ended at a point where the stream made a sharp curve and formed the end of the narrows. After scanning the area the Kid allowed Blackie to wade into and through the water. At the other side he set his course across the narrows, in the correct direction, with the ease of a sailor using a compass to navigate his ship. All the range ahead of him looked good, plenty of grass, enough water, and dotted with small woods in which the cattle might shelter during bad weather. A man who owned such a spread should have no need to jump his neighbors' land for more grazing.

Caution had always been a by-word for the Kid. A man

didn't live as he'd lived during his formative years* without developing the instincts and caution of a lobo wolf. Not even in times of peace and on the safe ranges of the OD Connected did the Ysabel Kid ride blindly and blithely along. Always there was caution, always his eyes and ears stayed alert for any slight warning sound or flickering sight which might herald the coming of danger.

So the two men who appeared on a rim half a mile off to his right did not take the Kid by surprise. He heard one of them yell, saw them set spurs to work and send their horses forward at a gallop. As yet he did not speed up the big white stallion. Blackie could allow the men to come in much closer before he need increase his pace any. The Kid knew his horse could easily leave behind the mounts of the Double K men, happen he felt like it. One word would see the white running away from the pursuers, leaving them behind as if they had lead weights lashed to their legs.

"Couldn't catch up even if they wanted to, old Blackie hoss," drawled the Kid. "Which same they want to, and are trying to."

After dispensing this rather left-handed cowboy logic the Kid relaxed in his saddle. When the two men passed behind a clump of bushes out of sight for a few moments he bent and drew his rifle from the saddleboot. With the old "yellowboy" in his hands he knew he could handle the two men and prevent their coming close enough to bother him.

There had been a time, just after the War, when the Kid's handling of the pursuit would have been far different. Then he would have found cover and used his old Mississippi rifle (he did not own a Winchester Model of 1866 "yellowboy" rifle in those days) to down one of the following pair for sure and probably both if the other did not take the hint. Those days ended on the Brownsville trail when he met the man who turned him from a border smuggler into a useful member of society. It had been Dusty Fog who prevented the Kid sliding into worse forms of law-breaking than the running of contraband and gave him a slightly higher idea of the value of human life. So the Kid contented himself in having the rifle ready. If the men became too intrusive he could easily take steps to dis-

* Told of in COMANCHE

courage them, but he aimed to let them make the first move.

For a mile the Kid rode at the same pace and the men, knowing the futility of trying to close with him and his fast moving horse, clung to his trail like a pair of buzzards watching a trail herd for weak steers dropping out. Only the Kid was no weak steer, he didn't aim to get caught or to drop out.

A woman's scream shattered the air, coming from a small *bosque,* a clump of trees to the Kid's right. He brought the big white stallion to a halt, looking in the direction of the sound. It might be a trick to lure him close, to hold him for the two following men, only that scream sounded a whole lot too good for pretence. Then his ears caught another sound, low, menacing, one which set Blackie fiddle-footing nervously. The hunting snarl of an angry cougar.

Without a thought of the following gunmen, the Kid headed his big white horse forward fast, making for the *bosque*. Once more the scream rang out, than he saw, among the trees, what caused the terror.

The young woman stood back up against a tree, her face pale, her mouth open for another scream. On top of a rock, facing her, crouched for a spring, with its tail lashing back and forwards, was a big, old, tom cougar. To one side, reins tangled in a blue-berry bush, fighting wildly to get free, eyes rolling in terror, a fine looking bay horse raised enough noise to effectively cover the sound of the approaching white stallion and its rider.

Only rarely would a cougar, even one as big as the old tom, chance attacking a human being without the incentive of real hunger and the human being bad hurt, or without being cornered. Probably the cougar had its eye on horse-flesh, it's favorite food, and would have ignored the young woman. However fear carries its own distinctive scent and the cougar caught it, knowing the human being feared it. So the big tom changed its mind, decided to take the woman as being an even easier kill than the horse.

Bringing his brass-framed Winchester to his shoulder the Kid sighted and fired all in one incredibly swift move. The cougar had caught some sound Blackie made and swung its head to investigate the new menace. Even before its cat-quick reactions could carry it in a long bound to safety at one side, the cougar took lead. The Winchester spat out, throwing back echoes from the surrounding trees, the cougar gave out with a startled squalling wail, sprang from the rock, back arched in pain and hurling at the young woman.

Moving so fast the lever looked almost like a blur the Ysabel Kid threw two more shots into the cougar, spinning it around in the air and dropping it in a lifeless heap almost at her feet. The young woman stared down, trying to back further into the tree trunk, not knowing she need no longer fear the animal.

"You all right, ma'am?" asked the Kid, coming down from Blackie, landing before the girl and holding his rifle ready.

For a long moment she did not reply. She stood with her face against the trees, not sobbing or making any sound, just frozen rigid with the reaction of her narrow escape. Then with an almost physical effort, she seemed to get control of herself and turned towards him.

"Yes, thank you," she said in an accent which sounded alien and strange to the Kid's ears. "I'm afraid I was rather foolish. Mr. Dune told me there were mountain lions in this area, but I'd always heard they don't attack human beings."

"Don't often," replied the Kid, knowing she wanted to talk, to shake the last of her fear away. "This'n most likely was hungry and figured you'd make an easier meal than the hoss."

Holding the "yellowboy" in his right hand and sweeping off the black Stetson with his left, the Kid looked at the girl his timely arrival saved. Without a doubt she was one of the most beautiful young women he had ever seen. Maybe a mite taller than a man'd want, but not so tall as to appear gawky and awkward. She had hair as black as his own, neat and tidily cared for. Her face would draw admiring glances in any company and she'd come second to none in the beauty stakes. Her eyes, now the fear left them, looked warm, yet not bold. She wore a black eastern riding habit of a kind he had never seen before. A top hat sat on her head and a veil trailed down from the brim to fasten on to her jacket belt. Her outfit did nothing to hide the fact that she was a very shapely young woman.

She dusted herself off, knocking the leaves from her dress. "He took me by surprise, my horse took fright and tossed me off. You came just in time. Thank you."

"It wasn't nothing," replied the Kid, feeling just a shade uncomfortable in her presence.

"I can't remember ever having seen you around the ranch," she went on. "Of course Papa and I only arrived two days ago and I haven't met all the sta—cowhands yet. Mr. Dune warned me about the cougar, but I wanted to see one close up."

"Likely this old tom," replied the Kid with a grin, stirring the dead cougar with his toe, "wanted to see a real live gal close up, too."

For an instant a slight frown came to the young woman's face, then it was replaced by a smile. When the Ysabel Kid grinned in that manner he looked about fourteen years old and as innocent as a pew-full of choirboys who had put tintacks on the organ player's chair. No woman, especially one as young as this, could resist such a smile. She smiled also, it made her look even more beautiful.

The Kid looked to the young woman. From the way she talked she must be the Double K's new boss's daughter. He decided to ask if this was correct, then try and explain the dangers of putting fences around property, especially across what had always been an open trail.

Only he did not get a chance. The big white stallion swung its head in the direction they'd come, letting out a warning snort. It stood with ears pricked and nostrils working, looking for all the world like a wild animal. Reading the warning, the Kid turned fast, but he did not try to raise his rifle for he stood under the guns of the two men who followed him across the range.

"Just stay right where you are, cownurse!" one ordered.

The Kid stood fast, only he didn't let his rifle fall. He kept it in his hand, muzzle pointing to the ground, but ready for use. Then the girl stepped forward, coming between the Kid and the two men. She brought a worried look to two faces for the men could not shoot without endangering her life.

"It's all right," she said. "The young man saved my life, prevented a mountain lion from attacking me."

Still the two men did not lower their weapons, nor relax. The taller made a gesture towards the Kid.

"He's not one of our riders, Miss Keller," he said.

"Aren't you?" she asked, turned towards the Kid. "I suppose you're trespassing really, but we can overlook it this time. Put away your guns, please."

For all her strange sounding accent she made it clear that when she gave an order she expected it to be obeyed. The Kid watched the men and the girl, thinking how her tone sounded like Dusty's cousin, Betty Hardin, the voice of a self-willed young woman who was full used to be obeyed. Her last words had been directed to the two men.

They scowled, clearly not liking the idea, but holstering their guns for all of that. Their duty was to patrol the range and discourage stray drifters from crossing. Neither had seen Tring's discomforted bunch returning from the abortive raid on Lasalle's place and did not know anything about the Kid's part in it. They did know that they should have stopped him getting this far in. They should also most definitely have never allowed him to get so close to Norma Keller, only daughter of the new owner of the Double K. However Norma had given orders and they were instructed to obey her.

Norma turned to the Kid and looked him over with some interest. Once more he felt like a bashful schoolboy—then he remembered, in the early days he felt just the same when Betty Hardin looked at him.

"What are you doing on my father's land?" she asked coolly.

"Just passing through, ma'am, headed north to Bent's Ford, that's over the Indian Nation line a piece."

"I know!" she answered. "Do you make a habit of riding across other people's property?"

For a moment anger flickered in the Kid's eyes. Then he remembered that the girl was English, likely they did things a mite different over there. Only now she was in Texas and would need to change some of her ideas. He held down his angry reply and said:

"This here's always been open range country, ma'am. In Texas folks don't stop a stranger from crossing their land as long as he does no damage and makes no grief for the owners."

"I see," replied the girl, and her entire tone had changed. "Of course one must remember this is a new—I'm sorry if I snapped. Never let it be said the Keller family failed to conform with the local custom. Would you care to come to the ranch and allow father to thank you in a more suitable manner?"

For an instant the two men looked relieved, but the Kid shook his head.

"Thank you, no, ma'am," he replied. "I've got to make Bent's Ford as soon as I can. Got me a riding chore out from there and I can't miss it. Say, whyn't you have these boys here skin out that ole cougar, or tote it back to your place and have it done. It'll make a dandy footrug and you'll likely have a story to tell folks about it."

"Why yes, that's a good idea," she answered and turned to the men. "Will you attend to it, please?"

The word "please" might be there, but the Kid got the idea the girl aimed to have her orders carried out for all of being polite. He knew he could now ride on without needing to bother about the two men. He held his rifle in both hands, ready to handle any refusal, or try at holding him, but the men turned to walk towards the cougar.

Quickly the Kid swung afork his big stallion. He booted the rifle, removed his hat once more and gave Norma an elegant salute.

"*Adios*, ma'am," he said, watching the two men.

"Good-bye," she answered, looking at the white with appreciation showing in her eyes for she knew a good horse when she saw one. "If you are ever in this part of the country again drop in and see us. My father would be pleased to meet you."

"I'll do just that, ma'am," the Kid replied, setting his hat on his head.

Turning his horse the Kid rode out of the *bosque* and headed north once more, making for Bent's Ford. He knew neither of the men would follow him now, they would be too busy with the cougar. However the Double K might have more riders on it, men who also aimed to keep strangers away. He allowed Blackie to make a better pace and did not relax, not even after he left the narrows and passed over the Texas line into the Indian Nations.

Norma Keller watched the two men as they profanely tried to load the cougar on to one of their horses, a horse which showed a marked reluctance at having anything at all to do with such a creature. Then she went to her own horse and calmed it down feeling annoyed that she had not cared for the animal earlier. Not until she managed to quieten the horse and freed it did her eyes go back to the men. By now they had managed to get the cougar's body across the back of the horse and lashed it into place.

A smile flickered across her face as she thought of the innocent looking boy whose arrival saved her life. He looked quite friendly and so young to handle a rifle so well. The three holes in the cougar's body (she smiled as she found herself no longer using the term mountain lion) could be covered by the palm of her hand and any one would have proved fatal. She hoped the holes could be covered and somebody could tan and cure the skin for her.

The smile stayed as she thought of the way that the youngster spoke. She made a mental note to remember this was not the East Riding of Yorkshire, but a new country with different ways. In England no worker would have dared address her on such terms of equality and she found the sensation stimulating. Norma Keller was no snob. The upper-class to which she belonged rarely were snobs, that was the privilege of the newly-rich, the intellectuals who felt unsure of their position in life. She felt no snobbish class-distinction against the Kid, nor any annoyance at the way in which he addressed her. He spoke politely, yet without in any way being subservient. She wondered who he was, where he came from, what his position in life might be. Then she smiled still more. It would be highly unlikely that she ever met the boy again. Or was he such a boy? He seemed to be ageless. She wished she might get to know him better. He seemed to be so much better natured and pleasant than the rather sullen men hired by Mr. Mallick while she and her father travelled from their home in England, the home they would never return to again.

"All set, Miss Keller," growled one of the men.

"Good," she replied, allowing him to help her mount to the side-saddle she used. "Let's get that creature home before it stiffens and can't be skinned."

They rode back through the *bosque* and out at the far side. Norma threw her eyes over the range, searching for some sign of her rescuer, but seeing none. So she rode with the two men, comparing them with him and not to their advantage. There was so much she wanted to know about this new land, so much they might have taught her, but they seemed sullen and uncommunicative.

For a mile or so they rode in silence, then she saw a rider top a rim and head towards them, a man who looked familiar.

"That's Mr. Dune, isn't it?" she asked.

"Yeah," grunted the taller man. "That Dune all right."

Norma frowned for she did not approve of employees referring in such a manner to their foreman. However she made no comment for Norma had already seen a different standard of behaviour seemed common in this new land she and her father picked for their home.

Coming up at a gallop Dune brought his horse to a sliding halt, eager to impress Norma with his riding skill. He was something of a range-country dandy and fashion-plate, dressed to the height of cowhand fashion. Although only a medium-sized man Buck Dune fancied himself as quite a lady-killer, a gallant with a string of conquests which covered the length and breadth of the west.

Since the girl's arrival at the ranch Dune had tried to bear down on her with the full force of his charm and personality. Her father had money, more money than Dune could ever recollect seeing at one time and Dune was more than willing to find acceptance into the Keller family circle. Only the charm which attracted girls in the better class saloons, dancehalls and cat-houses; plus a few women not from that class but who should have shown better sense; failed where Norma Keller was concerned. Towards him the girl displayed a cool attitude. She always answered his greetings, asked questions and listened with interest to his answers but always with calm detachment, oblivious to his swarthy good looks, his neatly trimmed moustache, or the faint scent of bay rum which always clung to him. She treated him as a valued employee and made it plain that was how things would remain.

This morning the girl's flat refusal to allow him to act as her guide when she went riding left him feeling as awkward and shambling as a barefooted yokel boy. It had been an unusual feeling and he still did not know if he liked it or not.

"Howdy, Miss Keller," he greeted, removing his hat in a graceful gesture guaranteed to prove his genteel upbringing. Then his eyes went to the cougar's body. "Where did you get that cat?"

"I had an adventure," she replied, smiling and forgetting

that he warned her of the presence of cougars on the range. She did not notice his surprise at seeing the one her rescuer had killed. "A young man shot it when it tried to attack me."

Dune threw a glance at the two gunmen. He had clean forgotten warning the girl about the danger of mountain lions. It had been no more than an excuse to get Norma to accept his offer of guidance and company. Now it seemed she had really met up with a cougar and he lost the chance of acting as a gallant heroic rescuer.

He forgot that matter in something more urgent. His eyes stayed on the two gunmen but he remembered just in time not to say too much before the girl. If the young man was no more than a drifting cowhand it would not be too bad, for he would be unlikely to return.

"You'd best get it right back to the spread and skin it out," he said, hoping the men would read his words right.

It seemed they did, for the one toting the cougar started his horse forward, Norma at his side. The other man held his mount back, reading the message in Dune's eyes.

"Who was he?" growled Dune after the girl had ridden away.

"Some kid on a damned great white hoss," replied the other man. "It sure could move. We saw it from half a mile back and hadn't gone two hundred yards afore we knew there wasn't a chance in hell of us catching up to him."

An explosive snorted curse left Dune's lips. He let the veneer of charm fall from him and showed what he really was, a killer without moral or scruple. Tring's bunch had returned to the spread, most of them toting shotgun lead and cursing about it, although all might have accounted themselves lucky the gun carried no worse than birdshot which did no more than pierce their hides.

They gave livid and profane descriptions of the trio of men who, according to them, jumped them, held them under guns and pinned down helpless. Dune found the descriptions tallied with three men he had heard much of, although had never met up with. He remembered the Ysabel Kid, the descriptions he'd heard of that tall, dangerous young man. The descriptions often contained references to the Kid's horse, a seventeen-hand white stallion which could run like the wind.

"A tall, young looking, dark faced kid, dressed all in black?" he asked savagely. "Got him a Dragoon Colt and a bowie knife."

"That's him."

"And that's the Ysabel Kid!" snarled Dune, spitting the words out like they burned his mouth. "Which way'd he go?"

"Said he was headed for Bent's Ford."

"Reckon he was?"

"That's what he said. Was headed north all right when we put him up."

The two men sat their horses for a moment. Dune dropped a hand to the butt of the Tranter revolver holstered at his side. If the Ysabel Kid was headed for Bent's Ford he was going for some good purpose. Dusty Fog wouldn't send off his left bower* at such a time without good cause. And the Kid had seen Norma Keller. He had seen far too much to be left alive.

"I'll take your hoss, ride a relay after him!" growled Dune.

"And leave me afoot?" answered the other.

"Shout to your pard. Tell him I've got to go into Barlock in a hurry, that's for Miss Keller to hear. They can send another hoss out from the spread."

"What'll I tell Mallick, happen he comes out and wants to see you?" asked the gunman, swinging from his saddle.

"Tell him I've gone to Bent's Ford. That black dressed breed's seen a damned sight too much. He's got to be killed!"

* Left bower. Originally a term used in playing Euchre and meaning the second highest trump.

CHAPTER SEVEN

Jackieboy Disraeli

IN all fairness to Mark Counter it must be said he did not intend to get into any trouble at all.

After visiting the Wells Fargo office and sending a telegraph message which would eventually be delivered to the OD Connected house in the Rio Hondo country, Mark headed towards where he could see Freda's buckboard halted before the general store. In so doing he had to pass the hospitable doors of the Jackieboy Saloon. He saw that Dusty had collected both their horses and taken them down to the store and so would not have wasted time entering the saloon if it had not been for what he saw happening inside.

Mark glanced through the batwing doors, then came to a halt. He was a cowhand, a good one, he was also a cowhand who had seen the treatment handed out to less fortunate members of his trade when they found themselves in a saloon and at odds with the owners.

None of the crowd looked at Mark as he entered. Their full attention centered on the group at the bar. It was this same group at the bar which brought Mark into the room in the first place.

There were three men in the center of the bar, only they hadn't come to it for pleasure, or if the cowhand of the group had he sure didn't look like he was getting any of it.

"The boss told you to clear out of this section. There ain't no work here!"

The speaker stood tall, as tall as Mark Counter and maybe thirty or forty pounds heavier. From the slurred manner of his speech and the battered aspect of his face he had done more than his fair share of fist-fighting in the raw, brutal bare-

69

knuckle manner. He had powerful arms and big hands, and was putting both to good use as he held the cowhand pressed back against the bar.

Held with the huge man's powerful hands gripping, gouging into his shoulders, the cowhand could do little. He stood six foot, had good shoulders and lean waist but he looked like a midget in the hands of the burly brutal bruiser who held him. His face twisted in agony. It was cheerful most times, maybe not too handsome, but friendly and pleasant. His clothes looked northern range fashion, they were not over-expensive, but his hat and boots both cost good money and his gunbelt, while not being a fast-man's rig, did not look like a decoration.

Standing to one side of the others a small, tubby man watched everything with drooling lips and a sadistic gaze. He was a sallow skinned man, his nose slightly large and bent. He wore a light dove-grey cutaway jacket of gambler's style, snow white trousers down which ran a black stripe, primrose yellow spats and a pair of shoes which shone enough to reflect the view around him. His shirt bore considerable frills and lace to it and his bow-tie had an almost feminine look about it. He stood relaxed at the bar, his posture nearer that a dancehall girl than of a gambling man. Taking a lace handkerchief from his cuff he mopped his brow.

"He understands now, Knuckles," he lisped in a falsetto voice which might have brought down derision on him, but did not. "Let him free."

On the order Knuckles released his hold. The young cowhand showed he had sand to burn. His right fist lashed around, smashing into the side of the huge man's bristle-covered jaw. It was a good blow, swung with weight behind it, but Knuckles did not even give a sign of knowing it landed. He grunted and his big left hand came back, slashing into the cowhand's cheek and sprawling him to the floor.

"He's not learned his lesson, Knuckles!" purred the tubby man. "Stomp him!"

Like an elephant moving Knuckles stepped towards the dazed cowhand, lifting a huge foot ready to obey. Through the pain mists the cowhand saw Knuckles towering over him, tried to force himself into some kind of action.

Two hands descended on Knuckles's shoulders. He felt himself heaved back and propelled violently away from the bar. A mutter of surprise ran through the saloon as the huge bouncer went reeling and staggering backwards. Not one of the watching crowd had expected to see a man brave, or foolish, enough to tangle with the huge bouncer of the Jackieboy Saloon.

Nor had Knuckles. Caught with one foot off the ground he could do nothing to prevent himself reeling backwards. He smashed down to a table which shattered under his weight and deposited him in a heap on the ground.

"You shouldn't have done that, cowboy!" said the tubby man. "Now you've made Knuckles angry."

Which could have been classed as the understatement of the year. Knuckles had gone past mere anger. He snarled with rage, foam forming on his lips as he rolled over on to hands and knees. One hand clamped on a table leg he came to his feet holding it like a club in his fist. He attacked with a rush as dangerous as the charge of a long-horn bull.

Not a person in the room spoke as they watched. The big blond Texan looked strong, but no man had ever stood up to Knuckles in one of his murderous rages.

With the table leg raised Knuckles came in fast. Mark watched him, seeing the strength, noticing the slowness. Knuckles had been a prize-fighter but like most of his kind fought with brute strength alone, by standing toe-to-toe and trading blows until one of them could take no more. His instinct for fighting had become settled into his routine and he could not believe that any other man fought in a different manner. So he expected, if indeed he troubled to think about it all, that Mark would stand there to be hit with the table leg. Believing this he launched a blow that should have flattened Mark's head level with his shoulders. Only it did not land.

At the last instant, when most folks watching thought he had left it too late, Mark sidestepped the rush. The table leg missed him and shattered to pieces on the floor. Carried forward by his own impetus Knuckles lost his balance once more. He staggered forward a step and Mark, with a grace and agility a lighter, smaller man might have envied, pivoted around and threw a punch. The blow, driven with strength, skill and precision, traveled fast and landed hard. It crashed into and mangled still more Knuckles's fight-damaged right ear.

Knuckles shot forward, head down and with no control over

his body. The man's close-cropped skull smashed into the bar front and shattered through it. He disappeared behind the bar, knocking the bartender from his feet and preventing him from grabbing up the ten gauge shotgun which lay under the counter for use at such times. With a yell the bartender went down, Knuckles's heavy body on top of him.

A concerted gasp rose from the watching crowd. Everyone expected Knuckles to come roaring through the hole in the bar and stomp the big Texan clear into the floorboards. In this they were to be disappointed for it would be another four hours before Knuckles could move under his own power again.

"I don't like you, you nasty man!" hissed the tubby man from behind Mark. "I don't like you at all!"

The words brought Mark around in a fast turn. He found his aid in handling the matter unnecessary. Even as the tubby man's hand started to lift from his pocket with something metallic glinting in it, the young cowhand took a hand. He rose to one knee, his right fist caught the man in the fat belly and folded him like a closed jack-knife. Then the cowhand came to his feet, the other fist lashed up to catch the tubby man's jaw, jerking him erect and over on to his back. A nickel plated Remington Double Derringer came from the fat man's pocket, left his hand to fly across the room as he fell. The gun looked dainty and fancy enough to have come from the garter of a high-class saloon girl, but that made it no less deadly.

"Freeze!" Mark barked, hearing the rumble of talk from the crowd and facing them with his matched Army Colts in his hands, lined in their general direction.

They all froze for not one member of the crowd failed to notice how fast the guns came out, nor how competently Mark handled them. Apart from the whining and moaning of the tubby man on the floor not a sound came for a long moment.

Mark's nostrils quivered. He could smell a rich perfume which seemed to be vaguely familiar, yet he could not remember for the moment where he last smelled it. This time he could locate the source for the fat shape sprawled on the floor reeked of it. The perfume should mean something, Mark knew. The fat man smelled of the perfume, it rose and hung around him like a cloud.

"Look here, mister," said one of the customers in a conciliatory tone. "We don't know what set Jackieboy there and Knuckles on to the cowhand. Reckon anything between you and him's your affair and he ain't doing nothing much about it. But I got a chance of filling a straight here."

"Go ahead then," replied Mark, holstering his guns. "Only don't blame me if you miss filling it."

The young cowhand had made his feet now. He looked around the room, then said, "We'd best get out of here. Likely somebody's gone for the law."

"Sure," Mark agreed. "What started all this fuss?"

"There you got me. I came in, bought me a drink. Then I asked if there was a chance of taking a riding chore in these parts and the next thing I knew they was both of them on me. The name's Morg Summers."

From his talk Morg hailed from the north country. He looked like a competent cowhand, one who could be relied on to stay loyal to any brand into whose wagon he threw his bedroll.

"I'm Mark Counter," Mark answered as they walked side by side across the room. "Happen you got no other plans I might be able to put a riding chore your way real soon."

They reached the doors and passed forth. From the moment their feet hit the sidewalk both knew they were in trouble. It showed in the shape of the eight men who lounged around in a half circle before the doors. They wore deputy marshal's badges and looked as mean a pack of cut-throats as a man could want to see. Only this looked like the town marshal had extra staff, for Lasalle claimed but eight men worked for Elben and two remained safely hog-tied in the Land Agent's office.

In the center of the group, with a pomaded blond hair, a moustache and goatee beard stood the town marshal himself, looking like a fugitive from a Bill-show. He had a high crowned white Stetson, a fringed buckskin jacket, cavalry style trousers with shining Jefferson boots. A gunbelt supporting a matched brace of ivory handled Remington Beals Army revolvers butt forwards in the holsters. All in all he looked far too well dressed to be honest and much too prosperous for a lawman in a small Texas town.

"What went on inside there?" he asked.

"Enough," Mark replied. "You want to tell that swish to

keep his tame bear chained afore somebody throws lead into it."

"Don't get flip with me!" Elben snarled. "I'm taking you both to jail on charges of assault and disturbing the peace."

"I got assaulted and my peace disturbed too," Morg answered. "You going to jail the folks who done it?"

"Shut your mouth!" Elben replied.

"Happen I ever get to be a taxpayer you sure won't get my vote," Morg threatened. "How about it, Mark?"

Mark knew the men wouldn't chance using guns against him unless they were pushed into it. He also knew he could not risk being taken to jail. Any time now the men down in Mallick's office might wriggle their way free, or might be found. Before that happened Freda must be taken safely out of town. Mallick didn't look the kind of man who would let her being a woman stop him from roughing her up or worse. Two against eight were poor odds, but Dusty was on hand and could likely get to them in time to help.

The game was taken out of Mark's hands. A man darted from the saloon, arms clamping around the big Texan from behind. At the same moment the rest jumped into the fray.

While still held from behind by a man who had some strength in his arms, Mark brought up his feet, rammed them into the chests of the deputies who came at him from the front. He thrust out the legs and reeled them backwards. The man holding him staggered, but still retained his grip. To one side Morg Summers proved that he could handle his end in a rough-house even against odds.

A face appeared before Mark, a snarling face surrounded with pomaded hair. Elben moved forward snarling, "You lousy cow-nurses're going to learn not to play rough in my town."

He moved his fist brutally into Mark's stomach, bringing a gasp of pain for Mark could do nothing to escape the blow. Even as Elben drew back his fist to hit again, Mark's boot lashed up. Fortunately for Elben the kick did not land full force. Had it landed with all Mark's strength the town marshal would not have risen for a long time. Even with the limited power behind it Elben jack-knifed over and collapsed holding his middle and croaking in pain.

With a surge of his muscles Mark flung the man who held

him first to one side then the other. The man lost his hold and
went to one side. Mark shot out a fist which sprawled an
attacker backwards, backhanded another into the hitching
rail. Then they were at him from all sides. He fought back like
a devil-possessed fury. This was Mark's element, in a fight
against odds, tangling with hard-cases.

By the time Morg Summers went down four of the deputies
lay stretched on the ground, one with a nose spread over most
of his face and and all carrying marks from two pairs of hard
cowhand fists. Sheer weight of numbers got them down in the
end. Mark saw Morg go down, staggered one of his attackers
and leapt to try and prevent the young cowhand taking a
stomping. A man behind Mark drew his revolver and swung it.
Mark heard the hiss of the blow and started to try to avoid it.
The barrel of the weapon caught him a glancing blow, but one
hard enough to drop him to his hands and knees. He stayed
there, head spinning, brain unable to send any instructions to
his body or coordinate protective movements.

"Get away from him!" Elben snarled, making his feet and
looking down at Mark with an expression of almost maniacal
rage. He waved back the remaining deputies who were preparing to attack the fallen Mark. "He's mine and I want to see his
blood."

Mark heard the voice. It seemed to come from a long way
off. The fight had been rough and not all the blows handed
out by himself or Morg. He could not shake the pain from
him, clear his head enough to protect himself. He did not see
Elben coming at him, nor was the marshal more observant.
Only one thing mattered to Elben, that he might take revenge
on the blood giant who humiliated him before the town. Snarling in fury he drew back his foot for a kick, looking down at
Mark. When he got through the big Texan wouldn't look so
handsome, nor so high and mighty. Mark knew none of this.
He shook his head to try and clear it and wondered why no
more blows landed on him as he tried to get up.

In Roylan's store, Dusty heard the girl's excited words. So
did the hired gunman, heard them and read their true meaning. He came up with a hand fanning his side, reaching for his
gun. "You're not—!" he began.

Dusty wasted no time. Nor did he rely on his guns to stop
the man. He came forward and left the floor in a bound, right,

foot lashing out into the gunman's face. The man's body slammed backwards into the counter and clung there. Dusty landed on his feet and threw a punch the moment he hit the floor. His right fist shot out, the gunman's head snapped to one side. He went clear over the cracker barrel, landed flat on his back and did not make another move.

Before Roylan could catch his breath, long before he could get over this unexpected turn of events. Dusty faced him, a Colt lined on his chest.

"You go help your pard, mister," Roylan said quickly. "I'll take care of this here unfortunate feller as was supposed to be protecting me. I've got the note from Mallick to cover me."

Without a word Dusty hurled himself from the building, holstering his Colt as he went. He saw the crowd along the street and headed towards it on the run. Roylan caught Freda by the arm as she started to go after dusty.

"Who is he?" he asked, sounding real puzzled. "What happened and what's coming off, Freda, gal. How the hell did he make that kick and down the gunny. Where'd you get the note from?"

"He's Dusty Fog and helping us!" the girl replied as she tore free from his grip and raced after dusty.

She answered two of Roylan's questions, but not the third. Freda did not know of the small Oriental man down in the Rio Hondo. A man thought to be Chinese by the unenlightened majority, but known to be Japanese by his friends. To Dusty Fog alone this man taught the secrets of karate and ju-jitsu fighting. They stood Dusty in good stead and helped him handle bigger men with considerable ease as had the karate flying high kick Dusty used to set up the deputy for a finish in a hurry.

Along the street Elben drew back his foot and made sure of his balance, the better to savor the forthcoming kicking. He heard the thunder of hooves, saw his men scatter and fell back to avoid being trampled by two horses which raced at him. He opened his mouth to bellow curses and his hands dropped towards his sides.

The taller of the riders unshipped from his saddle, landing between Mark and Elben. He stood tall and slim, almost delicate looking. His clothes were Texas cowhand except for the brown coat he wore, its right side stitched back to leave clear the ivory grips of his low tried Army Colt. His face looked pale, studious almost yet the pallor was tan resisting, not one caused by sitting indoors or through ill health. His right hand made a sight defying flicker and the Colt seemed to almost meet it in midair, muzzle lining full on Elben's middle and ending his move almost as soon as it began.

"Back off, *hombre*!" ordered the slim man.

His pard wheeled the big horse between his knees, halting it and facing the deputies. He held a Winchester rifle in his hands, lining it full on them and ending their attempts to draw weapons. In appearance he was as much a Texas cowhand as his pard. Stocky, capable and tough looking, with rusty red colored hair and a face made for grinning. Only he did not grin now, his eyes flashed anger and he looked like he was only waiting for any excuse to throw lead.

"Is Mark all right, Doc?" asked the rusty-haired cowhand.

"He'd best be," replied the slim man called Doc, watching Elben's hands stay clear of the guns as he backed away.

"This's law matter you've cut in on!" Elben snarled, trying a bluff.

It failed by a good country mile.

"Kicking a man when he's down!" Doc growled back. "That's about the way of a yellow cur-dog like you, Mister, happen you've hurt Mark bad you'd best go dig a great big hole, climb in and pull the top on you."

At that same moment Dusty arrived. He came on foot, but he came real fast. Halting before the gun-hung deputies he looked them over. He clearly recognized the two riders for he did not ask how they came into this affair, or even spare them more than a single glance.

"You lousy scum!" Dusty said quietly, his grey eyes lashing the men. "All of you and they whip you down, put half of you in the street."

"Just a minute, you!" Elben snarled, seeing Dusty's lack of inches and getting bolder. "I'm taking all of you in."

"You and how many regiments of Yankee cavalry, loud mouth? asked the rusty haired cowhand. "This here's Dusty Fog and that's Mark Counter you started fussing in with."

That put a different complexion on things. Elben knew the names well enough. From the way the big Texan fought he could most likely be Mark Counter and where Mark Counter was Dusty Fog mostly could be found. He could read no sign of humor in the rusty headed cowhand's face, only deadly serious warning.

Whatever Elben may have thought on the subject his deputies acted like they sure enough believed this small man really was Dusty Fog. They crowded together, those who could, in a scared bunch. One of them indicated the two new arrivals.

"That's Rusty Willis and Doc Leroy of the Wedge!" he whispered in an urgent, warning tone.

This gave the others no comfort. Not only were the two men named prominent as members of the Wedge trail crew, they also had long been known as good friends of Dusty Fog and Mark Counter. The Wedge hired hardy cowhands, men who could handle their end in any man's fight and the names of Rusty Willis and Doc Leroy stood high on the roll of honor of the crew.

Freda arrived, dropping to her knees by Mark, trying to help him to rise. She steadied him with her arm and gasped, "Are you all right, Mark?"

That clinched it. The girl gave any of the bunch who might have doubted them proof that the two Texans were who Rusty Willis claimed them to be.

Slowly Mark forced himself up towards his feet, the girl helping him. He pointed towards where Morg lay groaning. The young cowhand had taken a worse beating than Mark, due mainly to his being less skilled in the fistic arts than the big Texan.

"See to him, gal," he ordered.

Turning Mark walked towards Elben, fists clenched. Dusty caught his arm, held him back as Elben drew away.

"Leave it lie, Mark," he said. "Rusty, fetch that buckboard from down there by the store. Bring the hosses with it. And watch the door, there's one inside who might be on his feet again.

Rusty turned his horse without wondering at Dusty's right to give him orders. On the way to the store he substituted the rifle for his Dance Bros. copy of a Colt Dragoon revolver. He guessed that more than a dispute with the local law enforcement officers caused the trouble here. This town did not need all the number of deputies who had been in the fight.

"I'll take that loud-mouthed fighting pimp now, Dusty," Mark said, loosening his gun as he gave Elben the Texans' most polite name for a Kansas lawman.

"You'll get on your hoss when it comes and ride out," Dusty answered, then turned his attention to Elben's men. "And you bunch'll go down the jail and stay there. If I see one of you between now and leaving town I'll shoot him on sight. Not you though, marshal. You're staying here. Happen any of them have smart ideas you'll be the first one to go."

Kneeling by the groaning cowhand Freda looked down at his bruised and bloody face. She felt helpless, scared, wondering if the young man might be seriously injured. The cowhand called Doc Leroy dropped to his knees by her side and reached out a hand. She watched the slim, boneless looking hands moving gently, touching and gently feeling. Doc Leroy looked up towards Dusty, showing relief.

"Nothing that won't heal in a few days," he said. "Have to ride the wagon for a spell."

By this time Rusty was returning with the buckboard and horses. He had seen the man he took to be owner of the store calmly club down a groaning deputy who tried to rise from by the counter.

Bringing the buckboard to a halt by the party Rusty leapt down, helping Doc get the groaning Morg on to the seat by Freda's side. Morg clung on, then pointing to a pair of dun horses which stood hip-shot at the hitching rail, gasped they were his string.

"Rest easy, *amigo*," drawled Rusty. "I'll hitch them on behind."

Dusty and the others mounted their horses. The small Texan jerked his carbine from the saddleboot and looked down at Elben.

"We're leaving, marshal," he said. "You shout and tell those boys of your'n that the first shot which comes our way brings you a lead backbone. See, you'll be walking ahead of us until we reach the city limits."

"And then we'll go back and tear your lousy lil town apart board by board," Rusty warned.

Freda needed no telling what to do. She started the buckboard moving forward with Mark, gripping his saddlehorn, kept by her side. Elben shouted louder than he had ever managed before, warning his men not to interfere. He spent the walk to the edge of the town sweating and hoping that none of the others wanted his post as town marshal for they would never have a better chance of getting it. All they would need to do was to pull a trigger and he'd be deader than cold pork.

All in all Elben felt relieved when he reached the edge of town and obeyed Dusty's order to toss away his matched guns. He prided himself in those expensive Remingtons, but they could be recovered and cleaned later, whereas he possessed but one life which could not be recovered if lead caught him in the right place.

Not until Dusty's party had passed out of sight did Elben return to the town. He found the owner of the saloon, Jackieboy Disraeli, nursing a swollen jaw and in a fit of rage.

"What happened out there?" Disraeli screamed, sounding more like a hysterical woman than a dangerous man. "Why didn't you smash those men to a pulp for what they did to Knuckles and me?"

"That was Dusty Fog and Mark Counter, boss," Elben replied, hating having to call the saloonkeeper by such a name, but knowing better than to fail while Knuckles still lived. "They had that Lasalle gal with them and two of the Wedge crew. The girl was in to buy supplies."

Elben's voice shook. On the way back to town an awful thought struck him. He suddenly realized just what a risk he had taken. If his kick had landed on Mark Counter he likely wouldn't be alive now to think about it.

"So Lasalle's girl bought supplies," Disraeli hissed. "Then she must have sold out."

At that moment Roylan arrived with his story about how the deputy had been felled by Dusty Fog who then terrorized him and got away. The storekeeper tossed Mallick's note before Disraeli.

"Freda Lasalle had this and your deputy didn't say who Dusty Fog was," he said. "So I served her."

In this Royland cleared his name before blame could be fixed. He did not fear Disraeli and Mallick, but knew they could ruin him, so didn't aim to give them a chance. They had no proof of what happened in his place and he doubted if the deputy could say anything that might give the lie to his story.

Disraeli headed a rush for Mallick's office where they broke open the door and released an irate Mallick and his men. It took some time before the Land Agent could talk. He slumped in his chair, stiff and sore, glowering at Elben.

"We bring extra men to help handle the town and four cowhands ride all over you," he snarled, after hearing the story. "Elben, you're a— Hell-fire and damnation! They took that map I tore up and threw into the wastepaper-basket."

"I thought you destroyed it," hissed Disraeli. Only he, Mallick and Elben now stood in the office. "Why didn't you?"

"Because I didn't get a chance. They came before I could. Now there's only one thing to do. Get to Lasalle's place and kill every last one of them—and fast!"

CHAPTER EIGHT

The Ysabel Kid Meets
A Gentleman's Gentleman

A SMALL drifting cloud of dust on the horizon down to the south warned the Ysabel Kid he had somebody on his trail. He drew rein on top of a hill and looked along his backtrail. He saw the following rider at a distance where most folks could have made out only a tiny, indistinguishable blob. The Kid not only saw the man, but could tell he had two horses along. This in itself meant nothing for many men took their own string of horses along with them. The direction from which he appeared told a story. He came from the Double K area and the Kid knew few riders would get across without being halted by the hired guns and turned back in their tracks.

"He's after us, old Blackie hoss," drawled the Kid. "Dang my fool Comanche way of telling the truth when I'm questioned politelike. I should remember I'm a paleface, most times, and that as such I can be the biggest danged liar in the world without worrying."

The big white snorted gently, wanting to be moving again. With a grin the Kid started Blackie on his way again.

"Wonder what he wants?" he mused, talking to the horse, but never relaxing his wolf cautious watching of the trail ahead of him. The man was still too far behind to cause any menace. "Must be one of that bunch from this morning and looking for evens. Waal, he can have his chance when he comes closer."

Only the man did not seem to be pushing his horse to close up, nor riding the two mounts in rotation, travelling relay fashion. The kid knew he could make his tracks so difficult that he could delay the man—if he happened to be following the Kid's trail. The Kid told that pair of hired guns back on

83

Double K where he headed and the following man would not
waste time in tracking, but by riding straight for Bent's Ford
could be on hand when the Kid arrived. With that thought in
mind the Kid decided to continue to Bent's Ford, making sure
he arrived before the other man and so be able to keep a wary
eye on all new arrivals.

The sun was long set when the Kid saw the buildings, stream
and lake known the length of the great inter-state cattle trails
as Bent's Ford. The main house showed lights and even where
he sat the Kid could hear music from the bar-room so he did
not need to worry about disturbing the other guests by his arrival.

Why Bent's Ford had such a name when there appeared to
be nothing of fordable nature has been told elsewhere.* The
place served as a stopping off and watering point for the trail
herds headed north across the Indian Nations. On this night
however no herd bedded down near at hand. There were
horses in the corrals, two big Conestoga wagons standing to
one side, teamless and silent, the normal kind of scene for
Bent's most any night of the week.

The Kid rode steadily down towards the buildings. He could
almost swear the man following him had not managed to get
ahead during the dark hours. For all that he did not leave his
leg-weary white stallion in the corral. The horse stood out
amongst others like a snow-drift and would easily be noticed.
Also Blackie did not take to having strange horses around him
and could be very forceful in his objections.

Using the prerogative of an old friend, the Kid took his
horse to Bent's private stables and found, as he hoped, an
empty stall. He meant to attend to his horse before thinking of
himself. With Blackie cooled down, watered and supplied with
both grain and hay, the Kid left his saddle hanging on the
burro in the corner. He drew the old "yellow boy" from the
saddleboot and headed for the barroom.

Although busily occupied in wiping over a glass with a piece
of cloth, the bartender found time to look up and nod a
greeting to the new arrival.

"Howdy, Kid," he greeted. "Looking for Wes Hardin?"

"He here?"

"By the wall there, playing poker with the boss."

* Told in THE HALF-BREED

The bartender and the Kid exchanged glances and broad grins. The poker games between Wes Hardin, Texas gunfighter, and Duke Bent, owner of Bent's Ford, were famous along the cattle trails. In serious play and skill the games stood high for both men were past masters at the ancient arts of betting and bluffing known as poker. Yet neither had ever come out of a game more than five or so dollars ahead for they played a five to ten cent limit. This did not affect the way in which they played for they gave each deal enough concentration for a thousand dollar pot.

Before he crossed the room, the Kid looked around. The usual kind of crowd for Bent's Ford looked to be present. A few cowhands who spent the winter up north and were now either headed home or waiting in hope of taking on with another trail drive. Travelling salesmen, flashily dressed, loud-talking, boastful as they waited for stage coaches. A trio of the blue uniformed cavalrymen and a buckskin clad scout shared a table. None of them looked to have just finished a long, hard ride.

"Anybody new in, Charlie?" he asked.

"You're the first since sundown," the bartender answered.

"Check this in for me then," drawled the Kid, passing his rifle to the other man who placed it with the double barrelled ten gauge under the bar counter.

With his weapon out of the way, the Kid crossed the room towards where Bent played poker. He stood for a moment studying Bent's burly build, gambler style clothes and remembering the big man made this place almost single-handed, brought it to its present high standard by hard work and guts. Bent had been a cavalry scout, one of the best. He'd also been a lawman, tough and honest. And Bent was all man in the Kid's eyes.

With his back to the wall in the manner of one of his kind, Wes Hardin, most feared gunfighter in Texas, studied his cards. He was tall, slender, with a dark expressionless face and cold, wolf-savage eyes. Hardin wore the dress of a top-hand with cattle, which he was, he also wore a gunbelt which carried a brace of matched Army Colts in the butt forward holsters of a real fast man with a gun. He was that too.

"I'll raise you!" Bent said, fanning his cards between powerful fingers.

"Will you now?" replied Hardin. "I'm going to see that raise and up it."

The Kid watched all this, knowing the two men were completely oblivious of his presence. He moved around to see Hardin's cards, a grin came to his face and he did something no other man in the room would dare to do.

"Should be ashamed of yourself, Wes," he said, "raising on less'n pair of eights like that."

Slamming down his cards with an exclamation of disgust Hardin thrust back his chair and glared at the Indian-dark boy before him. The customers at nearby tables prepared to head for cover when guns roared forth.

"Hello, Lon," said Hardin, relaxing slightly when he saw who cut in. "What damn fool game you playing, you crazy Comanche. I was all set to bluff Bent clear out of the pot."

"Huh!" granted Bent. "You didn't fool me one lil bit." He raked in the pile of chips and started to count them. "Make it you owe me a dollar fifty, Wes."

"Bet you over counted, like always."

The two men glared at each other. They began a lengthy argument, each man casting reflections on the other's morals and general honesty. Things passed between them, insults rocked back and forwards, which would have seen hands flashing hipwards and the thunder of guns if spoken by a stranger.

Somehow the argument got sidetracked as, alternating between recrimination and personal abuse, they started to argue heatedly about a disputed call in a wild card game some three years before. Just what this had to do with the present disagreement passed the Kid's understanding as neither of the men had held the disputed hand, in fact had not even been in the pot where it came up.

A burst of laughter from the Kid brought an end to the argument and they turned their anger on him, studying him with plain disgust.

"What's amusing you, you danged Comanche?" Hardin growled.

"You pair are," answered the grinning Kid. "I've seen you both lose and win plenty without a word, in high stake games. Yet you're sat here whittle-whanging over who won a measly dollar fifty."

"You wouldn't understand it at all, Kid," Bent answered. "It's all a matter of principles, which same you've got none of."

"Man!" whooped the Kid. "Happen principles make folks act like you pair I sure don't want any."

Hardin's face grew more serious, though only men who knew him as well as the Kid and Bent would have noticed it.

"Where at's Dusty and Mark, Lon?" he asked. "I tried to make Moondog City, when I heard about Cousin Danny."*

"We handled it, Wes."

"Cousin Dusty all right now? He felt strong about that lil brother of his."

"He's over it now."

From the way the Kid spoke both men knew the subject was closed. He did not intend talking about the happenings in the town of Moondog. The sense of loss he felt at the death of Dusty's younger, though not smaller brother, still hung on. He did not offer to tell what happened when Dusty, Mark, Red Blaze and himself came to Moondog. They came to see how Danny Fog handled his duties as a Texas Ranger and had found him beaten to death. Danny Fog died because the town did not dare back him against Sandra Howkins' wolf-pack of hired killers. The Kid did not care to think of the days when he, Dusty and Mark stayed in Moondog and brought an end to the woman's reign of terror.

"Been any sign of the OD Connected herd yet?" asked the Kid, not only changing the subject but also getting down to the urgent business which brought him north.

"Nope, we haven't seen any sign of it," Bent replied. "You fixing to meet up with it here?"

"Was. Only we got us a mite of fuss down below the Texas line. Might take us a spell to handle it and we don't want Red Blaze coming down trail to help us, or waiting here for us to join up."

Due to having been followed the Kid was more than usually alert and watchful. So he saw the man who entered the saloon and stood just inside the doors, looking around. One glance told the Kid this man had not been on his trail, for the trailer had been a westerner and the new arrival anything but that.

He stood maybe five foot eight, slim and erect. His sober
_____
* Told in A TOWN CALLED YELLOWDOG

black suit was well pressed and tidy, his shirt white and his tie of eastern pattern and sober hue. Though his head had lost some of its hair and his face looked parchment-like, expressionless, he carried himself with quiet dignity as he crossed towards where Bent sat at the table. Halting by the table the newcomer coughed discreetly to attract attention to himself.

"Has Sir James' man arrived to guide us to his residence, landlord?" he asked in a strange sounding accent.

"Nope," Bent answered, having grown used to being addressed as landlord by this sober looking dude. "Did you pass anybody on the way north, Lon?"

"Nary a soul," replied the Kid. "You all expecting somebody, friend?"

Swivelling an eye in the Kid's direction, the man looked him over from head to toe. The Kid had ridden hard all day and his black clothes did not look their best, but he reckoned that to be his own concern. To the Kid it seemed this pasty-faced dude did not approve of him or his trail-dirty appearance. This annoyed the Kid, never a man to allow a dude to take liberties with him.

Bent knew this and cut in hurriedly, saying, "Mr. Weems here's expecting one of the Double K to come and guide him and his folks down to the spread."

At first Bent had not taken to Weems. Weems came down from the north with two big Conestoga wagons, each well loaded, but drawn by good horses of a type rarely seen in the west, great heavy legged and powerful creatures which Weems called shire horses. The two wagons had been driven by a pair of gaunt men dressed in a style Bent had never seen before. Two women rode in the wagons and, strangely to western eyes, they did not ride together. Bent suggested that the men shared a room and the two women another. The suggestion was greeted with horror by all concerned, the two drivers insisting it wouldn't be proper to share a room with Mr. Weems and the pretty, snub-nosed, poorly dressed girl stated firmly she could not possibly use the same room as Miss Trumble.

It took Bent a short time to understand the social standing so firmly ingrained in these English travellers. They did not live by the same standards as the men of the West. To the girl, Weems called her a 'tween maid, it was unthinkable that she should room with so exalted a person as Miss Trumble who appeared to be a housekeeper of some kind. So he arranged for the girl to use a small room while Miss Trumble and Weems took two of his expensive guest rooms and the two men insisted on spending the night in the wagons.

"You-all work for Keller, mister?" asked the Kid, his voice sounding Comanche-mean.

"I am *Sir James* Keller's man," replied Weems haughtily and laying great emphasis on the third and fourth words.

"Never took you for a gal!" answered the Kid, getting more riled at the thought of a dude trying to make a fool of him.

Once more Bent intervened in the interests of peace and quiet. "Mr. Weems is a valet, Lon," he said.

"A valley?" asked the Kid, sounding puzzled and wondering if Bent was joining in some kind of a joke.

"V-a-l-e-t, not v-a-l-l-e-y," Bent explained.

"A gentleman's gentlemen," Weems went on, as if that would clear up any doubts the Kid still held.

"Like Tommy Okasi is to Uncle Devil," Hardin put in, helping to clarify the duties of a valet in a manner the Kid understood.

"Never heard ole Tommy called anything as fancy as a valet," drawled the Kid although he knew now what Weems did for his living.

"There's not likely to be anybody up here today," Bent told Weems. "If your boss hasn't anybody here in the morning you could send a telegraph message to Barlock and let him know you've arrived here. Or you could see if there's anybody going down trail who'll act as a guide. But you won't be able to start until the morning either way."

"Thank you, I yield to your greater knowledge."

With that Weems turned and walked towards the bar. Bent looked down at the cards, then raised his eyes to the Kid's face. The struggle between possible financial gains at poker and his keenness at quartet singing warred for a moment and music won out.

"Say, Lon," he said. "Let's see if we can get up a quartet and have us some singing."

Always when the Kid visited Bent's Ford on his way north or south, Bent expected a session of quartet harmony. He possessed a powerful, rolling bass and enjoyed throwing it into the melody, backing the other singers. The Kid stood high on Bent's list of tenors and the Kid was always willing to oblige. Knowing Dusty did not expect him to return before morning, the Kid could relax and enjoy quartet singing in good company.

"Let's go and find us some more singers," drawled the Kid.

"Got us a baritone," Bent replied. "Whiskey drummer over there. Now all we want is another tenor. How about you, Wes?"

"Never took to singing since pappy used to make me get in that fancy lil suit and go into the choir back home."

"I'll get around and ask, Lon," Bent said, as Wes Hardin refused to be drawn into the quartet.

The Kid and Hardin headed for the bar while Bent made a round of the room looking for a second tenor without which no decent quartet could exist. The two Texans took beer, further along the bar Weems leaned with a schooner of beer in his hand looking off into space and speaking with nobody.

"Not another tenor in the place," said Bent in a disappointed tone, joining the other two at the bar.

His words carried to Weems who walked towards them.

"I suppose there is no chance of getting started for the master's residence tonight?" he said.

"Nope, none at all," Bent answered.

"Then may I join your quartet?"

The other men showed their surprise for none of them thought Weems to be a likely candidate for joining in a quartet.

"You?" asked the Kid.

"One sings occasionally," replied Weems calmly. "I recollect the time Sir James' butler and I formed a quartet with the head keeper and head groom. Of course they weren't in our class, but we felt the conventions could be waived at such a time. Without boasting, we made a pretty fair quartet."

The meaning of Weems' words went clear over the heads of his listeners. Not one of them understood the strict hierarchy of servants in upper-class households. Nor were they greatly concerned with such things as conventions, being more interested in getting buckled down to some singing.

One problem might present itself, the choice of songs.

Weems could hardly be expected to know old range favorites.

"Shall we make a start with *Barbara Allen*?" asked Weems.

"Take the lead, friend," replied the Kid.

It took them but the first verse of the old song to know Weems could handle his part and was no mean tenor in his own right. The room fell silent as the customers settled back to listen to real good singing.

After four songs, all well put over and with Weems showing he could lend a hand at carrying a melody even if he did not know the words of the tune, Bent called for liquid refreshment. This gave the Kid a chance to talk to Weems and to try to learn more about Sir James Keller.

"What sort of feller's your boss, friend?" he asked.

"Sir James?" replied Weems. "A gentleman and a sportsman. My family has served his for the past six generations."

"Why'd he come out here?"

"I never asked."

The Kid grinned, warming to Weems. If anybody had questioned him about some of Dusty, or Ole Devil's business he would have made the same reply, in much the same tone. Clearly Weems felt the same loyalty to his boss as a cowhand did to the outfit for which he rode. However the Kid hoped to try and learn if Keller knew what went on around and about his spread.

"Maybe he reckons to make a fortune out here," drawled Wes Hardin.

"We already have a fortune," sniffed Weems, just a trifle pompously. "The master felt we might have a better chance of development out here. After all there is so little scope left in England these days. The whole country's going to the dogs. Why shortly before we sailed a junior footman at Lord Granderville's, in *my* presence, addressed the butler without calling him mister."

To Weems this clearly amounted to the depths of decadence, a sign of the general rottenness of the times. To the listening men it sounded incomprehensible. If a Texan called a man mister after being introduced it meant he did not like the man and wanted no part of him.

Bent took up the questioning and Weems, with the mellowing influence of a couple of beers, talked of the life he had in England. He might have been discussing the habits of creatures from another planet as he described the strict social distinctions between servants. It now became clear to Bent why a between-stairs maid did not consider herself good enough to share a room with so important a person as a housekeeper. The term brought grins to Texas faces. In their world a house did not mean a home and housekeeper sounded like a fancy title for the madam of a brothel. Weems broke in to a delighted chuckle as the Kid mentioned this, trying to picture the puritanical Miss Trumble in such a capacity. He talked on but there was no snobbish feeling in his words. To him it stood as a way of life, one with a code as rigid as that which ruled the lives of cowhands in their loyalty to their brand.

During the talking, even though absorbed by Weems' descriptive powers, the Kid stayed alert. He saw the stocky man who entered the bar room and stood just inside looking around with watchful eyes. For an instant he looked at the Kid, then his eyes passed on, but the Kid had noticed just a hint of recognition in them. The Kid studied the newcomer, noted his dandy but travel-stained clothes, the low hanging Tranter revolver from the butt of which a right hand never strayed. The man looked like a tough hired killer, one of the better class than the pair he'd run across on Double K, or the group he helped chase from Lasalle's, but one of their breed.

Possibly the man might be a guide come to take Weems and his party to the ranch. His next actions proved this to be wrong. The man did not cross to the bar and ask for information about the Weems' party. He sat with his back to the wall and close to the door, and ordered a drink from a passing waiter. Which same meant if he came from the Double K it was not to meet Weems, but to follow the Kid.

"Let's have another song," suggested Bent, getting in another round of beers. "Give us the *Rosemay-Jo Lament*, Lon."

"Why sure," agreed the Kid. "Soon's I've been out back."

Shoving away from the bar, the Kid headed across the room and out of the door. He gave no sign of knowing the man might be after him, but sensed eyes on him as he left the building. Two horses which had not been there when he entered, stood at the hitching rail. That meant he guessed right, the man was the same who followed him north.

For some moments after the Kid's departure Dune sat at the table and waited. Then he emptied his glass in one swallow, rose and walked through the doors into the night.

The night lay under the light of a waning moon, but he could see well enough for his purpose. He glanced at the two horses, they had brought him from the Double K although he did not travel at speed. He might have caught up with the Kid on the range but did not fancy taking such a chance. He had ridden steadily, keeping reserve energy for a hurried departure. Clearly the Kid had friends in the bar-room and they were not going to take kindly finding him murdered.

With this thought in mind Dune led the two horses to the side of the main building and left them. Then he walked around behind the building, making for the long, three-hole men's backhouse which lay some distance away.

To discourage his guests from staying inside too long, to the discomfort of other guests, Bent had three-quarter length doors on each compartment of the backhouse. This left part of the top and bottom open and tended to make the occupants take only such time as was necessary.

Only one compartment of the backhouse appeared to be in use. Dune saw this and could tell that it held the Ysabel Kid, for a gunbelt hung over the top of the door, a white handled bowie knife strapped to it.

Dune looked around him carefully as he drew his Tranter revolver. Apart from a small bush some twenty feet away he could see nothing and even the bush was nothing to disturb him. He did not aim to match up with the Kid in a fair fight and he had a good chance of avoiding the need to.

Taking aim Dune threw his first bullet into the door. He knew that the .44 bullets would make light work of smashing through the planks at that range. Twice more he aimed and fired, taking only enough time to re-aim and place the bullets a few inches apart, so they would fan across the interior and catch the Kid as he sat on the hole.

No sound came from the compartment. Nothing at all. Dune realized this as he triggered off his third shot. Realized it and the implication behind the silence. Even had his first bullet struck and killed the Kid there should have been some noise, if only his death throes.

"Finished?" asked a voice from his left.

Dune swung around, trying to turn the Tranter. The Kid's black-dressed shape loomed up from behind the bush Dune had dismissed as being too small to hide even a child. His gunbelt might hang over the backhouse door and show the hilt of the bowie knife as bait for a trap—but the old Dragoon was in his hand.

With a snarled curse Dune tried to line his gun. The Tranter never saw the day when its butt lent itself to fast instinctive alignment and Dune had time for nothing else. He fired, the bullet missed the Kid although it came close enough to stir his shirt sleeve. With a roar like a cannon the old Dragoon bloomed out a reply, flame stabbing towards Dune.

The Kid shot the only way he dare. For an instant kill. His round, soft lead .44 ball caught Dune just over the left eyebrow at the front and burst in a shower of bone splinters and brains out at the back of the head. Such was the striking power of the old gun that Dune went over backwards, thrown from his feet. The Tranter fell from a lifeless hand even before his body hit the ground.

Shouts sounded from the main building. Windows of the upper floor rooms opened and people looked out. Then Bent and Wes Hardin, both holding weapons, burst into sight, racing towards the Kid. Other occupants of the bar-room came next including some of the staff carrying lanterns.

"What happened?" Bent asked the Kid who stood strapping on his gunbelt once more.

"Take a look. That *hombre* sure messed up your backhouse door."

Taking a lantern from a waiter, Wes Hardin came forward and let the light play on the door. His eyes took in the three holes. From their height and position he could guess at what would have happened had the Kid been sitting inside.

"Who was he, Lon?" asked Bent, for he handled law enforcement in that section of the Indian Nations.

"Never saw him afore, until he walked into your place tonight. Any of these folks know him?"

Bent allowed the onlookers to move forward, but none of them could say who the dead man might be. Dune's face, apart from the hole over his eye, was not marked even though the back of his head proved to be a hideous mess when exposed to view.

The two horses did not help either, one came from a south Texas ranch, by its brand; the other from a spread which specialized in the breeding and selling of saddle stock.

"Nothing in his pockets to identify him," Bent stated, making a check. "Sure you don't know him, Lon?"

"Nope."

Bent threw a look at the Kid, knowing the sound of his voice. When that note crept into the Kid's voice it was no use asking him questions. So Bent shrugged and turned to order his men to remove the body.

The Kid found Weems at his side. They watched men carrying away the body headed for the stables where it could be left until morning when it would be buried.

"You killed him," said the valet, his face looking ashen pale.

Tapping the door by the line of bullet holes, the Kid nodded. "I reckon I did. He wasn't in this much of a hurry to get in and even if he had been there's two more empty holes."

"And you didn't know him?"

"Nope. He could have mistaken me for somebody else. Say, I'm headed down trail in the morning. Happen you feel like it I'll show you to Double K."

Weems gave the matter some thought. This soft-talking, innocent looking young man had just killed a fellow human being. True the other man appeared to have given good cause for the action, but in England people did not treat killing so lightly. However Weems had his duty to his master. He must get the two wagon loads of furniture and property to the house as soon as possible. He decided to take a chance. Like his master, Weems had been escorted from Kansas by cavalrymen from Fort Dodge, their colonel being a friend of Sir James. However Weems's escort were ordered to return at Bent's Ford where a guide from the ranch would be waiting. The guide had not arrived and Weems wished for no more delay. Who knew what a position Sir James might find himself in, alone, without the services of a good valet in the raw, primitive west?''

"I'll be pleased to have you along," he said.

"We'll pull out at sun-up then," replied the Kid. "Now I'd best get back inside, likely Duke Brent'll want to see me some more about that *hombre* I had to kill."

CHAPTER NINE

Keep Back Or I'll Kill You

DUSTY Fog turned in his saddle and looked back along the trail to Barlock. What he saw satisfied him and he slid the Winchester carbine back into its saddle-boot.

"They're not following us," he remarked.

Rusty Willis scoffed at the thought. "Course not. They know I'm along."

"You don't smell that bad yet," grunted Mark. "How you feeling, Morg?"

The young cowhand from the north country managed a wry grin and tried to ease his aching body on the buckboard seat. he didnt want the men, all well known members of his trade, to think him a whiner.

"Like one time a hoss throwed me off then walked over me. T'aint nothing but half a dozen or so broken ribs, all us Montana boys are tough."

This brought howls of derision from the others. Freda watched them and smiled, wondering if cowhands ever grew up so old as to take life seriously. She also gave a sideways look at Morg Summers; he seemed capable and honest, not bad looking either if it came to a point.

"Say Freda, gal," Mark went on. "Morg here's looking for a riding chore and you're looking for a hand or so. Must be fate in it somewhere."

"I'd have to be able to call him something more than just Morg," she replied.

"Why?" grinned Mark, watching the flush which crept to the girl's cheeks. "All right. This's Morgan Summers, from Montana, 'though why he'd boast about that I sure don't know. Morg, get acquainted with Freda Lasalle; my pard

Dusty Fog; and this pair are from the Wedge, but don't hold it again 'em. They answer to Rusty Willis and Doc Leroy and if you can't sort out which's which you north country hands are even less smart than I allow you are.''

"Rusty Willis's the best looking one," Rusty prompted.

"Howdy Rusty," Morg replied, looking at Doc. "I'd recognize you from your pard's description."

All in all Morg allowed he had made the right impression on the others. He wanted to make a good impression on them all —especially the girl who sat so close besides him and handled the ribbons of the buckboard so competently.

"I think we can manage to hire you," Freda stated, wondering if her father would agree, then she looked towards Mark in a coldly accusing manner. "What started the trouble in town?"

Leaving Mark to explain, or to keep the girl occupied, for his explanation in the first place bore little resemblance to the truth, Dusty turned his attention to the two Wedge hands. He had not seen them in a couple of years, but they looked little different. Doc still looked as studious and frail as ever, and most likely could still handle his gun with the old speed and skill. Rusty clung to his old Dance Brothers revolver, a Confederate .44 calibre copy of the Dragoon Colt and he did not look any less reliable for that.

"Where at's the herd?" Dusty asked.

"Down trail a piece," replied Doc. "Rusty and me cut on ahead to Barlock to pick up some makings. You look like you've found some fuss up here, Dusty."

"Man'd say you were right at that," Dusty agreed.

Then he told the story of their visit to Lasalle's and what came out of it. He saw the change in his friends' faces as he spoke of that wire across the narrows and Mallick's threat that no trial herd would go through his land. They did not offer any comment until he finished then Rusty let out a low exclamation, obscene but to the point.

"Clay Allison's about two days behind us and to the southwest," he went on. "Johnny saw him on a swing around the herd. There'll surely be all hell on when old Clay hears about that wire."

Doc nodded his agreement and Dusty saw nothing to argue about in it. They all knew Clay Allison, a Texas rancher and one of the real fast guns in his own right. If he arrived and found his trail blocked he would have a real good answer, roaring guns.

A thought hit Doc Leroy and he reined in his horse, looking at Dusty.

"If those yahoos from the Double K hit Lasalle's they likely went for the other spreads at the same time."

An angry grunt left Dusty's lips. He should have thought of that in the first place. However he did not waste time in futile self-recrimination, or in discussing the chance of the Double K making visits.

He rode forward to the buckboard and interrupted Mark's description of how he and Morg were saving the virtue of a beautiful saloongirl when the marshal's bunch jumped them, with Morg protesting his innocence in the matter of rescuing beautiful saloongirls.

"Reckon you can get this pair of invalids back to your place without us along, Freda?" he asked.

"I reckon I can. If lies were health Mark's sure well enough. You're not going back to Barlock, are you?"

"Nope," Dusty answered. "So don't get all hot and bothered. Doc's just reminded me of something I should've thought of sooner."

"What's that?" she asked.

"The same thing that bunch tried at your place might've been done to your neighbors, only more so."

Freda gave a low gasp for she had not thought of the possibility either. She instantly became practical and helpful, pointing off across the range roughly in the direction of the Gibbs' place, then how they would be able to find the Jones' house.

"Want me along, Dusty?" Mark asked.

"Not this time, *amigo*," replied Dusty. "Three of us should be enough and I'd like somebody on hand at Freda's in case that bunch comes back."

Although he would have much rather rode with Dusty, Mark knew his small pard call the game right. Not only would an extra pair of hands give strength to the Lasalle house if an attack came, but Mark himself needed to get off his horse and rest. That fight in town had taken plenty out of him, enough to make him more of a liability than an asset in the sort of conditions Dusty, Doc and Rusty might be running into.

Knowing hired gunmen, Mark guessed Tring would be smarting under the indignity of failure and in being fanned off the Lasalle place by a load of bird shot. He might easily gather his bunch and make for the Lasalle house to avenge himself and Mark wanted to be on hand when he came.

So Mark stayed with the buckboard while Dusty swung off at a tangent, riding with his two good friends of the Wedge. Mark grinned at the girl's worried face and said, "Waal, there was ole Morg, with this beautiful blonde haired gal on his lap and all—"

"You danged white-topped pirate!" wailed Morg. "Whyn't you tell the truth for once in your life?"

"All right," grinned Mark. "She wasn't beautiful, She was about two hundred pounds weight, had seven double chins—"

"Let's ignore him, Morg," suggested Freda, interrupting Mark's flow of descriptive untruth. "You tell me what happened."

Which brought her no nearer to knowing the truth for Morg reversed the story Mark told, putting Mark in his place in every detail.

"That I can well believe," Freda remarked at the end. "Now—and I want to remind all and sundry that I am the sole cook at home—how about telling me what really happened."

"A wise man once told me never to argue with the cook," Mark drawled. "It all started when I saw Morg getting abused by that Jackieboy saloon bunch."

This time Freda heard the true story. She felt grateful to Mark for having saved Morg Summers and almost wished she had not slapped Mark's face back in town.

For a time after leaving the buckboard Dusty and the other two rode in silence. Beyond expressing their regrets at the death of Dusty's brother neither Doc nor Rusty made any other reference to the happenings in Moondog. They were all good friends with past dangers shared, so did not need to go into words to show their true feelings. Dusty turned the talk to the wire and the other two growled their anger. All agreed on one thing. The fence must go. Rusty and Doc were all for war, although Doc, more given to thinking of causes and effects than his *amigo* saw how a wire cutting war might affect the inhabitants of the area.

"I can't see Clay Allison sitting back peaceable and talking,

Dusty," drawled Rusty Willis, "even if Stone will."

"I'm going to talk to them both," Dusty answered. "I'll ride down trail in the morning and meet up with Clay. He'll stand firm maybe, if I explain things to him."

"What sort of things?" Rusty asked.

"Like what'll happen to these folks up here happen a war starts over their land."

"That'd tangle their lines for sure," agreed Doc Leroy. "It'd be them who go to the wall if the trail herds were held up and grazed their land out, to say nothing of the fighting that'd be going on."

Then Rusty saw it. He had seen an area blasted wide open by a range war between two big outfits. There were three smaller places around the scene of the war and at the end of it all lay empty and deserted, the owners either killed or run out by the opposing factions.

They rode across the range and struck a track made by wagon wheel ruts which, according to Freda's directions, ought to lead to the Gibbs' spread. After following the tracks for a couple of miles they topped a rim and looked down.

"You were right, Doc," Dusty said quietly and grimly. "Double K didn't just call on Lasalle."

Neither Doc nor Rusty made any reply to this, Rusty growled a low, barely audible string of curses, but Doc said nothing. His long, slim fingers drummed on his saddle horn as his eyes took in the scene below.

The corral fence had been smashed down. The house's front door hung on its lower hinges, the top having been smashed open. Not a single pane of glass remained unbroken at the windows. Nor did the destruction end with the corral and main house. The outbuilding doors had been burst in, their walls battered into gaping holes. Not a living thing showed about the place. Several dead chickens lay before the house and the body of a big bluetick hound sprawled stiff and still by the corral fence.

"Let's go!" Dusty growled and started his horse forward.

Slowly they rode down the slope towards the house. Not one of them spoke as they studied the wreck of a well-kept spread and a neat, clean house.

"Keep away!" screamed a woman's voice from the house. "Keep back of I'll kill you!"

Hysteria filled the woman's voice, but the three men did not stop. They rode slowly on and halted their horses by the corral. Dusty started to swing down from his saddle when Rusty's voice, tense and warning, stopped him.

"Dusty! The door! Turn slow and easy!"

Turning his head Dusty looked towards the broken door of the house. He found himself looking at the barrels of a ten gauge shotgun. Behind the shotgun, holding it waist high but aimed at them, stood a pretty, plump, red-haired woman. Slowly Dusty swung down from his saddle and took a step forward, hands well clear of his sides, eyes never leaving her face.

She would have been a happy woman, full of the joys of life, friendly and kind, most times. Now her face bore marks of the strain she was under and he eyes were red rimmed, swollen with tears. She came through the door, a smallish woman wearing an old gingham dress and with a face which told that she had been through living hell that day.

"Keep back!" she repeated. "Haven't you done enough? My husband isn't even conscious yet! He can't do anything!"

"Easy, ma'am," replied Dusty, watching her all the time and stepping closer. "We're not from the Double K."

He might never have spoken for all the effect his words had on her. it did not even appear that the woman heard his words. She brought up the shotgun a trifle and Doc bit down a warning shout just in time.

"Watch her, Dusty!" he warned in a voice which sounded nearer a whisper than a shout. "One wrong move and you'll be picking buckshot out of your back teeth. She's scared loco and'd do it without even knowing."

Slowly as a snail crossing a leaf, Dusty moved forward. He did not for an instant take his eyes from the woman's face, trying to hold her attention on him. So far she had not pressed the shotgun's trigger but one fast move could cause her forefinger to close and send the weapon's deadly charge into him. Despite his earlier scoffing Dusty knew even a charge of birdshot at that range would be more than lethal and would blow a hole like a cannon's bore in him. One quick move, one sudden sound even, might cause her to press the trigger.

It was as deadly and dangerous a situation as Dusty had ever been in. Perhaps the most dangerous. If this had been a man bad mean and set on killing, Dusty could have handled things differently. Only this was no man, but a terrified woman driven to the verge of madness, hysterical and not responsible for her actions.

Perhaps Doc Leroy knew the danger better than Rusty, than Dusty even. For a time, before circumstances sent him home to Texas and to become a cowhand working for Stone Hart's Wedge, Doc read medicine in an eastern college. He did not complete the course but spent every spare minute when in town working with the local medicine man, learning all he could. On the trail he handled the doctoring chores which fell to the cook in most cases. He would take care of injuries, splint and care for broken limbs, diagnose various illnesses and produce their cures, within the limitations of his medical supplies. He probably knew more about the extraction of bullets than most eastern doctors ever learned. On two occasions, when driven to it by the force of circumstances, he delivered babies. So Doc had knowledge of the effect of hysteria. He knew the full danger of Dusty going towards the woman and he felt more scared than he had ever been in his life.

Still moving slowly Dusty made his way towards the woman, edging to the right with the barrels of the gun following him like iron filings after a magnet. He knew his friends were now clear of the shotgun's charge and there only remained the problem of getting the weapon away from her without taking its charge full in his belly. For the first time he looked down at the gun, seeing that the right side hammer only had been cocked back, the left lying safe and down.

An inch at a time, moving with the same slowness which covered all his moves since dismounting, Dusty's right hand went up, gripped the brim of his Stetson and removed it. He was close to the woman, but not close enough to chance a straight grab, not while her finger rested on the trigger. However the gun aimed at him, his friends were in the clear. He had brought them into this mess and must get them out of it without injury if possible. That was the way Dusty Fog thought and acted.

"Just take it easy, ma'am," he said, keeping his voice gentle and fighting to hold the tension out of it. His eyes were on her face once more. "Afore you can shoot you'll have to cock back the hammers."

The woman's eyes dropped towards the breech of her shotgun. For an instant her finger relaxed on the trigger. Instantly Dusty slapped his hat around, knocking the shotgun's barrels to the right while he made a fast side step to the left. For all that it was close, very close. The gun bellowed, he felt the hot muzzle blast and the hot rush of air and burnt powder stirred his shirt, but the lethal load, not yet spread on leaving the barrel, missed him.

Jumping forward Dusty grabbed the shotgun by its barrels and dragged forward at it. The woman gave a scream of terror, she tried to fumble back the second hammer but Dusty plucked the shotgun from her hands. She stood for a moment, staring at Dusty, while Doc and Rusty came out of their saddles and the mount Dusty borrowed from Lasalle took off for home on the run.

"Catch my saddle, Rusty!" Dusty yelled, giving the old range request for aid; for while the horse a cowhand rode mostly belonged to the ranch's remuda it carried his more precious and vital item of personal property, his saddle.

The words seemed to shake the woman out of her paralysis. With a scream she flung herself at Dusty, coming all teeth and fingernails, a wild-cat ready to use primeval fighting equipment to defend her home and husband. Dusty did not dare take a chance. He caught her by the wrists, holding her as she struggled with almost super-human strength, feet lashing out and arms fighting against his grip. He saw Rusty take off after his departing horse and felt relieved. Nothing in the west caused so much anxiety as a riderless, saddled horse. Dusty knew Mark would be worried if his mount came back to Lasalle's empty. He did not want his big *amigo* coming looking for him and leaving the Lasalle house with only a small guard.

For a moment the woman struggled, until Doc caught her by the arms from behind and held her. Then she seemed to collapse into herself. The shotgun, thrown to one side by Dusty when he found need to prevent her scratching his eyes out, lay on the ground but she did not look at it. Instead she lifted dull, lifeless eyes to his face and spoke in a strangled voice.

"All right. Do what you like with me, but leave my husband alone."

Dusty and Doc released her, but Dusty took up the shotgun and removed its percussion cap to make sure the weapon could not be turned against him. Then he stood with his back to the two, allowing the tension to ooze from him. In his time as a lawman Dusty had found cause to use a shotgun on a man, it was not a pretty sight. A man did not just shake off, and laugh at it as being nothing, almost winding up the same way.

Knowing how Dusty must feel, Doc gently turned the woman to face him. "Now easy there, ma'am," he said. "We're not from the Double K."

"Freda Lasalle sent us over," Dusty went on, his voice sounding just a little shaky still, and not turning around.

At that moment Doc threw a look at the partly open door of the house. What he saw brought an angry growl for his throat and sent him running for the house. Dusty turned and followed, seeing what Doc saw and forgetting his personal feelings in the urgency of the matter. The woman turned, watching them, looking as if all her will had been drained out of her. Then she heard hooves and turned to see Rusty riding back, leading the Lasalle's horse. He swung down from the saddle, left his horse standing with its reins dangling and the runaway fastened to the saddlehorn. Coming towards the woman he threw a glance at the stiff body of the bluetick hound.

"Nobody but a stinking Yankee'd shoot a good dawg like that'n," he said in a tone that boded ill for the man who shot the dog if Rusty ever laid hands on him. "Where'd I find a spade, ma'am? I'll tend to burying him."

He got no reply, for the woman turned on her heels and fled to the house, Rusty did not follow, but headed for the damaged barn to see if he could find a shovel.

Dusty and Doc were already in the house. The building, made on the same lines as Lasalle's home, had once been just as neat, tidy and pleasant. Now the front room looked as if a whirlwind had passed through it. The table had been thrown over, chairs broken, the sofa's covers slashed open to expose springs and stuffing. The cupboards were shattered and broken, crockery lying in pieces on the floor. Just inside the door, face down, head resting on a pillow lay the woman's husband, a tall, powerful looking man of middle-age. His back carried marks left by the lash of a blacksnake whip.

"Don't touch him!" gasped the woman, entering the room just as Doc went to his knees by the man.

"Get me some hot water, ma'am," Doc answered gently.

"Happen they've left you anything to heat it in. And I'll want some clean white cloth. I've got to get that shirt off and tend to his back."

At last the woman seemed to realize that her visitors meant her no harm. She made an effort, then led Dusty to the kitchen. It appeared the Double K restricted their efforts to the out-buildings and the front room for the neat kitchen remained intact and she had already been heating water when they rode up.

"What happened, ma'am?" Dusty asked, leading the woman from the room as soon as she gave Doc the water and cloth. Doc was never too amiable when handling a medical or surgical chore and it paid to steer well clear of him at such times.

"Some of the Double K men came to see us early on. They told us to sell out and leave. Said they would be back after they saw the Joneses. Later on they came back. Ralph told them he didn't aim to quit and they jumped him. Sam tried to help, but one of them shot him down. They lashed Ralph to the corral and whipped him, while one of them held me, made me watch. Then they wrecked everything they could and rode away. They said they'd be back tomorrow. I thought you—I thought—Oh lord! I nearly k-killed you!"

"You were scared, ma'am," Dusty answered. "You couldn't know."

The sound of digging brought her attention from Dusty. She looked to where Rusty Willis, who at normal times wouldn't have thought of touching the blister end of a spade, dug a grave for the dog.

Then she turned and started to cry, the sobs ripping from her, tears pouring down her cheeks in a steady flow. The anguish she must have held bottled up inside while she tried to do something for her husband and about the wreck of her home, boiled out of her. She knew herself to be safe and in good hands. Now she could be a woman and cry out her misery.

Dusty let her get on with it, knowing she would be better once the crying ended. He waited by her side and at last she dried her eyes, turning to him once more and showing she had full control of herself.

"I should help your friend. I was a nurse for a time in the

War. After the men rode away I managed to get Ralph inside the house. I had laudanum in the medicine chest, they hadn't touched it. I gave Ralph some to ease the pain. I didn't know what to do for the best. Can your friend do anything for my husband?''

"Reckon he can, ma'am? There was a time when a trail hand for the Wedge took sick, like to die. Ole Doc there, he went to work and operated with a bowie knife and a bottle of whisky. He saved that hand's life. Yea, I reckon he can handle your husband's hurts all right.''

At that moment they heard the sound of hooves. Rusty dropped the spade and fetched out his Dance. Dusty turned, hands ready to bring out the matched Colts. He knew only one horse approached but prepared to tell the woman to head for the house. It didn't seem likely that Double K would send one man to visit the ranch, but one of the hired guns might have the idea that a woman left alone and in a state of terror would be easy meat.

"Don't shoot!" Joyce Gibbs gasped, seeing and recognizing the rider. "It's Yance. He works for Pop Jones.''

Riding at a fast trot the grizzled cowhand came towards the others. He halted his horse and threw a glance at Dusty and Rusty, then relaxed. Neither were the kind Double K hired.

"See they been here, too," he said in an angry tone. "They treat you folks bad, Mrs. Gibbs?''

"Ralph's hurt," she replied. "These gents came by and lent a hand. Have they been to your place?''

"Came in on their way through here. Told Pop to sell out and go. He allows to do it. Him and Maw's getting too old for fussing with that bunch. I'd've started shooting, but Maw said no.''

"When do they have to leave by, friend?" Dusty asked, stepping by Joyce.

"Double K allow to come in tomorrow and make sure we're ready to up stakes and pull out.''

Studying Dusty, the cowhand did not see a small, insignificant man, he saw a master of their trade, a tophand more than normally competent with the matched brace of guns he wore. Yance did not know from where Dusty and Rusty came, but he knew they looked like the kind of men who could handle the Double K bunch. He hoped they would stay on and help the Gibbs family who were real nice folks and deserved better than to be driven out from their homes. Yance was more than willing to listen to any words of wisdom the small Texan might hand out.

"You head back to your spread," Dusty told him. "I'll try and get a couple or so hands over to you in the morning. If they haven't made it by ten o'clock tell your boss to upstakes and head for Lasalle's. Don't stand and fight."

"You at Lasalle's?" Yance asked.

"Sure."

"I'll tell Pop. Only I sure hope that you-all can get the men to us. I'd like to tie into Double K with some good men at my back."

He wasted no more time in talk. Turning his horse he headed for his home spread, but he rode in a more jaunty manner. Joyce saw this and wondered who the small man might be.

"Who are you?" she asked, then her face flushed red for such a question was never asked in polite western society.

For once Dusty took no offense at the words. He introduced himself and Rusty telling her who Doc was. Then he kept her talking while Rusty finished the grave-digging and buried the dog.

"They broke a tea set my mother gave me for my wedding!"she said suddenly, recalling something. Tears glistened in her eyes as she said the words and she clenched her fists, trying to avoid breaking down once more for the reaction still hung over her.

"One thing I promise, ma'am," Dusty replied. "The man responsible for this lot here's going to pay for it."

CHAPTER TEN

The Coming of The Wedge

BEFORE Joyce Gibbs could sink into despondency again she saw Doc come out of the cabin and started towards him with Dusty at her side.

"I've fixed his back, ma'am," Doc drawled. "Cleaned the wounds and got them covered. It's bad enough. He'll likely carry the scars until he dies and it'll hurt like hell for a time. But there's no injury to his spine as far as I can tell."

"We can't move him, then?" Dusty asked.

"From where he lies to the bed is all," Doc replied. "Happen you mean can we take him out of here."

"That's what I meant. Rusty, lend a hand to tote him to his bed. Then get your hoss and head back to the herd. Ask Stone if he can send a few of the crew to lend a hand up this ways. Tell him what's happened and that I'll likely come down and see him in the morning, but to get the boys here if he can spare them."

"Yo!" replied Rusty, giving the cavalry affirmative answer.

"Lasalle's place is over that way. Happen you see it, call on in and tell Mark I won't see him until morning."

Joyce watched the men heading into her house. It took some getting used to, the way the two men jumped to obey the small Texan, a man she would have passed in the street without a second glance. Of course she had heard of Dusty Fog, but never would she have pictured him as this small, insignificant cowhand.

Following the two men into the house she watched the gentle way they carried her husband into the bedroom and laid him on the bed, face down. She also blushed at some of the *sotto voce* comments Doc heaped on his friends if they did not

109

handle Ralph in the manner he felt correct. Already the laudanum had started to wear off and Ralph groaned in pain.

"Just stay by him, ma'am," Doc said. "Until he's sane
enough to know better, I mean wtih the pain and all, and
strong enough to get out of it, we'll have to make sure he
keeps his face from burying into the pillow. I'd stay on, but
I'll see what Dusty wants first."

He left Joyce with her husband and headed out to find
Dusty watching Rusty ride off.

"What now?" Doc asked.

"We'd best put the hosses in the barn first, then get set for a
long wait and maybe a fight."

They took their mounts to the stable and found that the
damage had been done only to the outer walls. So they removed their double girthed saddles and left the horses in
empty stalls, then headed for the house, taking the saddles
with them.

Dusty spent the rest of the afternoon helping Joyce do what
she could about the damage to the house. They set the table up
and found that two chairs remained unbroken, but the rest
were smashed beyond repair. Dusty swore again that he would
make the men behind the raid pay for what they did and he
meant it in more ways than one.

"Your husband's awake, ma'am," Doc said, just before
dark as he entered the room. "Come on in and see him."

Joyce followed the slim Texan into the bedroom and found
her husband, his face lined with pain still, looking at her
although he still lay on his face.

"I'd like to thank you gents for helping us," Ralph Gibbs
said, looking at Dusty who followed his wife into the room.

"There's no call for that," Dusty replied. "I only wish that
I got here in time to stop them doing what they did."

"You fed our guests, honey?" Ralph asked.

"I did the best I could," she answered. "Used some of the
chickens the men killed, made up enough for us all. I'll fetch
you some broth in."

"You fixing on sticking here?" Dusty asked. "If you are,
I'll have some men on hand to help fight off that Double K
bunch when they come."

"I'm staying!" stated Gibbs firmly. "Although how I'll
manage for food I don't know. That bunch told me the only

way we could buy supplies was to sell out to Mallick and he'd give us a note for the store."

"I've got an answer for that," Dusty said quietly. "How about your market herd, did you get it gathered?"

"Not yet. I wanted to hire a couple of hands for a roundup but there's none to be had out this way."

"We'll see what we can do," promised Dusty. "So—Douse the lights Doc. We've got callers."

They all heard the rapid drumming of hooves and this time not just one horse but several.

Doc quickly doused the light in the room and Dusty darted across to blow out the lamp on the dining-room table. The house plunged into darkness and Dusty stood by a window. He heard a soft footfall and saw Doc coming towards him.

"You ought to be with her," Dusty said.

"That's what I thought," replied Doc and his teeth gleamed white in a grin. "Only I done fetched in, cleaned and loaded that old ten gauge and Mrs. Gibbs done got it by the window, swears to fill the hide of the first Double K skunk she sees out there. She'll do it, too, or I've never seen a gal who could."

"I reckon she will," agreed Dusty for he knew Joyce had regained control of herself and was the more dangerous for it. Now she could handle the shotgun in cold determination and she knew how to make the most of it.

Nearer thundered the hooves. Clearly if these were the Double K they did not expect trouble from Gibbs or his wife. Joyce suddenly realized the riders did not come from the direction of the Double K and she turned from the window to call out this information to Dusty. A voice let out a cowhand yell from the darkness, before she could speak.

"Hey Dusty, Doc! Don't go fanning any lead. It's us."

Which left a lot unexplained to Gibbs and his wife, but apparently satisfied the two men in the dining-room. After a brief pause a match rasped and the table lamp lit once more. Joyce saw Dusty resting his carbine against the wall then open the door they had repaired.

"I can't think of a better reason for shooting!" he called to the men outside, then looked across the room towards Joyce. "It's all right, ma'am. They're friends."

Saying that Dusty stepped out of the house to greet his old friends of the Wedge trail crew.

Six men sat their horses in a half circle before the front of the Gibbs' house. Six men who, apart from the OD Connected crew or some of his illustrious kin, Dusty would rather have seen than any others at such a time. Rusty Willis was one, leaning on his saddlehorn at the right of the party. Next to him, tall, slim, still retaining some of his cavalryman's stiff-backed grace, sat Stone Hart. He would have been a hand-some young man had it not been for the sabre scar on his right cheek, a memento of a cavalry clash in the War Between The States. He wore cowhand clothes neither better nor worse than those of the others, but about him hung the undefinable something which sets a leader of men apart from the others. Stone Hart was such a leader of men. He rode as trail boss for the Wedge and that took a leader, not a driver of men.

"Rusty allows you found some trouble, Dusty," Stone said, his voice an even cultured deep south drawl.

"You called it right, Stone," Dusty agreed, then threw a glance at the woman in the doorway. "Can they light a spell, ma'am?"

"Of course they may," she answered, annoyed at being so lax in her hospitality. "Please get down, gentlemen."

Now she was no longer scared and half-hysterical, Joyce could tell quality when she saw it. Every man in that group looked like a tophand, even the medium sized, stocky man with the drooping moustache and the woe-begone look on his face. The rest did not look like hired hard-cases, but they did look like remarkably efficient fighting men. He alone did not fit into the picture, or the sort to be tied in with such an outfit as the Wedge. Later she found this man, Peaceful Gunn by name, would move easily two inches out of his way if he ran into trouble. His element was a fight into which he could plunge, all the time insisting he was a peace-loving and easy-going as a dove. Joyce knew something of wild animals and knew the dove, for all its being regarded as the bird of peace, was in reality amongst the toughest and most trouble-hunting of birds, always ready for a fight.

Next to Peaceful sat a tall, wide shouldered, freckle faced and handsome young man with a fiery thatch of red hair. He wore cowhand clothes and belted a low handing Army Colt. He rode as scout for the Wedge. Folks said Johnny Raybold, as the red head was named, could eat as much as would founder a good-sized horse although he preferred something more nourishing than grass. he had other good qualities and could be relied on in any man's fight.

While the other three men were not members of Stone Hart's regular crew, all carried a look of tophands who knew what their guns could be used for. They were the usual type of men he hired, tough, salty, loyal to the brand they rode for. Stone introduced them as Tex, Shaun and Billy.

The men trooped into the house at Joyce's invitation. She watched Peaceful as he peered around him a shade nervously. His moustache, which was capable of more expression than most folks could get from their entire face, dropped miserably and gave him the appearance of a terrified walrus.

"Where they at?" he asked in a tone which suggested they might be hiding under the table ready to jump him. "It's getting so a body can't ride a trail these days without running into fuss."

The rest of the men ignored Peaceful's words. Johnny Raybold gave out a whoop and held out a hand to Dusty.

"Where at's thishere wire, Dusty?" he asked. "And where's Mark 'n' the Kid?"

"What you want them for?" groaned Peaceful, his moustache drooping like the wilted lily on a cheap undertaker's lapel. "They'll only help wind us up in more trouble."

This brought howls of derision from the others who all knew Peaceful much better than did Joyce.

"Should head for the badlands and go 'round," he went on miserably. "That way we won't wind up in fuss with them gents who strung the wire."

"Get mum, all of you," Stone growled, bringing an end to the argument which was developing, even before it started. "We all know you'd be fit to be tied if I even thought of going round."

"Rusty tell you it all, Stone?" Dusty asked, while Joyce went to fetch coffee for her guests.

"What he knew about it. What's on that tricky Rio Hondo mind?"

"I figured that Double K might come back and that'd we'd give 'em a real Texas welcome, only I needed a few friends on hand to tote 'round the tea and biscuits for the guests."

Stone Hart smiled. He'd known Dusty for a few years now

and they'd sided each other in a couple of tight spots in that time. One thing he did know for sure. The situation up here must be very grave for Dusty to send for help during a drive. Dusty knew trail driving, knew it from the angle of hand and as trail boss, so he would not lightly send and ask for men.

"Stake 'em out the way you want," he said, setting the seal of approval on Dusty's actions and giving permission for orders to be passed to his men. Stone hired the men, it should be to him to make any arrangements for their employment, but he knew Dusty had a better idea of the situation and knew what would be needed in offence and defence.

"I'll have Johnny staked out on the range about a mile out towards the Double K, waiting for the first sound of their coming. When they get here I want some of the boys in the out-buildings, some here. I want that bunch boxed in and held tighter than a Yankee storekeeper's purse strings."

"Get to it, Johnny," drawled Stone. "Which's the way Double K'll most likely come ma'am?"

"That way," Joyce answered, a finger stabbing in the direction of the Double K house. "But they might not come that direction."

"It's likely they will," Dusty replied. "They don't know about Stone and the boys and'll likely think they've got nothing to worry about. So they'll come the easiest direction."

"Dusty could be right at that, ma'am," Stone put in.

Joyce noticed the trail boss never looked straight at her and tried to keep the unscarred side of his face to her all the time. She felt sorry for him, he must have been a really handsome young man before the Yankee sabre marred his face. Even now a woman would not find him revolting; the scar looked bad, but could have been far worse. Much as she wished to tell him her thoughts she knew any reference to his injury would offend Stone. He would not want a stranger to mention it.

The men stood around Joyce's table and drank their coffee, all except Johnny who knew what was expected of him and faded off into the dark astride his big iron grey night horse. Only Peaceful seemed to be worried by the forthcoming possible visit and Joyce got the feeling that he did not care as much as he pretended.

"What do you want from the rest of us, Dusty?" asked Rusty Willis.

"Stone, Doc and I'll stay at the house," Dusty answered with a grin. "And don't go saying we're pulling rank on you—because we are. Rest of you pick out your places and wait until you hear Johnny come back. Put your hosses in the barn, but keep them saddled. If Double K hit, I want them. Not one's got to get back to their spread."

"These Double K bunch, Cap'n Fog," put in one of the new Wedge hands, "How'd you want them, alive or dead?"

"Whichever way you have to take them."

Dusty's reply came in a flat, even voice, but every man present knew what he meant. Shoot if you must and if you must shoot, shoot to kill, that was Dusty's meaning. It was the way of a tough lawman, of the man who tamed Quiet Town. Such would be the orders he gave to his deputies when they went after a dangerous outlaw in the line of duty. In the same manner Dusty now spoke. He did not want killings or trouble, but if Double K forced them on him he would try and prevent his side from taking lead if he could.

"How about me, Dusty?" asked Joyce after the men went to their posts. She used his given name, having received no encouragement to carry on with his formal rank and title, and knowing far better than call a cowhand "mister" after being introduced.

"If they come, get in the bedroom with your man. Let Doc handle the fighting, he'll be in there. Stone, Johnny and I'll be out here."

"Don't you think it might be better to send that miserable looking man back to the herd?" she asked. "He looked terrified when he went out to the barn."

Two faces looked at her, trying to see if she was joking, then Dusty and Stone started grinning.

"You mean Peaceful, ma'am?" asked Stone.

"I don't know his name. Nobody got around to introducing me to any of you."

Taking the hint Dusty introduced her to Stone. She knew the Wedge boss by reputation but nothing more. He and Dusty seemed much alike in many ways. Polite, courteous, yet masterful. Men who gave orders and knew their strength without being over-aggressive or bullying. She could see how they extracted such loyalty from the men under their command.

"How many men do you have, Stone?" Dusty asked, forgetting the matter of sending Peaceful to the safety of the herd.

"My regular crew and nine more."

"Seventeen, huh? Double K have at least that many at the spread and more in town. You'll be needing half of your men to hold the herd back down there for a day or two while we sort this wire trouble out."

"There's folks relying on me taking their herds through, Dusty," Stone pointed out.

"I've thought about that too."

"What're you fixing to do then?"

"Wait hereabouts for Clay Allison to come closer, ride down tomorrow and meet him, ask for help."

Stone grunted. "I never knowed the Wedge to need Clay Allison to do our fighting for us."

"He's not fighting for you. He's fighting for himself, for every herd that comes up the trail, for every man who died making this trail and keeping it open in the early days," Dusty answered. "And I hope to keep it from busting into an open fight if I can."

"It'll come to fighting, happen Clay reaches here and the wire's still up," Stone answered.

"Not the way I want to play it. With him and your boys I reckon we have enough hard-country stock to make Double K think twice about locking horns."

"Would Clay Allison make all that much difference?" Joyce asked, looking from one man to the other.

"Enough, ma'am," Stone answered.

He knew Clay Allison, respected the man as a rancher and a trail boss of the first water, but there had never been any close ties between them. To Stone the end of a trail meant little more than selling his herd at the best possible price, paying off his hands, working out each ranch's share of the profits and taking his cut to be added to the bank balance with which he hoped one day soon to buy a ranch of his own.

To Clay Allison, already a rich rancher owner in his own right, the end of a drive meant fun, hoorawing the trail-end town, celebrations, wild and hectic parties with his hands and anyone who cared to join in the fun, before heading back home to Texas. Happen there should also be a chance to tie

into some loud-mouth Kansas lawman who boasted he jailed
Texans one handed, left-handed at that, then Clay Allison's
trail-end was made complete.

So, beyond their mutual loyalty to the south in the War and
their combined interest in keeping open a trail to the Kansas
markets, Clay Allison and Stone Hart had little or nothing in
common. Yet Stone knew Clay's name packed considerable
weight as a fast-gun fighting man. With him along, backed by
the Wedge's men, Dusty might be able to make the owner of
the Double K open the trail without blood being shed.

"I'd like to leave three men here and send three across to the
Jones spread, if that rides all right with you, Stone," Dusty
drawled. "Just for a couple of days happen all goes well."

"Sure, I'll see to it," Stone replied. "We've made good
time up to here and the beef could stand a couple of days' rest.
I'll leave Rusty, Doc and Billy here."

Hearing the words Joyce could almost have sung with
delight. She knew Rusty looked like he could take care of
himself and any of the other hands, apart from the one called
Peaceful, would also be a good man to have around. She
decided Doc was being left to help care for her husband,
although he did wear a fast man's gun-rig, she doubted if so
studious a looking young man could make best use of it.

"Which spread's the further from Double K?" Dusty
asked. "You or Jones?"

"We are."

"Be best to have Peaceful up there then. Should be far
enough away from Double K to keep him happy," Dusty said.

"But we're farther from Double K—!" Joyce began, thinking Dusty misunderstood her words.

"Yes'm, that's just what we mean," grinned Stone.

Leaving Joyce to try and work logic out of the words, Dusty
and Stone got down to discussing the events leading up to this
night gathering. Joyce sighed, deciding she would never
understand cowhands. She went into the bedroom to find her
husband sleeping comfortably and Doc sitting by the window,
cleaning his Army Colt.

Sitting his horse about a mile from the ranch house Johnny
Raybold looked around him, studying the open range. Then
he swung down and squat on his heels, letting his iron grey
stallion stand with reins dangling. Tied or loose the big horse

would not stray far from him, and never played up or tried to avoid him when he went to it. That was a quality Johnny often needed in his task as scout for the Wedge.

Johnny drew his Winchester from the saddleboot and then settled down for a long wait. He took out his makings, rolling a smoke and hanging it from the corner of his mouth, but did not offer to light it. The horse moved to one side and fell to cropping the grass.

"Fool chore this, ole hoss," he said quietly, after being on watch for an hour. "Bet Chow put Dusty up to it."

Snorting softly the horse moved closer to its master. Johnny grinned, realizing that Dusty could not have seen the Wedge's cook for a couple of years and could hardly have worked up this business with chow. It made him feel better to lay the blame on somebody for being sent on a chore that he, with the exception of the Ysabel Kid, could handle best.

Johnny knew little or nothing of the trouble in this section of the Panhandle country. He had been with the rest of the crew when Rusty Willis returned on the run with a message for Stone. Johnny found himself one of the group Stone selected to ride with him, leaving his segundo, Waggles Harrison, in charge of the herd. Why they came still remained something of a mystery to Johnny. He did not particularly care. A good friend needed help and Johnny needed to know no more.

Listening to the night noises Johnny stayed where he was, quiet, relaxed and without moving restlessly. Often he had done this kind of work and knew how to keep his mind alert and working without it interfering with his watching and listening. He thought of nights spent sitting by a fire, listening to the baying of coon-hound music as a redbone ran a line in the darkness. To Johnny no sound in the world came so sweetly as the trail song of a good hound dog. He thought of his return to Texas for the fall. He'd head down and see some kin who owned good hounds and—

Suddenly the thoughts ended. Johnny came to his feet in a lithe move. He stood with the rifle held before his body, face turned towards the sound which took his thoughts from hound music. For a moment he stood, listening to the night sounds and catching once more the faint crackle of shots in the distance.

Now Johnny had a problem on his hands. He did not know

if Dusty could hear the shots while in the house. So Johnny needed to decide if to stay here or head back with the word would be best. Then he decided. Dusty would want to know about the shooting, especially as there did not appear to be any sign of the Double K.

Johnny turned, he went afork his stallion in a bound, catching up the reins and starting his mount running towards the house.

In the house Joyce poured her coffee for her guests before making for the barn and serving the other men. She stifled a yawn and said, "They might not be coming tonight after all."

"Might not," agreed Dusty. "But—"

They all heard the thunder of a fast running horse's hooves and made for the door of the house. Outside they could just hear the crackle of shots. Joyce's face lost some of its colour.

"Lasalle's!" she gasped.

By now the other men were from the barn. A sudden bright flash showed down where the shots sounded, followed by a dull booming roar.

"Dynamite!" Dusty snapped. "Loan me a hoss, Stone. I've got to get down there."

Stone wasted no time. "Peaceful, loan Dusty your hoss. Stay here with Doc. The rest of you hit those kaks and let's ride."

For a man who professed to have no other aim in life but to avoid trouble, Peaceful showed some reluctance to being left out of the rescue party. He did not argue for he knew Mark Counter was out there some place, most likely where that explosion sounded. He led his big horse from the barn and jerked the Spencer rifle from the saddleboot.

Dusty went astride Peaceful's horse in a flying mount, grabbed the reins and put his pet-makers to work. The horse was no livery plug to accept a stranger on its back, but it sensed a master rider and did not try to make a fight. It set off across the darkened range at a gallop. The other men followed. They rode fast, pushing their horses. For all they knew, their help might be needed at Lasalle's place.

In the lead Dusty rode with fear in his heart. The dynamite had gone off at the Lasalle place and his *amigo*, a man as close as any brother, might even now be dead, blown to doll-rags by the Double K hired killers.

CHAPTER ELEVEN

The Hit At LaSalle's

"I'LL see that five thousand dollars and up another five," Freda Lasalle announced calmly, after studying the three kings in her hand once more.

The Lasalle's sitting-room looked bright and cheerful enough. Lasalle sat at the side table, reading a book and throwing his amused gaze at the high stake poked game at the dining table where his daughter backed feminine intuition against the skill and knowledge of the other two. Female intuition did not seem to be all it was cracked up to be for Freda owed Mark and Morg Summers about five hundred thousand dollars so far.

"I sure can't see how you always get the cards," she objected, after the betting as her three kings fell before Mark's low straight.

"Unlucky in love, lucky at cards," Mark answered.

An over-done snigger greeted his words, coming from Freda who reached for the cards. The game only started to stop her worrying about the fate of her friends and the non-arrival of Dusty, Rusty and Doc. On his ride to the herd Rusty had missed Lasalle's place and so none of the occupants knew what might have kept Dusty away. At last Mark insisted they played cards, needling Freda into the game to prevent her worrying.

To Morg Summers the night could go on for ever. He now held the position as official hand of the Lasalle spread and Freda seemed very friendly. Morg wondered how things stood between the girl and Mark Counter, felt just a little jealous and decided he did not have a chance against such a handsome and famous man's opposition. However he got the idea that Mark would be riding out as soon as the trouble came to an end and felt better about things.

The redbone hound sprawled before the empty fireplace for Mark would not allow a fire. Suddenly the dog raised his head, looking towards the front door and letting a low growl rumble deep in his throat.

"Douse the lights!" Mark snapped, thrusting back his chair. "Get to your places. Move it!"

His very urgency put life into their limbs. Morg blew out the lamp on the table and Lasalle doused the other. They could all hear the horses now, a fair sized bunch of them by all accounts. It looked like Tring had returned and meant to make up for his last visit and so brought plenty of help.

"Hit the back, Morg!" Mark ordered. "George, take that side and watch the barn. Freda, keep well down, gal. Don't none of you start throwing lead until I give the word."

For once Freda did not make any comment to Mark's orders. She knew when to have a joke and when to obey fast, without question. Mark had been in charge of the preparations for defending the house ever since they returned from town. He threw all his considerable knowledge into the matter. First he scouted around and found a secluded draw about two miles from them and on the side away from Double K. Into this went all the ranch's remuda along with Dusty and Mark's horses and their pack horse. Then, although he ached in every muscle and bone, Mark looked the house over and found but little needed attending to, beyond dousing the dining-room fire and making sure all the weapons were fully loaded.

Now the attack had come. The riders were on top of the slope and coming down towards the river. Suddenly shots thundered out, lead smashed into the house but its walls kept them out. The window panes shattered and bullets raked the room, but so far all the shooting came from the front.

Mark's matched guns were in his hands as he flattened on the wall by the window. He looked back across the room, eyes trying to pierce the darkness. From the look of things the opening volley hit nobody. He could see Lasalle's shape by the side window looking out towards the barn and outbuildings, holding his Le Mat carbine ready for use. Morg had already taken his place in the hands' bedroom and so would be clear. That only left Freda.

"Mark!" whispered a scared voice at his side, a voice trying to hide its fear. "I've brought your rifle. Papa and Morg are in place and ready. Why did those men start shooting?"

Before Mark could make a reply the Double K men came sweeping down the slope and into the water. He guessed that whoever had charge of the raid thought the occupants of the houses were all asleep and hoped to startle and confuse himself and his friends. The men knew of the hound's presence and that a chance of moving in silently was unlikely to succeed. So they hoped to startle, suddenly waken the people in the house and rush in on them before they recovered.

It was a real smart plan. Except that Mark and the others were fully awake and ready.

Suddenly Mark swung around towards the shattered window. He brought up his right-hand Colt, thumbing four rapid shots into the darkness, firing into the brown without taking sight. He heard a yell and guessed some of the lead took effect. The attackers yelled their surprise. He heard the frantic churning of hooves in water as they brought their horses to a halt or tried to change directions. Mark grinned and darted to the other window, beyond the door.

"Pour it into them, Dusty!" he yelled, firing three more shots, and trying to make out his two *amigos* were with him.

He heard the crash of his rifle from the window just vacated and twisted his head in time to see Freda flatten herself back against the wall. The girl once more showed she had courage and could think for herself. She guessed at what he tried to do and lent a hand.

The riders came ashore and fanned out, riding along the side of the house towards the barn. Lasalle cut loose with the old Le Mat, turning four of his nine bullets adrift towards the men. He did not think he had managed to hit anyone but his little effort caused a rapid swing about and dart to cover.

Not all the men had headed for the barn, a few went the other way but Mark already had thought of this and was by the other side window which stood open. He lined his right-hand Colt and used its last two loads on them. This time he saw a man crumple over, cling to his saddlehorn and turn his horse away.

"Freda!" Mark snapped. "Watch 'em, gal. I'll reload."

It took some time to strip foil from a combustile cartridge, nick the bottom to ensure the percussion cap's spark of flame struck powder, and place it in the chamber of the Colt, turn the chamber, work the loading rammer and force it home. Mark had done the drill so often he could manage it in daylight or dark, but he felt satisfied with himself that he remembered to have the spare loads laid out on the table, along with an open percussion cap box. He loaded both his guns and even as he did so fresh developments came.

The men from Double K, being met with a hot fire on three sides of the house, took stock of the situation. From the guns, and the yell they heard, it looked like Dusty Fog, Mark Counter and Lasalle were all in front and, unless Dune called it wrong, the Ysabel Kid had left for Bent's Ford. So it appeared the defenders had committed an error in tactics and left the rear unguarded. With this in mind a group of men moved in, swinging behind the barn, leaving their horses and running off across the range, meaning to come in at the rear.

"Hey, Freda!" Morg's voice came in an urgent whisper. "Bring me some shells for my rifle, please."

"I'll be right there," she answered.

"It's no use you-all trying to make me jealous, gal," drawled Mark. "I'm allus true to one gal—at a time."

"She doesn't show very good taste, whoever she is," replied Freda hotly, but in no louder voice than Mark used. "I wouldn't be your gal, Mark Counter, not even if you were the last man in the world."

"Gal," replied Mark, his teeth gleaming in a grin as he watched her back off from the table, keeping down. "Was I the last man in the world I'd be too busy to worry."

Freda gave a snort and thought of a suitable answer, although she doubted if her father would approve of it. She collected a box of bullets and headed for the bedroom to find Morg standing by an open window and looking out. He had his rifle in his hands, but her ten gauge lay on the bed by his side.

"Hi, there," he greeted. "Sure is quiet back here. Say, has that mean ole Mark been abusing you again?"

"He sure has. Whyn't you act like a knight in shining armour and go in there to demand satisfaction."

"Me?" grinned Morg. "I'm satisfied already. Who wouldn't be? Got me a starlit night, a real pretty gal to talk to and—hand me up the scatter, gal."

None of the speech had been in a loud tone, but the last few words came in an urgent whisper. Freda took up the shotgun, exchanging it for the rifle he offered her. Then she peered through the window and watched the dark shapes moving by the backhouse and coming towards them.

Gripping the shotgun Morg rested its barrels on the window ledge and drew back the hammers. The double click must have sounded loud in the still of the night, the group of men out back came to a halt for a moment. Then, apparently deciding the clicks to be imagination they moved forward, their weapons glinting dully in their hands.

Morg now had a problem. Never had he been in such a spot and he had never turned lead loose at another man. He did not want to shoot at the men, to kill without a warning. Then an idea came to him.

"She's loaded with nine buckshot, gents!" he called. "Hereby I lets her go! Yahoo! Hunt your holes, you gophers!"

His first words brought the men to an uneasy halt. The rest of his speech had the effect of making the men turn about and head for cover. He aimed low and cut loose with both barrels. A man yelled, staggered, but reeled on. Morg knew some of the lead had gone home but that the man he hit was not seriously hurt.

He passed the shotgun to Freda who whispered she would reload for him. At the shot, lead slashed from all sides at the house. A bullet smashed into the window frame, showering broken glass and splinters which caused Freda to cry out and twist around. Morg gave an angry growl, grabbing his rifle to throw shots at the spurts of flame around the building.

"Are you all right?" he asked.

The concern in his voice brought a thrill to Freda, a thrill she could hardly explain even to herself. Before she could answer the firing died down and Mark's voice came to her.

"How's it going back there? Is the roof still on?"

"Why shouldn't it be?" Freda replied, running a hand across her face and knowing the flying splinters missed her.

"I heard you fire that fool shotgun off!"

It took Freda a moment to catch Mark's meaning. She wished she could find a real smart answer. Then she remembered Morg's question and turned to him, seeing he watched her.

"I'm all right thanks, Morg. How about you?"

She laid a hand on his arm, he released the rifle with one hand to reach and trap the hand, holding it gently.

"Lord!" he said. "If they'd hurt you I'd—"

Freda bent forward, her lips lightly brushed his cheek. This was not the action of a well brought-up young lady. She and Morg met for the first time that afternoon, sure he had taken on to ride for her father but that did not mean he took on for any other reason than he needed work. All those thoughts buzzed through Freda's head after her impulsive action.

"There's nothing between Mark and me," she whispered.

"There's no gal any place waiting for me," Morg whispered.

Then they kissed, oblivious of everything. Two young people who suddenly found themselves in love. Then Morg gently moved her away from him and swung to the window. Any man who tried to harm Freda was going to get lead and would need to kill him first.

Unaware of romance blooming in the back of the house Mark Counter moved from front to the left side of the dining-room, watching through the windows, letting the Double K men do the shooting, saving his lead for when it would be needed to break an attack.

He flattened by the side of the window which looked out across the range. Men darted forward, coming towards the house. Then a shout from the other side reached his ears although he could not make out the words. The approaching party came to a halt and took cover rapidly.

Mark's fighting instincts warned him something was in the air. The men had been moving in undetected, or at least without warning that they had been detected. Yet they had taken cover in a hurry. This was not the actions he would expect of an attacking group coming in to their objective unsuspected. Anything unusual in an attack worried Mark and made him the more alert.

"Freda!" he called. "Freda!"

The second word brought her to his side. She realized that he no longer sounded easy-going and friendly.

"Go and warn both your pappy and Morg to be ready for something to start. That bunch out there have something tricky on their minds."

"What?" she asked.

"I wish I knew, gal."

The coldness of his voice made her feel as if a chilly hand laid itself on her. She knew Mark had guessed what the smart move might be—and that it was something terrible.

After delivering Mark's message to her father Freda returned to the bedroom and told Morg. He gripped her hand in his.

"Are you scared?" he asked.

"Not now I'm with you."

At the right side window Lasalle knelt watching the barn into which a fair part of the attacking force went. Due to Mark's prompt action on returning from Barlock they would find little to destroy and would not burn the building until after the attack. A lighted barn blazing merrily would make them much too easy targets for the defenders, so the barn and other buildings were safe during the attack.

Nursing the Le Mat, feeling the weight of the Army Colt in his waistband, he watched for the first sign of his attackers. He wished he could take time out to reload the fired chambers, but still had a fair few shots left and a load of grapeshot in the lower barrel, just waiting to be used.

Lasalle was no longer the defeated, tired man who rode to his ranch that morning, ready to call "calf-rope" and run. Now he stood firm, grimly determined to fight for his home, to defend it with his last breath.

A small group of men eased out of the barn, moving cautiously towards the house. Lasalle watched them, wondering if his best move would be to open fire now, or let them come in closer and make sure he hit at least one of them. He did not want to kill, but knew it might be necessary to get himself clear of this mess. He knew they did not suspect he watched them, or they would not be advancing so openly on him.

Just as he decided to throw a warning shot, the group halted. He saw a flicker of light, a glow as if a man had turned around and lit a match, shielding the flame with his body. Apparently one of the men had lit a cigarette or cigar, for something glowed redly in the darkness.

In a flash Lasalle knew something to be dead wrong. He knew that in the heat and madness of battle men often did strange things like singing, praying, crying or shouting. But they did not stop to light cigarettes. Nor did men sneaking up on a night attack a defended building.

Resting the barrel of the carbine on the window he took a careful aim. Drawing back the hammer he fired a shot and saw the man holding the red, glowing thing rock under the impact of lead, then go down, dropping whatever he held so that it spluttered on the ground by him.

Instantly consternation and pandemonium reigned amongst the party around the shot man. They yelled, shouted, and one bent, grabbing at the spluttering red glow on the ground. The others seemed to panic and not one of them thought to throw lead at the house. Lasalle aimed again, switching to the grapeshot barrel and touching off a shot, sending it into the body of the man bending to grab the thing from the ground.

Then the others turned, racing away, not merely running, but fleeing in terror, discarding their rifles as they went. They left a man sprawled on his back and another crawling on hands and knees, screaming after them.

"Dave! Stace!" he screamed in a voice none of the others who heard it would forget. "Come back he—!"

The rest ended in a thunderous roar and a sheet of flame which ripped the night apart, turning it for a brief instant, into day. The house shook, the remaining window glass shattered in the explosion's blast, but the walls held firm.

"Get to the windows!" Mark roared. "Pour it into them!"

His words came not a moment too soon. Hooves thundered, feet thudded and men shouted as they raced towards the house. Freda dashed into the front room with Morg's rifle in her hands. She reached the window and fired through it at the horsemen rushing up from the river. She heard the rapid crashing of Mark's rifle, saw a man drop from his horse and fired again. From the bedroom sounded the booming roar of the shotgun. Her father's Le Mat spat at the side and lead raked and ripped into the house.

"Mark!" Freda screamed, seeing a shape loom up at the window on the undefended side.

Mark turned, levering two shots, the first struck the wall close to the window, the second slammed into the man's face and threw him back from it.

A man sprang from his horse, landed before Freda's window and grabbed the rifle in her hands. She screamed, her finger closed on the trigger and flame lashed from the barrel. She saw the man reel back, smelled burning cloth and flesh, then screamed and fell to the floor in a faint.

His rifle empty, Mark let it fall to the floor and brought out the matched Colt guns. Now he was at his most deadly for he could handle the Colts like twin extensions of his own arms. Flame spurted from the left gun, causing a rapid withdrawal from the side window just as a man tried to throw down on him. A sound before the house brought him around, throwing a bullet into the shoulder of a mounted rider and causing him to turn his horse and head away.

Lasalle cut loose with his Le Mat, shooting fast and emptying the cylinder. Then he let the gun drop and drew the Army Colt to shoot again. He stopped one man with the Colt, which surprised him as he had never been much of a hand with a revolver.

At the back Morg's shotgun brought a hurried end to the attack and left one man moaning on the ground. The young cowhand felt sick, but the heat of the excitement kept it down. He had put lead into a man, maybe killed him. It was not a pleasant thought.

Then it was over. The defence had been too hot and accurate for hired guns to face. They broke off, dragging their dead and wounded with them, making for their horses. They split into two parties, one throwing lead at the house while the other mounted dead and wounded on horseback for they wished to leave as little proof as possible. Those were Mallick's orders when he organized the attack by almost the full Double K crew with the intention of wiping Lasalle's place from the face of the earth. Dusty Fog and Mark Counter had good friends who would come and investigate should they be killed. Nothing which might point to Double K must be found. The same applied now. Sure the men in the house knew who was responsible for the attack—but they couldn't prove it and Elben was the only law around.

"You can light the lamps now," Mark said as the men rode away, splashing through the water. "The mauling we gave them—My God! Freda!"

Almost before he reached her side Morg had arrived and Lasalle ran to where the girl lay on the floor.

She groaned and Mark struck a match, looking for some sign of a wound. He saw the fear and panic in her eyes. She stared wildly at him.

"What—where—!"

"Easy gal. They've gone," Mark replied. "Are you hit?"

"I killed one of them!" she gasped. "I shot—"

"Drop it, girl!" Mark's voice cracked like a whip. "It was him or you. Now lie easy until we find if he hit you."

Morg lit the lamp and stared at the girl in a distracted manner. Not until then did he feel the trickle of blood running down his face where one of the last shots threw splinters into him. Freda saw it and nothing could have shaken her out of the hysteria quicker.

"Morg!" she gasped, getting to her feet. "You're hurt!"

"Not him," Mark put in. "You can't hurt a feller from Montana by hitting him on the head."

The girl threw Mark a cold look and eased Morg into a chair. She saw the wound to be more messy than dangerous and prepared to care for it. Lasalle watched all this and a slightly puzzled look came to his face. Mark grinned and suggested they took a look outside.

Freda froze as she reached a hand to Morg's head. "That explosion!" she gasped. "What caused it?"

"Dynamite," Mark answered flatly. "Come on, George. Let's make sure they've left clean. Where's that old Bugle dog?"

Having shown commendable good sense and headed for the girl's bedroom when the shooting started, Bugle now came out, wagging his tail. He followed the two men to the door of the house. He stood outside and his head swung to one side, his back hair rose and he growled.

"Back in, *pronto*!" Mark snapped. "Freda, douse the lights."

Once more the room plunged into darkness and Bugle

headed for the safety of his mistress's bedroom.

"Get the guns loaded!" Mark growled. "We might need them."

The horses came nearer and Lasalle's house lay silent. Mark felt puzzled at the turn of events. He thought that after the mauling they took Double K would stay well clear. They might be sending a small group of determined men in, hoping the house suspected nothing, although Mark could not think how the group managed to get in the direction from which they came so soon after departing the other way.

"Yeeah!"

Loud in the night it rang. The old battle yell of the Confederate Cavalry. Mark realized that Dusty would send one of his friends to the Wedge to collect help and reinforcements. The explosion must have brought them on the run but they knew better than ride up unannounced to a house which had just been under attack.

"Hey Mark!" yelled Dusty's voice. "Answer up, *amigo!*"

"Come ahead and quit that fool yelling!" Mark called back. "What for you all waking folks up in the middle of the night?" He holstered his guns and threw a look across the room to where Freda and Morg were much closer than needed for first-aid or reloading weapons. "You can put the lamp on again. Unless you'd rather stay in the dark."

Freda and Morg gave startled and guilty exclamations, moving apart hurriedly and trying to look unconcerned as Lasalle lit the lamp.

"You're so sharp you'll cut yourself, Mark Counter," Freda gasped. "Why don't you go out and meet Dusty?"

"Why sure," agreed Mark. "Reckon you pair would like to be alone."

The nearest thing Freda could lay hands on that wouldn't be too dangerous was the discarded deck of cards. She grabbed them up and hurled them at Mark. He side stepped, grinned, winked at the blushing Morg, then stepped out to greet his friends.

CHAPTER TWELVE

The Map

"YOU all right, *amigo*?" Dusty asked, swinging down from the borrowed horse and walking towards Mark.

"Why sure. They didn't get any of us."

"What happened?" asked Johnny Raybold, showing his relief at finding Mark safe and unharmed.

"They hit us foot, hoss and artillery," Mark replied, hearing the others as they came from the house behind him.

"Get any of 'em, Mark?" Rusty Willis inquired.

"Not less'n these folks can shoot," scoffed Johnny. "He couldn't hit the side of a barn if he was in it."

Mark ignored the comments from his good friends. He stepped forward to greet Stone Hart and then introduced him to Lasalle, Freda and Morg. They were all invited in, but Johnny and Rusty turned their horses and headed across the stream to make a sweep across the range and make certain the Double K pack had headed home.

"I reckon there were getting on for twenty or more of them," Mark said, as the men gathered around the Lasalle's dining-room table and Freda, with Morg's help, went to the kitchen to make coffee. "They came down on us loaded for bear."

"That's a mean bear, needing dynamite to move it," Dusty answered quietly.

"That's the part of it I don't like," growled Stone. "Dusty, they've gone too far now. We'll have to paint for war."

"Likely. Comes daylight Mark and I'll head down trail and get Clay to come up here. Then we'll clear this whole section out. It'll be open season on anybody wearing a gun and riding for Double K."

133

Lasalle looked at the faces around the table. Tanned faces which showed little of their thoughts. Not one of them looked like the sort of man to back down once they set their mind to a thing.

"Why did they hit us tonight?" he asked.

"Way I see it, they had to make a grandstand play. They'd hit Gibbs and left him with his hide peeled by a blacksnake whip," Dusty answered. "Which same Pop Jones had called it quits. That left you. If you stayed on the other two might take heart and stand fast. You had to be brought down."

"But not with dynamite, Dusty," Stone Hart objected. "That's going a mite strong even for a bunch of hard-cases with the local law behind them."

"Maybe," Dusty drawled. "I'll feel happier when I've got Clay Allison here so we can make us some talk to the owner of the Double K."

"Something struck me about this Keller," Lasalle put in. "None of the Double K crowd even refer to him. When they say boss they always mean Mallick."

"Maybe haven't seen enough of Keller to call him boss," Mark answered.

"Or maybe he's not the real boss of this she-bang," Stone suggested. "It could be that Mallick's behind all this for his own benefit. Nobody's seen Keller from all accounts."

They were words of wisdom, although none of the others knew it. However before the subject could be followed further Rusty Willis returned with word that Johnny had taken off after the Double K men and would not be back for a couple of hours. Rusty had taken time out to circle the house on his return.

"Looks like you got at least four, maybe more," he said, then looked at Lasalle. "Was I you, I'd keep my gal inside comes morning."

"Why?"

"It's not a sight for her to see. Out where the dynamite went off," was the simple reply. "I'd say at least two of them were there, but it's kinda hard to tell for sure."

"Two's right," Lasalle said, his voice showing strain and a shudder running through his body. "One of them was wounded. I hit—"

"Drop it!" Mark snapped, gripping the man's shoulder in a

hold which made him wince and brought an end to his words. "You didn't ask them to come here in the night, or to try and dynamite your home. And it damned sure wasn't your fault they came to die."

"Mark's right at that, friend," agreed Stone Hart. "You stopped a man killing you, your daughter, Mark and that young feller in the kitchen. To do that you shot a man who was trying to throw dynamite at your place. It was his choosing, not you'rn."

Dusty thrust back his chair and came to his feet. He went to the kitchen door, opened it, closed it again, without Morg and Freda knowing for they were in each other's arms and kissing. Dusty knocked on the door, turning to wink at the others. Then he opened it and walked in. Now Freda busied herself at the stove and Morg seemed fully occupied with cutting bread for her.

"We'll be staying here for the night, Freda," he said. "Stone and the boys don't have their bedrolls along."

"I'll fix it," she replied, face just a trifle flushed.

An hour later Freda went to her room and climbed into bed. She heard the men settling down in the dining-room and wondered if she would sleep again, so great was the feeling surging inside her as she thought of Morg Summers. She doubted if sleep would ever come to her again.

Yells and whoops woke Freda. For a moment she lay on her bed, blinking in daylight which flooded her room. Then she gasped for she saw the sun hung higher in the sky than usually was the case when she rose. Rolling from her bed she sat on the edge, rubbing her eyes. Then she went to the window and peered out. She stared at the sight before her, wondering what had gone wrong for it seemed that Johnny Raybold and Rusty Willis were attacking Dusty Fog.

Freda had undressed and wore her night-gown now; she could not remember doing it the previous night, but appeared to have done so. Grabbing up her robe she quickly climbed into it. She saw Rusty grab Dusty from behind, locking hands around his waist from behind. Johnny had landed on the ground, but was getting up and charging into the attack.

The girl could not think what started the fight. She wondered why none of the others stopped it. With bare feet slapping on the floor, Freda darted from her room and through the kitchen. She tore open the door and went out. To her amazement her father and the other men sat around watching the fight and clearly enjoying it.

Even as the girl appeared Dusty bent forward, reached between his legs to grab one of Rusty's. Then he straightened and Rusty let out a yell and fell backwards with Dusty sitting down hard on him.

"Eeyow whooof!" Rusty bellowed, the air rammed from his lungs in the cry.

By this time Johnny was on his feet and charging forward. Dusty left the recumbent Rusty's body in a rolling dive forward. His hand clamped on Johnny's ankle in passing and heaved. Johnny gave a wail and lost his balance. He lit down on his hands, breaking his fall with the skill of a horseman taking a toss from a bad one.

Dusty retained his grip on the ankle and grabbed Johnny's free leg. He bent the legs upwards, crossing the ankles and sitting on them. Johnny's mouth opened and he let out a howl.

"Yowee!" he yelled. "Yipes, uncle, Dusty. Uncle!"

Never had Freda felt so completely baffled by a turn of events. She stared at her father, then at Mark and Stone who calmly smoked cigarettes, finally at Morg who seemed to be enjoying the scene.

"What happened?" she gasped, watching Dusty rise after receiving Johnny's surrender howl. "What happened?"

"That?" grinned Mark as the men got to their feet. "Why that's just Johnny 'n' Rusty showing Dusty how it's done."

"But—but—I thought—!" began a very irate Freda. *"Cowhands!"*

With that final yell, realizing that no young lady should be seen dressed, or rather undressed, in such a manner, she turned and fled to the house.

Johnny grinned wryly as he took up his hat. Ever since Dusty demonstrated the arts of ju jitsu and karate to them in Quiet Town, Rusty and he had tried to disprove its effectiveness. Whenever their paths crossed with Dusty's, the two Wedge hands banded together to show their friend they could lick him—only they never managed to do it.

"Say, Dusty," Johnny drawled. "You dropped this paper. Is it anything important?"

He held out a scrap of paper and Dusty frowned. Then the light dawned and Dusty thrust a hand into his levis pocket. He drew out the torn papers taken from Mallick's office on the previous day.

"It might be at that," he said. "Let's go inside and see if we can sort it out."

"I'll get the boys out to those two spreads first," Stone replied. "Then I'd best go down trail to the herd."

Dusty left Stone to attend to the matter and entered the house. He went to the table and sat down, spreading the pieces of paper out before him. Turning them so they all faced the same side upwards he started to fit them together. He found little difficulty in getting the scraps in order and forming a completed whole. A map lay before him, complete in design and outline, but without a single name to say what it might be a map of. It showed land contours, water-courses, woods even, yet not a single letter to identify the range it covered. An oblong outline ran around the inner edge of the map but it meant nothing to him.

"Where in hell is it a map of?" he said, more to himself than to Lasalle who stood by the window.

"Let me take a look, Captain."

For a long moment Lasalle studied the map, frowning and cocking his head on one side.

"I forgot about the pieces," Dusty drawled. "Picked them up in Mallick's office yesterday, but things happened a mite fast and I didn't get a chance to look at them earlier."

Then Dusty tensed slightly. He took a long look at the map, then reached into his pants pocket. He shook his head, rose and crossed the room to where a box of Winchester bullets lay. Taking one out he returned to the table and bent over the map. He drew a line from the lower edge about six inch from the right side to about an inch from the top, then still using the bullet's lead as a pencil, made a right angle turn and a line to the right edge.

"Does it look any more familiar now?" he asked.

Lasalle looked down at the map, he gave an explosive grunt of surprise as he saw the whole thing with the eye of a man who knew how to make a map.

"It sures does!" he breathed. "That's the Lindon Land

Grant. You didn't quite get the lines right, Captain Fog, but I recognize the physical features of the map now. But the way this is drawn it makes the Grant appear to cover all our range and right up to the badlands.''

"Yeah," Dusty said quietly. "That's just how it looks."

Just at the moment Stone Hart entered from sending off his relief forces to the Gibbs' and Jones' places. He came forward and looked down at the map, seeing its significance.

"What do you make of it, Dusty?" he asked.

"I don't know for sure. But it'd take a trained man to make a map like this, wouldn't it?"

"Sure," Stone agreed. "This's been line-drawn from the original I'd say."

At last Lasalle found himself in a position to offer advice on something beyond the ken of the two Texans. He spent his service career in the Confederate Army Engineers and knew considerable about making maps.

"It was," he said. "The man who did it knew his work."

"A Government surveyor'd be able to do it I suppose?" Dusty asked.

"A well trained one would," Lasalle agreed.

"What're you thinking about, Dusty?" Stone asked, seeing the interest Dusty showed, although most people could have noticed no change in the small Texan's face or appearance.

"Just a hunch, Stone. I'll tell you more about it when I've met Clay."

He refused to say any more and Stone knew the futility of trying to get more out of him. After breakfast he still knew no more about Dusty's hunch but did not bother, he knew he would learn about it when Dusty had every detail worked out and not before.

"I'll head down to the herd and tell Waggles we're staying a spell," Stone said. "Johnny's gone ahead, should get them afore they head the cattle up."

They had finished breakfast and were preparing to start out. This time Mark would be riding with Dusty and they left warning that neither Lasalle nor Morg were to move far from the house and that they keep all weapons loaded.

"If they hit at you," Stone went on, after Dusty gave his grim warning, "get inside and fort up. Then make some smoke, burn rags or something, get smoke coming up from your chimney and we'll come a-running.''

"One thing, George," Dusty finished, turning his big paint stallion's head from the ranch. "Try and stick that map together for me."

"Sure, Captain Fog," Lasalle promised. "If you reckon it's important."

"I reckon that map's the middle of all this fuss," Dusty replied quietly. "Let's go, Mark. And don't worry if you hear riders coming up from the south on towards dark, George. It'll most likely be us."

After his guests left, Lasalle went around his buildings with Morg at his side. They looked at the ragged hole left where the dynamite went off and Lasalle could not restrain a shudder, even though the other men had been up at the first hint of dawn to clear away the ghastly horror.

"We'll do like Captain Fog said, Morg," Lasalle stated. "Stay around the house and tidy things up today."

"Sure, boss. Say, can I have a talk to you—about Freda and me?"

"I reckon you can," Lasalle replied. "Let's go to the barn. I wonder how Pop Jones and Ralph Gibbs'll find things today?"

At the Jones place a wagon stood before the door as Peaceful Gunn and his party rode up. The old man and the cowhand called Yance watched the trio of Wedge hands approach as they lifted chairs into the back of the canvas-topped wagon. "Howdy folks," greeted the man called Shaun, his tones showing his Irish birth. "Cap'n Fog sent us along to help you."

"Knowed I shouldn't come here with this pair!" Peaceful moaned, eyeing the Colt the cowhand held. "Nobody'd trust me with villainous looking *hombres* like them at my back."

"Sure and here's me a descendant of kings of auld Ireland being spoke ag'in by this evil-doer," replied Shaun, in his breezy brogue. "'Twas foolish to put all that gear into the wagon when we'll only have to be moving it out again."

Then the Jones family and their hand started to smile. These were the men promised to lend a hand with the defense of the house. Pop looked right sprightly for a man who had been on the verge of losing his home. He took out a worn old ten gauge and set percussion caps on the nipples ready for use.

"Let's us get this lot back into the house," he suggested.

With eager hands to help the work was soon done. At Peaceful's suggestion they left the wagon standing outside, then Shaun turned on his Irish charm and got a very worried looking Ma Jones to smile.

"You don't sound like any Texan I ever heard," she said at last.

"I'm the only Texas-Irishman in the world," Shaun replied. "Can't you tell from me voice, a Texas drawl on top of a good Irish accent. Say, ma'am, you wouldn't know how to make an Irish stew, would you?"

On being assured that Ma not only could, but would, make an Irish stew, Shaun gave his full attention to making plans for the defence of the house.

Five hard looking men rode towards the Jones place shortly after noon. In the lead came Preacher Tring, sitting his horse uneasily for the Kid's birdshot onslaught had caught him in a most embarrassing position. This did not tend to make Tring feel any better disposed to life in general and the small ranch owners in particular.

He growled a low curse as he saw the wagon standing before the Jones' house and without a team. Clearly Pop Jones thought the Double K were playing kid games when they said get out. Right soon Pop would get a lesson.

Then the men put spurs to their horses and rode fast, coming down on the ranch and halting the mounts in a churned up dust cloud before the house. Tring dropped his hand towards his hip, meaning to draw and pour a volley into the house.

"Don't pull it, mister!" said a plaintive voice from the barn. "You'll like to scare me off."

All eyes turned to look in the direction of the speaker and all movement towards hardware ended. This might have been due to a desire to keep the nervous sounding man unafraid—or because all they could see plainly of him was the barrel of a Spencer rifle, its .52 calibre mouth yawning like a cave entrance at them.

"Is it the visitors we have, Peaceful?" a second voice inquired.

The wagon's canopy had drawn back and a Winchester

slanted at the Double K men, lined from the source of the Irish voice. Then a third man sauntered into view from the end of the house, also carrying a rifle, while a shotgun and a fourth rifle showed on either side of the open house door.

"Who are you?" Tring asked.

"We work here," Shaun replied. "Who are *you*?"

"Tell that pair of ole—!"

A bullet fanned Tring's hat from his head. The lever of Shaun's rifle clicked and the Double K men tried to keep their horses under control without also giving the idea they could reach their weapons.

"Just be keeping the civil tongue in your head, *hombre*!" Shaun warned. "And if you've no further business here, let's be missing you."

Tring had brought only four men with him as he did not expect any trouble in handling the Jones family and because the ranch crew had taken a mauling on their abortive attack at the Lasalle place. He knew he and the others had no chance of doing anything better than get shot to doll rags at the moment. However a second party of men were at the Gibbs place, attending to Mallick's orders. Tring decided to gather them in and return to the Jones house. When he came he would not leave a living soul at the house.

It was a good idea. Except that the other party were having troubles of their own.

They came on the Gibbs place, six of them, almost all the unwounded fighting strength of the Double K out on the business of clearing the two weakened small outfits out of the Panhandle country.

One of the men jerked his thumb towards where a tall, slim, studious young man leaned his shoulder against a corral post, clearly having been working on repairing the fence.

"Hey you!" he barked.

Doc Leroy looked up almost mildly. "Me sir?"

"Yeah, you! what in hell are you doing?"

"Fixing the fence," Doc answered.

From the house window Joyce watched with a quaking heart. She wondered why Rusty and Billy were not on hand to help Doc.

"Then start to pull it down!" ordered the man, a man she recognized from the previous visit.

"Now that'd be plump foolish," said Doc.

The man's hand dropped towards his gun and froze immobile a good inch from its butt.

Doc's right hand made a sight defying flicker, the ivory handled Colt came into it, lining on the man, the hammer drawn back.

"Just sit easy, *hombre*," Doc said, but his entire voice had changed. "And pray I don't let this hammer fall."

A footstep behind her brought Joyce swinging around. She found Rusty had entered from the back and was making for the front door, his rifle in his hands.

"Ole Doc sure is surprising, ain't he?" grinned Rusty and stepped out to lend his friend moral and actual support just as Billy emerged from the barn, complete with Henry rifle.

"Mrs. Gibbs!" Rusty said over his shoulder. "Come out here, ma'am and bring your scattergun." Joyce complied and Rusty indicated the men with the barrel of his rifle. "Any of them here yesterday?"

She stabbed up the shotgun, lining it on the man who did all the talking. "He was the one who shot Sam."

"Drop your guns, all of you!"

The words cracked from Rusty's mouth and the men obeyed. Then they were told to move to one side. Rusty put down his rifle and removed his gunbelt. He walked forward, going to the man Joyce indicated. His hands shot out, grabbing this man and hauling him from the saddle.

Rusty slammed the man on to the ground. His right fist shot into the man's stomach and ripped up a left as he doubled his man over. The man stood taller than Rusty but he never had a chance. He tried to fight back, but against Rusty's savage two handed attack he never stood a chance.

After a brutal five minute beating the man lay in a moaning heap on the floor and Rusty, nose bleeding and chest heaving, looked at Joyce.

"Any more of 'em here?" he asked.

"You leave them, boy," Doc answered coldly. "These gents have just volunteered to mend the corral."

The men most certainly had not intention of volunteering, but they were given no real choice in the matter. Under the guns of the three Wedge hands the men went to work. They might have hoped that Tring and his bunch would come to their aid but Doc put a block to such hopes.

"Happen anybody should come up and start throwing lead at us," he told the men, "we'll throw some back and you bunch'll get it first."

So, while hating fence building, or any other kind of work, the men hoped that Tring and his bunch would not come and try to rescue them.

Luckily for them Tring did not come. He started thinking after he left the Jones place and decided that Gibbs most likely had backing. The odds in the game were coming to a point where Tring no longer fancied them. Along with the others of his party he headed back to Double K and waited to hear what the Gibbs raiding party found. They did not return until after dark and came in looking sorry for themselves after working harder than any of them had done for years.

At dawn the following morning every man pulled out, heading for Barlock where they aimed to have a showdown with their boss, get such money as they could and pull out.

The Double K lay silent and peaceful after the men left. All the dead had been disposed of and the wounded taken into town, so only Sir James Keller and his daughter remained on the premises.

CHAPTER THIRTEEN

His Only Name Is Waco

THREE thousand head of longhorn Texas cattle wended their way across the range country. They kept in a long line, feeding as they moved. To prevent them from breaking out of their line, rode the trail hands, the point men at the head of the column, then the flank and swing men and at the back came the drag riders. Behind them moved the remuda and bringing up the rear two wagons, one driven by the cook, the other controlled by his louse.

The scene was one Dusty Fog and Mark Counter had seen many times. Yet they never grew tired of looking at it. This was the scene which brought money to Texas, allowed it to become the great and wealthy State it now was.

For a moment the two men sat and watched the trail hands riding the herd, horses jumping into a sprint to turn some steer which tried to avoid its destiny by breaking from the line. The steer would be turned back and another try the same move a few yards further on.

"Look restless," Dusty drawled.

"Maybe Clay ran into fuss," Mark replied. "There he is, the old cuss, right out front with Smiler and a kid I've never seen before."

Dusty had also noticed this. He studied the three riders about half a mile ahead of the herd. They saw Mark and Dusty at the same time and Clay Allison's hat came off to wave a greeting. Then both parties rode at a better pace towards each other.

Although they had not met for four years, Clay Allison looked little different, tall, slim, well dressed, even though trail dirty. He managed to keep his black moustache and short

145

beard trimmed and neat, the matched guns at his sides were also clean and hung just right for a real fast draw. Smiler, tall, gaunt and looking more Indian than the Ysabel Kid, lounged in his saddle at his boss's side.

The boy at Clay's right took Dusty's attention, held it like a magnet. Not more than sixteen years old, but he still wore a brace of Army Colts in low hanging fast draw holsters. He had blond hair, a handsome face but looked cold and sullen. His clothes were not new, but they were good and serviceable.

Dusty bit down an exclamation for the boy looked much as had his brother Danny. Except that this kid looked meaner, the sort who either built himself the name as a real fast man with a gun—or found an early grave.

"Howdy Dusty, Mark," greeted Clay Allison. "Didn't expect to see you on this trail. You got a herd ahead?"

"Nope, but Stone Hart has," Dusty replied. "There's some fuss up ahead, Clay. Bad trouble. Let's pull off to one side and talk it out."

Waving his hand to one side Clay Allison nodded his agreement. They rode well clear of the herd, then swung down from their saddles. The youngster did not follow immediately but sat his horse for a moment watching the approaching herd.

"Who's the boy, Clay?" Dusty asked, nodding towards the youngster.

"His only name is Waco," Allison replied. "Been with me for nigh on six months now. I met up with him down in Tascosa. He was in a bar and all set to take on half a dozen Yankee soldiers. So I cut in and helped him. Been with me ever since. That boy's fast, Dusty, real fast. And he knows it."

At that moment the boy whose only name was Waco rode to join the four men as they stood under the shade of a cottonwood tree's branches. The horses were allowed to stand and graze to one side and Allison nodded to the herd as they passed.

"They've been so spooked up for the past few days that you have to ride a mile from 'em to cough or spit."

Dusty grunted his sympathy. He knew how uncertain the behaviour of a bunch of longhorn cattle could be. They might go through a howling gale or a thunderstorm without turning a hair, or they might just as easily spook and take to running at their own shadows. It all depended on how they felt.

"What's ahead, Dusty?" asked Allison.

"Wire."

"WIRE!"

Three voices said the word in a single breath. Clay Allison, Smiler and Waco each spat the word out as if it burned their mouths.

"Who strung it?" asked Smiler.

"Now that's a problem," Dusty admitted. "It's across the narrows on the old Lindon Land Grant."

"Lindon never block the trail," Smiler went on, speaking more then he had spoken in months.

"Lindon sold out to an Englishman," Mark replied, watching the boy called Waco and paying particular attention to the way Waco studied himself and Dusty. "I reckon Dusty's not satisfied that the new owner's behind the wire-stringing though."

Dusty glanced at his big *amigo* and grinned. It looked like he couldn't fool Mark or keep his thoughts from the big cowhand after all these years. Before Dusty could make a reply to Mark's words, Waco put his say-so in.

"This Englishman got you scared, or something?" he asked.

"Or something, boy," Dusty answered, knowing youngsters of Waco's type.

Yet somehow Dusty got the idea there was better than the makings of a fast-gun killer in the boy. The face, while sullen, looked intelligent and did not carry lines of dissipation. Not that it would stay that way long. Clay Allison might be a rancher, but Dusty knew the kind of men he hired. Good hands with cattle, but a wild onion crew form the Pecos, men who handled their guns better than average and liked to show their skill. A boy growing and spending his formative years in such company had one foot on the slope and the devil dragging at his other leg.

"Boy!" Waco hissed.

"Choke off, Waco!" Clay snapped.

Waco relapsed into silence, watching Dusty now with cold eyes. He had been an orphan almost since birth, his name came from people calling him the Waco-orphaned baby on the wagon train where his parents died. In time it became shortened to but one name, Waco. He had been reared by settlers, but never took their name even though they treated him with such kindness and love as could be shared for they had nine children of their own. He grew in a raw land and carried a gun form the day he was old enough to tote one. Now he rode for Clay Allison's CA spread and he didn't let any man talk down to him, especially not a short growed runt like that cowhand talking to Clay. It surprised Waco considerable that Clay would waste time in talking with such a small and insignificant man.

"What're you down here for, Dusty?" Clay went on.

"I'd like you to bring your herd to a halt for a day or so and come up trail with me. Bring a few of the boys. I've got Stone Hart along. Between us we ought to be able to wind this up without starting a war."

"Wind hell!" Clay barked. "That wire's got to go and I say it ought to go around the feller who strung it's neck."

"He's got around twenty guns backing him," Dusty answered. "And there's a whole slew of folks up that way, small ranchers, who can't stand a war fighting over their land."

Whatever his faults, and they were many, Clay Allison respected the property and persons of people less fortunate in the matter of wealth than himself; as long as they did not encroach on his holdings or make trouble for him, which the small ranchers up here did not. He nodded his head, seeing what Dusty said to be the truth. He also knew Dusty would not be back here unless he had some definite plan. However he did not feel happy about being too far from his herd while they acted so spooked.

"Tell me about it as we ride," he suggested.

"You sure want some help," Waco suddenly put, in facing Dusty.

"How do you mean?" asked Dusty.

"Come high tailing it down here to ask Clay to fight your fight for you."

"That's enough, boy!" Dusty's voice took a warning note.

"Don't call me boy!" Waco snapped. "I'm a man grown with these guns on."

"Then try acting like one."

The words met with the wrong reaction on Waco's part. His right hand dropped towards his gun. He did not make it.

Dusty caught the warning flicker in the youngster's eyes, his left hand crossed his body, fetching out the Colt from the right holster, lining it with the hammer drawn back under his thumb. For a long moment he stood like that, the others not moving either. Waco stood still, not entirely scared but numb and unbelieving. He thought he was fast with a gun, but this small man did not just stop at being fast. Somehow it did not matter to Waco if lead smashed into him. He had made his play and failed, he knew the penalty for failure.

With his thumb trembling on the gun hammer Dusty waited and watched. Then suddenly he lowered the Colt's hammer, spun the weapon on his finger, holstered it and turned to walk to his paint horse.

Letting out his breath in a long sigh Clay Allison followed, then Smiler also turned and walked away. Only Mark and Waco stood where they had dismounted to hold their talk, under the shade of a cottonwood tree.

"He didn't have the guts to drop the hammer!" Waco sneered. "The d—"

Mark's big hand clamped on to the youngster's shirt, lifting him from his feet and slamming him back into a tree as if he weighed no more than a baby. Then Mark thrust his face up close to Waco's.

"Listen good to me, you hawg-stupid kid. Only one thing saved you from being killed or wounded bad. Dusty's brother was killed a few months back. You look a lot like him, except that he was a man, not just some trigger-fast-and-up-from-Texas kid."

With a contemptuous gesture Mark thrust Waco from him. Then he turned to go and collect his horse. Waco's face flushed with rage, his hand lifted over the butts of his guns.

"Turn around!" he snapped.

Mark turned, noting the stance. "What's on your mind, boy?"

"Nobody lays hands on me and lives to boast about it."

They faced each other, hands over the butts of their guns. The other three rode away, not knowing what went on behind them for their attention rested on the cattle.

Just what started the stampede they never discovered. It could have been any of a number of things, or none of them. It most likely stemmed from the ornery nature of the Texas

Longhorn steer, a breed of cattle never noted for the stability or gentleness of its behavior.

Whatever the cause, one moment the herd moved along in its normal manner. The next saw every steer bellowing and leaping forward, galloping into wild stampede which swept aside the hands, made them draw clear or be run down.

"Stampede!" roared Clay Allison. "All hands and the cook!"

The old range cry brought every man forward at a gallop. Now they must try to reach the point of the herd, turn it, make the leaders swing around until they joined on the rear of the column, then keep them running in a circle until they tired and came to a halt. Only it would not be as easy as all that. Those wild-eyed racing steers would not willingly turn.

Clay's shout and the noise of the stampede reached Mark and Waco's ears. To give him credit Waco dropped his aggressive pose even before Mark relaxed and the youngster made his horse's saddle before Mark reached the bloodbay. Their difference of opinion was forgotten. Only one thing mattered now. To ride and help turn the herd.

Racing his horse at a tangent Waco came boiling down on the herd's point ahead of the other men. He urged the horse on, cutting down so as to try and slam into the lead steer and make it swing. The horse he rode knew its business, had been trained for cattle work. It ran well, then put its foot in a gopher hole and went down. Waco heard the terrified scream of the horse as he flew over its head. His instincts as a horseman saved him, allowed him to land on his feet, running. Then he stopped and turned, the herd headed straight at him now, the leaders seeing a hated man-thing on his feet and at their mercy instead of on a horse where he was their master.

The youngster turned, he saw his horse struggling to rise, terror and pain in its rolling eyes for its leg had broken. His right hand dipped and brought out the Army Colt to throw a bullet into the horse's head and end its terror and misery. Then he turned and tried to run but high heeled cowhand boots were never meant for running on and a longhorn steer could keep a horse hard-pressed to catch it.

Nearer came the steers, their horns, which could go to a six foot spread, lowered and ready to rip into him. Waco knew it would be no use turning and trying to shoot his way clear. He found a situation where his skill with a gun stood for nothing and all he could do was run.

"Waco!"

A single shout reached his ears, ringing above the noise of the herd. He twisted his head and saw a paint stallion bearing down on him. He saw the small man who he dismissed as nobody, and nothing and who he tried to draw on, cutting in ahead of the cattle, coming across the widening front of horns. Waco knew that if Dusty slowed down the herd would be on them before they could make a move to escape the rush.

Dusty knew the danger also. He measured the distance between the running youngster and the onrushing herd. This would be tricky, one false move, a wrong step on the part of the seventeen hand paint and they would all be under the hooves of the stampeding herd.

Bending low in the saddle Dusty prepared to grab Waco's waist band. He gave quick, tense instructions.

"Get set, boy. When I grab you, make a jump. I'll sling you across the back of the saddle. Then hang on with all you've got."

Waco heard the words, felt the presence of the big paint at his side. Then a hand grabbed him by the pant's belt and he felt himself heaved up. He had not expected such strength, his feet left the ground and he felt himself dragged towards the paint's back. Then he grabbed the cantle of the saddle to help out, hauling himself to hang across the horse's rump. The double girths of the rig took the strain and stood it. Waco writhed, he felt a horn brush his leg, then the paint ran the gauntlet of the herd, cutting to one side of them. The leaders did not aim to be so easily cheated of their prey. They swung after the paint, with its near helpless bundle hanging over the rump and slowing it.

Racing his big bloodbay stallion ahead of any of the others, Mark brought it full at the lead steer. Seeing the huge horse tearing at him, the steer started to swing slightly. Mark gave it no chance to reverse towards Dusty but crowded in once more. Clay Allison came up, followed by his brothers Ben and Jack. Between them the four men started to swing the stampede around, away from where Dusty brought his horse to a halt and lowered Waco to the ground. He did not leave the youngster for there was still the danger of a stray longhorn coming up and the longhorn did not fear a man afoot.

"They've got 'em!" Dusty said with satisfaction. "Making 'em do a merry-go-round. That'll slow 'em down."

Waco did not reply. He looked at the small man, only he no longer saw Dusty as being small. He knew he owed the other man his life, not once, but twice. Dusty could have killed him back there when he tried to draw. Then at the risk of his own life Dusty came to rescue him. This was a kind of man Waco had never met before and did not know what to make of. Clearly Dusty gave no thought to the incident back under the cottonwood, his full attention being on the herd.

They watched the circle made, and the steers began to slow, being kept in a circle all the time. Slowly the movement came to an end but the hands continued to ride their circle.

Clay Allison and Mark swung from the herd, riding to where Dusty and Waco stood waiting.

"You came close to being the late Waco, boy," Mark said.

"Yeah," agreed Clay. "I never thought to see you alive when your hoss went down. Reckon you owe Dusty something."

Slowly Waco turned, his eyes on Dusty.

"I reckon I do. I'm sorry for what happened back there Dusty."

A smile flickered on Dusty's face. He knew what the apology meant to Waco. It had been torn from him for he had never felt he owed any man a thing, now he owed Dusty his life.

"That's all right, boy. You did the man's thing back there when you shot that hoss rather than leave it to be stampeded under by the herd. You might have got clear with no trouble if you hadn't."

"It was my hoss, never let me down. I couldn't let it down at the end."

Smiles came to faces of the watching men. Then Clay pointed back to the remuda which approached them.

"You've got your pick of any hoss in the bunch, boy. Go take it."

A grin came to Waco's face, softening the sullen expression. Until this moment Clay never referred to him as anything but his own name. It looked like Dusty had stuck him with a fresh title. Somehow he did not mind. The word "boy" was now spoken in a different manner. Now Dusty regarded him as a boy who would one day grow into a man.

"I'll lend you a hand to get your saddle out, boy," Mark drawled. "Come on."

There were good horses in Clay Allison's remuda. One of them caught Waco's eye. He took up the rope from the saddle he'd laid on the ground. With a quick whirl he sent a hooley-ann loop flipping out to settle on the neck of a big young paint stallion, a seventeen hand beauty as yet untrained in cattle work. This horse he led out. It had been three saddled, ridden the three times which a bronc-buster considered all that was necessary before handing the horse into the remuda and since then little ridden. Clay brought it along to test out anybody who wanted to ride it, only Waco aimed to be the only man who ever did.

"You've picked a mean one there, boy," drawled Mark, on whom the implication of the choice was not lost. "He's got a belly full of bed-springs that need taking out before he'll be any use."

"Then I'm going to have to take them out," Waco replied.

Dusty and Clay watched the herd settle down before they offered to do anything else. Clay sat his horse and cursed the fool steers which had run off a fair amount of beef in the stampede.

"Keep 'em here and range feed for a spell," Dusty suggested. "Two, three days on this buffalo grass'll put the meat on them again. And by that time, happen you go along with me, we'll have this wire trouble fixed and the narrows opened again."

"I'll go along."

"Leave the herd here, with Ben and Jack, get half a dozen or more men you can rely on not to start a shooting match unless they have to, ride to the Lasalle place, and we'll pick Stone up on the way. Then I'll tell all of you what I aim to do."

It said much for Clay Allison's faith in Dusty that he agreed to this without inquiring what Dusty's plans might be. He felt fully satisfied that Dusty not only had a plan but could also see that same plan through given a bit of aid.

Calling his brother Ben over, Clay told of Dusty's arrangements. Ben listened and gave his agreement. Then he jerked his thumb along to the remuda where Waco and Mark were saddling the big paint.

"Waco sure picked the beauty this time," he said. "Told me you said he could have hand-choice of the remuda and he wanted the paint, so I told him to go ahead. Why in hell did he pick that hoss out of the rest?"

A grin twisted Clay's lips and he glanced at Dusty's big horse which stood grazing to one side.

"I wonder why?" he said.

Three times the paint threw Waco, but each time he got up and mounted again. He showed he could really handle a horse and the fourth time on he stuck there until the horse gave in. Not until then did he join the other men at the fire and took the mug of coffee offered by the cook. His eyes were on Dusty all the time, his ears working to catch every word Dusty said. Not until then did he fully realize who Dusty was for nobody had introduced him.

After the meal Clay selected six men, including Waco, to ride with them and see about moving the wire.

"We're r'aring to go, Cap'n Fog," said one of the men.

"Then un-rear!" Dusty snapped. "There's a time to talk and a time to fight. We'll try talk first."

"Hell they ain't but a bunch of hired guns, way you told us, Dusty," Waco objected.

"You're just as dead no matter who puts the lead into you, boy," Dusty answered. "And a lot of innocent folks might get hurt at the same time."

Usually Waco would have scoffed at the idea of worrying about other people. This time he did not. He sat back and waited to hear what the others said on the subject.

"We'll do whatever you say, Dusty," Clay stated firmly. "Then if talk don't work we can always try making war."

The Lasalle house had a crowd in it after dark that evening, not counting the Allison hands who lounged around outside, letting their boss make the talk while they ate some good fixings.

In the dining-room Dusty, Mark, Clay Allison, Stone Hart and Waco sat with Lasalle and Morg. The girl came in and joined her father after serving a meal from the supplies the CA crew brought along. They had barely got down to business when Johnny Raybold arrived, bringing word that although visited by the Double K men the Jones' and Gibbs' houses were fine and without a worry in the world.

"Never seed ole Peaceful looking so miserable," he concluded, to show that all really was well.

"I thought I'd send him visiting to earn his pay," Stone remarked.

"I sure earned it," Johnny grinned. "Mrs. Gibbs done made a pie for the boys, had it all a-cooling on the window. Only it's not there any more." Here Johnny rolled his eyes in ecstasy and rubbed his stomach. "Man, that Mrs. Gibbs sure is one good cook. Not that you-all aint, Miss Freda."

This latter came as he caught an accusing gleam in Freda's eyes and remembered visiting the house and praising her cooking.

"I bet you say that to all the cooks," she replied.

"I do, I do. But I sure don't want to meet up with Rusty, Doc'n Billy for a spell, not 'til they get over losing their pie."

"Now that's a shame. That sure is a shame," Dusty drawled. "Because you're headed over there right now, then on to Jones'. I want them here with their wagons in the morning so we can take them into town for supplies."

"Sure," Johnny replied, secure in the knowledge that no reprisals could be taken on him while he rode on urgent business. "I'll tell them."

"Just one man with each wagon," Dusty went on. "The other two stay on and guard the house."

"Yo!" Johnny replied and left the room.

"What's your plan, Dusty?" Clay asked.

"Easy enough. We're going into town tomorrow in force. And we're serving notice on the Double K bunch that they get out of town. After that I'm getting some questions answered by Mr. Mallick, the Land Agent, whether he wants to answer or not."

"And after that?" Stone put in.

"I want to get this fence business ended one way or the other. I aim to run Elben out of Barlock so the Double K doesn't have the backing of the law. Then, if I have to I'm going to see Keller and show him the error of his ways."

CHAPTER FOURTEEN

The Freeing Of Barlock

THE town of Barlock lay sleepily under the early morning sun. Few people walked the streets. In the office of the Land Agent an emergency meeting had been called. Mallick sat at his desk, sullen and scowling. Jackieboy Disraeli sat in a chair with a pout like a petulant schoolgirl on his face. To one side, by the door, stood Knuckles, leaning against the wall and looking about as intelligent as the wooden planks behind him. Before the desk stood Elben, and a man from the Double K, a hired gun who had slipped away early in order to have a chance at making some money at the expense of his friends.

"So you came here with a warning?" asked Mallick, in a mocking tone as he watched the man's face.

"Yeah."

"Why?"

"I reckoned it'd be worth something for you to know what Tring's fixing to do," replied the gunman.

Mallick looked at the man, and his voice still stayed mocking. "I see. So Tring and the rest are coming here to make us pay them for work they botched and couldn't complete."

"Yeah."

"And you thought you would warn us out of the goodness of your heart?" piped Disraeli, also watching the man.

"I reckoned it'd be worth at least a hundred dollars for you to know," answered the man, throwing a contemptuous look at the fancy dressed man.

The sudden anger which came to Disraeli's face should have warned the man of his danger, but he was more interested in talking himself into money, then getting away from town before the others arrived. Disraeli snapped his fingers and pointed at the man.

157

With a slow, almost beast-like snarl Knuckles left his place. He moved faster than one might have thought possible for so bulky a man. The gunman heard Knuckles and started to turn, his hand dropping towards the butt of his gun. Knuckles drove out a big fist, throwing it with all his power. Like the arrival of a thunderbolt it smashed into the side of the man's head as he turned. He flew across the room, his head snapped over and hanging at an unnatural angle. The others watched him hurl into the wall, hit it and slide down.

Crossing the room, Elben bent over and looked down at the man. Then he lifted scared eyes to Disraeli and Mallick. The Land Agent stood staring, but Disraeli remained in his seat, sadistic pleasure etched on his face.

"He's dead!" Elben said. "His neck's broke."

"So?"

There was challenge in Disraeli's one-word reply, mockery too, for Disraeli liked nothing better than to see stronger men who might have treated him with derision and mockery but cowered before the awful might of Knuckles. He watched Elben, seeing the marshal's eyes flicker to Knuckles who ignored the man he had struck down and killed and was now leaning against the wall again.

"I only told you," Elben answered. "What do you want us to do with him?"

"That's for you to decide," Mallick answered. "It was self defence on Knuckles' part. Now get down to your office and come back in a couple of hours with some of your men and clear that carrion out of here."

After the door closed on Elben's departing back, Mallick and Disraeli exchanged glances.

"I think we're finished here, don't you?" Disraeli asked.

Mallick nodded. "I think we are. What next?"

"We run. I have a friend in New York who can get us on a boat for Europe and we can disappear into some big city if we find that the law is after us. That is one advantage to being of my race, Mallick, the brotherhood of my people will shield us from the Gentiles."

"And what about me?" asked Mallick.

"You too, old friend. A little more money might help us though."

They exchanged glances. Both had money from their

scheme, although not as much as at first expected. The hiring of gunmen took much of the cream from their profits but the same men had been a necessity.

"Keller has the money to complete the purchase," Mallick remarked. "And for his running costs as he calls them. And he had a collection of jewelry, as you told me when you first put this idea to me. He'll be at the ranch, alone except for his daughter and with that bad ankle won't be any a problem. He'll never suspect anything until too late."

An evil gleam came to Disraeli's eyes. "Yes that's the idea!" he said, slapping his hands together like an excited girl. "I'll have revenge for my brother and see that accursed Sir James Keller suffer."

"Let's destroy all the papers on the Lindon Land Grant, and do a thorough job this time!" Mallick said. "Then we'll get the wagon, the money, and go to the Double K."

Half an hour later only the ashes of burned paper lay in the waste-paper basket, the body of the gunman sprawled by the wall. The doors were locked, that at the front bolted also for Mallick's party left by the rear.

They called at the saloon where Disraeli emptied his office safe, took all the money and the deeds to the business from it. Then, after making sure that no incriminating papers remained the two men went to where Knuckles had a fast two horse carriage awaiting them. They left town and took cover in a wood while Tring and his men rode by, then they headed across the range in the direction of the Double K.

When he found the birds had flown Tring cursed savagely. A look over the painted lower half of the Land Agent's office windows showed him the room held only the body of a man who would have sold them out. The safe door hung open and clearly Mallick was gone. So had his partner Jackieboy Disraeli, when they came to the saloon. A boot sent his office door flying open but once more the Double K had arrived too late.

"We'll take it out of here boys," Tring said waving a hand towards the saloon. "And anything more we need this stinking lil town's going to give us."

His plan only partially succeeded. The men headed for the bar where scared bartenders poured drinks and emptied the till for Tring and the hired gunmen. They drank and then one of the men standing by a window and watching the street, gave a warning shout.

Silence fell on the room. They heard the sound of hooves, many hooves and gathered to see who came to town. Mutters of surprise and fear rose from amongst the men as they recognized the men who led the well armed party into town.

"There's Dusty Fog and Mark Counter!" one man said. "We never touched either of them when we hit Lasalle's."

"Naw. They weren't staying in the house 'cause they was scared neither," another went on, putting forth the reason one faction of the raiding party offered for Dusty and Mark not coming after them in revenge for the attack on Lasalle's. "They was waiting for help."

"And they got it!" a third put in. "That's Clay Allison and Stone Hart up front and some of their boys along."

"They coming in here?" asked a fourth man, casting an eye on the rear door.

"Nope, going through."

They formed quite a party, coming down the main street. The four men in the lead each famous in his own right. Behind them came the Gibbs and Jones' wagons, driven by the women and flanked by men. Stone had called a further four men from his herd, bringing the fighting force to fourteen, but they were fourteen who might have made a troop of cavalry think twice about attacking.

"There's the stores, Clay," Dusty said. "Get to it."

In his store Matt Roylan looked at the two gunhung deputies who now lounged at the counter and decimated his profits by their constant dipping into cracker barrel or candy jar.

"How the hell does your boss expect me to make a living with you scaring trade off?" he asked.

"Whyn't you go and ask him?" answered one of the men, then looked towards the door.

Horses and a wagon had halted outside. Then boots thudded on to the sidewalk and up to the door. It opened and two tall men stepped inside, two men with low hanging guns, although one of them did not look more than sixteen years old.

"The name's Clay Allison," said the bearded man and jerked a thumb to where Ma Jones stood by her wagon. "The lady aims to buy supplies and I'm here to see she gets them. Understand?"

The two deputies understood. So did Roylan. He removed his apron, walked around the end of the counter and shot out a hand to grip each collar of the gunmen. With spirit and delight he hustled the two men across his business premises, doing what his heart craved to do ever since they first came here. He heaved the two astonished deputies through the door, ran them to the edge of the sidewalk and hurled them off. With a delighted grin Roylan looked down at them.

"That was gentle!" he said. "The next of you shows his face in here gets it damaged!"

One of the deputies sat up, mouthing curses. His hand went to his side, to grip the butt of his gun, eyes glowing hate at Roylan's back as the storekeeper turned to Ma Jones.

Waco lunged through the door, his right hand Colt coming clear and lining on the man.

"Loose it!" he snapped. "Then on your feet and find a hoss. The next time I see you I'll shoot."

Watching this Clay Allison felt puzzled and then smiled. Waco would have shot the man without a chance had this happened yesterday. Waco also felt surprised at the change in his outlook. His first instinct had been to shoot, to send lead into the gunman. Then, at the last instant, he held his hand. He knew Dusty Fog had said no killing unless it became necessary. He could not see Dusty, or Mark, wanting truck with a fool trigger-fast-and-up-from-Texas kid who cut down a man in cold blood.

So Waco watched the man get to his feet, then kept the two deputies under observation as they walked away. He stood aside and let Roylan and Ma Jones enter the store.

"I had to do it, Ma," Roylan said. "So did Banker O'Neil. They threatened his wife and family unless he went along with them. It's over now."

She nodded. "It looks that way."

Mrs. Gibbs traded with the other store. She found that her escort would consist of Stone Hart, Rusty Willis and Peaceful Gunn. They made for the store where Peaceful and Rusty insisted on entering first, to sort of watch things and kind of make sure the deputies didn't get too festive when Mrs. Gibbs entered. This was Rusty's idea. Peaceful moaned about it being safer inside than on the streets where already Dusty's men were letting out their wild cowhand yells, firing guns into the air and doing all they could to produce the local law.

In the store Jake Billings leaned his old frame on the counter and glowered at the pair of deputies, one of whom lit his third free cigar from Jake's private stock.

"You pair's supposed to be deputies," he said. "Whyn't you get out there afore those cowhands ropes the town and hauls it back to the Old Trail with them."

"Not us. We're special deputies," replied one of the men, his face bearing marks of Mark Counter's big fists.

They looked at the door as Rusty Willis and Peaceful Gunn entered. The two cowhands separated, crossing the store to halt one by each deputy. Peaceful removed his hat and held it in his right hand, mopping his brow with a large red handkerchief and letting his moustache droop in an abject manner.

"Them rowdies out there," he said in his usual mournful and whining tone for such an occasion. "They're causing so much fuss that I'll just get me some t'baccy and light out afore the marshal comes and jails everybody in sight."

If anything could have lulled the suspicions of the two deputies, Peaceful words were most likely to succeed. Neither of the hard-cases gave him another glance. The second deputy looked at Rusty who stood by him and took up a heavy skillet.

"Chow asked me to get him one of these," he drawled, looking at the deputy. "You reckon this'n'd be all right?"

"How the hell would I know?" snapped the deputy, then looked to where Stone and Mrs. Gibbs came through the door. "What do you want?"

"The lady's here for her supplies," Stone answered.

"Then she can get the hell out of—!" began the deputy by Peaceful.

His speech did not end. Peaceful moved at a speed which amazed Joyce, when she thought of his usual lethargic movements. His hat lashed back, full into the man's face. Two pounds of prime J. B. Stetson could hurt when lashed around with the full power of a brawny arm. The gunman's hand, almost on his gun butt, missed and he gave forth a startled, pain-filled yell.

The second man sent his hand flying towards his gun and almost made it. At his side Rusty gripped the heavy skillet by the handle and swung it sideways, using the edge like an axe blade against the man's stomach. With a croaking cry of pain the gunman doubled over, holding his middle. Up lifted the pan to come down with a resounding and very satisfying clang, on to the temptingly offered head. Billings let out a whoop of delight, but the gunman gave only a moan to show his disapproval of Rusty's actions.

With tears in his eyes, the deputy Peaceful assailed with his hat dropped a hand towards the butt of his gun. Steel glinted in Peaceful's hand, the bowie knife which mostly rode at the peace lover's left side, now lay in his hand, its clipped point driving at the man's stomach, Joyce let out a gasp of fear for she expected to see the deputy drop writhing in agony and spurting blood on the floor.

At the last instant Peaceful changed his aim slightly, the knife rose and then cut down, the razor sharp lower edge ripping through the leather of the man's gunbelt causing it to drop. The deputy's hand clawed air for his holster now hung mouth down by the pigging thong and his gun lay at his feet.

"I'm a man of peace, I am!" warned Peaceful and cut again, this time through the gunman's waist band causing him to grab hurriedly at his pants. "And if I sees you again after you go through that door I'll prove it!"

Taking the hint, and holding his pants up at the same time, the deputy headed past Joyce and out through the door. She watched him go and smiled a little. It appeared that the hardcase Double K were not as hard as she at first imagined.

She knew why her friends acted in the way they did. Stone Hart might be accepted as a master trail boss, but his name did not carry the same weight as Clay Allison's in gun fighting circles. So Stone and his men arranged to take care of the deputies before announcing their presence, or at least to make sure that the two deputies could be rendered harmless by having Rusty and Peaceful on hand before Stone brought Joyce intot he building.

"About these supplies, friend?" Stone asked.

Billings grinned. "You can have them, Joyce. I didn't dare go again Mallick until I had some backing. But I got it now. What do you want?"

"It telled you we ought to've gone round!" Peaceful wailed. "I—"

Joyce spun to face him and stabbed an accusing finger at his face. "You're a fake!" she yelled. "And if you ever mention peace and quiet to me again I'll drag you east by the ear and make sure you get some."

The threat brought a heart-rending sigh from Peaceful. "There," he told Rusty miserably. "For this here lady I forget me true and beautiful nature, and that's all the thanks I get."

Since the arrival of the Texans there had been a steady departure from the Jackieboy Saloon. Men who took pay for their fighting ability drifted out, mounted their horses and rode out of town. The word had passed around that Barlock would be unhealthy for any hired gun who took pay from Double K and they aimed to stay healthy as long as they could.

One of the men who went was Preacher Tring. Unlike the others he did not have his horse before the saloon, but left it saddled and ready down by the civic pound. He left the saloon by its rear entrance, having an idea that his prominence in matters of the Double K, including the attack of the Lasalle house and attempted dynamiting, would put him high on the list of those most wanted by Mark Counter and Dusty Fog.

Tring went to the civic pound, a walled corral in which stood the horses of Elben and his deputies. His own horse waited at the rear and he passed around to the rear of the corral. Just as he was about to mount and shake the dust of Barlock for ever from his feet, he saw a man come around the side of the town marshal's office and halt standing facing the rear door of the building.

A hiss of satisfaction left Tring's lips. The man was Dusty Fog. More he clearly did not suspect Tring's presence or he would never have been foolish enough to present his back in such a tempting manner.

Never again would Tring have such a chance of killing Dusty Fog. The small Texan's back was to him, his attention fixed on the rear door of the marshal's office. Tring's horse stood saddled and only needed mounting for a rapid departure to safer pastures once he sent lead between Dusty's shoulders. Ever since Dusty drove him from the Double K, Tring had nursed hatred and swore he would be revenged. Now it seemed he would be given his chance.

Not suspecting the danger behind him, Dusty Fog stood watching the rear door of the town marshal's office. He took

no part in the general freeing of Barlock and clearance of the
Double K hired guns. For himself, Dusty reserved the duty, if
not the pleasure, of handling the matter of Mallick's tame
lawman.

Dusty never made any move without good reason. His reasons for removing Elben were simple. The man wore a law
badge. He might not have been elected by true democratic
principles but he held the badge and while he wore it he had
certain rights and privileges. So Dusty aimed to see Elben and
use moral persuasion, of his own style, to make Elben resign
from office. In other words Elben was to be offered the
chance of resigning, or being resigned forcibly. Dusty did not
intend allowing Mallick the protection of a law badge when
they met and discussed the matter of the Lindon Land Grant.

The office door opened and Elben emerged carrying a
saddle and looking back across the room. Dusty knew at what
Elben looked. On the front porch Mark Counter stood waiting
and Elben wondered when the blond giant would come after
him to take reprisals for the attack upon his person on Mark's
last visit to town.

Whatever his other faults, and they were many, Elben
counted himself as being smart enough to know when to yell
"calf rope" and get clear of danger. He had seen the eviction
of his deputies from the stores and the departure of Double K
men so knew his term of office was due for a sudden termina-
tion at the hands of the enraged citizenry of Barlock.

With that thought in mind Elben took his saddle which he
kept in his room. He emptied the office safe of various little
trinkets and keepsakes presented by people around town, including the donations made by various sources to his election
campaign funds. These he stuffed into a saddlebag, took up
the saddle and headed for the back door, aiming to collect a
horse and ride out.

"Going someplace?"

The words brought Elben around in a startled turn. He
stood with the saddle in his right hand, his left hovering over
the butt of his gun. Then he stiffened and his hovering hand
froze for he recognized the small man standing before him.

"Yeah, Cap'n," he said. "I'm going someplace."

He thought of the money in his saddlebags. Money extorted
from various people around town. To be caught with it was

likely to wind him up in jail for a fair time and he didn't want such a thing to happen. Yet he did not see how he could avoid it.

At that moment Elben saw Tring sneaking along the side of the corral behind Dusty. This would be his chance for Tring held a gun and clearly aimed to use it. Elben watched the man raising the gun, licked his lips with the flickering tip of his tongue and prepared to take a hand. He could get off a shot into Dusty Fog even as Tring fired, showing his heart to be in the right place. Then he and Tring would be free to make good their escape. For a share of the loot Tring would carry his saddle while he rode bareback until they had time to halt and get the saddle on Elben's mount.

Elben tensed slightly as Tring aimed the gun. At the same moment he heard a voice yell one word.

"Dusty!"

A tall, blond youngster burst into view around the corner of the office, his hands fanning down towards the butts of his guns. Instantly everything burst into wild and sudden action.

Hearing the yell and seeing the danger, Tring turned his gun and fired at the newcomer, his bullet fanning by Waco's cheek. Even as he did so. Dusty flung himself backwards and to one side, hands crossing and fetching out his matched guns. At the same instant Elben let his saddle fall and clawed out his right hand gun to take a hand in the game.

Dusty's matched guns roared, slightly less than three-quarters of a second after his first move. He threw his lead at Tring, shooting to prevent the man correcting his aim and cutting Waco down. In doing so Dusty put his own life in peril for he had his back to Elben and the ex-town marshal's gun was already sliding clear.

A warning flicker caught the corner of Waco's eye, brought his attention to Dusty's danger. He ignored Tring, ignored the fact that the next bullet from the gunman might hit him. He aimed to save Dusty Fog's life even if he died doing it.

Even as Dusty's lead smashed into Tring, rocking him over into the corral fence and sending him down, Waco shot Elben, shot him in the head, aiming for an instant kill to prevent him being able to trigger off even one shot.

"You fool kid," Dusty said quietly, but there was admiration in his voice. "Why in hell didn't you put lead into Tring?"

"Figured you could handle him, and that *hombre* behind you sure didn't aim to play spit-balls," Waco replied.

One look at Elben told Dusty the marshal offered no danger to him now. He heard running feet as men came to investigate the shooting. then he holstered his guns and walked towards Waco.

"You risked Tring killing you to save me," he said, speaking quietly.

"And you hauled me out from under that stampede," Waco replied. "Figured to get even, but," he looked at where Tring lay sprawled by the corral, "you're still one up on me."

Mark reached the scene first, coming with guns in his hands. He holstered the weapons, looked at the scene before him and read its implications. He had seen Waco leave the store and pass between the two buildings, disobeying Dusty's orders, but could also see that likely Waco's disobedience saved Dusty's life.

"Why'd you come here?" he asked.

"Me'n Clay'd done our lil piece down at the store and I figured to see how this here moral persuasion worked," Waco replied with a grin.

"You did the right thing, boy," drawled Mark and slapped Waco on the shoulder. "For once."

A grin came to Waco's face. He doubted if he could have been given greater praise than that.

"Let's get to the Land Agent's office, Mark," Dusty said. "These gents here can attend to the bodies."

After unlocking the rear door with a powerful kick from Mark's right leg, Dusty led the way into the office. Mark and Waco followed on his heels and they stood behind Dusty, looking at the body by the wall, then at the charred remains of many papers lying in the waste-paper basket.

"Looks like we got here too late," Dusty said.

Mark did not reply. He went to the body and looked down at it, seeing the bruise left by a fist and the way the neck hung. It had taken a man with exceptional strength to deliver such a blow and one man sprang to Mark's mind.

One thought led to another, Mark's nostrils quivered as he sniffed at the sickly scent which still hung in the office.

"Remember that first time we came to see Mallick, Dusty?" he asked. "We smelled this same scent in here then. Thought it might be some calico cat Mallick had been entertaining. Only I

know it wasn't. That fat little swish* who owns the Jackieboy
Saloon uses it. And the trained ape he had with him was strong
enough to have bust this feller's neck with a punch.''

"Best go along to the saloon then," Dusty replied.

As Dusty expected, the saloon's owner had departed with
Mallick and nobody appeared to know where they had gone.
However, on going outside to see that everything in the streets
was peaceful and the Double K men cleared out of town,
Dusty met Matt Roylan. After the storekeeper thanked him
for freeing Barlock from the clutches of the gunmen, Roylan
remarked that he had seen Mallick, Disraeli and Knuckles
making a hurried departure in the direction of the Double K.

Before any more could be said an interruption, in the shape
of a fast riding man, stopped the conversation. They all recognized George Lasalle and wondered what brought him into
town at such a speed.

"Captain Fog!" Lasalle gasped, even before his horse slid
to a halt. "Miss Keller came to visit us this morning. Her
father thinks he bought all our land. She asked Freda and
Morg to go back with her to the Double K house to see and explain things to her father."

"Dusty's face looked suddenly grim. He turned to the
listening men and they saw that he considered the situation to
be very grave.

"Mark, Waco!" he snapped. "Get your horses. Mallick's
headed for the Double K and happen he finds Freda and Morg
there all hell's due to pop!"

* Swish: HOMOSEXUAL

CHAPTER FIFTEEN

Mallick's Plan

THE redbone hound raised his head and gave a low growl which caused Morg Summers to drop the hammer, come to his feet and reach for his gun. It made Freda Lasalle lay aside the bowl of peas she had been shelling, while sitting on the front porch, so she could talk with Morg as he repaired a section of the flooring damaged in the fight. Freda threw a look to where her shotgun leaned by the door for she caught the sound of horse's hooves.

"One horse, gal, coming easy," Morg said, but did not relax. He raised his voice: "Boss! We got callers!"

This brought Lasalle to the door of the barn. He stepped from the door and crossed the open to the house, a hand resting on the butt of the Colt in his waistband. On the porch he looked at the other two, then at the dog which, having done his duty in giving a warning, now lay on the porch with an eye on the open house door in case a sudden departure to the safety of his mistresses's bedroom be called for.

"A gal," said Morg, as the approaching rider came into view on the river bank, then turned her horse and rode to where the bank sloped down towards the ford, her eyes on the house.

"And a pretty one," Freda answered.

"Sure. Rides good too," said Morg, his hand going out to gently squeeze her arm. "I bet she can't cook as well as you do. And I never saw a riding outfit like that afore."

Woman-like, Freda's first look had been at the newcomer's clothes. Even at that distance she could tell the clothes were good quality and well-tailored. She had never seen a woman wearing a top hat or an outfit like that worn by the newcomer

169

but grudgingly admitted the clothes looked good and the girl had a figure to show them off.

Sitting her horse with easy grace, Norma Keller rode along the river bank, studying the small house and the three people before it. She reached the top of the slope and rode down towards the water. Then she remembered something the army captain who commanded their escort from Dodge City told her one night. Halting the horse at the edge of the water she raised a hand in greeting.

"May I ride across?" she called.

"Come ahead," Freda answered, watching Norma and seeing the easy way the other girl rode through the water and towards the house.

"Good morning," Norma greeted, halting the horse. "I appear to have lost my way. I saw smoke from your chimney and rode this way. It puzzled me somewhat. Mr. Mallick did not mention that there were any tenants farming on our property."

"Tenants—farming!" snorted Freda, more annoyed because the other girl drew praise from Morg than for any other reason.

"I'm afraid this isn't your land, Miss Keller," Lasalle put in, guessing who the girl must be for he had heard upper-class British accents before.

A slight frown came on Norma's face. "That's strange. I pride myself on being a good judge of distance and I thought I had at least another two miles before I came to the end of our property."

Lasalle saw the light immediately. He also had to admit the girl was a good judge of distance for there would be another two miles or so more—if the Lindon Land Grant covered the area shown on the map he fixed together for Dusty Fog and which still lay in the side-piece drawer.

"I think there's something you should know, ma'am," he said, stepping forward. "Would you come inside please."

"Thank you," replied Norma. "I would like directions to the house though."

"You must have a cup of coffee first," Freda put in, her hospitable nature coming to the fore. "We haven't had a chance to meet you so far."

"Thank you again," smiled Norma. "I think I will stay. I

haven't met any of the neighbors yet. Papa managed to crock his ankle up and we haven't managed to get around much as yet."

She slid down from her saddle without needing any help and, a point in her favor, attended to the horse before she came on to the porch. She looked down at Bugle for a moment and he beat his tail on the porch floor.

"I say," she said. "He's a redbone, isn't he?"

"Sure is, ma'am," agreed Morg. "Real good one, too."

"Papa hopes to bring some foxhound and staghounds from England if the hunting is worthwhile," she replied. "Are there any foxes about?"

"A few," Lasalle replied. "But more chance of cougar, or bear."

"I never thought of hunting such dangerous beasts with hounds," Norma remarked. "It sounds interesting."

The girl's attitude surprised Lasalle and puzzled him. She did not appear to have any idea of the trouble the Double K men caused throughout the Panhandle country. In fact, from the way she acted, she did not appear to know there were other people in the country. Lasalle decided to show the girl the map and tell her how Mallick and his men acted in her father's name. It would be interesting to see her reactions.

With that in mind Lasalle escorted Norma into the dining-room and seated her at the table. Then he crossed to the side-piece and took out a map and a deed box. Norma glanced at the kitchen where Freda had gone to make the coffee and slam things about. A smile crept to Norma's face for she had not failed to notice the other girl's hostile looks and read them for what they were, the jealousy of a young girl very much in love.

"Have you seen anything like this before, ma'am?" Lasalle asked, spreading the map before her on the table.

She looked down at it, then raised her eyes to his face.

"It appears to be a map of our est—ranch," she answered. "But what is this piece marked off for?"

"I can show you better on this map," Lasalle replied, opening the metal deed box to take out and open another map of the area. "This is the correct shape of the Lindon Land Grant. This part down here is not a part of the Grant. There are, or were, four small ranches on here."

Norma frowned. "I'm afraid I don't understand," she said.

"The map Papa received from Mr. Mallick showed that we own all the block of land. I forget how many thousand acres it came to. What does this mean?"

"I think I'd better start at the beginning and tell you everything," Lasalle replied, taking a seat and facing the girl.

Starting at the beginning and hiding nothing, neither making things worse nor better, Lasalle told Norma of the happenings since Mallick offered to buy them out. The girl watched him, her face showing horror as he spoke of one family driven from their home and the other three attacked, brow-beaten, having pressure brought to bear on them to sell and clear out.

Looking at the shattered windows, the bullet holes in the walls and sidepiece, Norma's lips drew tight and grim.

"You mean that my father's employees did this?" she asked. "Attacked your home, whipped that poor chap and wrecked his home?"

"They did."

Strangely it never occurred to Norma to doubt Lasalle's word. She thought of the sullen men at the ranch, of little incidents, like that party which returned late one night cursing and making a lot of noise. Norma fancied her judgment of character and liked this family even though they had not introduced themselves nor she to them.

"Papa and I have only been here a few days," she said. "And with Papa having crocked his ankle he hasn't been able to look over his property. He loathes riding in a carriage of any kind. But he must be told. Would you come with me to the ranch and help me explain?"

"We will," agreed Lasalle.

"And of course Papa will discharge all the men and make restitution for the damage caused in his name," said Norma. "I promise you that not one of the men will remain here when they return from their work today."

"What work's that, ma'am?" Morg asked.

"I don't really know. They all rode out early this morning and I haven't seen anything of them."

Three faces looked at each other, Lasalle, Freda and Morg exchanged glances which were pregnant with expression.

"Morg, take Miss Keller and Freda to the Double K. I'll head for town to warn Captain Fog!"

"Be best!" Morg agreed.

All thought that the hired guns might be gathering to make one last final onslaught on the small ranchers. In that case a fighting force such as Dusty gathered would be of vital importance.

Freda dashed into her bedroom to change for the trip while Morg left to catch and saddle two horses. Lasalle and Norma talked on and the more they talked the more sure of Sir James Keller's innocence Lasalle became.

The door to Freda's bedroom opened and Norma looked towards it, a smile came to her lips.

"I say, that is a fetching outfit," she said, studying the shirtwaist, jeans and high heeled cowhand boots Freda now wore. "I must get something like it. I'm afraid these togs are more suited for a Hunt meet in Leicestershire than for out on the range."

In a few seconds Freda had lost her jealous suspicions and was talking clothes with Norma like they had been friends for years. The girls took their horses and with Morg riding on one side, Norma on the other, Freda headed them in the direction of the Double K house.

Talk passed amongst them as they rode across the range. Norma wanted to know so much that the sullen hard-cases who formed the ranch crew could not, or would not explain. She managed to preserve a nice balance of keeping Morg answering her questions without giving Freda anything to complain about. In fact Freda could tell of conditions in this section of the range far better than Morg. Norma told the other two of her adventure with the cougar and Freda recognized the Kid's description.

When the Ysabel Kid did not return from Bent's Ford, Freda had worried but Dusty and Mark told her not to. They stated flatly that Double K didn't hire a man capable of catching up to, or downing, their *amigo*. Sure the Kid hadn't returned, but most likely he had good reason for it. Red Blaze might need help with the herd, some word from Ole Devil Hardin might have been received, or the Kid might be around, staked out on the plains somewhere, watching every move the Double K made. Their very confidence reassured Freda. From what Norma, they knew each other's names by now, said the Kid had been busy on his way north.

They came to the big old Double K house, a fine, stoutly

built, two story wooden structure strong enough to act as a fort in time of trouble. Right now it looked silent and deserted, a few horses in the corral moving about, but not a sign of life. The bunkhouse and cookshack looked empty, devoid of life, the chimney of the latter showing no smoke to give evidence that a cook prepared food for all hands.

"They're not back yet," Freda said and Norma nodded.

Morg loosened his gun in its holster as they rode towards the house. He felt worried about the emptiness, it did not seem right. He wondered if Norma might be leading them into a trap.

The front door of the house opened and a tall, burly man stepped out, leaning on a cane. He wore a round topped hat—known as a fez or smoking cap in more refined circles—a dark green smoking jacket, well pressed trousers. On one foot was a shining black shoe, the other had bandages around it. His face looked tanned, healthy, but not vicious. It looked very much a man's face and one Morg felt could be trusted and who would make a real good boss.

"Papa!" Norma said, dropping from her horse and going to the man. "I'd like you to meet two good friends, and neighbors, Freda, Morg, this is my father."

"Pleased to meet you," Sir James Keller said. "Come in and I'll see if I can scare up a drink. The blasted cook took off this morning with the others. Don't know what they're playing at."

"They're not playing, Papa," Norma replied seriously. "Come inside. Freda's father told me some distressing news."

The inside of the house still looked much the same as when Lindon owned the place for it had been sold furnished. Freda remembered the library into which they were taken, it looked out on the north range. The window was open and the room cool after the ride. Keller proved an excellent host, he produced chairs for his guests and seated them at the desk.

"Like to offer you something," but I'm not much at cooking," he said. "Do you have trouble with your help, Miss Lasalle?"

Freda smiled at Morg. "If I don't watch him. Morg's our only hand. We don't have a large spread like this, and I'm the cook. If you like I'll throw up a meal for you. I'd like to."

"Then Norma can help you," Keller replied with a grin.

"Time she learned how to cook."

"I can cook," smiled Norma. "It's just that I don't like eating what I've cooked." Then her face lost its smile. "You had better hear what I discovered first, Papa."

Keller threw a look at his daughter's face, then took his seat behind the desk. Norma told what she learned at the Lasalle's house. He did not speak until she finished. Then he slapped his hand on the table top, a hand which looked as hard as any working rancher's.

"I see," he said.

"Wish I did, sir," Morg drawled.

"It's easy young feller, very easy. I was thinking of making a change of scenery. Decided to come out here. I'd been out west three years ago, hunting, and liked the look of it. So Norma and I held a conference and decided we'd buy a place out here. Arranged it through the British Embassy, they contacted various chappies and got wind of the Double K. Felt it might be an omen, two K's and all that, so we said we'd take it. Got it at so much an acre, deuced great oblong of land."

"Only it isn't oblong, papa," Norma put in. "Mallick sold us land which was owned by other people."

"And then he tried to drive us out, make us sell for a fraction of the value of our places," Freda put in hotly, seeing the light for the first time. "So that he could show you the full area you have bought."

"By gad!" boomed Keller. "So that's the bounder's game. I left it in his hands to keep things going for me, after I put down the deposit. It appears he ran it all right."

"But why'd he wire off the Old Trail?" asked Morg. "He must have known that'd make trouble when the herds came up."

"I don't know!" snapped Keller. "All I know is I aim to horsewhip the bounder when I lay hands on him."

At that moment the door opened and Keller started to rise, his face showing anger. Freda's nostrils caught a whiff of a sickly sweet scent she seemed to recognize, one she did not attribute to Norma for the English girl had better taste than use such vile stuff. Along with the others Freda started to turn and a gasp of horror came to her lips.

Mallick stood in the doorway, a revolver in his hand, lining on the men. Behind, holding the fancy Remington Double

Derringer, stood Disraeli and looming over them, empty handed but no less deadly, Knuckles.

"I'm here, Keller," Mallick said.

The men moved into the room, Knuckles leaning a shoulder against the door while the other two stepped inside. Morg stood half risen from his seat, his hand clear of his gun. He was no gun-fighter and his reactions did not have the ability to make split-second moves. Under the guns of the two men he could not take a chance at drawing his weapon and fighting back.

"Drop the gunbelt, cowhand," Mallick ordered. "Kick it this way."

Morg did as ordered. He knew he had no chance but to obey. He felt Disraeli watching him all the time. Felt also that the fancy dressed little man had not forgotten what happened in the saloon. Slowly Morg unbuckled the belt and lowered it to the ground, kicking it to one side.

"Stay where you are, Sir James Keller!" hissed Disraeli. "No heroics or we shoot down the two girls then this man. Ah! I thought that would stop you. You English gentlemen, with your high and mighty code of morals. You would attack us and risk being killed if only your life was at stake. But not to endanger the lives of these others."

"It sounds as if you know English gentlemen," Keller replied quietly.

His words brought a snarl of hatred from Disraeli. "I know you. I know you well. So did my brother. So did my brother Emmanuel. You remember him, Sir James Keller?"

"I can't say I've had that pleasure," replied Keller calmly. "Now may I ask what you want here?"

"We want money," replied Mallick. "The money to complete the sale of this ranch."

"With or without the part you don't own?"

Mallick growled out something in his anger. "So, I thought Miss Lasalle was here for something. It makes no difference. We want every cent you have in the house. And all your collection of jewelry."

"Really?" answered Keller, still as calm as ever.

"Don't fool with us, Keller," warned Mallick. "We've too much at stake to play games."

"We could always let Knuckles have fun with the girls," purred Disraeli.

"One thing's for sure," Morg put in. "You wouldn't have any use for fun with a gal."

Smiling, a vicious smile which did not reach his eyes, Jackieboy Disraeli minced across the room. His hand lashed out, the Remington's foresight raking Morg's cheek and rocking his head back. Morg started to rise and with an almost beast-like snarl Knuckles bounded forward. With speed and agility which was surprising in such a man, Disraeli stepped aside. Knuckle's huge hands shot out, closing on Morg's throat and squeezing.

"Stop him!" Mallick barked out the order. "You hear me, Disraeli, stop him."

At the same moment Mallick jumped forward and caught Freda's arm, holding her as she tried to throw herself at Knuckles. Disraeli looked at Mallick, a slobbering sneer on his lips. Then he gave the order and Knuckles opened his fingers, letting Morg flop back into his chair. The young cowhand sucked in breath and looked ready to throw himself into the attack again.

"Tell him to sit still, Miss Lasalle!" Mallick ordered. "I might not be able to stop Knuckles again."

"Morg!" Freda gasped. "Don't move."

"Look here, Mallick!" barked Keller, standing up and ignoring the gun Mallick swung towards him. "Get this lot over and let's have you out of my house so I can start making up for what you've done to people around here."

"It's just like we told you," Mallick replied. "I want the money you've bought along to complete the purchase of this place and any more you have, as well as that collection of jewelry you own."

"And who told you about that?" Keller asked.

"I did!" Disraeli spat out the words. "I did. To avenge my brother, Emmanuel."

"You seem to think I know this brother of yours," Keller replied, speaking to gain time, in the hope that something might happen to get them clear of the danger they found themselves in.

"You knew him. You and your accursed kind knew him.

You ruined him. You brought him to be hanged. Have you forgotten Emmanuel Silverman. My brother!"

"Silverman," said Keller softly. "Silverman is it. I remember him. Money-lender, owner of crooked gambling hells, sweat-shop owner. I remember him and it is true I helped lay the trap which brought proof of his guilt. And he killed two women trying to escape, shot them in blind panic—"

"Stop!" Disraeli screamed.

"Keep Knuckles back!" Mallick snarled the words out. "Do it, Disraeli, or by God I'll kill him. We want something from Keller and he can't give it to us if he'd dead or unconscious."

For a moment Disraeli stood with his mouth hanging open. Then slowly, with an almost visible effort, he got control of himself.

"You helped hang my brother and I swore I would have my revenge," he said. I learned of your plans to come out here, Sir James Keller. I came ahead. I met Mallick and we managed to get ourselves in, he as Land Agent and I in a saloon. Then we offered this Lindon Land Grant for sale and you took it. Mallick thought only of the profit, his percentage of the sale and the extra for the small ranch properties. I thought of revenge. We sold you several thousand acres of land which did not belong to the Lindon Grant, and hoped to drive its owners out, to sell to you at a profit. I thought of stringing the wire across the trail. Soon the trail herds would be coming north. When they saw the wire they would attack the man who ordered it to be there. And they would blame you for that. I would have avenged my brother."

"In a most courageous manner," Keller replied.

"Cut the talk!" Mallick snarled. "How about that money, or do I turn Knuckles loose on your gal?"

"You're welcome to what money I have," Keller replied. "A matter of a thousand dollars."

"Don't fool with me, Keller!" snarled Mallick.

Keller shrugged and sat at his desk. "I've never felt less like fooling. My good chap, do you expect me to carry the amount this place costs in a valise? I intended to pay for my place, when I was satisfied with it, by a certified order on the First Union Bank in Dodge City. I brought a thousand along as running expenses and no more."

For a long moment Mallick stared at Sir James Keller who met his stare and then looked away. Mallick turned towards Disraeli and snarled:

"He's telling the truth, damn it to hell!"

"And as for my collection of jewelry, as you call it," Keller went on. "I left it in the bank at Dodge City, in my strongbox. So it would appear that you can't have that either."

Disraeli gave a scream of rage and frustration. The hand holding the Remington quivered. For a moment Keller expected a bullet to slam into him for the man stood facing him and lining the gun. Norma, face pale, tensed, her hands opened and curved into talons as she prepared to try and defend her father. Morg watched this, he knew that the girl would jump Disraeli at any moment. He knew the little fat man would shoot her out of hand, then cut down Keller. There was only one way to stop, or delay it.

"Hey, swish!" he said. "You watch yourself, or I'll let Freda hand you alicking and sh—"

With a howl of fury Disraeli swung around. He seemed ready to burst into tears and screamed. "Get him, Knuckles! Gouge his eyes out!"

Gamely Morg flung himself at the huge man, straight into the huge hands which clamped on to his throat. Morg felt himself lifted and shook like a dog in the big man's hands. Desperately he lashed out a kick at Knuckles, felt his boot connect with the man's shin but Knuckles gave not a sign of knowing it landed. Only his grip on Morg's throat tightened.

Shooting out a hand, Mallick grabbed Norma Keller's wrist and dragged her to him, thrusting his revolver barrel into her side. His move ended Sir James' attempt at opening the top desk of the drawer wherein lay a magnificent ivory butted 1860 Army Colt.

"Freeze, Keller!" Mallick snarled.

His warning went unheeded by Freda. With the ferocity of a bobcat defending its young she threw herself straight at Knuckles. She screamed, although it was doubtful that she knew the screams left her lips. Full on the huge man's back she hurled herself, one arm locked around his throat, the other trying to rip hair out and failing changed to scratching at his face.

Letting out a howl like a fattened shoat that had felt the but-

cher's knife. Disraeli jumped forward. His left hand caught
Freda by the neck of her blouse and dragged at it, trying to get
Knuckles free. The buttons on the blouse popped but the girl
clung on. Then Disraeli raised his other hand to bring the gun
down on to Freda's head. He struck hard but the girl's hair
prevented the worst of the blow, even so it knocked Freda
down.

Snarling like a wild animal Disraeli raised his hand again.
Sir James Keller started to open his desk drawer. His daughter's life lay in the hands of Mallick but he could not see either
the girl or cowhand killed in cold blood.

Faintly, as from a long way off, Freda heard words, Mallick
snarling a warning, Disraeli cursing her in his high-pitched
voice. Even more faintly she heard the thunder of approaching
hooves. Then everything went black.

CHAPTER SIXTEEN

Waco's Decision

THE Ysabel Kid felt puzzled as he rode by the side of the leading wagon. By now they were so far into the Double K range that he could make out the empty, deserted look of the buildings, and still no sign of the hired guns who had roamed the range on his way north.

He looked up at Weems and the housekeeper as they shared the wagon's box with the taciturn driver.

"That there's the house, Bill," he drawled. "Looks a mite too quiet for me."

"I'm afraid you have the advantage over me there, Kid," Weems answered as he squinted his eyes and tried to make out more than a few tiny buildings.

Since leaving Bent's Ford on the day after the Kid's rather hectic arrival Weems had changed. With the Kid he acted in a friendly manner and even thawed out to some small extent with the menials, the two grooms, as he called them, who drove the wagons and the 'tween-maid who was the lowest of the low amongst female employees. He still made them keep their places, but he relaxed slightly under the Kid's influence.

Much to his surprise, Weems had found the Kid to be anything but an uncouth savage. True he lacked some formal schooling, but he made up for it in matters practical and there was little he did not know about how to live most comfortably while travelling in Texas.

For his part the Kid found Weems to be far from helpless and a man with some knowledge, even if shy on other vital subjects. He enjoyed the trip down from Bent's Ford and would be sorry to part from his new friends at the end of it.

After another mile Weems could study the buildings. He

grunted as he looked the main house over.

"Not exactly like our country house in Yorkshire," he said. "A sturdy enough structure though."

"Reckon," replied the Kid.

His eyes took in the general deserted aspect of the ranch buildings and he did not like what he saw. Three saddled horses before the front of the main house, a two-horse riding wagon behind the big barn, like somebody didn't want it seen. To the Kid it spelled out but one thing, trouble.

The wagons rolled nearer, coming down from the north towards the buildings. His right hand near the butt of the old Dragoon Colt, the Kid sat relaxed but watchful and alert for trouble.

A scream shattered the air, coming from the big house, followed by more.

"What's that?" Weems gasped.

He spoke to the Kid's back for on the first scream a touch of the spurs sent Blackie racing for the house. As well as he could tell the screams came from the room towards which he now made.

Through the window he saw Knuckles choking Morg. Mallick holding a gun on Norma while Sir James stood at his desk, hand still on the drawer of the desk. He also saw Disraeli drag Freda from the huge man and raise the Remington Double Derringer to strike down at her. Of all the people in the room, the Kid knew only Freda. How she came to be at the Double K he could not guess, who the rest might be he also did not know. He could tell who sided with Freda from how they behaved.

The big white stallion raced towards the house but at the last moment, when it seemed certain to collide with the wall, Blackie turned. The Kid, ready for the turn, left his saddle. He held his Dragoon Colt in his right hand as he flung himself through the air. Hands covering his head, the Kid went through the window carrying its glass and framework in a shattered wreck before him.

He lit down on the floor, rolling like he'd come off a bad one. Disraeli released Freda and allowed her to slump to the ground. Flame spurted from the small Double Derringer and splinters kicked to one side of the Kid's rolling body. He lined the Dragoon and touched off a shot. The bullet ripped into

Disraeli's chest and tossed him backwards across the room. At the same moment violent action broke out amongst the others.

Snarling like an animal Knuckles hurled Morg to one corner and turned to face the Kid who lay on his back, the smoking Dragoon still in his hands. Seeing the huge man bearing down on him the Kid knew his danger. Knuckles might not carry a gun but was no less dangerous for it. His huge hands and great strength along with his beast-like rage, were fully as dangerous as any gun once he got close enough to lay hands on a man.

Only he did not get close enough. The Kid's big old Dragoon boomed out again and Knuckles at last met a force his strength could not withstand. One third of an ounce of soft round lead ball, .44 in calibre, powered by forty grains of prime du Pont powder, drove up, entered his mouth and shattered its way out through the top of his head. the force of the blow knocked Knuckles back so he crashed into the wall and slid down never to rise again.

The Kid's sudden and unexpected arrival took Mallick, Keller and Norma by surprise. Keller thrust back his chair and came to his feet. Mallick turned his gun away from Norma, thinking to line it on the blackdressed shape. Then Norma took a hand, reacting with cool courage even as the Kid's gun cut down Disraeli. She drew back her boot and lashed out a kick, the riding boot catching Mallick on the front of his shin. The man let out a howl of pain, released her arm and staggered back. Norma's face lost all its color as she saw Knuckles take lead. With a gasp she slid to the floor in a faint.

Gun in hand, Mallick still did not make a fight of it. He saw Sir James open the desk drawer and saw the Kid starting to turn. Then he flung himself back through the library door slamming it behind him. He raced along the hall to the main door and spun around to fire a shot. He backed through the main doors, firing again and sprang to the ground outside.

Behind him, from the house, he heard running feet and sent another bullet through the door. From the house sounded a piercing whistle then a voice yelled one word:

"Blackie!"

Hooves thundered behind Mallick. He started to turn and saw a huge white stallion charging at him. Saw its laid back ears, the bared teeth, heard its wild fighting scream. Desperately he tried to turn his gun, he fired one shot which missed.

He never had the chance to fire another. Blackie came at him, rearing high on its hind legs, the fore hooves lashing out. One ripped into the top of Mallick's head, crunching home with wicked force. Mallick screamed once, then he went down under the savage and awful fighting fury of the enraged white stallion.

The Ysabel Kid and Sir James Keller came from the library side by side although as yet neither knew who the other might be. They were not at the front door when they heard the screams.

"God!" gasped Sir James. "What's that?"

"Stay here, friend," replied the Kid who knew all too well what "that" was. "And keep those gals inside."

With that the Kid plunged out to get control of his horse. He hoped that Weems would show enough good sense to either stay well back, or keep the womenfolk to the rear of the building. That bloody wreck on the ground was no sight for female eyes, or male eyes either, happen the man had a weak stomach.

Quickly the Kid quieted his big white stallion, getting the fighting fury out of it. Then he led Blackie around the house and saw the wagons rolling up at a good speed. He went into the saddle in a lithe bound and rode to meet them.

"Take them around back, Bill," he said. "And keep the women out here, don't let them go around front. There's been a mite of trouble."

After entering and seeing the master's library and passing through to the front of the house, Weems decided the Kid had, as he often did, made quite an understatement when he spoke of a "mite of trouble".

Even before the men could do more than take Freda and Norma to another room, they heard hooves. The Kid, gun in hand, went to the front door, followed by Sir James and a shaken, but armed, Morg. They saw three men riding fast towards the ranch house.

"Don't shoot!" Morg croaked, speaking through a throat which seemed to burn red hot. "They're friends."

"I'd never have knowed," drawled the Kid, holstering his Dragoon Colt as he went to meet Dusty Fog and Mark Counter and a tall, blond-haired boy he had never seen before.

In a few moments Morg managed to introduce Dusty and the others to Sir James Keller and Weems explained the Kid's presence. Then they went inside to start the work of cleaning up.

It was two days after the death of Mallick and his partner. The spacious dining-room at the Double K held a large bunch of men. Dusty, Mark, and Kid were on hand, Waco, who had been like a shadow to Dusty for the past two days of wire removal and starting to clean up after the departed gunmen, sat to one side of the OD Connected men. Stone Hart and Clay Allison represented the trail driving interests. Lasalle, Ralph Gibbs, sitting awkwardly in his chair, and Pop Jones had been asked to come, along with Matt Roylans and the Barlock banker. Weems, back to his official capacity, glided around and served drinks from the stock brought in the wagons along with much of Sir James' belongings.

"From what Mallick told me," Sir James said. "He planned to sell me several thousand acres beyond the true boundary of the Double K and showed on the map I received from him. I paid by deposit and was to complete the deal when I'd seen the property. Then he set out to try and buy the small ranchers out as cheaply as possible or run them out. He did not expect me for another month, but our ship made better time than we expected and I brought my daughter ahead with an escort supplied by an army friend. However I'd managed to crock my ankle and so could not ride around and that gave Mallick a chance to force the last three spreads out."

"How about the wire?" Clay Allison asked.

"Bought in my name by Disraeli and put up to try and make trouble between the trail herds and myself. He hated me for something that happened in England and helped Mallick arrange this entire thing. He hoped I would either be ruined or killed by the enraged trail crews."

"He near on had his way," drawled Stone Hart. "Happen Dusty hadn't been on hand and seen what was coming off; well I reckon I might not have stopped to think. You was on to Mallick from the start, weren't you Dusty?"

"Not right at the start. I guessed most of it when I pieced together the map I found in Mallick's office, and tied it in with the hit at the Lasalle house when they tried to dynamite us out.

That meant we'd hit on to something vital and Mallick wanted us dead before we could use it. Didn't know what part Disraeli had in it though. We'd sniffed that scent he used in the office and tied him in with Mallick. So I figured they were trying to sell land they didn't own.''

"Well," said Sir James. "It's over now. Norma and Freda have both recovered from the shock of what happened in my study. It was just a bluff on the part of Mallick saying I intended to take over the bank notes. So he could put pressure on the small ranchers. Of course I insist on paying for all damages caused by my men.''

"There's no call for that," objected Ralph Gibbs. "They weren't your—"

"They rode for my brand and ignorance of their actions is no excuse. I ought to have known what they were doing. By the by, Ralph, did you and your lady talk over my offer?''

"Yeah. We'll take you up on it. And we both thank you for making it.''

Only Dusty of the others knew of the offer. Full compensation for his injuries and the damages for his property. Then if he wished, to sell his land to Keller, and take over as foreman of the Double K, with a house built on the property. Joyce and Gibbs discussed the matter at length and decided to give up trying to run a one-horse spread one step ahead of bankruptcy and take the security of a good post as foreman of the Double K.

"The only thanks I'll need, old son," Sir James said with a grin. "Is that you get this spread working. How about getting hands?''

Sir James suddenly grinned again and remembered his position as host. He changed the subject and for a few minutes the men talked over past happenings and future plans. Then the party broke up for the trail bosses wished to get back to their herds and the others to their various tasks.

On the porch Sir James Keller shooks hands with Captain Dusty Fog. Of all the others Dusty had got on best with the Englishman for they were much alike and, had Dusty been born in the same circumstances as Sir James he would most likely have carried the same three letters before his name.

"I owe you a lot, Dusty," Sir James said. "You can rely on

me to keep the Old Trail open. Give me time and I might even make a Texan.''

"Yeah," Dusty agreed, shaking hands with the other man while Mark and the Kid waited with the horses ready to ride north once more after the OD Connected herd. "You might at that. We'll come down this way and see how you're settling in. And don't worry, you'll have hands coming looking for work, maybe even some of the old crew when word gets out. Ralph Gibbs'll pick you good men.''

He turned and went to his horse where Freda Lasalle stood.

"You remember to come in and visit any time you're out this way," she said.

"We'll do that, gal," Mark promised. "See you sometime.''

Waco stood by Clay Allison and watched the three men riding away. He felt empty, lost and sick. Some instinct told him that his destiny stood before him. The chance to change from a trigger-fast-and-up-from-Texas kid to a respected man. But he took on with Clay Allison to finish the drive and a *man* did not walk out on his responsibilities just because it suited him to do so. He must finish his drive and hope to meet the man who he now regarded as his idol again.

"Dusty was telling me as how he needed another hand to help him with the OD Connected herd," Clay remarked. "Asked if I could spare one. So I said I'd more hands than I need. Could let one go all right.''

Now it lay before Waco. The chance he wanted. He knew his life would change, his very outlook must change if he rode after Dusty Fog. He knew he would most likely work harder than ever he did with Clay Allison. Against that he knew that he must get clear of Clay Allison, or forever be marked with the CA brand. Sure he might become a tophand, but always folks would say, "He rode for Clay Allison" and think twice before hiring him just for cattle work.

For the first time in his life Waco faced up to what he was becoming. Five men died before his guns since he left his adopted home. Five men failed to beat him to the shot in arguments which might have been passed over. Each time the other man asked for death. But there came a time when a man with intelligence asked himself where it all would end.

Waco had the answer. It could end here—or with him riding the same trail as many another fast Texas boy.

He held out his hand to Clay Allison, reading Clay's hope that he would follow Dusty Fog, reading the thought behind it, that Clay did not want Waco to become like him.

"Thanks, Clay," Waco said.

He mounted the big paint stallion and rode after Dusty Fog.

The Making of a Lawman

Author's note:

While complete in itself, the events in this book run concurrently with those in THE TROUBLE BUSTERS.

For Mike Legat, who agreed to try my Rockabye County stories.

I

A Special Kind of Man

"To all this I swear, so help me God," said the boy whose only name was Waco, completing the oath which made him a deputy town marshal of Mulrooney, Kansas.

While pinning the badge to his black and white calf-skin vest, the youngster could hardly hold down a faint, unbelieving grin. Six, or even three, months ago the suggestion that he might become a peace officer would have been met with derision. Yet there he stood, faced by Mulrooney's mayor and town marshal, a member of the civic law enforcement body.

Just over six foot in height, with a frame developing to its full power, Waco dressed and looked what he was, a Texas cowhand. His black J.B. Stetson hat, distinctively shaped, gave as clear an indication of his place of birth as did the star motif carved on his high-heeled boots. The hat hung on a peg by the door, exposing his curly blond hair to view. Tanned by the elements, his handsome face had strength, although the blue eyes no longer bore a wolf-cautious glint and his mouth smiled more easily than previously. Tight-rolled and knotted about his throat, the scarlet bandana trailed long ends over a blue shirt almost to the waistband of the levis pants. The gunbelt around his middle had been tooled to his fit and carried a pair of staghorn-handled 1860 Army Colts in holsters designed for speed on the draw. Something in the way he wore the rig warned it was no mere affectation.

Looking at Waco, Mayor Woods felt a momentary doubt at his suitability for the post. The town was one of those which had grown up along the trans-continental railroad, hoping to gain its livelihood from the almost numberless longhorn cattle brought north in search of a market. Being Mulrooney's leading citizen and partially responsible for its conception, the mayor

7

wanted it to prosper. In which case the correct kind of law enforcement would be essential.

Could a boy not yet eighteen give the type of service required?

Only the previous day Mayor Woods had seen Waco draw his right hand Colt with blinding speed and kill a man trying to shoot a friend. Yet, inexperienced in such matters, the mayor realised that being an efficient peace officer called for more than a fast draw and accurate shooting. True some trail-end towns asked no more of their marshals than gun-skill, but Mayor Woods thought that to be a short-sighted policy and not what Mulrooney required.

The worry over the age side of the matter might also apply to another of the three deputies—and even to the man Mayor Woods had selected to be the town's first marshal.

Almost as tall as Waco, and lean as a steer reared in the greasewood country, the Ysabel Kid seemed even younger. At first glance the sight of his handsome, almost babyishly innocent face, the all black clothing, walnut-handled Dragoon Colt buttforward in the low cavalry draw holster at the right side of his belt and ivory-hilted James Black bowie knife sheathed on its left, might tend to raise a mocking smile. Then one noticed the Indian-dark features, red hazel eyes and rapidly reached the conclusion that here stood no mere dressed-up boy trying to pose as a tough, mean man. Young he might be, but the years had been spent learning hard lessons that had prepared him well for the future. However, he too failed to comply with the popular conception of a trail-end town lawman.

While the third deputy certainly seemed fitted for the part, it was a specialised one. Big Sarah Shelley wore a plain gingham dress instead of the garish costume she used when serving behind the bar of Mayor Woods' Fair Lady saloon. Red-headed, good-looking tall and buxom, although hard-fleshed and far from flabby, she looked ideally suited for her work as matron in charge of handling female prisoners.

If the two male deputies appeared an unusual selection, the man chosen by Mayor Woods to be marshal—chief law enforcement officer of the town—seemed, on the face of it, even more so.

At most he stood no more than five foot six, with dusty blond hair and a pleasantly good-looking face. Although dressed in expensive, well-made range clothes, he gave them the appearance of being somebody's cheap cast-offs. Nor did the excellently

8

made gunbelt, with matched, white-handled Army Colts in its two cross draw holsters, greatly add to his stature or noticeability. All in all, at first glance, he looked like an insignificant nobody. Closer inspection revealed that his face had strength of will and intelligence, while his lack of inches failed to prevent him from possessing the muscular development of a Hercules.

During the Civil War, as a seventeen-year old Confederate States cavalry captain, that small, insignificant cowhand built a reputation equalled only by the great Turner Ashby and John Singleton Mosby; although he gained it on the less-publicised Arkansas battle-front. After the War ended he had been called from his work as segundo of the biggest ranch in Texas and sent into Mexico on a dangerous, exceedingly delicate mission which he had carried out successfully.* Since then his name had gone out as a cowhand of the first water, trail boss second to none, the lawman who tamed a wild Montana gold town after three less able officers had died trying.† Texans boasted of his uncanny bare-hand fighting skill which rendered bigger men helpless; or told about his wizardry in the matter of rapid drawing and straight shooting with his two long barrelled Army Colts.

Small he might be, but nobody ever thought of Dusty Fog in a matter of mere feet and inches. In reputation or actual deeds he stood as tall as any man.

In addition to acting as the OD Connected's segundo, Dusty also rode with its floating outfit. On the large spreads of the great open-range grazing days, a group of six or so cowhands were employed to work the extremities of a ranch. Accompanied by a chuck wagon, or taking food along on mule-back, they acted as a mobile ranch crew. During his trip into Mexico, Dusty had met and hired the Ysabel Kid and Mark Counter to form the nucleus of the OD Connected's floating outfit. However, the general state of unrest in Texas caused them to spend more time trouble-shooting in various places than riding their ranch's ranges.

Bringing the OD Connected herd north, Dusty heard rumours of the two new towns and saw one or the other would shorten his drive. So he and the Kid headed for Brownton while Waco and the fourth member of the floating outfit came into

*Told in THE YSABEL KID.
†Told in QUIET TOWN.

Mulrooney.* From what Dusty saw, Brownton was no place to take his herd. Despite the fact that Mark Counter had received a wound in the Fair Lady Saloon, Dusty concluded that Mulrooney offered his trail crew a fairer deal than its rival metropolis. His decision struck Mayor Woods almost as a god-sent gift. Being fresh from the East, none of the citizens knew enough to handle the law. In the mayor's opinion, Dusty Fog ideally filled her needs. Especially with the backing of his friends.

Take the Ysabel Kid as a start. There stood a man whom any honest peace officer would count fortunate to have at his side.

Not that such had always been the case. Until meeting Dusty that day on the Brownsville trail, the Kid had been regarded as something of a one-boy crime wave; a border-smuggler with one foot on the slippery slope that led to real law-busting. The meeting changed all that and now the Kid's early upbringing made him a most useful member of range-country society.

Born the only son of a wild Irish-Kentuckian and his French Creole-Comanche wife, the Kid spent his boyhood living as a member of the *Pehnane* band of his mother's tribe. There he learned all those things a brave-heart warrior needed to know†, skill with weapons, ability to read sign or discover hidden enemies, horse-savvy of a high degree. Fortunately for the peace of Texas he never found the need to use his training while among the *Pehnane*, although it came in handy at various times in later years. Maybe the Kid did not rate high as a gun-fighter, being only fair with his Dragoon Colt, but he claimed few peers in the matter of handling a knife or a rifle.

Like the Kid, Waco was a product of the times. Left an orphan in a Waco Indian attack on a wagon train, he grew up among the large family of an impoverished rancher. Although treated as one of the family, some urge set him drifting at the age of thirteen. Even then he carried a gun, a battered but operational old Navy Colt. Four years later he wore a brace of Army Colts and bore a log-sized chip on his shoulder. Working for Clay Allison's wild onion crew had given him truculence and might have sent him on the trail of Wes Hardin, Bad Bill Longley or other fast-handed *Tejano* boys running from the law after a killing too many.

*Told in THE TROUBLE BUSTERS.
†Told in COMANCHE.

10

Then fate stepped in. Waco met Dusty Fog, the fastest of them all. From the time that Dusty saved the youngster's life, hauling him clear when a stampeding herd threatened to run him down, Waco became a changed person.* With Clay Allison's blessing, Waco quit the CA and rode north as a member of the OD Connected. During the last weeks of the drive a change in him had become apparent. No longer did he regard all men as potential enemies. He smiled easier, took part in night camp horse-play. Sure he still wore his guns, but under Dusty's tuition he restrained his eagerness to use them.

All in all Dusty felt satisfied that he could run the law. He knew Texans, could handle them and figured he could deal with the railroad workers, buffalo-hunters or others who would also use the town. Mayor Woods and the Town Council gave him a free hand, promised no interference with his methods. Backed by the Kid, Waco, Big Sarah and Mark, when the latter recovered from his wound, he reckoned that he could make Mulrooney a decent town and one in which everybody received a fair deal. In that desire he had the blessing of the mayor.

While there might possibly be other female mayors in the United States, it was unlikely that any of them equalled Freddie Woods in the matter of beauty. Five foot eight in height, with raven black hair topping a regally beautiful face, she would turn heads in any crowd. The sober, if expensive, black suit and white blouse she wore for performing a civic function set off a truly magnificent figure with rich mature curves. The fact that she ran a saloon did nothing to detract from her acceptance by the most influential people in town. Everybody knew the British aristocracy had eccentric ways and Freddie Woods had been born the Right Honourable Winifred Amelia Besgrave-Woodstole. Why the rich, talented, beautiful daughter of an English lord had come to the United States and wound up running a saloon in a trail-end town has been told elsewhere. She came, gained election as mayor and now worked to give the voters satisfaction.

With the oath-taking ceremony over, Freddie looked at the young faces before her.

"I'm not going to make a speech," she said. "Just do what you're hired for and we'll be satisfied."

"We'll do just that," Dusty promised. "Lon, you'd best—."

*Told in TRIGGER FAST.

11

Hooves thundered along the street outside the office, punctuated by ringing cowhand whoops, screeches and shots.

"Could be this's where we start to earn our pay," the Kid commented, crossing to the window and looking out.

Much what he expected to see greeted the Kid's gaze. Galloping along came a trio of trail-dirty, unshaven young cowhands. None of them belonged to the OD Connected, which had paid off the previous night and had given the citizens of Mulrooney an idea of what celebrating trail-drivers meant. While raising a considerable ruckus, the trio did not endanger other lives, but kept to the centre of the street and sent their bullets straight up into the air. Heading for the Fair Lady Saloon, they saw the marshal's office building and brought their horses to a halt.

"Yeeah!" whooped the tallest of the three, a well-made, good looking youngster. "Let's smoke the John Law's hole some."

With that he threw a shot at the building. Glass shattered as the bullet struck a window. It was a most satisfactory sound, one which delighted the trio and stirred up the desire to hear more. Restraining their fiddle-footing horses, they tossed more lead at the building. Not all of it hit the windows, but enough struck home to increase their delight.

Catching Freddie around the waist, Dusty swept her down behind the desk. At the same moment Big Sarah dived through the open door leading to the cells in the rear of the building. Out flashed Waco's Colts and he started for the door, ready to do battle.

"Hold it, boy!" Dusty barked.

Reluctantly, showing his surprise, Waco skidded to a halt by the door. The building's walls had been constructed strongly enough to stop revolver bullets and he flattened himself to the right of the door as lead drove into the thick timber. Despite the anger he felt, he stood still and waited for further orders.

"You fixing to let 'em get away with this, Dusty?" Waco demanded.

"Well no, I don't reckon I am," Dusty replied with a smile. "Only I don't want to shoot them either."

"Would you mind getting off my chest, Captain Fog?" Freddie put in a mite breathlessly, still on the floor with the small Texan holding her down.

"I thought you'd never ask," he replied and started to rise.

Derisive howls and yells rose from the three cowhands. Then, having failed to produce the local law, they tired of the pastime and headed for the Fair Lady at a wild gallop. Bringing their horses to a halt, they tossed reins across the hitching rail and tramped into the building.

"What the he—," Waco began, then rephrased his words for Freddie's benefit. "What're you figuring on doing about them yahoos, Dusty?"

"Go along and remonstrate with 'em," Dusty replied.

"I'd toss 'em in the pokey!" yelped Big Sarah indignantly, emerging from the rear. "To hell with that there remon— whatever you said."

"We'll let Dusty try it his way first," smiled Freddie. "Mind if I come along to watch?"

"Come ahead," Dusty replied and walked towards the front door.

At that hour of the morning, the Fair Lady had not yet opened for business. Only the fact that the swamper did his work inside caused the doors to be unlocked. Behind the bar, Donna—another of the girls who tended to the customers' needs—checked on stock ready for the day's trade. Neither she nor the swamper, a grizzled old timer, showed any great pleasure at the trio's arrival.

"We're not open yet, boys," Donna warned.

"Let's have some glasses then, ma'am," the tallest cowhand replied. "Monte, you go fetch that bottle that's done kept us warm and comfy all the way in."

"I surely will, Tack," answered the shortest, who sported an early attempt at moustache-growing. "Boy oh boy, we sure showed that marshal that we'd come to town."

"That we did," enthused the third member of the trio. "He never even showed his lil Kansas head outside at-all."

Leaving to collect the bottle of cheap whiskey from Tack's saddle pouch, Monte returned with it and news.

"The marshal's done coming," he told his delighted companions.

"We'll have him buy us a drink, Brother Tack," grinned the third youngster.

"Sure will, Brother Del," agreed Tack. "Why 'twouldn't be fitting for him not to set them up for some of Colonel Charlie's boys."

"We'ns ride for Colonel Charlie Goodnight, ma'am," Del

13

told Donna with an air of pride and superiority.

"I bet he lies awake at night praying that his good luck lasts," the buxom blonde answered and waited expectantly for the arrival of the town's newly-elected marshal.

If the trio felt any concern at the approach of the marshal, they failed to show it. Having just completed their first drive, they wished to give the impression of being well-travelled veterans. Fed on highly-spiced accounts of how a trail crew acted when in town, they had come into Mulrooney as they believed would be expected of them. Already, in their opinions, they had made a good start by asserting their Texas superiority over the Kansas lawmen. All that remained for them to do was buckle down and show those Kansan grasshoppers how Colonel Charlie's crew whooped up a storm on hitting town.

Leaning with their backs to the bar, the trio watched the batwing doors swing open. On the way to town they had drunk enough to dull their perceptions. So they failed to take in the significant signs which ought to have spelled danger to rangewise minds.

"It's the law, Brother Tack," announced Del, standing at the right of the group.

"Naw," corrected Monte from the left. "It's the marshal's lil son playing at sheriffs 'n' owlhoots. Don't he look the fiercest thing that ever growed?"

"Trouble being that he stopped growing a whole heap too soon," Tack answered, setting down the whiskey bottle on the bar. "Hey, bar-lady, is this here half-portion the best your town can afford in the shape of a lawman?"

Standing with the other deputies and Freddie outside the batwing doors, the Kid raised his eyes to heaven as if searching for strength.

"Lordy lord!" he breathed. "I allus figured cowhands didn't have a lick of good sense. But these three're plumb foolish."

"They'll likely learn," Waco growled, deeply annoyed and bristling at the insults to his hero.

"And soon," guessed Big Sarah.

Freddie remained silent, watching Dusty and wondering how he intended to handle the matter. Running the law in a trail-end town took a special kind of man. Unless Freddie missed her guess, the next few minutes would prove whether Dusty had the necessary qualifications.

14

While advancing to the bar, Dusty studied the cowhands and assessed the situation. Leading men since his sixteenth birthday had given him the ability to read them and gauge their potential. Everything he saw told him that gun-play would not be needed. None of the trio looked that kind of proddy. Sure they all wore guns, a Texan who did not being something of a rarity, but none showed signs of coming close to his own standard. However they needed firm handling, as a warning to themselves and others that the law could not be flouted in Mulrooney.

If the cowhands had consulted with him previously they could hardly have stood more suitably for Dusty's needs. Almost shoulder to shoulder they lined the bar and eyed him with tolerant contempt. Then they learned the error of their ways.

As a boy, possibly to divert attention from his small size, Dusty had developed and improved a natural tendency to being ambidextrous. The ability to use either hand for every purpose often came in useful—and did at that moment.

Suddenly, giving no hint of what he aimed to do, Dusty drove up both his hands, arcing them outwards. With the speed and co-ordination that enabled him to draw and shoot in under a second, he crashed a back-hand blow into Monte and Del's jaws. He hit with such force and so unexpectedly that the two cowhands spun away from Tack along the bar.

Even as realisation knifed into Tack, he found troubles of his own. Down swung Dusty's left fist and rammed with considerable force into the cowhand's belly. While Tack might be as tough as working ten to eighteen hours a day could make him, he still felt the punch. Pain doubled him over and the air belched from his lungs in a rush.

Nor had Dusty finished. Catching Tack by the rear of the collar and seat of the pants, he heaved the youngster at Del with enough force to tumble them in a tangled heap to the floor. Monte started forward, hands reaching out at Dusty and a desire for revenge in his heart. Swivelling around fast, Dusty clamped his two hands around Monte's right wrist. Then, carrying the trapped arm into the air, Dusty pivoted underneath it and snapped it down. Letting out a bewildered wail, Monte felt his feet leave the ground. For a moment it seemed that the room spun around and he lit down upon the sprawling bodies of his companions.

For a moment the trio lay winded and dazed. Finally they

rolled apart and sat up to stare about them. Only they no longer looked at a small, insignificant man. In some manner Dusty seemed to have put on height and heft until he stood taller than any of them. Monte expressed his companions' feelings.

"Hey!" he yelped in an aggrieved tone. "Where'd the lil feller go?"

2

Cowhands are Only Part Of It

"On your feet!" Dusty snapped and the trio obeyed with considerable speed.

"What're you fixing to do with us, marshal?" Tack asked worriedly.

"Take you to jail for whooping up the town and damned near shooting the mayor."

Instead of distressing the trio, the latter piece of information seemed to amuse them. Broad grins creased their faces.

"We-all did that?" gurgled Monte, slapping a hand against his thigh. "Ain't that a pistol. We'ns near on done shot their mayor."

"And I didn't find it amusing!" interrupted a cold feminine voice.

So engrossed in staring at Dusty had the trio become, and delighted that they had given their companions at the herd such a good lead in the matter of hoorawing the town, that they failed to notice the batwing doors opening. Followed by the three deputies, Freddie stalked across the room. The cowhands turned, eyes raking Freddie from head to foot with frank juvenile admiration. Tack found his voice first, jerking off his hat.

"I sure bet the mayor didn't neither, ma'am," he said.

"I am the mayor!" Freddie replied.

Slowly the grins faded as the import of the words sank in. Three pairs of worried eyes darted from Freddie to Dusty, seeking confirmation of the remarkable statement and hoping to

16

see denial instead. While the rest of the trail hands would regard scaring a male mayor as a piece of good-natured fun, the same did not apply when that civic dignitary was a woman.

"Are you the for-real, sure-enough female lady mayor of this here town, ma'am?" gulped Del.

"I'm the for-real, sure-enough female lady mayor of this town," Freddie confirmed. "And I don't take to having lead whistling around my ears."

"Ma'am," said Monte fervently as he made a belated removal of his hat. "We didn't know you was in there."

"If we had," Del went on, "why we wouldn't've thought of shooting that ways, ma'am."

"You should've thought on it afore you started," Dusty growled. "Let's head for the pokey."

"We'ns work for Colonel Charlie Goodnight," Tack pointed out.

"Which same he's just going to fall on your necks with whoops of joy when he hears what you've been doing," Dusty drawled.

"You-all don't know Colonel Charlie, happen that's what you reckon," Del put in, an uneasy feeling forming that his employer would not regard the trio's behaviour as commendable.

"Reckon I don't know him?" Dusty smiled. "I rode with him on that third drive he made to Fort Sumner after the War."

"You was on that drive?" Tack asked, with less disbelief than he might have shown earlier.

"On it!" the Kid put in. "Boy, he was Colonel Charlie's segundo."

Which explained a whole lot more to the Texans than it did to Freddie. All three knew the name of Goodnight's segundo on that fateful third drive to Fort Sumner, a journey which helped pave the way for the longer trails north to the Kansas market.

"Lordy lord!" Del breathed, admiration glowing in his eyes. "You're Dusty Fog. No wonder you licked us so easy."

"What's going to happen to us, Cap'n Fog?" Tack inquired respectfully.

"I told you, you're going to the pokey. There're two windows bust—."

"Ole Tack here's the bestest window fixer in Medina County, Cap'n," Del began hopefully. "He could fit in new glass—."

"Who pays for it?" Dusty interrupted.

"Well now," Tack answered, hesitantly feeling into his pockets. "I'm bust."

"Me too," Del groaned.

"I ain't got but three dollars, 'cepting what the boys gave me to bring back the makings and stuff for them," Monte went on.

"I'll tell you what," Freddie remarked, recalling something Dusty had told her about cowhands the previous day. "The backhouse hole needs to go down deeper. If you three put it down, I'll pay for the windows and Tack can fix them."

"Dig?" yelped Del.

"I ain't never took to working on the blister end of a shovel, ma'am," Monte went on.

"Then you can wait in a cell until I've seen Uncle Charlie and asked for your fine money," Dusty told them, inwardly grinning at the way Freddie handed out a punishment.

"Can't say as how I'm took with that idea either," Monte groaned. "You're sure enough kin to Colonel Charlie. That kind of meanness goes in families, they do reckon."

Watching the trio's expressions, Freddie found increasing difficulty in maintaining her coldly regal pose. She could read the growing realisation that a trap had closed around them. All three knew just how Goodnight would regard finding them in jail. They could also visualise their companions' reactions to hearing what had caused the delay in the arrival of much-needed supplies of tobacco and the like. Despite a cowhand's antipathy to handling a shovel, all three felt it better to dig than be held in jail.

"We'll do it," Tack decided. "Happen we work at it, we'll be done soon enough to get back to the herd in time for supper."

"Digging's thirsty work," Freddie smiled. "You boys had better take a drink before you start."

Grins creased three faces and Tack took up the bottle they had brought in with them. Just as he started to pour out the drinks, he recalled his manners.

"Maybe you'd have one along of us, ma'am?"

"Thank you," Freddie replied, accepting the offered glass and raising it towards her lips. Then she sniffed at it instead of drinking. "What's this?"

"Whiskey, ma'am," Del answered.

"Is it?"

"Sure is, ma'am. Done bought it off a feller who met us on the range."

Ignoring Del's comment, Freddie took the bottle's neck between the extreme tips of her forefinger and thumb.

"Dispose of this slush, Donna," she ordered. "Give these gentlemen some decent liquor."

Watched by the cowhands, Donna dropped the bottle into the trash bucket behind the bar. Then she took one of the saloon's stock and poured out the drinks. The cowhands drank appreciatively and forgot any objections to losing their bottle.

"Whooee!" Tack commented, setting down the empty glass. "What've we been drinking all our lives?"

"On likker like this I can dig that there hole with my two bare hands," Del continued. "Lead me to it, ma'am."

"Tell you what," Dusty remarked. "Lon here's riding out just now. Give him the money. He'll buy that stuff for your pards with the herd and take it to them."

If any Kansas lawman had offered such a suggestion, it would have been regarded with at least suspicion. However the cowhands knew they could trust Dusty Fog. So Monte handed over the money and a scrawled list of goods to the Kid. Then the three cowhands trooped off to begin working out their fines.

Watching them go, Dusty felt sure that he had handled things just right. Back at the herd after finishing their chores, the trio would pass the word of their treatment. Soon news would spread that the law in Mulrooney treated cowhands fairly. Most of the trouble in other Kansas trail-end towns came from the citizens and lawmen cheating or abusing the visitors. That was one thing Dusty aimed to prevent at all costs.

"You handled that really well, Dusty," Freddie complimented.

"So did you," he returned. "It won't always be this easy though. Cowhands are only a part of it."

"If they drink stuff like this regularly," Freddie said, waving a hand to the glass of whiskey Tack had offered her and which still stood on the bar, "I can see how they would get mean."

Picking up the glass, Dusty sniffed at it and pulled a wry face. "It's the real, genuine snake-head base-burner for sure."

"They must use twenty-rattle sidewinders' heads in it," the Kid went on after following Dusty's example.

"I never saw a rattlesnake with twenty rattles on its tail," Freddie began.

"That's 'cause you've never been to Texas, ma'am," Waco informed her. "Why we've rattlers there with—."

"I'll bet you have,' she interrupted, but in such a friendly manner that he neither took offence nor felt snubbed. "What I don't see is the connection between rattlesnakes' heads and the whiskey."

"They drop the heads in to give it a kick when they're brewing it," the Kid explained. "Makes that fire-water so fierce that I don't know how they keep it bottled up."

"It's lucky those bunch hadn't drunk more than a couple of snorts apiece," Dusty put in, looking worried. "Happen they had, they might've been some harder to handle."

"They can buy better stuff than this at any place in town," Freddie said.

"Only they're not buying it in town," Dusty replied. "Let's go. When those three've put the hole down deep enough, see they fix the windows at the office, Sarah."

"Sure, Cap'n," the woman answered. "Where'll you be?"

"Around and about somewheres. Lon's heading out to the OD Connected camp to see about spreading the word that Brownton's bad medicine."

"You don't have to do that for us, Dusty," Freddie remarked.

"I'm not doing it for you," he assured her. "Those yahoos in Brownton 're fixing to trim the trail crews to the bone. They've got a civic ordnance that says nobody who supported the Confederate States, which means any Texan whether he supported it or not, can tote a gun in their town. That'll mean the trail-hands who turn in their guns're unarmed in a town full of folks who aren't. Any cowhand who goes home with his teeth and two eyes in his head'll be lucky, because that's just about all he will take. So I figure word ought to go out to warn them what to expect. What they do after that is up to their trail boss."

"They won't be treated like that here," Freddie promised.

'If I thought they would,' Dusty answered. 'You'd still be looking for a marshal." Then he looked at his two male deputies. "Come on, we've got work to do."

"I just knowed you'd get around to saying that," Waco groaned, darting glances around the room. "Where-at's Babsy, ma'am?"

"Upstairs resting," Freddie replied, "being, as you Texans put it, plumb tuckered out from all the fussing last night."

Although the girl in question had come from England to act as Freddie's maid, she had proven adept at providing the kind of entertainment saloon audiences enjoyed. Blonde, vivacious, buxom in a small way, her spirited renderings of Cockney songs and dances added to the general festivities celebrating the arrival of the first herd to Mulrooney. Waco found her especially attractive, but hoped to meet her again under less crowded conditions. However it did not seem that she would be making an appearance and Dusty showed signs of wanting to be on his way.

"Tell Mark that we'll be in to see him later," the small Texan requested.

"I bet he's up there in that big soft bed snoring like ten razorback hawgs," the Kid went on.

"Trust him to get shot when there's work to be done," Waco commented and followed the other two into the street.

"How'd you have handled it, Boy?" Dusty asked as they left the saloon.

"I dunno. Gone in with a gun in my hand, likely," the youngster replied.

"Which could've sparked off a shooting," Dusty told him. "Throwing down with a gun's only part of being a lawman. You'll get on better by learning how to handle people. Those three kids aren't bad, just happied up a mite—."

"They just hadn't drunk enough of that wild mare's milk to make them mean," the Kid interjected.

"That's for sure," Dusty agreed, but put aside his thoughts on the matter so as to continue making his point to Waco. "With kids like that you don't need a gun. Just show them who's running things, treat them fair, then you'll get no trouble."

"Not as long as they drink decent whiskey," the Kid continued. "Which they sure wouldn't've been had they finished that bottle they bought."

"That's for sure," Dusty admitted.

"Mind that time over to Newton when a feller was peddling snake-head gut-rot to the trail hands outside town?" the Kid went on.

"I'll never forget it," Dusty replied.

"What happened?" asked Waco.

"This jasper got a smart notion for making money. He stocked up with cheap whiskey and took a wagon on to the range. Used to peddle it to the trail-hands. Up that close to the

21

sale-pens they figured they could loosen off a mite and bought a couple of bottles. Only some of the hands got a mite too loose. After belting the bottles, a couple of them started grandstanding a mite reckless for some Eastern folks who'd come out to see a real, genuine trail herd."

"Which same their fooling spooked the herd into a stampede," the Kid continued as Dusty paused. "Near on three thousand head went down on to Newton like the devil after a yearling. Seeing them coming riled up the cattle already in the railroad holding pens so that they bust down the fences and the whole damned boiling went through the middle of town."

"Two folks were killed, maybe another dozen hurt, and a helluva lot of damage was done in or around town," Dusty went on grimly. "Paying off for the other stock killed or lost and the damage his herd caused broke the rancher. His crew lost their pay. Two of them got shot trying to rob a store on their way back home. They were broke, damned near starving."

"There's some might say it served them right as they'd been the pair who started the stampede," the Kid drawled. "Only a thing like that doesn't end easy."

"That's for sure," Dusty agreed. "Up to that time Newton'd been a decent sort of town. Folks treated the cowhands fair, everybody got on well enough. Only it stopped after the stampede. Then there was nothing but trouble. They brought in a real mean fighting pimp as marshal, started making fuss with the trail crews. All of it came about just because some stinking yahoo wanted to make a quick profit."

"There's some who'd claim the cowhands didn't have to buy the likker in the first place," Waco said. "Only them who'd say it don't know cowhands and've never driven a trail herd."

"It's not going to happen around here!" Dusty stated, ignoring the youngster's comment.

Except under certain circumstances, Dusty raised no objections to other men drinking. The way he saw it, any man had the right to decide on such matters without interference from others. One of the conditions where he felt liquor had no place was on a trail herd.

Every man of the trail crew needed his wits constantly about him when handling a herd of between two and three thousand head of half-wild longhorn cattle. So drinking and trail-driving did not mix. Most trail bosses banned the carrying of hard

22

liquor—except for the inevitable medicinal whiskey bottle in the chuck wagon—during the drive. Although they frequently complained about the ban, every experienced trail hand secretly admitted its necessity. Cowhands were not saints; their line of work did not call for abstemious, gentle souls. But the majority of them accepted the no-liquor rule when on the trail.

Consequently they built up quite a thirst between towns and, like sailors in port, tended to make up for lost time on their arrival. While not given to drinking in excess, Dusty regarded it tolerantly and as an understandable human failing. What he wished to avoid was the kind of premature drinking which had sparked off the stampede and its consequences in Newton. So far the majority of Mulrooney citizens wanted only to make a reasonable profit from the trail crews and wished to remain on friendly terms with the Texans.

Under such conditions, provided cowhand rowdyism remained in bounds, harmonious relations were assured. From what Freddie claimed, and Dusty had so far seen, the saloons stocked decent whiskey. However cowhands primed on the raw, cheaply-made liquor that Tack's party had brought into town might easily, if inadvertently, spark off an incident that spoiled everything.

"You knew that rancher, Dusty?" Waco asked. "The one in Newton?"

"I knew him. It was Hill Thompson."

" 'Smokey' Hill Thompson, the owlhoot?"

"That's what he became," Dusty admitted. "Like I say, he went broke. The carpetbaggers took over his spread for non-payment of taxes and he went bad. But I knew him in the War, and after. There wasn't a better, stauncher man in a day's long ride."

"You tried to reach him with enough money to pay the taxes, Dusty," the Kid put in. "But he'd shot up that damned State Police posse and gone on the dodge before you got there."

"Thing being, what's to do about that jasper who's peddling whiskey on the ranges out here," Waco remarked, guessing that Dusty wanted the subject closed.

"What'd you suggest we do?" Dusty asked.

"Stop him," the youngster answered bluntly.

"How?" Dusty said.

"How'd you mean, 'how'?" Waco demanded. "Just ride out

23

there and tell him to quit is how."

"There's no law against selling whiskey," Dusty reminded him.

"Except to Injuns," the Kid went on.

"Yeah," agreed Dusty, eyeing the Kid in a calculating manner. "Except to Indians."

"Now just what've you got in that tricky Rio Hondo mind, Dusty?" the Kid inquired, knowing his small companion pretty well.

"Just a kind of fool notion," Dusty replied. "Let's go see if there's any answer to that telegraph message I sent off this morning, shall we?"

On arrival at the Wells Fargo office they found that an answer had just arrived.

"I was fixing to send it on to you," the agent told Dusty, handing over a buff-coloured official message form.

"Thanks," Dusty answered, then read it.

"Just like back home," drawled the Kid, accepting and studying the paper. "Only I can't see how it helps us."

"It's like you said, Lon," Dusty answered, retrieving the paper and placing it in his vest pocket. "Selling liquor to Indians's plumb illegal. Let's go?"

"Maybe somebody'll tell me what in hell's going on!" Waco yelped as they left the Wells Fargo office.

"I'd surely do it, boy," the Kid replied. "Only I'm damned if I know myself."

3

Prevention Licks Trying to Find a Cure

From behind a rim some three miles outside Mulrooney's city limits, Dusty and Waco watched the Kid preparing to make a purchase. Leaving his huge white stallion well clear of the light two-horse wagon, he walked over and began to talk with the two men. Finding the pedlar who had sold Tack's party the snake-head whiskey had not proved difficult and Waco waited to see what happened next. When sure that the Kid had transacted business with the men, Dusty nodded in satisfaction.

"Let's go, boy," he said.

"I hope this works," the youngster remarked as they walked to where a pair of big, well-made paint stallions stood ground-hitched and waiting.

"And me," Dusty replied. "Prevention licks trying to find a cure any day."

If Abel Hockley had any idea what brought the two lawmen out on a visit to his wagon, he failed to show it. Pocketing the Kid's money, he darted a glance at the burly, buckskin-clad, uncleanly man seated on the wagon box. Then he twirled the stout walking cane in his right hand before resting the tip of its ferrule on the toe of his right boot.

Tall, slender, in his late middle-age, with a lean face that sported a moustache, goatee beard and rat-trap mouth, Hockley dressed in elegant city fashion. Coming closer, Waco studied the man and concluded that the elegance had run to seed. The fancy shirt's cuffs were frayed, the collar dirty, the hat showing much use and boots patched. Thrusting out prominently to catch the eye, the butt of an Adams Navy revolver showed beneath his jacket.

"Howdy," Hockley greeted, watching the two Texans swing from their saddles. "Anything I can do for you?"

"Sure," Dusty replied, letting his paint's reins fall free and walking forward. "Start up that wagon and get the hell away from here."

"How's that?" the pedlar spat out.

"You heard. Take your wagon and go."

"You asking official-like?"

"You could say that."

Hockley's eyes flickered down to the badge on Dusty's vest. Shield-shaped, it bore the words 'CITY MARSHAL, MUL-ROONEY, KANSAS' inscribed on its surface and differed from the star badge used by the sheriff's office. From Dusty, Hockley turned his gaze on Waco. The youngster also wore a shield, but his stated he was a deputy marshal of the same town.

"Don't see any sign of a town hereabouts," the pedlar finally commented.

A town marshal's jurisdiction ended at the city limits. Once past them, he possessed no more authority than any other citizen. Which partly accounted for Hockley's lack of concern at seeing the Texans ride up. Except in the larger cities no licence was required to sell intoxicating liquor. Even if the saloonkeepers in Mulrooney had learned of his activities and objected to losing trade, they had no legal way of stopping him; and if they had, their town marshal could not be used to enforce the ban.

"I reckon you can read," Dusty said, taking the telegraph form from his vest pocket and handing it to the pedlar.

"Sure I can," Hockley growled.

"Then read that out aloud, so's your *amigo* there can hear and understand."

Looking just a touch puzzled, Hockley glanced down at the paper, then stared again and his scowl deepened.

"Marshal Fog, Mulrooney," he read. "Accept your offer. You and all your deputies appointed deputy sheriffs. Letter confirming follows. Bracker, sheriff, Edwards County." Slowly he raised his eyes to Dusty. "So?"

While Hockley understood the message's meaning, he could not see how it affected him. According to what he read, Hockley was facing two men appointed as deputy sheriffs of Edwards County. That meant they could handle law enforcement anywhere within the county's boundaries instead of being confined to Mulrooney's city limits. However he knew his rights and that, unless he broke the law in some way, even members of the county sheriff's office could not order him to move.

Being well aware of the distinctions between county and municipal powers, Dusty had taken steps, on being asked to become Mulrooney's marshal, to ensure he possessed both. That morning he had telegraphed Sheriff Bracker and offered to serve as unpaid deputy sheriff. Clearly Bracker saw the wisdom of such an arrangement and accepted the offer.

"So I'm telling you again to move and keep going," Dusty answered flatly.

If Hockley felt like casting doubts on the message's validity, he restrained himself admirably. To do so would be tantamount to calling Dusty a liar—to which charge a Texan knew only one answer. Instead the pedlar put on an expression of injured innocence and righteous indignation.

"Since when's selling whiskey been again the law?" he demanded.

"Well now, that depends on who you sell it to," Dusty replied.

"How's that?" Hockley growled, tapping the tip of his cane against the boot.

"Like when you sell it to an *Indian* for one thing," Dusty told him.

"I know that," Hockley stated, confident that—for once—he did not contravene the law in such a manner.

Then an uneasy feeling gripped the pedlar; the kind of sensation one got at poker when beginning to realise that what had been taken for a bluff was really a power-packed genuine hand. Noticing the emphasis Dusty placed on the word 'Indian', he turned his attention to his most recent customer.

"My grandpappy's Chief Long Walker of the *Pahnane* Comanche, mister," drawled the Kid.

"And that means you've sold liquor to an Indian," Dusty went on.

"He's no Injun, he's a half-br—!" Hockley began hotly, then clamped his mouth shut so quickly that he almost bit off the end of his tongue.

That tall, dark cuss might look as innocent as a church pew full of choir-boys singing for the bishop, but Hockley was not fooled. Any adverse comments upon his mixed blood would come bouncing back on the speaker's head, followed by something real painful.

"You sold the whiskey to my Injun half," the Kid told him.

Anybody who knew the effect white man's whiskey had upon the red brothers agreed to the wisdom of trying to prevent its sale to them. However the rule hardly applied in the Kid's case. Racial discrimination as such only rarely reared its head on the Western frontier. Cowhands in particular accepted a man for what he was worth, not because of accidents of birth, blood or social standing. If a man of mixed blood lived up to the code of the land, he was regarded as having 'made a hand' and was accepted.

The Ysabel Kid had never been considered as other than a worthy member of rangeland society. That applied even in his border-smuggling days, the running of contraband being regarded in most circles as no more than a protest against an unfair imposition foisted on the public by politicians in far-off Washington. At no time in his hectic young life had he gained a reputation for being dangerous when wet down by fire-water.

Although Hockley did not recognise the Kid, his instincts

27

warned of a trap. Pure coincidence could not have brought the other two Texans along just after he sold the whiskey to the dark youngster. Nor did it seem likely that the two peace officers had guessed, without prior knowledge, at the customer's mixed blood.

Further evidence of complicity flashed to Hockley's mind. In the background, well clear of any lead that might start flying, the peace officers' horses stood range-tied by their hanging reins near to the dark youngster's mount. Yet that huge, magnificent white stallion looked meaner than a bull wapiti bugling for mates in the rutting season. Such a horse would not tamely accept having other stallions so close unless it knew them pretty well.

Which meant Hockley had fallen into a neatly laid trap. If, as he suspected, the saloonkeepers in Mulrooney had sent their law to move him on, he had presented that cold-eyed *big* marshal with an excuse to do so. Should he refuse and be arrested, a jury of Mulrooney citizens could be relied upon to find him guilty. Or so he believed, basing the assumption on how he himself would act in their place.

Anger filled Hockley at the thought of how he had let himself be tricked. The wagon held all the whiskey his bank roll could buy, and which he hoped would realise an enormous profit. On learning of the incident in Brownton which had caused Dusty to leave the town, Hockley had guessed what might happen. Concluding that Mulrooney now stood the best chance of grabbing the trail-herd trade, he established himself in a position where passing customers might easily find him. To be driven off by the law, or arrested for selling liquor to an Indian, would ruin his chances and see him broke. While that would not be an untried sensation, he saw no reason to repeat it. Not when there was an easy way out.

"We can't—talk—about this, now can we, marshal?" he asked.

"How much?" Dusty answered.

"Hell, I don't make much out here—," Hockley began.

"This *hombre* sure lives dangerous," drawled the Kid. "Selling liquor to us poor heathen savages and bribing peace officers."

"I bet he even spits on the sidewalks in Kansas City," Waco went on.

Seeing that bribery stood no chance of succeeding, Hockley decided to make another attempt at straightening out his affairs. In his anger at the possible loss of a good business opportunity,

28

he clean forgot the name he had read on the telegraph form. Or maybe he failed to connect the name 'Fog' with that small, insignificant Texas cowhand.

"Now looky here, young feller—," he said indignantly, raising the walking cane as if intending to make a gesture of pointing it at Dusty. On the wagon box, the burly man tensed slightly.

Springing forward, Dusty lashed out and slapped the cane aside with his left hand. To Waco's amazement, there came the crack of a shot and flame sparked from the bottom of the cane's ferrule. Dusty whipped his right hand upwards, lashing the back of it across Hockley's face. The blow caused the man to stagger and Dusty followed it with a left handed punch to the jaw. Dropping the smoking cane, Hockley sprawled backwards and crashed into the near-side team horse.

At the first movement by Dusty, the man on the box started to rise and draw his gun. Despite being taken by surprise, Waco responded instantly. Down flashed his right hand, fingers closing around the staghorn handle of the off side Army Colt. With the effortless-seeming, but incredibly swift way of a true master, the youngster brought out his Colt, cocked it and fired all in one flowing movement. Before the man's gun could line on any of the Texans, Waco's bullet ripped into his shoulder and knocked him backwards off the box. In falling, he released his hold on the gun. While not as fast as Waco, the man had followed much the same procedure in making the draw, cocking the hammer as the gun cleared leather and squeezed the trigger ready for use. Freed of restraint, the hammer fell before the trigger could return and hold it. So the gun barked and, although the bullet missed, the muzzle-blast's flame burned the off-side horse's rump.

Following his normal type of trading, Hockley often found need for rapid changes of location. So he invariably used a light wagon and selected fast, spirited horses to haul it. Even on what amounted to legitimate trading he and his assistant followed certain precautionary rules. Trail bosses often objected to their men being distracted and sold liquor before the herd was safely penned; and most of them were tough enough to back up their objections. So while Hockley served the customers, the other man remained on the box to control the team while the brake remained open.

At almost the same moment both horses received an unprovoked attack. Hockley's collision with the one at the left caused

29

it to rear, while the sudden burn and sound of the shot set the other plunging forward. Free from impediment by the brake, the wagon lurched into movement and the horses started off across the range at a gallop.

"Stop it, Lon!" Dusty ordered, drawing and lining his left hand Colt as Hockley reached towards the Adams.

"Nigger!" yelled the Kid and his horse started towards him on the run.

One look at Dusty warned Hockley not to continue with his attempt to take revenge. Such speed on the draw only very rarely was achieved without a corresponding ability to shoot accurately and he stood much too close to the other to take chances. So he moved his hand and glanced to where his assistant sprawled un-moving on the ground. Not caring greatly whether the man be alive or dead, Hockley swung his attention to how the Kid was carrying out Dusty's command.

Darting towards the approaching horse, the Kid went into its saddle with a flying bound. Comanche trained, the white would stand indefinitely without being fastened to anything and did not even need its reins left hanging as an inducement to staying put. Clamping his legs about the saddle, the Kid uncoiled the reins from the horn and steered his mount in the direction of the departing wagon.

That enormous stallion could run like a greyhound and found no difficulty in catching up on two harness horses encumbered by even a light wagon. Aware of his mount's potential, the Kid studied the situation and gave thought to obeying Dusty's order. Already the wagon was rolling down a gentle slope, but some distance ahead the ground fell away more steeply. Going down the steep section would be easy enough for a skilled driver in control of his team, yet dangerous when they ran uncontrolled. Anything he aimed to do must be done before they hit that steeper slope.

A signal told the white what its master needed and it lengthened its stride. To the watching men it seemed that the wagon was going at no more than a walking pace, the way the white closed up on it. Drawing alongside the box, the Kid prepared to board it. He took his outer foot from the stirrup, bent his leg under him on the saddle, freed the other boot and hurled himself across the gap separating him from the wagon. Once on the box, he slid the reins from around the brake handle, but made no attempt to operate the lever as an aid to stopping the wagon.

All too well the Kid knew the effect liquor of the kind Hockley sold had upon the drinker. No armchair moralist, he still hated men like the pedlar for what they did to the Indians by selling their poisonous brew. While the man had so far only dealt with cowhands, the Kid did not doubt that he would just as willingly sell his wares to Indians. So the dark youngster aimed to see that the chance did not arise.

Gripping the reins in his left hand, he leaned forward over the box and took hold of the pin coupling the single-tree to the wagon bed. At first he could not draw the pin out and hung in a precarious position as the wagon bounced over the rough ground. Lurching over a rock, the wagon shot forward enough for the pin to come loose and the Kid plucked it out of its hole.

With the team freed, the Kid straightened up again. Flinging the reins and pin from him, he cut loose with a Comanche war whoop loud and wild enough to scare a dead Osage scout white-haired. The yell acted as a spur to send the team horses bounding forward at a better pace. Freed from the weight of the wagon, they drew ahead of it although it continued to roll forward. Already the incline was growing steeper and the wagon's impetus kept it on the move.

Unguided or not, the team horses possessed sufficient instinct for self-preservation to turn away from the more severe incline ahead of them. Finding no reins-inspired compulsion to continue downwards, they swung off to one side. Without the pull of the horses, the wagon went on its inanimate way guided by the force of gravity.

Coming to his feet, the Kid bounded from the box. He lit down with an almost cat-like agility while the wagon trundled on at an ever-increasing pace. Whistling up the white stallion, the Kid mounted and followed the departing team horses. Behind him the wagon careered on downwards accompanied by the jangling clash of breaking glass. Then its near front wheel struck a bigger, firmer rock and shattered under the impact. Tilting crazily, the inoperative remains of the wheel spiked into the ground beyond the rock. Unable to halt so abruptly, the wagon started to somersault over. A hideous cacophony of shattering bottles and splintering timbers rose into the air, making music to the Kid's ears as he caught up to and halted the pair of harness horses.

Curses rose in a wild, almost insane flood from Hockley as he watched the wrecking of his property. However, still covered by Dusty's Colt, he made no more.

"Got the hosses, Dusty," drawled the Kid amiably, coming up to the men. "But dog-my-cats if the wagon didn't sneak away from under me."

"You done it on purpose!" Hockley snarled.

"Did I?" asked the Kid with a mildness of tone that did not match the cold glint in his eyes.

"Damn it, I'll see the sher—!" Hockley began.

"No you won't!" Dusty put in. "Because if you don't pull right out of this neck of the woods, I'll jail you the next time we meet."

"Jail me?"

"That's what I said."

"Do you reckon you can make that selling likker to an Injun charge stick?" the pedlar demanded.

"Maybe I couldn't," Dusty replied. "But you tried to kill me with that fancy cane-gun. That's attempted murder. Fact being no jury'd blame me for killing you defending myself against another try—even if you didn't make one."

"The law—!" Hockley started.

"Doesn't cover what you're doing," Dusty interrupted. "So I'm telling you right now. The next time I catch you selling that snake-head rot-gut to cowhands on the range, I'll kill you where you stand."

Watching the small Texan, Waco could almost believe the threat would be carried out. From all appearances Hockley did not doubt it. All the last attempts at bluster left him. Although the fury and hatred still flickered on his face, it was tempered by fear. However he made a final attempt at putting on a bold face.

"You'll hear more ab—."

It seemed to be Hockley's day to have speeches cut off in mid-sentence. Dropping from his white's saddle, the Kid stepped between Dusty and the pedlar. A face, suddenly changed to a tight-lipped Comanche Dog Soldier's war mask, thrust itself up close to Hockley's and a pair of red hazel eyes glared into his.

"Mister!" said the Kid in a deep-throated *Pehnane* grunt. "You see to your hired man, then climb on to those hosses and get the hell gone from here afore Dusty kills you now."

"Which same I wouldn't want to see him do that," Waco went on. "So I may just have to save him the trouble."

32

"Which same *I* wouldn't want the boy to have that on his conscience," the Kid stated. "So I just might do it myself."

Looking at the trio of grim faces, Hockley realised that his life had never been in more deadly danger. One wrong move, a further word out of place, could easily bring lead crashing into him. Possibly Dusty Fog would not kill him unless given adequate cause, but the other two might have fewer scruples. With that thought in mind the pedlar started towards the team horses.

"You hired him and got him shot up, mister," Dusty said. "So you see to him now."

Throwing a glance at the groaning, wounded man who was sitting up holding his injured shoulder, Hockley gave a disinterested shrug. "He can go to hell for all of me."

"Take another step and you'll be lying alongside him," Dusty warned as the man continued to walk.

"What the hell do you want now?" Hockley almost screeched, spinning around and glaring at the Texans. "You've come here and busted my wagon——."

"It's called the responsibility of an employer," Dusty answered. "See to that feller. Take him with you—and don't come back."

4

Pick out the Leaders

While Hockley obeyed Dusty and tended to the hired man's wound, Waco went over and picked up the cane. At first glance it seemed ordinary enough, but the weight was more than bamboo, silver decorative connecting bands and a curved walnut handle ought to be. Walking back to Dusty, the youngster turned the cane and looked at the ferrule. A hole of about .36 calibre ran up the centre of the cane, drilled into a steel tube hidden under the coating of bamboo. Closer examination showed rifling grooves cut into the hole.

"That's slick," he remarked, joining Dusty. "I never saw a dingus like this afore."

33

"He counted on it," the small Texan replied and took the cane. "It's a Remington cane-gun. I thought it might be from the way he kept it on the toe of his boot."

"So's he'd not plug the muzzle with dirt," Waco guessed.

"Sure. Although Thomas, the feller who designed this sort of gun for Remington, fitted it with a piece of cork that'd blow out with the bullet and keep dirt out of the barrel. It worked, only it doesn't pay to take chances."

As he talked, Dusty drew back the cane's handle until a flat spring-catch flicked into place and held it open. Then he showed the youngster where to insert the self-consuming paper cartridge and percussion cap. Waco next learned that the tip of the catch holding back the casing could be used as a rear-sight and the location of the small stud which served as a trigger. By the time Hockley had finished bandaging the other man's shoulder, Waco knew how to load and fire the Remington-Thomas Model of 1858 cane-gun.

"Reckon he'll be back, Dusty?" Waco asked as they watched Hockley riding away without attempting to retrieve his hide-out weapon.

"I don't reckon so," Dusty replied and looked at the Kid. "When're you thinking of starting?"

"Huh?" replied the dark young man innocently.

"Work. Earning all the money the tax paying citizens of Mulrooney're going to pay you," Dusty explained.

"Oh, that."

"Sure. I told you to do something, didn't I?"

"I done it. The wagon stopped a mite sudden, but I done it for sure."

"You've done one itty-bitty chore, not a day's work," Dusty told him. "Get on that white goat and go earn your keep."

"Damned if I don't go back to smuggling for a living," grumbled the Kid as he went to his horse. "Leastwise then I'll only do one day's work a day, not three days all rolled into one."

With that he swung into his saddle, saluted Dusty by applying the tip of the thumb to the nose and waggling his fingers. Before the small Texan could make any adequate reply, the white stallion turned and loped across the range. Grinning more cheerfully than he had since learning of the whiskey-pedlar's activities, Dusty walked with Waco to the waiting paints. They mounted and rode back in the direction of Mulrooney.

A feeling of well-being and content filled Waco as he rode at Dusty's side through the fringes of the town. Already a good piece of work lay behind them and with the afternoon well advanced he gave thought to the evening. He decided to spend the time improving his relations with Babsy, a pleasant occupation. All such notions departed when, after leaving the horses at the livery barn, he and Dusty arrived at the marshal's office. They found Big Sarah standing at the desk, feeding shells into one of the ten-gauge shotguns from the wall rack. Relief showed on the woman's face at the sight of the Texans.

"I'm sure pleased to see you, Cap'n Fog," she stated.

"What's up?" Dusty asked.

"Shamus O'Sullivan, Fritz Voigt and Frenchy Rastignac're down at the Fair Lady with their gang of gandy-dancers, fixing to hang a railroad lamp outside the front door."

Such an action might not appear a cause for alarm to some people, but Dusty knew it to be a situation calling for immediate action. Hanging the lamp outside the saloon signified that the railroad workers considered it to be their private domain. Any cowhand who saw it would regard it as a challenge, an infringement on their liberty, and feel compelled to take up the matter.

"Let's go talk to them about it," Dusty said. "Put up the scatter, Sarah."

"I don't reckon I'll be needing it now," grinned the women, removing the shells and returning the gun to the rack.

On the way along the street Dusty explained the seriousness of the situation to Waco.

"How'd we handle it?" the youngster asked.

"That depends on how they want to play it," Dusty replied. "The first thing to do when you're handling a crowd gathered for fuss is to pick out the leaders and deal with them. This time we know their names. You won't always have that much of a start. So we'll play it like we don't and see how you get along—if there's time to do it, that is."

While Dusty realised the gravity of the affair, he did not forget that his only backing was a youngster inexperienced in the work of a peace officer. He knew Waco to be brave and not likely to panic, but wanted the youngster trained as a lawman. So he was prepared to delay dealing with the gandy-dancers, railroad construction workers, long enough to give Waco a practical lesson.

"Maybe I should've loaded up that fancy cane-gun and

brought it along," Waco said with a grin, having left the weapon at the office.

"That'd be as much use as an udder on a bull," Dusty replied. "If you figure on quieting a crowd, tote along a ten-gauge scatter-gun. One look at those big black-eyed barrels and it's surprising how peaceable folks can get."

Arriving in front of the Fair Lady, Dusty and Waco paused to look through the window. There being only the gandy-dancers present, Dusty delayed his entrance while Waco gained experience.

Some twenty men of European extraction had gathered before the long mahogany bar. Ignoring the very attractive sight of Freddie clad in her working clothes, or Babsy dressed saloongirl fashion, Waco studied the men. Three caught his eye, being in the centre of the crowd and in conversation with Freddie.

Holding a railroad engine's lamp was a big, brawny black-haired man so obviously Irish that he might have been painted bright shamrock green. To his left stood a blond, crop-headed German almost as large. At the right of the trio, the third of Waco's selection looked almost weedy compared with the other two, being shortish, slender man of Gallic appearance. Yet something about him made Waco regard the third man as a leader rather than one of the led.

"Good choosing," Dusty complimented when Waco pointed out the trio. "I'd say you called them right."

"As right as the off side of a hoss," agreed Sarah. "Those three used to come in while the town was being built and what they said went with the rest of the rust-eaters."

"Then they're the ones we'll dicker with," Dusty said. "Leave me do the talking and start the doing, boy."

"Sure," Waco replied, too impressed by the serious way the other spoke to make any further comment.

Followed by his two deputies, Dusty stepped through the batwing doors. What he heard on entering showed him that they had come not a moment too soon.

"I tell you, Miss Freddie," O'Sullivan was saying, waving the lamp. "With this here hanging out front all the cowhands, buffler-hunters and other riff-raff will know this's under railroad pertection."

"And I'll lose their trade," Freddie replied.

"Divil the bit," O'Sullivan assured her. "We'll let it be knowed that any as wants can come on in—As long as they treats you civil and don't get under our dainty lil feet."

"Hey, Shamus," Voigt hissed in a dramatic stage-whisper, nodding towards the batwing doors. "Just take a look at what's come in."

"Sure, and 'tis a cowhand," the burly Irishman said, after directing a long stare at Dusty. "But what's that thing on his vest?"

"A badge, *mon ami*," Rastignac told him.

"So it is. Now there's an evil thing somebody's gone and done, pinning a great, big, heavy badge on him that ways," O'Sullivan commented. "And what can I be doing for you, me lad?"

"I hear tell you're fixing to hang that lamp outside," Dusty replied.

"That we are."

"You know doing it'll mean trouble?"

"Not as long as what it's there for's respected by one and all," O'Sullivan answered.

"You know it won't be," Dusty pointed out. "And that being the case, I'm not letting you hang it."

"*You're* not?" Voigt growled.

"You caught on real fast," Dusty drawled.

"Just how do you and your deputy there aim to be after stopping us then?" demanded O'Sullivan, nodding in Waco's direction as the youngster stood behind Dusty with hands thumbhooked into his gunbelt.

"Any way we have to," Dusty assured him. "Stay here as long as you like. Have your fun, but don't try hanging up that lamp."

"And if we says we're going to hang it, regardless?" asked O'Sullivan, then answered the question. "I suppose you'll put lead into us?"

"You reckon you could stop us without them guns?" Voigt inquired.

What happened next handed the gandy-dancers the surprise of their lives. Reaching down, Dusty untied the pigging thongs holding the bottom of his holsters to his legs. Just as unconcernedly he unbuckled and removed the belt, handing it to Freddie. Then he looked at the trio and grinned.

"They do say showing licks telling about it, and proves more," he said.

"You means to rassle with us?" O'Sullivan gurgled in a disbelieving tone.

"I'd prefer it one at a time," Dusty replied. "But that's your choice."

"One at a—!" the Irishman croaked, eyes bugging out while his companions stared in speechless amazement at the small Texan.

"It'll have to come sooner or later," Dusty told them. "So we might just as well get it over with right now."

"And no hard feelings at the end of it, win, lose or draw?" O'Sullivan wanted to know.

"Like you'd say, devil the bit of it," Dusty answered. "If you win, the lamp goes up. If you lose, it doesn't."

"And fairer you couldn't be," boomed the Irishman. "We'll let Pierre here give you the first whirl."

"That's the only fair way," Voigt agreed.

"As long as he doesn't hurt me," finished Rastignac with a wink, peeling off his jacket.

Taking in the Frenchman's slight build, it seemed strange that he should be one of the leading lights of a hard-muscled, brawny gang of gandy-dancers. Any thoughts that Dusty might have had on Rastignac being merely in such an exalted position by virtue of friendship with O'Sullivan and Voigt ended at his selection to fight first.

Quickly a circle formed, large enough to permit the fighters plenty of moving space. Waco stood by Freddie's side and exchanged a glance with her, both wondering if Dusty might be biting off more than he could chew. For his part, Dusty concentrated on studying his opponent and noting certain significant details.

From all appearances, Rastignac knew more than a little about fist-fighting. He adopted the ready stance rapidly replacing the old bare-knuckle style in pugilistic circles back East, right fist cocked ready, left held across to guard his jaw. However he appeared to have learned the style badly, for his foot placement might have been faulted by a purist. Although positioned about a shoulder's width apart, the left foot at the rear pointed sideways instead of both being aimed to the front.

If Dusty noticed the apparent fault, he overlooked it. In fact he showed very little sign of being ready to defend himself. Grinning confidently, Rastignac prepared to attack. Only he did not use his fists. Up lashed his left foot, rising with speed, power and skilled precision. Always before his *savate* attack had come as

38

a complete surprise when used against men unaware of the French Creole style of foot-and-fist fighting.

Unfortunately Dusty not only knew of *savate*—including how its foot placement differed from ordinary boxing—but possessed a real good method of countering the attack. On a visit to New Orleans in the early days of the Texas Republic, Dusty's uncle, Ole Devil Hardin, had met and hired a small Oriental man most folks thought to be Chinese. Actually Tommy Okasi hailed from the Japanese Islands and brought with him certain strange skills. To Dusty alone of the Hardin, Fog and Blaze boys, Tommy had passed on the secrets of *ju-jitsu* and *karate*, alien fighting arts virtually unknown at that time in the Western Hemisphere.

Faced by such an attack many men would have tried to grab the leg, but Dusty knew a far better—and safer—way of dealing with it. Swiftly he brought his hands down, crossing his arms just above the wrists. Instead of making an attempt to catch the leg, he allowed it to pass into the lower section of the X his arms formed. Only when the kick's upward rise had been blocked and brought to a halt did he make the next move. Catching hold of the toe of Rastignac's boot in the right hand and its heel in the left, Dusty gave it a surging, twisting heave. A howl of mingled pain and surprise broke from the Frenchman as his other foot left the floor. Unable to stop himself, he somersaulted over and landed with a thud that drove all wind or cohesive thought from his body.

"I'd say it was you next, mister," Dusty remarked, looking at Voigt.

The soft-spoken words cut through the excited chatter of the crowd and silenced it. While the gandy-dancers had expected Dusty to tangle with Rastignac, although not with the result just witnessed, they had doubted if he would take on either Voigt or O'Sullivan.

"Don't you b'ar-hug him too hard, Fritz," warned one of the crowd. "You'll likely squeeze him in two halves."

"I just give him *ein kleine bischen,* make his eyes pop out of his head and break a couple of ribs," Voigt answered. "I'm not wanting hurt a lawman too bad."

With that the German advanced on Dusty. It seemed that the small Texan did not take the threat too seriously, for he moved to meet Voigt. Watching them, Freddie sucked in a deep breath and opened her mouth to give a warning. Having seen Voigt give a man *ein kleine bischen* bear-hug, she knew just what it meant. Yet Dusty made no attempt to avoid the reaching arms. In fact he appeared to walk straight into them. Although unused to opponents willingly entering his grasp, Voigt did not intend to look a gift-horse in the mouth. Curling his brawny arms around Dusty's torso, he prepared to give a crushing pressure.

"Oh lord!" Freddie breathed, wondering what had prompted Dusty to act in such an apparently reckless manner.

She learned quickly enough.

Like his every action since entering the room, allowing Voigt to gain the hold fitted into Dusty's plan. He knew that for the most part the gandy-dancers were not gun-fighters and displaying superlative skill in that respect would have only a subsidiary interest for them. Proving that he could beat them at their own style of fighting was the way to deal with them. Once that had been established, he figured there would be no trouble keeping the railroad workers' high spirits within bounds.

Although Dusty allowed Voigt to obtain the bear-hug, he made sure that his own arms stayed outside the other's grasp. That did not worry Voigt—at first—for he reckoned the agony of his pressure would prevent his victim doing anything effective. Which theory might have worked better had it been given a chance to mature. Even as the brawny arms started to tighten about his middle, Dusty cupped his hands and clapped them over Voigt's ears.

In making the move Dusty tried to achieve a compromise between too little power and striking so hard that he burst the German's ear drums. It seemed that he succeeded. On the hands slapping home, Voigt's body went rigid and his arms relaxed. Thrusting the German away, Dusty followed up with a style of attack none of the watchers had ever seen. Although he drove his hand into Voigt's belly, he did not close it into a fist. Instead he used the *hira nukite*, the level-piercing hand of *karate*, taught to him by Tommy Okasi. With the fingers extended and together, thumb bent across the palm of his hand, Dusty stabbed Voigt full in the solar plexus. An explosive croak broke from the German and he staggered back, holding his middle as he folded over. Again Dusty struck, still with his hands held in that alien manner. Only this time he chopped the heel of each palm into the sides of Voigt's neck, tumbling the man to the floor like a back-broke rabbit.

"Now there's something you don't often see," Freddie commented, first of the audience to recover from the shock of seeing Voigt's dreaded bear-hug broken with such ease.

"He's a tricky one for sure," O'Sullivan agreed, a shade uneasily.

"Two down and one to go," Dusty drawled.

Realising what that meant, O'Sullivan gave rapid thought to his social position. He held an enviable standing among the gandy-dancers, being known as their unofficial leader. Many concessions came his way from the bosses of the construction crews, in return for which he maintained a form of law and order among the other workers. Such a position came and was retained by his ability to beat his companions physically. Should he tangle with the small Texan and be bested, the loss of prestige would have a serious effect on his standing. Yet refusing to take up the challenge was just the same.

Although not a man given to deep thinking, O'Sullivan could on occasion make a rapid decision.

"Sure and we all know you can fight, friend," he said, waving a hand to his fallen companions. "So let's try something different, shall we?"

"Such as?" Dusty inquired.

"A friendly game of 'Douse-The-Candle'."

A faint grin twisted Dusty's face at the Irishman's suggestion, for he knew it meant a rougher version of wrist-wrestling. While Dusty's knowledge of *ju-jitsu* and *karate* gave him an advantage in a straight fight, he knew that he stood no chance at all in the contest O'Sullivan suggested. So did the majority of the crowd and one member of it in particular.

Standing unnoticed on the stairs, ready to help if the need arose, Mark Counter decided the time had come for him to intervene. Not that he would have gone unnoticed without such a centre of attraction as Dusty's actions offered. Six foot three in height, golden blond curly hair topping an almost classically handsome face, Mark stood out in any crowd. Great shoulders, hinting at the enormous muscular development underneath, spread wide the material of a costly, made-to-measure shirt. From there he tapered down to a slim waist and curved out to long, powerful legs. Along with his green silk bandana, all his clothing hinted at wealth. The gunbelt about his middle, carrying ivory-handled Army Colts in carefully tooled holsters, told another story. Although showing the finest 'Best Citizen's Finish' Colonel Colt's Hartford factory could produce, the revolvers were purely functional fighting weapons, hanging just right for rapid use.

Dandy dresser the elegant blond giant might be, but he possessed few peers in the various cow-land arts. Third son of a big South Texas ranch owner, rich in his own right since a maiden aunt died and left him her considerable fortune, Mark still preferred to ride as a member of Ole Devil's floating outfit. Nor did his sartorial tastes make him a less useful member of that efficient fighting force. Few who saw him in action during a rough-house brawl soon forgot the scene. Already his great strength had become legendary. Calamity Jane often told how he single-handedly lifted her wagon out of a gopher hole* and performed other feats of muscular prowess in her presence†. Nor did Miss Martha Jane Canary for once stretch the truth. Riding as he did in the shadow of the Rio Hondo gun wizard, Mark's ability with his Colts rarely gained its just acclaim. Yet many gentlemen experienced in such matters put him second only to Dusty Fog in speed and accuracy. Anybody who took Mark Counter for no more than a dandy stood a good chance of regretting it.

However Mark did not appear to be in a position to make his full contribution to the affair at that moment. He had been shot in the shoulder during a brawl on his arrival in Mulrooney. While Waco's intervention had prevented any further injury, the blond giant's left arm hung in a sling. For all that he moved forward.

"Don't you reckon Dusty's just a mite light to take you on at 'Douse-The-Candle'?" he asked, elbowing through the crowd

"And who asked you to bill in?" O'Sullivan demanded indignantly, swinging around to see who was interfering.

"I'm Dusty's deputy," Mark replied. "So I reckon I can take some of the work off him."

"With a busted wing?" O'Sullivan asked, nodding to the sling.

"I only use one hand for 'Douse-The-Candle'," Mark told him. "If you don't mind, it'll be my good one. Get the candles out and lit, then let's give her a whirl."

*Told in TROUBLED RANGE.

†Mark's other meetings with Calamity Jane are told in THE WILDCATS, THE FORTUNE HUNTERS, THE BIG HUNT and GUNS IN THE NIGHT.

"Mark!" Freddie gasped. "You may burst open your wound."

"Nope," he grinned. "I'm fixing to use my other hand."

Once again O'Sullivan assessed the situation. While a defeat over the small Texan might save his face, he knew there would be sceptics who commented on the disparity between their weights. Although slightly smaller than Mark, he weighed a little heavier and did not figure there ought to be too much trouble in licking the blond Texan.

"I'll douse it quick for you," O'Sullivan promised and nodded to Freddie. "Could we trouble you for two candles, ma'am?"

Taking seats on opposite sides of a small table, Mark and O'Sullivan waited for the final preparations to be made. Collecting two candles from the bar, a gandy-dancer lit them and dribbled wax on to the table to hold them in position where the contestants' hands would arrive at the conclusion of the bout. Then Mark and O'Sullivan placed their right elbows on the table and interlaced fingers.

"Start us off, Miss Freddie," Mark suggested. "If that suits the Irish gent here."

"It'd be a honour," O'Sullivan answered. "Go to it ma'am."

"I'll count to three and say 'go,'" Freddie told them. "One—two—three—go."

Instantly O'Sullivan started to press at Mark's hand, with the intention of forcing it down on to the flickering candle flame. Already the Irishman had felt the hard solidity of the Texan's hand, but did not expect any great difficulty in forcing it over. Only that did not happen. Instead he met a rock-like resistance that refused to yield.

Around the table startled exclamations rose from the gandy-dancers. Sitting up, groaning and holding his head, Voigt muttered curses in German. However Rastignac caught him by the arm, helped him rise and pointed to the table. Any ideas the German might have formed about resuming hostilities with Dusty ended. Sinking into a chair, he accepted the drink Babsy brought and watched the game of 'Douse-The-Candle' run its course.

Slowly the confidence oozed from O'Sullivan's face, being replaced by a mixture of strain and amazement. No matter how much pressure he exerted, he could achieve nothing. Then slowly but inexorably Mark started to force the Irishman's hand down. Not that he brought an end to the game immediately. Twice

43

O'Sullivan strained every muscle to bring his hand to the vertical. Then slowly it sank a few inches. Gathering in his reserves of strength, Mark threw it all into a final effort. Down went O'Sullivan's hand, crushing the reduced candle under it and dousing the flame.

"The saints preserve us!" the Irishman yelped, shaking his hand in an attempt to restore life into it. "If you can do that with one arm in a sling, bucko, I'd hate to see what you can do when well."

"I've never met a man who came so near to licking me," Mark replied. "This calls for a drink, I'd say."

"That it does, that it does," O'Sullivan agreed. "And I reckon seeing's how you've bested us, we'll not be hanging the lamp—."

"They've not bested us all!" put in the youngest member of the railroad men, and the only one to wear a gun in a holster tied to his leg. "We come here to hang that lamp and I'm going to do it."

"The hell you are, Wicker!" O'Sullivan growled.

"Don't you or anybody else try to stop me!" Wicker warned, hand hovering with spread fingers above his Colt's butt. "I'm taking that lamp and hanging it just like we planned."

At which point Waco became aware that Dusty had not yet strapped on his gunbelt. For once the small Texan had failed to take the elementary precaution, feeling there would be no need for guns with the situation so well in hand. He also knew that it was too late to rectify the mistake. Then Waco took the matter out of his hands.

"Come ahead," the young Texan said. "All you have to do is pass me."

5

You'll Never Know How Lucky

With that inborn instinct all westerners gained, the crowd knew what it must do. So gandy-dancers and saloongirls fell back, standing well clear of the two young men. Much as Dusty wanted to interfere, he knew he could not without implying a lack of trust in Waco. At the small Texan's side, Freddie watched with a growing feeling of concern. Not that she feared for Waco, having seen how fast he could draw a gun. Inexperienced she might be, but she guessed killing the gandy-dancer would make trouble. Maybe not that night, but later it would be remembered and Wicker, despite being the aggressor, raised to the status of a martyr. Freddie could still remember the expression on Waco's face as he burst into the saloon to kill the man who shot Mark. Unless she was very mistaken, only the blond giant's intervention had prevented more of his attackers from feeling the youngster's lead. So when Waco gave out his quiet challenge, she expected the worst.

"You reckon I can't pass you?" Wicker snarled.

"That's for you to find out," Waco answered.

Much of Wicker's time had been spent in practising his draw and he expended hard-earned money on fodder for his Colt. Like most youngsters of the day, he revelled in stories of the great gun-fighting names and longed to emulate their achievements. Working among gandy-dancers offered few chances to display his talents, for they tended to be fist- or knife-fighters, with various erotic variations thrown in. At last he found himself faced with the real thing, in the kind of position he had dreamed about.

Only a nagging doubt bit into him. Apart from a very few cases, western peace officers received their appointments by virtue of exceptional gun-skill. So far two of those Texan John Laws had proved more than able to handle the best the railroad could offer. Maybe the tall, blond youngster came up to their high standard in his own line. However Wicker did not wish to back down.

"I'm coming!" he warned and hoped his voice did not sound as strained to the others as it came to his ears.

"Come or go," Waco answered evenly, raising his right hand to wave at the lamp. "But that dingus stays right whe—."

Sensing the chance Waco's action offered, without having the knowledge or experience to question it, Wicker stabbed his hand down at his gun. While such a move might pass as fast when performed against his even less skilled gandy-dancer admirers, it failed to come even close to the standard required when used against Waco.

45

At the other youngster's first movement, Waco sent his left hand from hanging with deceptive negligence at his side to around the near Colt's butt. Out came the gun and roared while Wicker still tried to draw his clear of its holster.

There had been a time, not too long past, when Waco would have killed Wicker on the spot. Only since meeting Dusty Fog he gained a slightly higher opinion of the value of human life. When he stepped in between Wicker and the lamp, Waco did so out of a sense of duty. He knew neither Dusty nor Mark could stop the young railroad worker at that moment and so moved in to do so. And he came prepared to halt Wicker any way he found necessary. Instinct and knowledge told him of Wicker's indecision, allowing him to gauge the other's true potential.

So, instead of planting the .44 bullet in Wicker's body, Waco drove it into the boards between his feet.

Shock numbed Wicker at the sound of the shot and he stared with unbelieving eyes to the smoking Colt in Waco's left hand. Even as he watched, the Colt performed a pinwheel on the young Texan's forefinger and flipped back into its holster all in one continuous move.

"Still fixing to come on?" Waco asked.

"And that he's not!" O'Sullivan put in grimly. "Give it up, Wicker lad. We've had our fun and nobody's been hurt—."

"Speak for yourself, *mon ami*," Rastignac put in, rubbing his rump and wincing. "I'll never be the same again."

"There's some'd say any change'd be an improvement," O'Sullivan sniffed, then went on. "None of us's been hurt bad. Let's keep it that way."

"Mick's right," Freddie continued. "Donna, pour out a round of drinks on the house. Then for Pete's sake let's start making some money."

The prospect of free drinks prevented any comments on Wicker's failure as a gun-fighter. Gathering at the bar, the gandy-dancers reached for the glasses which Donna's deft hands filled. O'Sullivan turned and grinned broadly at Dusty.

"You'll be taking something with us, marshal?"

Before Dusty could answer, cowhand yells and drumming hooves sounded on the street outside. Giving a shrug, the small Texan nodded towards the doors.

"Some other time, Mick. Right now I've got to go earn my pay. Let's go see who it is, Waco."

46

"There goes a real big man, and I'll lick the pants off anybody who says different," O'Sullivan boomed, then nodded to Mark. "Well, almost anybody."

"You'll get no argument on that from me," the blond giant answered, watching his companions leave.

"And you leave off that damned gunbelt, Wicker boy!" O'Sullivan growled, turning to the young railroad man who stood clutching a whiskey glass in a hand that shook a trifle. "You're lucky not to've been shot."

Thinking of how Waco had been when they first met, Mark nodded in sober agreement.

"You'll never know how lucky," he said. "Set up another round on me, Donna!"

"And when you've done it, you're going back to bed," Freddie whispered into his ear.

"The night's young—," Mark began.

"I could always have the girls undress you and carry you there," Freddie smiled. "And you know they'd do it if I told them."

Recalling how the girls had pitched into the bunch of buffalo-hunters who tried to cause trouble on the day he arrived, Mark did not doubt that.

"Maybe I should stick around," he suggested. "That Wicker kid might get all liquored up and try something loco like looking for evens. I don't reckon Waco'd hold back twice."

"I didn't think he'd hold back once," Freddie confessed. "Don't worry about Wicker. I'll make sure that he behaves."

"Reckon you can?"

"Do *you* reckon I can't?" countered Freddie. "Go on, that fool trick you pulled took more out of you than you're wanting to show."

Which, being the truth, Mark conceded. Guessing he could safely leave matters in Freddie's hands, and hearing nothing to tell him he might be needed in the street, he returned to his room upstairs and went to bed. Although Wicker drank enough to raise his courage, he did not commit such a foolish act as going after Waco to resume hostilities. At the first hint that he might, Freddie gave Donna a signal and herself carried the drink the bar-maid—as Freddie called the female bartenders—had prepared to the young man. Flattered by the attention, Wicker drank it. Shortly after he fell asleep and did not wake until back at the

47

construction camp. There, giving the matter sober reflection, he decided that he lacked the necessary ability to make a gun-fighter and stopped trying.

While Waco heard nothing of it, he probably saved a young life on his first day as a deputy. If Wicker had continued trying to pass off as a proddy gun-hand, he would have eventually met a man with less scruples than the young Texan and gone the way of the foolhardy.

Any hopes Waco nourished of asking for Dusty's opinion of his conduct in the saloon died as they reached the sidewalk. Down before their office almost all of Colonel Goodnight's JA trail crew milled horses in the centre of the street. Forcing his mount from among the others, one of the cowhands drew his revolver and rode towards the office.

"Let's get the town clowns out here and show them that the JA's arrived, boys!" he whooped.

Before either Dusty or Waco, running along the street, could intervene, a screech, like a cougar finding the wild hogs had ate its young might give, rang out. Hurling from the shadows at the end of the jail, the young cowhand Tack bounded on to the hitching rail and from there flung himself at the potential window-breaker. As he hooked one arm around the offender's neck, Tack used the other hand to knock up the revolver and its bullet sped harmlessly into the air. Then the two of them slid from the bucking horse, landing on the ground as it went off along the street.

"Best catch it, boy," Dusty said. "I'll go talk some to them."

An enraged cowhand sat up, cocking a fist ready to strike at his attacker. Then recognition came and he held off the assault long enough to demand an explanation.

"What in hell fool game you playing at, Tack?"

"I'll tell what!" the window's defender yelled back no less heatedly. "I done dug a hole with a shovel to earn enough to pay for that glass and stuck it in with my own two lily-white lil hands. So I'll be tarnally damned if I'll see it all busted up again."

"How come you-all took to digging and fixing windows, Tack boy?" asked a grizzled veteran of the cattle industry. "Don't Colonel Charlie pay you good enough without that?"

"The marshal here allowed that I bust it and he didn't like sitting in a draughty office," Tack replied.

"You mean that there marshal got all mean 'n' ornery?" demanded another of the cowhands. "Made you ride the blister end of a shovel and fix up a window that got busted accidental-like."

"He for sure did," grinned Tack, seeing Dusty approaching.

"Such doings should be stopped instanter-like!" stated the cowhand Tack had pulled from his horse.

"Or even sooner," continued yet a forth hand. "Where-at's this mean ole Kansas lawman?"

"Coming up right now," Tack informed him, delighted with the way things were going.

Although the trail crew turned with some hostility to face the approaching lawman, much of it died away on seeing him. While the sun had gone down, the street was sufficiently illuminated for them to tell that no ordinary Kansas trail-end town marshal was coming their way. Nor did Dusty's small size fool cold sober cowhands, even those who did not know him. All knew they faced a master of their trade and a man more than ordinarily competent in handling his guns. Any faint doubts which may have lingered fled as the oldest cowhand present spoke.

"Air that you, Cap'n Fog?"

"This's me," Dusty agreed. "And I'm town marshal here."

Even those of the trail crew who did not ride with Goodnight on the third drive to Fort Sumner had heard of Dusty Fog. The men who made the drive recalled him all too well and knew better than cross his path in what he considered to be his duty.

"That danged Injun never allowed that you was marshal," the old timer said aggrievedly. "And me sharing my makings with him."

While the Kid delivered news of Brownton's peculiar ideas, he had failed to mention who ran the marshal's office in Mulrooney. Questioned later on the lapse by the indignant old timer, he replied, "I figured you'd learn soon enough."

Rising and dusting his clothes, the potential window-breaker studied the front of the office and exclaimed, "I never see a finer piece of glass-fixing. It'd be plumb sinful to destroy a work of art like that."

"Which same I'm scared of riling Cap'n Fog as well," grinned the old timer. "So I per-poses, seconds and thirds that this-here fool meeting adjourns to the hotel, sees Colonel Charlie for our pay and goes out to spend it. If we're going to wind up in pokey, let's get good and drunk first."

"Go to it," Dusty told them. "Only keep your guns in leather and horses on the streets."

With that he stood aside and watched Waco hand over the runaway horse to its owner. Exchanging laughter and cheerful comments, the trail hands followed the old timer on his way to carry out his suggestions.

"It's going to be a lively night tonight, boy," Dusty told Waco as they watched the departure. "And afore it's through you'll wish you'd six arms and at least eight legs."

"Did I do right, facing down that young cuss at the Fair Lady?" Waco asked a touch worriedly.

"Do you reckon you did?"

"I figured that he had to be stopped."

"You figured it right and acted righter," Dusty assured him. "Sure he had to be stopped. But if you'd thrown that bullet into him, the gandy-dancers'd've remembered it. They'll not forget the way you acted either, and it'll pay better than shooting that fool kid. Now they know how well you can handle a gun—and that you know just how much to use it."

"What now?" asked the youngster, looking relieved at receiving Dusty's approbation. He had been worried about how the small Texan might regard his actions in dealing with Wicker and felt satisfied now he knew.

"We'll grab a meal and do like I said in the Fair Lady, make a start at earning our pay," Dusty replied.

"Now me," Waco said. "I'd reckon we've already done pretty fair at that."

With the meal over, Waco began to find out just how much work a conscientious peace officer did in a day. A marshal of Wild Bill Hickok's type spent most of his time sitting in card games, or loafing in a favourite saloon, only appearing if called upon to quell a disturbance. Wyatt Earp became conspicuous only when little danger threatened, he had plenty of tough backing, and somebody of importance was on hand to witness his 'heroics'. Although not a professional lawman, Dusty had been trained to try to prevent trouble breaking out, rather than arrive and attempt to halt it once started.

So he and Waco took to the streets, keeping an unobtrusive but unceasing watch. The youngster, cowhand at heart, bewailed the fact that nobody had warned him that being a deputy entailed so much foot-work or he would never have taken the fool chore. He also listened as Dusty explained the various specialised aspects of what they did, whether it be breaking up a fight or something which, on the face of it, appeared to be the most simple routine.

"Try that door," Dusty told him as they walked by a warehouse near the railroad depot. "Make sure it's locked."

"Sure," Waco replied and started to obey.

"Hold it right there!" Dusty snapped as the youngster reached towards the door's handle.

"What's up?" Waco hissed, right hand fanning gun-wards.

"Suppose there's somebody inside, robbing the place," Dusty said, walking forward. "He hears you trying the door and figures its a watchman, or somebody coming and throws lead. What'd it do to you, stood where you are?"

"Make a hole in my fool hide, I reckon," Waco answered as he studied his position in relation to the door. "Only there's nobody inside."

"If there is, time you've learned different it's too late. No matter whether you're certain the place's empty, always stand to the side and reach around to try the door. That way you stand a better than fair chance of being missed if anybody is inside and cuts loose.'

"You must reckon I'm awful green."

"Sure. But I figure you've got good enough sense to learn."

"What happens if somebody's inside and shoots?" Waco asked after moving to the wall and reaching around to try the door handle.

"A whole lot depends on how many of 'em you reckon're inside and if you've got an amigo with you," Dusty replied. "If the place's only one room and the door's weak enough, bust in fast with a gun in your hand."

Continuing on their way, Dusty explained other matters arising from Waco's question. Always eager to learn, Waco listened and stored the knowledge away for future use. In later years, as an Arizona Ranger, county sheriff and finally U.S. marshal,* he found Dusty's teachings invaluable and following the precautionary rules laid down by the small Texan often saved his life.

*Told in SAGEBRUSH SLEUTH, ARIZONA RANGER, WACO RIDES IN THE DRIFTER and HOUND DOG MAN.

Not wishing to crowd too much detail on to the youngster at one time, Dusty failed to mention one elementary, but vital, rule. Knowing Waco's ability in the line that rule covered, he felt that no explanation would be needed. Later events proved him wrong.

6

Innocent as Lon Looks, or Guilty-Looking as Hell

"I tell you, Lon, this here's a fool, no-account, no-good chore," Waco stated as he walked with the Ysabel Kid through the rear streets of Mulrooney on the morning of his second day as a deputy marshal. "Damned if being a lawman's not worse than following a plough or herding sheep."

"Now me, I wouldn't know about that, not having done either of 'em," the Kid replied.

"No, and you didn't do none of the walking last night!" yelped the youngster indignantly. "All you done yesterday was bust up some poor feller's wagon and trail 'round the country bumming smokes offen cowhands. Ole Dusty made me *walk* near on a hundred miles. We stopped cowhands shooting up main street, gandy-dancers and buffalo hunters chawing each others' ears off in fights, toted drunks to jail. Then what happens?"

"You tell me," suggested the Kid, having returned at midnight from spreading the word about Brownton's welcome to various trail drives.

"I'll tell you for sure!" Waco yelled. "That mean boss we got hauls me out of bed near on at day-break, when I figured that being a peace officer I could sleep town hours, and has me help get all those jaspers we'd stowed away in the pokey on their feet."

"They'd got to clean out the cells afore going afore the judge. Or would you want to be the boy who does it?"

"Like ole Pickle-barrel says, they mussed 'em up, leave them do the cleaning," Waco answered, referring to the swamper from the Fair Lady Saloon who had been hired by Dusty to act as jailer.

"Then what's gnawing at your craw, boy?" grinned the Kid, knowing just how little the youngster's complaints meant.

"So we has them get everything good and clean. Comes time for them to go to court and I'm figuring on riding a chair at the back while the judge fines 'em— So then what does Dusty say?"

"I'd never guess."

"He says, 'You and Lon go take a walk around town!' That's what he says. 'Take a *walk*,' he says. And me with a damned great slab of crowbait just eating up hay and corn like it's going out of fashion, then getting all feisty through not being rid. Dammit, I walked all around this town last night."

"It looks better in daylight," commented the Kid.

"Nothing looks better when you're walking!" Waco objected.

Despite his complaints and protests, the youngster knew why Dusty had given the order. The time might come when their lives would depend on knowing what lay behind the buildings of the main street, or how to reach a particular part of town by an inconspicuous route. Which gave a serious purpose to the stroll without lessening his objections to performing that most distasteful business, walking.

So far only a portion of the buildings were occupied, the original settlers having combined their resources to erect properties for sale to people attracted by their town's prosperity. Dusty had sent out his two deputies to learn which places were still empty and note the location of tempting prospects for robbery.

"There's one place we shouldn't need to worry about," the Kid remarked, nodding to a good-sized house standing in a large square of land surrounded by a picket fence.

"That's for sure," Waco agreed "They're starting to fix it up."

"They never waste any time," the Kid replied.

Several women wearing nuns' clothing worked around the property, digging the ground or tidying up the outside of the building. Waco strolled over to where a small novice was applying white paint to the picket fence.

"Howdy, ma'am," he greeted. "You-all settling down all right?"

Although the girl turned a pert face towards him, she did not

53

offer to reply. A shadow fell across the fence and Waco found that another member of the convent had come over. The newcomer equalled big Sarah in size and heft, had a face with strength of will and humour in its lines and wore a slightly different style of habit to the novice.

"We're under a vow of silence here, young man," the big woman told him in a broad Irish brogue. "So Sister Teresa's not allowed to answer you."

"Thanks for telling me, ma'am."

"But how come the vow doesn't apply to me?" smiled the woman. "That's what you're wondering, isn't it?

"Yes'm," admitted Waco with a grin.

"Somebody has to deal with people from the outside, and it falls on the senior sister until the mother superior arrives. You're one of the town marshal's deputies, are you?"

"Sure, ma'am."

"Tell your marshal that if he needs any help I can give to come and ask."

"I'll do that, ma'am," Waco promised and rejoined the Kid. "What do you reckon to that, Lon. These gals aren't allowed to talk."

"I've heard tell of it afore, down in Mexican convents," the Kid replied. "Come on, they're one bunch who won't concern us."

After touring the convent's side of the town, Waco and the Kid swung over to the other section beyond the railroad tracks. There they saw what they regarded as an ideal site for a brothel; not knowing that Freddie, realising the need would arise for such an establishment, had planned the placing of the building with that use in mind when helping to lay out the town.

Before going back to the office, the deputies called in at the livery barn to check on their horses. Another large corral next to the barn's sizeable compound held the stock of the town's freight company. Halting to look over the harness horses, they leaned against the corral fence.

An old timer carrying a dinner-pail in one hand and coffeepot in the other came through the alley between the barn and the freight outfit's warehouse. Ambling up to the deputies, he directed a spurt of tobacco juice into the water of the horse-trough halfway between the corral and the building.

"Danged uppy shiny-butts," he said.

"Who, us?" asked the Kid.

"Naw! Them two milk-faced dudes up to the office there. Can't leave all their fool paper-work to go out and eat, so I have to tote it to them. Which same I wouldn't mind if the office was on the ground, but I have to go up them steps to hand it over."

Following the direction of the oldster's indignant glare, the Kid and Waco looked to where a flight of stairs led to a first floor outer door.

"Sure is a sinful sin, brother," the Kid declared.

"You never said a righter word," the old man agreed and walked slowly away. Then he halted and looked back. "That safe they've got up there's mighty strong. You boys don't need to stand guard on it."

"That went right by me," the Kid replied.

"Didn't you know? They've got a big old Chubb safe up there to hold the company's wealth."

"We didn't know," admitted Waco.

"I wouldn't've mentioned it, only you pair being lawmen it's all right."

"Let's hope nobody else mentions it," the Kid said as the old man continued his interrupted delivery. "I reckon Dusty'll want us to keep an eye on the back here, safe or no safe."

On hearing about the safe, Dusty confirmed the Kid's guess by telling them to make periodic checks on the rear of the freight outfit. Not that they needed to start right off, first they could relax at the office and clean the weapons—Winchester rifles, shotguns and a long-ranged Sharps buffalo gun—supplied for their use.

The rest of the day went by without serious incident. Hearing from the first arrivals of the fair manner in which the town was run, other trail crews held down their boisterous behaviour to reasonable levels. As for the railroad workers, the story of how the law had handled O'Sullivan's gandy-gang lost nothing in the telling. No other construction crew felt like chancing such leniency should they cut up extra rough.

During the day three separate visits were made by citizens of Brownton, all with the intention of studying the situation. Their findings caused some alarm and despondency, also a desire by a number of citizens to migrate to Mulrooney's richer pastures.

At noon on the third day Waco accompanied Dusty and the other deputies to meet the east-bound train on its arrival from

Brownton. There the youngster saw how Dusty dissuaded various unwanted elements from taking up even temporary residence after their desertion of what they regarded as the other town's sinking ship. After some very plain talk from Freddie Woods, who came along to give civic approval of Dusty's actions, a madam called Lily Gouch received permission to buy the property selected as a brothel. Other business people also gained access, but a number of petty crooks, card-sharks and confidence tricksters continued with the train when it pulled out. During the weeding-out process, Waco saw Dusty apply an iron fist without a velvet glove and learned from the sight.

One man who arrived from Brownton not only received admittance but, despite being a professional gambler, was made welcome. Having known Frank Derringer as an honest player and friend, Dusty offered to take him on as a deputy marshal. Among Mulrooney's civic ordnances, one gave the marshal's office the right to examine any gambling device and to order its destruction should it prove dishonest. While a straight man himself, Derringer knew how to detect crooked moves or equipment as a means of self-defence. His agreement to Dusty's suggestion not only put a valuable weapon in the hands of the law, but paved the way for Waco to gain a very thorough knowledge of all aspects of gambling.

Although he had an arrangement to take Babsy on a buggy ride that evening, the first opportunity to present itself since becoming a deputy, Waco agreed to accompany Dusty and Derringer to an inspection of the gambling devices at the Fair Lady and Wooden Spoon—the only other saloon yet open. The tall, slim gambler fixed his badge to the lapel of his black cutaway jacket. He wore a white broadcloth shirt, string tie, striped trousers and town boots, while an ivory-handled Army Colt hung in a tied-down holster on his right leg. Unless Waco missed his guess, the gun had seen some use.

"Where's Lon?" Derringer asked as they left the office.

"Down to the store teaching the owner how to shoot," Waco replied.

"Lon giving shooting lessons?"

"Why sure. He allowed it to be his civic duty to help a tax-paying citizen learn how to defend hisself—and that Sarah Birnbaum's a right pretty lil gal."

Which explained the Kid's eagerness to instruct Storekeeper

Birnbaum in the art of handling a gun.

A trio of men rode by Dusty's party and swung their leg-weary mounts in the direction of the Wooden Spoon Saloon. Although Waco studied them as they passed, he attached little importance to their arrival. Unshaven, clad in range clothes that showed hard wear and each with a low-hanging gun at his side, to Waco they looked just like the majority of trail hands who came north with the herds. Nor did he read any significance in the way they tossed their reins over the hitching rail on dismounting, instead of fastening them to it. Most of Clay Allison's crew did the same, in case a very hurried departure should be necessary.

However the youngster noticed one thing of interest. In the days when he rode for Clay Allison, the sight of another man's horse about to throw a shoe would not have passed without comment. As a deputy marshal he felt that he ought to warn the man in case the deficiency had not been detected.

"Hey, mister," he called, moving slightly ahead of his companions. "Hold it a min—."

At the first word the three men turned. They had already left the horses and were about to step on to the sidewalk. Surprise flashed on to the faces of the two outside men at discovering that the two cowhands and professional gambler they had passed wore law badges and were coming towards them. Although at first the centre man showed no concern, his companions clearly had no desire to make the acquaintance of peace officers. Both immediately started reaching for their guns and he followed their lead.

Two things kept Waco alive that day; Dusty's knowledge of a lawman's most basic rule and the small Texan's ambidextrous prowess.

"Look out, boy!" he yelled, thrusting Waco aside with his right hand while the left flickered across to the butt of the off-side Colt.

For all that Waco came close to death.

Although last of the trio to start moving, the centre man beat the other two to the shot. Flame ripped from the barrel of his Colt and the bullet missed the staggering youngster by inches. If Dusty had failed to recognise the danger, or had moved less rapidly, the lead would have torn into Waco's body. Before the man could change his aim or fire again, Dusty's Colt barked and

57

he shot to kill. There was no other way. Already the man had shown considerable ability at throwing lead and proved he had reason to fear the approach of law enforcement officers. Taking chances with such a man paid off only in grieving kin-folks and tombstones. So Dusty sent a .44 calibre conical bullet into the man's head and ended his menace instantly.

While the centre man might be good, his companions came nowhere near his standard. Counting himself no better than fair, Derringer still outclassed them and he stood third on the law's side.

Off balance and staggering, Waco partially repaid his error by beating Derringer and the remaining two men into action. Bringing out his right hand Colt, he cut loose and nailed the man at the left through the shoulder. As his victim spun around, Waco did no more than thumb-cock the Colt and ignored the fact that the other still held a gun.

Then the youngster learned his second lesson in a few seconds, although it had been one Dusty had failed to mention on the first evening outside the warehouse. Swinging his Colt, Dusty sent a shot into the wounded man as he hung against the hitchingrail and tried to lift his gun. Dusty acted fast, without a moment's concern for the other's condition and was fully prepared to continue shooting if the situation warranted it. However the impact of the second bullet made him open his fingers and the revolver fell to the ground. For a moment the man hung on the rail, then slid downwards. Startled by the shots, the three horses bolted.

An instant after Waco fired, Derringer brought up his own Colt. Having time to spare, even though it amounted to no more than a split second, he angled his shot to injure rather than kill. Letting out a screech as lead burned into his shoulder, the third man jerked backwards. His feet struck the sidewalk and he sat down on it. Hurt or not, he showed a remarkably quick grasp of the situation and threw his gun aside. Nor did he act a moment too soon, for Derringer knew the rule of a peace officer which Waco had yet to learn.

"Don't shoot!" the man yelled, clutching at his right shoulder with the left hand. "Don't shoot. I'm done."

"Move in on them and watch them good," Dusty ordered and, as they advanced, went on, "Boy, never as long as you're wearing a lawman's badge call out to a man you don't know, or go towards him after you've stopped him, without being ready to draw your guns."

"I only—," Waco began.

"I know what you aimed to do and don't blame you for doing it. But innocent as Lon looks, or guilty-looking as hell, don't make the mistake of not being ready to draw. And if you have to throw down on a man, keep shooting at him as long as he holds his gun no matter whether he's standing or lying."

Cold-blooded it might seem, but the advice proved valuable to Waco in later years. The youngster had killed four men already, but each time in a plain shoot-out and never when working as a peace officer. So, despite Dusty's assumption, he did not know the rule every successful western lawman followed.

A crowd quickly gathered, bursting out of the Wooden Spoon or dashing along the street. Leaping from the sidewalk, some cowhands caught the fleeing horses and led them back towards the saloon. Ignoring the questions fired his way, Dusty told Waco and Derringer to gather up the trio's weapons. While that elementary precaution was being taken, he studied the trio. The first man lay dead, a hole between his eyes mute testimony to Dusty's deadly skill. Although hit twice, the second time in the chest, the next man might pull through if given medical attention soon enough. Due to Derringer's consideration, the third member of the party had no more than a minor wound. Though he would not be able to handle a gun for a spell, he would live. Something more than the wound seemed to be bothering the third man and he looked at Dusty.

"How'd you know?" he whined and released his shoulder to point at the dead man. "Stayley there reckoned word couldn't've got here."

While not sure what the man meant, Dusty decided it might be worthwhile trying a bluff to learn.

"It arrived."

"Th—The money's in Stayley's saddle pouches. All of it. Just like when we took it out of the Wells Fargo box."

"Where was that?" Dusty asked.

"Six miles south of Newt—," the man began, then chopped off his words as he realised that Dusty ought to know the answer.

"A Wells Fargo coach, huh?" Dusty said thoughtfully.

"I've got nothing to say," the man replied.

Guessing that he would learn no more at that moment, Dusty

let the matter lapse. If it came to a point, he did not want the matter aired in public.

One did not need to be a genius to guess what had happened. After robbing a Wells Fargo stagecoach close to the town of Newton, the trio had come to Mulrooney. From the condition of their horses, they had made a fast ride. Probably their intention had been to mingle with the other visitors until after the hunt for them died down. If they had kept their heads when Waco called to them, the plan would have stood a better than fair chance of working. No word of any hold-up had reached Mulrooney and, despite noticing the way in which they had left their horses, Dusty had no cause to suspect them of breaking the law.

7

Maybe you Didn't ask Him Right

Coming up at a run, the Ysabel Kid saw there would be no need for his intervention. Before he could return to continue sampling Sarah Birnbaum's cooking, he found himself actively involved. Dusty told him to see to the removal of the body, guard the doctor while the two wounded men received attention and to make sure that the trio's horses went into the civic pound for disposal.

"Would that be all, Cap'n Fog, sir?" he asked, seeing chances of further culinary pleasures disappear.

"It'll do for starters," Dusty replied. "Waco, fetch their saddlepouches with you while we go over the Wooden Spoon's games. Then we'll see what that jasper was talking about."

While Dusty felt certain there would be no cause for complaint, he insisted that the examination of the saloon's gambling equipment be carried out. Later, when other places opened, he wanted proof that he had dealt in the same manner with everybody. He wanted to learn more about the stage hold-up, but could not make a start until after the men's wounds had been treated. So he might just as well fill in the time usefully. However, to prevent accusations at a later date, he took the precaution of fastening and sealing the saddle pouches in the presence of the saloon's owner—a member of the town council—and did not trouble to look into them before doing so.

After the check, which proved negative but gave Waco a chance of learning something of crooked gambling, Dusty left the saloon ready to investigate the activities of the trio before they came to Mulrooney. However Mark brought news that sent them to look in on a private card game at the hotel. The game proved dishonest and the ensuing formalities further delayed Dusty's plans. In addition the Kid had not yet returned from the doctor's office with either of the wounded men. So Dusty locked the saddle pouches in the safe and sent the old jailer to telegraph the authorities at Newton, requesting information about the hold-up.

Although it was Waco's night off watch, and ignoring the fact that he had a date to take Babsy for a buggyride, he remained at the office to watch Derringer demonstrate the operation of various crooked gambling devices found at the hotel. So engrossed did the youngster become that he arrived late at the rendezvous, sparking off a quarrel with the pert little blonde that later proved to have most beneficial results.

It seemed that the fates conspired to prevent Dusty satisfying his curiosity. The doctor, new from the East, young and very keen to aid suffering humanity, put both wounded men under such heavy opiates that even the lighter injured of the pair would not be able to speak before morning. Realising that the doctor had acted as he thought for the best, Dusty withheld the blistering comments which rose at the news. All he could do was telegraph Sheriff Bracker at the county seat and ask for information on a man called Stayley.

As things turned out, the doctor's actions did not delay the investigation. A Texas rancher noted for his rivalry with Colonel Goodnight arrived with his herd and paid off his trail drive crew. Only unceasing vigilance by Dusty and all the available deputies prevented trouble breaking out between the two groups of celebrating cowhands. So there would have been no chance of interviewing the men, even if either could have talked.

Next morning, leaving Derringer and the tall, lean, leather-tough old jailer known as Pickle-Barrel to deal with the ordinary overnight prisoners, Dusty prepared to interrogate the man wounded by the gambler-deputy. Brought from the doctor's

61

house while still unconscious, the man had been held in one of the three single-bunk cells reserved for dangerous prisoners. When the Kid fetched him into the office and seated him before Dusty's desk, he looked pale but in reasonably good condition apart from his wounded shoulder.

Studying the lean face, with its hooked nose, rat-trap mouth and weak chin, Dusty could not place it with any outlaw of his acquaintance. Not that he felt too surprised at the failure. While he possessed a fair knowledge of Texas law-breakers, he had not previously found the need to familiarise himself with the Kansas crop. Nor did the office possess anything that might help make the identification. In a well-established town, a new marshal might expect to find a collection of wanted posters gathered by his predecessors. Mulrooney had not been built long enough to accumulate such aids.

"How's the shoulder?" Dusty asked.

"It hurts like hell. Are you turning me loose?"

"Nope."

"Why're you holding me?"

"Don't you know?" asked Mark, standing at the man's right side while the Kid hovered at his left.

"What's your name?" demanded Dusty before the man could reply, sitting on the edge of the desk in front of him.

"Tom Smith."

"I met one of your kinfolks," drawled the Kid. "Only you don't feature him."

"Not enough to be real close kin," agreed Dusty. "Would Smith just be your summer name?"

"Summer and winter both," the man replied, gaining confidence as he took in the youthful appearance of the trio. "What'd you fellers start shooting at us for yesterday?"

"To stop you throwing down on *us*," Dusty replied. "Why'd you do it?"

"Maybe he figured you'd recognised him from his picture on a wanted dodger, Dusty," Mark suggested.

"You ain't seed no picture of me on a dodger," Smith stated, with such confidence that the Texans believed him.

"Not even for that stage hold-up six miles south of Newton?" Dusty asked.

"How'd you mean, marshal? I don't know about no hold-up any place."

"Did Stayley?"

"I only met him on the trail into town. When you three fellers jumped us, I figured you must be some fellers looking for evens with him."

"Then why'd you draw?" Mark said.

"Wouldn't you? Hell, those three fellers'd seen me ride in with Stayley. They'd not wait to ask who I was afore shooting."

Clearly the delay had given Smith a chance to think up excuses for his actions. Dusty had feared that it might, but had hoped the opiates would keep the man unconscious long enough to prevent him examining his position. However Dusty felt that he ought to be able to learn enough by careful manipulation of the man.

"Let's take a look at those saddle-pouches, Mark," the small Texan ordered. "Lon, go ask Dongelon to come over and check the seals before we break them."

After the owner of the Wooden Spoon arrived and made sure that the seals placed on in his presence still remained intact, Dusty opened the first of the pouches. A low curse broke from Smith and he started to rise as Dusty tipped the contents on to the desk. Nor did the man alone show surprise, for nothing more important than a heap of newspapers slid into view. Only for a moment did the shock crease Smith's face, then a calculating glint replaced it and he sank back into the chair.

"Where is it?" Dusty demanded, after the other pouches and the trio's bed-rolls had failed to yield anything incriminating.

"Where's what?" Smith countered innocently.

"You expected the money to be in there," Dusty said.

"Me? I didn't expect a thing."

"Then why did you tell us that Stayley had it in his saddle pouch?"

"I must've been out of my head with pain. Getting shot makes me that way."

"Do you get shot often?" Mark wanted to know.

"Naw! Why should I?"

"Now me," drawled the Kid. "I allus shoot owlhoots."

"I ain't no owlhoot!" Smith yelled and a foxy grin creased his face. "Say, if there was money in Stayley's pouches, maybe you bunch took it."

"Now you don't mean that like it sounds, do you?" asked the Kid, his bowie knife sliding from leather.

"I was only joking," gulped Smith, turning his eyes from a face that no longer looked young to an eleven-and-a-half inch long, two-and-a-half inch deep, razor-edged blade.

"Don't joke with us!" Dusty barked. "We don't joke with thieves."

"Could be he's innocent, Dusty," Mark suggested.

"I've been telling you that I am!" Smith wailed.

"I believe you, like I believe in Santa Klaus and fairies," stated the Kid.

"You'll let me go then?"

"Well no, I can't say that I will," Dusty replied. "See, you nearly shot a deputy out there. So I'm holding you for attempted murder."

"I never got off a shot!" Smith squealed.

"Can you prove it?" drawled the small Texan.

Smith gulped down something that appeared to be blocking his throat as he realised that he could not. Only his companions, neither of whom could testify, and the peace officers knew exactly what happened outside the Wooden Spoon. If the marshal and his deputies claimed that Smith had fired at the young one, a jury of town folk would believe it.

"If you aim to railroad me, I'm in no shape to stop you," Smith said.

"I'm right pleased you know it," Dusty replied. "Put him back in his cell."

Watching the man led away, Dusty felt puzzled. The discovery that the pouches held no money had come as a surprise to Smith. Yet, after one brief show of emotion, he had settled down and seemed almost content with his position.

"What do you make of that, Dusty?" Mark inquired, returning from locking Smith in the cell.

"Something stinks about it. He almost looked happy when he saw the money'd gone. Why in hell doesn't Wells Fargo in Newton answer our telegraph message?"

If the men in question had heard Dusty's words, they could not have answered any more promptly. The office door opened and a youngster entered carrying an envelope.

"This message just come in, Cap'n," he said. "The agent told me to get it over here as fast as I could."

Taking the message form, Dusty learned why Newton had delayed in answering his request for information. A stagecoach carrying ten thousand dollars had left Newton heading south. Attempts to contact the way station at which it would halt for the night had failed due to the telegraph wire being down. Alarmed by the message Dusty sent, a posse rode out along the stage trail. They found the telegraph wires had been cut and, re-establishing contact with the way station, learned the coach had not arrived. By that time a careful search could not be made, but men went along the trail. Pure luck led them to where the coach had been driven into a dry wash, its dead driver and guard being inside and the horses taken away. Finally the Newton agent requested that Dusty held Smith until their special investigators could come to Mulrooney and interrogate him.

"And that's just what we'll do," Dusty told Mark.

At which Waco made a belated appearance and told the others that one of the vacant saloons was being taken over by its new owner.

"We'd best go look them over," Dusty said. "Hey, Pickles!"

"Yo!" replied the jailer entering the office.

"Be real careful with that jasper in the solo cell. He's likely mixed up in a stage robbery and double killing."

"I'll watch him with both eyes," Pickle-Barrel promised.

Although he had been employed in the menial task of swamper at the Fair Lady, the old timer had proved to Dusty's satisfaction that he possessed the required attributes for a jailer. Actually Pickle-Barrel had only taken work as swamper until his present position became available. He had scouted for the Army until rheumatism slowed him down to a point where further work of that nature would be suicidal. However he could still take care of himself in a tight corner and knew all the safety precautions to take when dealing with dangerous prisoners.

After introducing himself to the newly arrived saloonkeeper, a big, buxom woman called Buffalo Kate Gilgore—whom he had last seen operating a place in Brownton—Dusty watched her meeting with Freddie Woods and sensed rivalry in the air. However, he guessed Kate could be relied upon to keep a straight place and did not foresee the extra work the rivalry between the two women would give him.

A meeting with the various trail bosses and town's leading citizens followed, to arrange for means of entertaining the cowhands on Sunday without opening the saloons. Between them Dusty and Freddie had already formed a plan. While the term 'rodeo' was not yet in use, they used many of the contests such affairs would later offer as a means of letting the cowhands show various skills and find work to occupy otherwise idle and mischievous hands.

On his return to the office, Dusty found a big, bluff-looking man waiting. Dressed in a town suit and boots, although the tie had been removed and a Stetson hung on the peg by the door, the newcomer gave the impression of spending much time out of doors. A Remington Army revolver rode a crossdraw holster at his left hip and a county sheriff's badge glinted from his vest.

"Cap'n Fog?" the man asked, a faint hint of surprise in his voice. "I'm Tom Bracker."

"Howdy, sheriff," Dusty replied, shaking hands. "Hope I haven't kept you waiting for too long."

"Pickles's been showing me over the place. It's a right good lay-out. Whoever planned it knew what they was at."

"That was Mayor Woods."

"It figures. That's one smart lady—and a real looker too."

"They don't come prettier, or smarter," Dusty agreed.

"How's the town settling in?" Bracker inquired, taking the seat Dusty offered him.

"Fair enough. Not many places open yet, but Kate Gilgore came down from Brownton. Likely there'll be more."

"Knew Kate back in Hays. She runs a straight place. That's more than you can say for the rest of the Brownton bunch. Say, I looked in on that Smith jasper. Can't say as I can place him."

"Does the name Stayley mean anything to you?" Dusty asked.

"Don't it to you?" Bracker inquired.

"Nope."

"If it's who I reckon, Joe Stayley, you've picked up a three thousand dollars bounty—and a peck of trouble."

"Is he wanted that bad?"

"He is up here and out to Montana. He's Tricky Dick Cansole's right bower."

"Tricky Dick?" Dusty repeated. "I'm sorry, sheriff—."

"Make it 'Tom'."

"Running trail herds in didn't give me any call to know your Kansas owlhoots, Tom."

"I thought Tricky Dick was better known than that," Bracker mused. "Likely it's only a matter of time afore he is. He's real smart, works with a small, hand-picked bunch and's pulled off some nifties."

"That Smith *hombre* doesn't strike me as top-grade stock," Dusty commented.

"Or me," the sheriff admitted. "You say they came straight over here from a hold-up. Did they have any money along?"

"The saddle-pouches where it was supposed to be came up empty when we opened them."

Apparently the news did not surprise Bracker, for he merely nodded. "That's Tricky Dick's way all right. Every time his bunch pull a robbery, the fellers who do it stash away the loot someplace safe and ride hard. Then if they get caught, they've nothing to prove they did it. Thing I don't get is why Stayley grabbed for his gun when your deputy shouted to him—Sure, Pickles and Frank Derringer told me how it happened."

Thinking back to the incident, Dusty found various facts leaping to mind. "The other two made the opening moves," he said. "Once they'd started, what else could Stayley do but back them?"

"Not much," admitted the sheriff. "Only why did the others make the play?"

"I've got a feeling that at least Smith didn't know the money'd gone. If he didn't, he wouldn't want a lawman searching them as the money'd give them away."

"You mean that Tricky Dick aimed to double-cross them?"

"If nothing worse."

"It could be," Bracker said thoughtfully. "Or he hadn't used them before and didn't want them knowing too much about how he worked until he knew them a whole heap better."

"I don't know enough about this Tricky Dick to start guessing which one's right," Dusty said. "Say, you'll have time to identify Stayley if we go now. They haven't buried him yet."

"Let's go take a look," Bracker offered. "I've only seen his face on wanted dodgers, but I've got one with a good description of him along."

Going to the undertaker's parlour, the sheriff and Dusty arrived only just in time to view the last remains before the coffin lid was screwed into place. To give him his due, the undertaker had done a good job and the lawman studied the ashy-pallid face.

"It's Stayley," Bracker stated, comparing the features with the wanted poster he held. "Whoever made this drawing's good.

That's three thousand dollars your office's picked up."

"We made an arrangement with Freddie Woods," Dusty answered. "All bounties go into the civic funds."

Bracker nodded approvingly. "I've never been much on taking them myself. Say, about that money. Have you talked to Smith about it?"

"Nope. Trouble being by the time we got around to it, he'd thought up some slick excuses for what happened.'

"How come?"

"One thing and another kept coming up. You know how it is in a trail-end town like this. Half or more of the time you're wishing you'd a regiment of deputies on hand. Like I said, by the time we got around to him, He'd thought up the answers."

"Maybe you didn't ask him right," growled the sheriff.

"With a feller from the *Kansas City Intelligencer* in town?" Dusty asked mildly. "That'd be buying trouble."

A point which Sheriff Bracker understood all too well. Being a 'liberal' newspaper, the *Intelligencer* looked after the underdog's interests. A favourite target for the paper was any peace officer who rough-handled criminals; though the liberal-intellectuals who ran it never gave space to the brutal treatment honest Texas cowhands received from the Earps or others of their kind. Backed by a number of influential men at the state capital, possibly so that they would not become targets for its attacks, the *Intelligencer* could easily blast the career of any peace officer it crossed. Dusty's prominence on the Southern side during the Civil War, along with the fact that most of his deputies hailed from Texas, made him a likely target for *Intelligencer* investigation. In which case Bracker did not wish to become involved in the process of asking Smith 'right'.

Although no liberal-intellectual, Dusty did not approve of the beatings or torture many peace officers of the day used to extract information from captured outlaws. Not that he regarded criminals as misunderstood victims of circumstances who needed only understanding and kindness to turn them into useful citizens. While that might be true in a few cases, most men took to crime in their ways. However he realised that rough-handling a prisoner made the victim look sympathetic to the public and only rarely produced any useful results.

Having seen Belle Boyd, the legendary Rebel Spy, interrogate

68

a prisoner and having discussed the subject with her,* Dusty knew of far more subtle ways than the crude methods most peace officers employed to gain information.

"We'd best leave him to the Wells Fargo fellers," Bracker remarked as they walked back to the office. "Anyways, I don't reckon he's important."

"He could be real important to Tricky Dick," Dusty replied.

"How come?"

"It's just a hunch, but I think Smith's counting on his boss to get him out of jail."

"Why?" Bracker demanded.

"Because Smith figures he's the only one with any idea where the money from the hold-up might be. That's why he's sitting quiet instead of telling us all he can to get even with Tricky Dick for double-crossing him."

Before Dusty could go further into his idea, a man dashed up to say a fight had broken out in the Wooden Spoon. So the two lawmen headed in that direction and temporarily forgot the possibility that Smith was guessing correctly.

8

Nobody's Taking my Guns

"Damn and blast all women!" Waco growled bitterly, slipping a combustible cartridge into the chamber of the Remington canegun taken from the whiskey pedlar. "If it wasn't for them, I could be out watching the fun instead of sitting my butt-end down here, cleaning guns."

"Women're the cause of all the trouble in the world," Dusty told him, entering the office.

After breaking up the fight at the Wooden Spoon, Dusty and Sheriff Bracker grabbed a meal and prepared for more work. If the previous nights had been rowdy, Saturday out-did them all. Every member of the marshal's office staff and Bracker found

*Dusty's meetings with Belle Boyd are in: THE REBEL SPY and THE COLT & THE SABRE.

plenty to do. Any ideas the sheriff might have brought with him about needing to teach the Texans practical law enforcement ended rapidly. In fact he soon saw that he was working with masters of his trade. Another thing to strike him was the air of friendly enjoyment shown by visitors and residents alike. Due to the early spadework put in by Dusty and the deputies, Mulrooney already bore a reputation as a fair, tolerant place, yet capable of halting anybody or outfit that went too far.

Finding none of the veiled hostility and open money-grabbing of other trail-end towns, the cowhands reciprocated by keeping their fun within bounds. Hard workers, they played just as energetically. If a rope, horse or gun formed a frequent aid to their fun, it was because in many cases the cowhand owned nothing else. With money in their pockets, gained by gruelling hours of hardship on the way north, they sought only to enjoy themselves. The more they had to pay for damage caused, the better time they felt they had had. If, as often happened, the cowhand went broke, he could ride south and find food offered in exchange for information by the trail crews on their way to the rail head.

Dusty knew all that and explained it to the Mulrooney citizens. In their turn, they showed tolerance and accepted a few broken windows or disturbed sleep as the price for making a good living out of the trail herds.

Of course there were incidents which wound up by one or more of the revellers being hauled off to jail, but Bracker saw no objections raised to that even by the arrested parties' friends.

Although Mark had volunteered to keep the office on Sunday, while the rest of the Texans, Big Sarah and Pickle-Barrel went out to keep the peace among the folks attending the various sporting events, things did not work out as planned for Waco. A pretty, vivacious little red-head from Buffalo Kate's saloon became attracted to the young deputy, which almost sparked off a hand-scalping brawl with Babsy. In the interests of peace Dusty sent Waco back to the office and kept the two girls well clear of each other.

Figuring that the Wells Fargo special agents would come in on the afternoon train, Dusty left the sporting events in good time to meet them at the office. He found Waco in a dark humour, somewhat disgruntled with women in general and Babsy in particular. While waiting for his companions to return, the youngster had passed his time by cleaning the office's assault armament.

While the cane-gun did not come into that category, it stood on the rack with the rifles and shotguns. Dusty intended to take it south with him as a present for his uncle. The time might come when Ole Devil, confined to a wheel-chair since failing to ride the paint Dusty now used as a personal mount,* might find a need for such a device. So, after completing the others, Waco attended to it.

"Did anything else happen down there?" the youngster asked, fitting a percussion cap on to the nipple.

"I managed to keep them apart, if that's what you mean," Dusty grinned. "Damned if you're not worse than ole Mark, way you get the gals fussing over you."

"All I wanted was a peaceable afternoon," Waco objected, reversing the cane and fixing the open screw-in ferrule to the mouth of the barrel.

"Which's what you've had," Dusty pointed out, sitting behind the desk.

Footsteps sounded on the sidewalk and two men walked by the office window, then halted at the door. Waco laid the cane on the desk top and perched his rump on the edge, then looked as the door opened. While the men who entered wore town suits and derby hats, they had weather-beaten faces and sported range-fashion gun-belts with Army Colts in tied-down holsters. Nor did Dusty find the contrast incongruous. A Wells Fargo special investigator might work out of one of the big city offices, but he spent a good proportion of his life in the open and exposed to the elements.

"Howdy, marshal," greeted the taller man, advancing to the desk. "I'm Haver and this's Tarrick. We're from Wells Fargo."

"I've been expecting you," Dusty answered, rising to shake hands. Then he sat down again, expecting the men to ask for information.

"We've come for that feller you took prisoner," Tarrick told him. "So if you'll turn him over to us, we'll tend to his needs."

"Suppose you gents show me something to identify yourselves first?" Dusty countered.

Anticipating the request, Haver had already reached into his jacket and produced a wallet. He slid it across the desk and it fell to the floor on Dusty's side. Even as Dusty bent over to pick it up, certain facts sprang to mind. He recalled how the two men

*Told in THE FASTEST GUN IN TEXAS.

had darted glances around them on entering, almost as if they feared a trap might be laid for them. More significant, for men in their position learned the value of remaining alert, neither had made any mention of the money. It almost seemed that Tarrick knew such a question would be a waste of time.

Even as the thought struck home and Dusty started to straighten, he found it came too late. Haver's right arm bent, elbow pressing against his side. Instantly a Remington Double Derringer shot into his palm, propelled there by a device like the spring card hold-out machines used by crooked gamblers. Strapped around the wrist and hidden by shirt or jacket sleeve, the hold-out machine usually carried selected cards or a pre-arranged deck to be brought into play at a favourable stage of the game. It also could be made to hold a small hide-out gun, a fact Dusty knew but had overlooked until too late.

"Come up slow and easy, marshal," Haver ordered. "And you sit still, or he gets it, young feller."

While Waco might have only recently learned one important rule concerning firearms, he needed no telling when to sit tight. Bucking the odds at that moment would have been fatal, if not for himself, to Dusty. So he remained seated on the edge of the desk and kept his hands motionless. Any hope of making a move lessened as Tarrick's revolver slid from leather and lined on the youngster.

"What now?" Dusty asked, obeying the order by coming erect at a leisurely pace.

"Like Tarrick said, we'll take your prisoner—," Haver replied.

"Which of you's Tricky Dick?"

"Neither of us, short-stuff," grinned Tarrick. "And we ain't Wells Fargo men, comes to that."

"I'd figure so much for myself," Dusty admitted.

"No sir. We left 'em with bust heads in the men's room at a whistle stop down the tr—."

"Shut it, Walt!" growled Haver. "And you pair shed your guns."

"Nobody's taking my guns," Dusty answered quietly.

"We are," Tarrick told him. "Off your body if you make us."

"Go right to it," Dusty replied, using the same even tone. Only you hit me any place other than between my two eyes and I'll take at least one of you with me before I go."

"The shots'll bring folks running," Waco went on.

"That's one thing we don't need to worry on," Haver answered. "Near on everybody's out back of town. The railroad depot crew could hardly wait to see the train off and get out there."

"Time anybody gets back, you'll both be wolf-bait," Tarrick put in.

"You're still not taking my guns," Dusty warned.

For all the calm manner in which he spoke, Dusty did not make the mistake of underestimating the danger. Seated behind the desk with his knees in the roomy leg-hole, he could not hope to draw his guns quickly enough to save himself. Yet he had no intention of surrendering them to the two men. Doing so would in no way alter their plans if they meant to kill him.

The matter went deeper than that. While law enforcement in the West might tend to be disorganised, already a tradition had grown among the better class of peace officers that a lawman must never surrender his gun. Trained in that belief, Dusty intended to force the issue and hope for a break. Not that getting one was likely when dealing with such men. A Remington Double Derringer lacked accuracy, but across the width of the desk could plant its fat .41 calibre bullet into a man-sized target easily enough.

"Hell, Dusty!" Waco put in. "There's no sense in getting killed to hold that Smith jasper. I say hand him over."

"The kid's showing sense, marshal," Haver commented. "Let the gunbelt drop, boy, then go and do it."

"Sure," the youngster answered, still sitting on the desk but unbuckling his belt. He nodded to the cane-gun and went on, "I near on got my leg bust in a fight at the Fair Lady last night and can't stand on it too good. I'm riding that walking-cane to get around. Which's why I'm here 'stead of out watching the fun."

"Don't try anything smart like sliding that belt to your pard," Haver warned, darting a glance at the cane and seeing nothing suspicious.

"Not me!' Waco promised and lowered the belt to the floor at the side of the desk.

"Happen you've got any ideas about whomping me on my pumpkin head with that cane, forget 'em," Tarrick continued.

"Mister," the youngster replied, lowering himself carefully from the desk like a man with an injured leg and casually gripping the cane, "that's the last thing I plan to do."

With that he lifted the cane from the desk, lining it by instinct

73

like hip-shooting a Colt, and pressed the stud trigger.

At first Dusty had been taken in by Waco's acting, so well did the youngster play the part. Not until the mention of the fictitious injury did the small Texan guess what his companion had in mind. Studying the two men, Dusty saw no hint that they failed to accept Waco's behaviour as genuine.

Maybe Haver or Tarrick would have been more suspicious if Waco was older, a professional gambler instead of an obvious cowhand, or the normal type of trail-end town lawman. The Remington-Thomas cane-gun helped with the deception by virtue of its design and special features. Although its tip pointed towards the men and could be easily seen, no hint of its deadly nature showed. Most such items on the market bore a wooden tampion to act as a ferrule and could only be fired after its removal. Not so the Remington-Thomas. That carried a screw-on hollow metal ferrule, the barrel hole being closed by a piece of cork carefully fitted for size and held by friction. While the makers recommended removing the ferrule, the gun could be fired safely with it still in position. One of the things Waco had done while using the gun for target practice was to re-fit the cork plug shot out by Hockley and paint it the same colour as the ferrule. Small wonder the two men failed to recognise the danger until too late.

Propelled by gasses caused from igniting the combustible cartridge's powder charge, the bullet passed along the gun's barrel, carried out the cork plug and ranged up to catch Tarrick in the mouth. Shock twisted the man's face and he staggered backwards. While his Colt bellowed, its barrel no longer lined at Waco and the bullet missed to ricochet from the corner of the safe.

Surprise caused Haver to swivel his head in Waco's direction as the cane-gun revealed its true purpose. In doing so he allowed the Derringer to waver slightly out of line.

Instantly Dusty thrust back his chair, sending it skidding across the room, but he did not rise. Instead he hurled himself forward and down through the desk's leg-hole. Never had he been more grateful for wearing his Colts in cross-draw holsters than at that moment. Drawing either gun from a butt-to-the-rear holster in the cramped confines through which he passed would have been almost an impossibility. While difficult, he managed to slide the left side Colt out with his right hand as he passed beneath the desk.

When he emerged at the other side, he came out shooting. Not just shooting but getting off his shots in the fastest possible manner when using a single-action revolver. Although some fire-arms' manufacturers produced double-action weapons, allowing the hammer to be cocked by pressure on the trigger, the Colt company preferred the more rugged and less complicated single-action for the majority of their products. While this allowed the weapon to operate with a minimum of working parts, an advantage in an age when repairs must be carried out by a local gun-smith who owned few tools, it meant the hammer needed manually cocking before it fired.

To overcome this slight disadvantage, Western gun-fighters had developed the art of fanning the hammer. True very few of them achieved success using such a method, but there was no quicker way of getting off shots from a single-action revolver. And in really skilled hands it could be surprisingly accurate at short range.

Dusty possessed that kind of skill. As he came into view, his right elbow rammed tight against his side to help control the gun. Whipping across his left hand, he forced over the hammer with its heel. Already his right forefinger held back the trigger, so the hammer did not engage and slammed down upon the waiting percussion cap on being released.

Still sliding forward, Dusty continued to fan the hammer as fast as he could circle his left hand around and repeat the cycle of operation. He shot fast for a definite purpose, to save his own life. While Waco had given him a chance and his unexpected action kept him out of Haver's line of fire, he did not know how quickly the man would recover from the surprise and change the Remington's aim. Black powder burned into a thick cloud of propellant gas and Dusty hoped to churn enough of it out to make him an uncertain target even if the bullets missed.

Only they did not miss. Three times in very quick succession lead ripped up into Haver's body and hurled him backwards. Nor did they strike a moment too soon. Already the wicked little hide-out gun had started to slant down and flame sparked from the upper of its superimposed twin barrels. Dusty heard a 'whomp!' at the side of his head as the Derringer's bullet churned into the floor alongside him. Then Haver toppled over backwards, crash-ing down some distance from where he had been standing.

Dropping the cane as soon as it had served his needs, Waco

bent and caught hold of his left hand Colt's butt. While he used his right hand and knew by the feel that it held the wrong gun, he wasted no time in changing. Instead he sent the holster flipping from the Colt and whirled in time to see Haver go down. Then the youngster swung towards Tarrick.

Blood gushing from his mouth, the man hung against the front wall. He had dropped his gun on being hit and showed no signs of further resistance. Even as Waco moved forward, shock and pain slid Tarrick unconscious to the floor. At the same moment Waco heard Dusty let out a pain-filled curse.

"Did he get you?" the youngster asked in concern, swinging towards the small Texan.

"No. I spiked a splinter into my butt-end as I slid through," Dusty replied and rose to his feet. "Thanks, boy. You handled that just right."

"I was scared as hell I'd not get away with it."

"The day you're scared, I'll vote Republican," Dusty said and rubbed his rump, then drew free the long splinter. "It was close, boy. If I never have a closer one, I'll be happy."

"And me."

"You'd best get the doctor for that jasper you shot. I'll do what I can for him until you get back."

Knowing that the need might arise for reaching some place in town faster than on foot, Dusty had arranged that one of the deputies kept his horse out back of the building while on watch. Collecting his waiting paint, Waco rode out of town and headed for the sports area. There he found and notified the doctor who left immediately. Using his initiative, the youngster next located the sheriff and told what happened. Like the doctor, Bracker returned to the marshal's office.

"There's not much chance for him, Captain Fog," the doctor stated after examining Tarrick. "The bullet's torn his tongue apart; even if I can stop the bleeding, he won't be able to eat."

"That's what I figured," Dusty replied.

"And that other man, Smith's companion, died late last night."

"So you told us."

"Doesn't it mean anything to you, Captain?" the doctor demanded.

"If you mean, am I sorry, the answer's 'yes'," Dusty answered quietly. "But I'd do it again under the same conditions. This's a rough country, doctor. There's not much law in it. Maybe the time'll come when a man doesn't need to strap on a gun in a morning, but until it comes I'll do what I have to do."

"Those two men died—," the doctor began.

"It was their own choosing," Dusty pointed out. "If that feller with Smith hadn't been stopped, he'd've killed one of us. Those two here might have just left Waco and me in a cell when they took Smith and pulled out; but it was a chance I couldn't take."

"Captain Fog did what he had to do, doctor," Bracker put in. "Sure he had to do some killing, but this territory's a mite safer for honest folks because of it."

"Let's get this feller into a cell," Dusty suggested, wanting the discussion over. "It'll be easier for him than lying on the floor."

The doctor nodded. While he might be new to the West, he had heard of other trail-end towns. Suddenly he realised that the one reason Mulrooney did not see the wild times of the other towns was because of Dusty's handling. So he chopped off his intention of continuing to raise the moral issues of the affair and supervised the removal of the wounded man.

"Now what happened, Dusty?" asked the sheriff once Tarrick was lying on a bunk in one of the cells.

"It's like we figured, Tom. Tricky Dick doesn't know where the money is."

"How'd you know that?" Waco inquired.

"Why else would he send two of his men here to get Smith out?" Dusty asked.

"But Smith didn't know the money'd gone," the youngster objected.

"He didn't," Dusty agreed.

"Then how'd he be able to find it?'

"That's a right smart question," Bracker put in.

"He's an idea where Stayley could have hid it," Dusty replied.

"Look, Dusty," Waco said slowly. "I might be hell with the gals—."

"You sure are," grinned Dusty.

"But I'm not smart like you," the youngster continued, ignoring the interruption. "So just sort of explain things real slow, easy and in itty-bitty words that dumb lil ole me can understand."

"It's easy enough. Stayley couldn't say to the others 'Wait here while I sneak off secret-like and hide the money.' And there's a limit to how many times he could find excuses to leave them before they got suspicious. I'd say three or four at the outside. Smith knows those places and a search around them'd likely turn up the money."

"That figures," Bracker admitted. "Only why doesn't Tricky Dick just follow their line instead of trying to pry Smith loose?"

"It's near on fifty miles to Newton, by the line those three'd take and none of it easy trailing country, or they don't know their business," Dusty guessed. "Also there'll be posses out hunting for them. Nope, Tricky Dick's best bet is to get Smith out, learn where Stayley could've hid the money and then pick it up."

"Maybe one of them pair's Tricky Dick," Waco suggested.

"Not if the description I've got's anywhere near right," Bracker answered. "He's a middle-sized jasper, looks like a swish, but he's tougher than any no-bullfighter* when the chips go down."

"He'd have to be to handle fellers like Stayley and those two," Dusty commented. "Thing now is, will he send some more of his boys, or try himself the next time?"

"You reckon he'll make another go at freeing Smith?" Bracker asked.

"Likely," Dusty replied. "He's taken so much trouble that he'll have to go through with it to show the rest of his bunch he's still the big man."

"Could be they'll fight shy of trying and expect him to do it," Bracker said. "Which means Tricky Dick'll be handling the next try hisself."

"Let's hope he does," Dusty answered. "Maybe we can nail his hide to the wall with Smith for the bait."

"Wells Fargo're going to want Smith pretty bad," Bracker pointed out.

"Could be," Dusty admitted. "Only I reckon we'll have something to say about that."

---

*Swish, no-bullfighter : effeminate.

9

Just a Half-Smart Lil Texas Boy

There was a heated scene in the marshal's office when the two real Wells Fargo special investigators finally reached Mulrooney. Once again the Cansole gang had cut the telegraph wires to prevent word of their exploits being passed ahead of them. Even after the investigators had been found in the men's room at the whistle-stop and freed, a considerable delay had ensued before contact could be made with the outside world. Travelling up by a special train sent out for them, the two men arrived at Mulrooney expecting the worst to have happened.

Smarting under the indignity at having been tricked into entering the room at the whistle-stop, clubbed insensible then left bound and gagged, they showed relief on learning that the rescue bid had failed. Their pleasure ended when Dusty flatly refused to turn Smith into their tender care. All he would do was allow them to interrogate the prisoner in his presence and he used the myth of the *Kansas City Intelligencer* reporter's presence to damp down any tendencies to take revenge for their mishaps.

"Damn it, marshal!" one of the investigators growled, when Smith continued to pretend innocence. "We're getting nowhere with him. If I can just—."

"Not in my jail," Dusty interrupted firmly.

"Then turn him over to us!"

"I reckon he'd be safer here—and if it comes to a point, you've nothing to prove he was mixed up in the hold-up. So I'm holding him for the attempted murder of a deputy marshal."

Anger glowed in the investigator's eyes, but a suggestion of another reason for Dusty's refusal died unsaid. Small he might be, but Dusty Fog stood in no man's shadow when it came to salty toughness. He would take the strongest objection to a

79

suggestion that he might be holding Smith in the hope of laying hands on the hold-up money for his own use.

"J.B. Hume won't like this when he hears, marshal," the investigator contented himself with saying.

"Tell him to take it up with me," Bracker put in, having stayed at the office to witness the interview. "I'm backing Cap'n Fog all the way."

In the face of such opposition the Wells Fargo men realised they could do nothing. So they stamped indignantly from the office and headed for their Mulrooney depot to telegraph James B. Hume, the company's able chief of detectives. An answer came back promptly, but as a complete surprise. Hume ordered his men to give the local law every co-operation and to leave Smith in the marshal's hands. Grudgingly the pair returned to tell Dusty the news, little guessing that he had communicated his plans for using Smith as bait to Hume before they arrived.

With that matter attended to, Dusty started to plan for foiling further efforts by Cansole to rescue the prisoner. Even should no attempt be made, Dusty felt that Smith might respond to hints of being double-crossed by helping the law find the hold-up loot.

So, on Monday morning, Smith went before the local judge who ordered he be held in custody for a week to allow a full investigation into the attempted murder of a deputy town marshal. That decision came about as a result of a consultation with Dusty. While it might not be in accordance with the strict letter of the law, both the small Texan and the judge felt it would be worthwhile. So Smith found himself faced with another seven days in the Mulrooney jail. During that time both he and Dusty hoped that Cansole would try again.

Preparing for the attempt, should it come, Dusty warned his staff to remain constantly alert for tricks and to watch everybody who tried to make contact with Smith. Not that Dusty thought Smith would be stupid enough to part with his information before being rescued. The outlaw had sense enough to know that once Cansole learned where to look for the money, he need no longer waste time, or risk losing more men, in further rescue bids.

Despite the threat of other jail-breaking attempts, the normal routine of the office had to go on. Towards noon on Monday the man who had bought Buffalo Kate's Brownton saloon arrived in Mulrooney, backed by several hard-cases, to take revenge on her for what he regarded as trickery. Only the arrival of Dusty and shotgun-armed deputies saved Kate. Being challenged by the vengeance-seeker, Dusty fought and killed him with duelling swords, the man making the mistake of believing such weapons offered him the best chance when dealing with a known gun-fighter.

Nothing further of note happened on Monday, except that the smouldering feud between Freddie Woods and Buffalo Kate received further fuel when the latter used information given by the former to hire a top-grade attraction to appear at the Buffalo Saloon and stole the majority of the trade.

Much as Dusty wanted to remain on hand around the jail, circumstances on Tuesday prevented him from doing so. Various civic dignitaries organised a banquet for the cattle-buyers, trail bosses and other important visitors. As segundo and trail boss of the great OD Connected, Dusty received an invitation to attend. So did Mark Counter, going along to represent his father's R Over C spread and other Texas Big Bend interests.

It was Frank Derringer's night off watch. Although he offered to help out, Dusty felt the need would not arise. Called to deal with a disturbance at the Fair Lady—a gandy-dancer claimed his pocket was picked while he watched a game of strip-poker between Babsy and three other girls—the Kid and Big Sarah left Waco in charge of the office. On their return, Waco decided to make the rounds. From the start, the youngster had showed such an affinity for peace officer work that the Kid did not hesitate to let him go alone.

Although considerable noise was coming from the Fair Lady, the rest of the town seemed peaceful enough. Then Waco heard the crack of a shot and a crash of breaking glass. Halting for a moment, he decided the sound came from the Buffalo Saloon and headed in that direction on the run.

While he might be conscious that he was handling his first lone-hand work since becoming a deputy, Waco did not forget the lessons Dusty had taught him. Instead of dashing straight into the saloon, he halted on the sidewalk and looked through one of the big front windows. A hold-up might be in progress, or a shoot-out between two enemies, either of which offered con-siderable danger to a peace officer who burst in unprepared to deal with them.

Nothing so dramatic met his gaze, although what he saw did not fill him with joy. The strip-poker game at the Fair Lady had sucked in most of the trade, as Freddie hoped when she organised it, but the Buffalo had managed to draw some custom. Not that much drinking, gambling or other business was being done, for employees and customers alike sat and stood in attitudes of strained immobility staring at the two men who monopolized the front of the long bar.

Waco sucked in a deep breath as he looked at the men. Each equalled his height, one lean, the other heavier. From their smoke-blackened and blood-stiff buckskin clothing, the sheathed knives at their belts and moccasin-covered feet, he took them to be buffalo-hunters. Unshaven, long-haired and dirty, they most likely were just back from a hunt. Probably they had sold their hides and started a celebration before taking a bath, hair-cut, shave and change of clothes. By all appearances, they carried enough whiskey internally to feel festive—and, like cowhands, they found their fun by shooting off guns.

Even as Waco watched, the heavier of the pair cut loose with a revolver shot that burst a bottle on the table before a scared-looking town dweller. Not to be out-done, the second hunter shattered a beer schooner. Buffalo Kate, looking angry and concerned, stood on the stairs leading to the first floor rooms. Unless the youngster missed his guess, she aimed to try to stop the men. Only he could not see them taking orders from a woman.

In any case, it was his duty as a deputy town marshal to go in and keep the peace. So he must enter and do something; the problem being what to do. Maybe the pair did not intend to hurt anybody, and cold sober could shoot accurately enough, but they had drunk sufficient to become unsteady. At any moment one of them might waver in his aim, putting the bullet into human flesh, not an inanimate object. Even if it did not happen, the reckless shooting had to be stopped. Let word once go around that buffalo-hunters had shot up a saloon unchecked and some cowhand was certain sure to try to uphold the honour of his profession by out-doing them. Sooner or later somebody would be hurt.

Darting a glance towards the marshal's office, Waco could see no sign of the Kid. While not afraid for his own sake, the youngster wished he had a more experienced man along to guide him. Knowing how easily the carefully built reputation Dusty had

82

created might be spoiled, he did not wish to do the wrong thing. A glaring error of judgement on his part might easily ruin all Dusty's good work. Yet, on the final analysis, he felt that Dusty would rather have him do something and be wrong rather than nothing, permitting a breach of the peace.

"Now was I a real smart Kansas lawman, I'd quick enough let windows in their bellies from the street and then go in to tell 'em to quit," Waco mused as he walked towards the batwing doors. "Trouble being I'm just a half-smart lil Texas boy. So I'll have to do it the hard way."

"Yahoo!" whooped the heavier man as Waco reached the doors. "I'm as tough as a hickory log. I can dive deeper and come up dryer than any man on the Great Plains."

Sucking in a deep breath, Waco pushed open the doors and stepped through. Every eye in the room turned his way and a slight air of expectancy ran through all but the two trouble-makers. They swivelled whiskey-wild faces his direction, taking in his empty hands and the badge on his vest.

"You wanting something, boy?" demanded the lean jasper, twirling his Colt in a manner which showed liquor had not fumbled his reflexes to any great extent.

"Now you-all wouldn't be fixing to spoil our fun, would you?" his companion continued, lining a Starr Army revolver in Waco's direction with disconcerting steadiness of hand. "Me 'n' Eli here wouldn't care for that."

Catching Buffalo Kate's eye, the bartender waited for a signal to take a hand. The woman hesitated, not sure what to do for the best. Since her arrival in Mulrooney, she had developed the greatest respect for all the local law officers. If possible she wanted to help for that reason, but another one sprang to mind. She knew Dusty, Mark and the Kid regarded Waco as their protege and like a favourite younger brother. If he should be shot down, the men who did it were sure to pay. Yet that could easily start bad trouble between the cowhands and buffalo-hunters, for both factions would side with their own.

Just as Kate prepared to signal to the bartender, she caught Waco's eye and the youngster shook his head. Such was her faith in the marshal's office that she refrained from passing a sign for her bartender to gather up the sawed-off ten gauge from under the counter. As the shotgun lay at the far end of the shelf, the bartender let out a faint sigh of relief.

83

"All I came in for's a drink," Waco assured the men, walking forward.

Used to the normal run of Kansas lawmen, who would have entered behind a lined shotgun—provided they did not send in two loads of buckshot first—the buffalo-hunters accepted his explanation. Yet neither relaxed to any great extent, which precluded any chance of drawing and covering them, even if doing so would solve the problem.

"You look kind of young to be wearing that badge," Eli commented.

"The marshal's my uncle," Waco explained with a disarming grin.

"So he figured the town might's well pay and feed you 'stead of him, huh?" asked the second man, lowering the Starr.

"Don't talk it out loud," Waco said urgently. "The tax-payers might hear. Say, that was mighty slick shooting I saw you doing —Near on as slick as I've ever seen."

"He reckons he's seed better'n us, Zeb," Eli growled.

"Maybe he'd like to see some more," the other buffalo-hunter replied.

"Now what I calls shooting's what I've seen Uncle Dusty do," Waco put in before the men could decide what action to take. "Why I've seen him stand like where I am now and shoot a whiskey bottle as it slid along the bar top. Now *that's* what I call shooting."

"Yeah," said Zeb, sounding a might subdued.

"There's not many can do it," Waco went on. "It's too hard for most."

"Hah! It ain't all that hard," snorted Eli. "Least-wise not for buffalo-hunting gents like us."

"I've seen Uncle Dusty hit five out of six. Now there's real lead-slinging."

"G'wan!" Zeb snorted. "He missed one, didn't he?"

"I've never seen it beat," Waco replied.

"By cracky, you will this time!" Eli yelped and swung towards the bartender. "You slide a whiskey bottle down there, feller."

Directing a glance at his boss, the bartender saw her nod. While Kate did not know what Waco was planning, she guessed more than mere boasting lay behind his words. So she went along with him, wondering if he hoped the sound of the shooting would bring Dusty and the others to help deal with the men.

"Ready?" the bartender asked, taking one of the empty bottles from beneath the counter.

"Go to it," Waco replied and looked at the men. "You have to let it get right to the end afore you cut loose."

Whatever his motive, Kate realised that Waco aimed to minimize the damage to her property. If the men allowed the bottle to reach the end of the bar before shooting, provided they came anywhere near close to their target, the bullet would end its flight harmlessly in the building's wall. The outer timbers were of sufficient thickness to prevent a revolver bullet bursting through. So she moved slowly down the stairs, watching every action the trio made.

The bartender sent the bottle sliding along the polished top of the counter with a deft flick of his wrist. Bringing up his Starr, Zeb fired and missed, the bottle coming to a halt on the edge of the counter. However Eli had been watching Waco all the time and presented no opportunity for him to make a move.

"Missed," grinned the youngster.

"Dang it, so did your uncle!" Zeb replied hotly.

"Skim another down and leave me try a try," Eli suggested.

Puzzled by Waco's actions, the bartender still felt no inclination to make a move himself. If Kate gave him the sign he would, but until then he felt content to go along with the young Texan's wishes.

Like Zeb, Eli discovered that shooting a sliding bottle proved a tricky proposition.

"Dag-nab it!" the lean hunter wailed as the bottle stopped unbroken by his bullet. "That danged mirror threw light back into my eyes. Maybe I ought to do something about it."

"Busting it'd sure be a heap easier than hitting that bottle," Waco agreed, determined to prevent such an expensive piece of damage.

Slowly Eli lowered the Colt from pointing at the mirror. The young deputy's words had carried all around the room. So if Eli did throw lead into the mirror, everybody would reckon it was because he lacked the skill to hit the bottle. Conscious that he upheld the honour and dignity of the buffalo-hunting fraternity, Eli could not allow such a thing to happen.

"Damn it, send her along again!" he growled.

Once more the bottle made its glide along the counter.

Although both men fired, no shattering of glass gladdened their ears.

"Danged if you didn't put me aim off, partner," Zeb said.

"I never figured you'd blast off in my ear just as I pressed the trigger," Eli protested. "You leave me do it next time."

If Waco had hoped to cause a rift between the two men, he failed. The misses merely increased their desire to shatter that hateful bottle. Eli tried again with no better result. Then Zeb made another attempt, shooting twice and bursting the bottle with the second bullet.

"Done it!" he whooped.

"Lemme have one, barkeep!" yelled Eli, not wishing to be outdone.

More by luck than skilled aim Eli managed to shatter the bottle, although it had almost come to a stop when he hit it. A point which Waco immediately brought out in a loud tone.

"Uncle Dusty hits them at full slide," he announced. "Not when they've just about stood still."

"Yeah?" snorted Eli. "Well as soon as I've reloaded, I'll show you how its done."

"Just let me fill my old Starr's chamber," Zeb went on. "Then I'll hit six outa six. I was just getting the range."

"You mean you gents're empty?" asked Waco with deceptive mildness.

"Sure am, boy," agreed Eli.

"And me," confirmed Zeb.

Then both of them froze, staring into the barrels of the matched Army Colts which flashed from Waco's holsters and lined on them.

"Now you just put up your guns and we'll take us a walk down to the jailhouse."

"What—!" Eli squalled.

"Why you—!" Zeb bellowed.

But they stood very still, for neither had drunk enough to dull their perceptions at such a moment. The speed with which Waco drew, and the way he thumb-cocked the hammers and pressed back the triggers *after* the barrels had left leather and slanted away from him, did not go unnoticed by the men. Faced by such mastery, even with a fair load of whiskey in them, they knew better than to make any foolish moves.

"By cracky, boys," Buffalo Kate said, coming forward. "He

sure out-foxed you."

Then the humour of the situation struck the crowd. They suddenly realised that the youngster's actions since entering the saloon had been for a purpose. Nor did the difference between his method of disarming the pair and that which most Kansas lawmen would have employed go unnoticed. A man started to laugh and others took it up. All the tension went from the crowd as they howled their mirth. Slowly the baffled anger faded from the faces of Eli and Zeb, then they too joined in the laughter as heartily as anybody.

"Everything all right, Waco?" asked the Kid, walking in with his Winchester cradled over the crook of his right arm.

"I reckon so," the youngster replied. "These gents've just been showing me some right fancy shooting and now they're fixing to show me how fancy they are at sweeping up broken glass."

"How's that?" Eli asked, watching Waco's Colts return to leather.

"I figure you owe it to Miss Kate," the youngster told him. "Busting bottles all over the place."

"Which same it'd be easier than spending a night in the pokey," the Kid went on.

"I'll be damned if I believe anybody could hit a bottle at full slide," Zeb stated indignantly.

A grin twisted Waco's lips as he faced the bar. "Skip one along, friend."

Obediently the bartender picked up a bottle and sent it along at, if anything, a faster pace than the others. Waco's right hand dipped and rose, the room's lights glinted dully on blued steel, then his Colt roared from waist high. Glass flew as the bottle disintegrated in full motion and a concerted gasp passed around the room. Twirling the Colt into leather in almost a continuation of the draw and shot, he looked at the men.

"I'd do the other five, but the tax-payers buy fodder for my gun and'd rawhide me for wasting 'em," he said. "Miss Kate, set these gents a drink up on me and then hand them a brush each."

"Now there's a lawman I could get to like," grinned Zeb. "I heard this was a straight town, Kate—and it's true."

"You the best hand with a gun in the marshal's office, friend?" Eli asked, dropping the over-familiar condescension and 'boy'.

"There're two better than me," Waco replied.

"In that case, I'm leaving my gun empty," the lean buffalo-

87

hunter stated. "Hand me a drink, then watch me go to sweeping."

"What'll Dusty say about me letting them do all that shooting?" Waco asked as he left the saloon with the Kid.

"That you did just right. Any other way and you'd've had to salt lead into that pair of hide-hunters."

"So I figured. Maybe I should've jumped them sooner."

"You did it just right," grinned the Kid. "Now stop fishing for compliments and let's get back to the office."

10

You're Not What I'd Call Welcome

Dusty confirmed the Kid's summing-up of Waco's actions when told on Wednesday morning and praised the youngster for the shrewd manner in which he had handled a tricky situation. So for the first time Waco felt himself capable of holding down his full end of the office's work.

While the youngster was learning fast and gaining confidence with each day, he had yet to come into conflict with the commission of a crime. Due to Dusty's policy of having a 'welcome committee' awaiting the arrival of every train and stage-coach, weeding out undesirables, the word went out that Mulrooney was bad medicine for petty criminals. None of the paying visitors who went broke regarded it as a fault of the town, for they received fairer treatment than in other such places along the railroad.

One of the girls employed in Lily Gouch's house stole a client's wallet during the transaction of business. However Lily, realising that she might never find another town which allowed her to operate without paying substantial bribes to various civic authorities, acted fast. In addition to returning the wallet, contents intact, to its owner, she gave the thief a beating calculated to make her fight shy of the touch of leather between her fingers for life. The other girls took the hint and there were no further incidents of that nature in the house.

Under the peaceful air of Wednesday morning, the town

seethed with excitement. The feud between the Fair Lady and Buffalo saloons grew hotter, causing considerable interest among citizens and visitors alike. While the game of strip-poker had put the Fair Lady ahead, nobody expected Buffalo Kate to stand back and accept defeat mildly. Nor did she. When the Buffalo opened for business on Wednesday, the girls wore dresses cut considerably shorter than accepted as usual, even in saloons. Naturally such an attraction hauled in trade and the town waited eagerly to see how Freddie planned to top it.

"Did Babsy tell you anything, boy?" asked the Ysabel Kid as he stood with Waco and Frank Derringer watching the noon train pull in to the depot on Thursday. "I'd sure admire to lay a bet on it with Mark—if I could be sure of winning."

"She never told me a thing," the youngster grinned. "Like I told Mark, when he asked so he could bet against you."

"Damned if the office's not crawling with sharps," Derringer commented, then nodded towards the train. "Here they come."

"You're bossing this drive," the Kid answered. "Point her the way you want to go."

In addition to being the office's gambling authority, Derringer possessed another asset. Travelling around in search of high-stake games of chance, he had come to know many of the assorted petty criminals Dusty wished to deny access to Mulrooney. So the gambler always attended the arrival of trains or stagecoaches and put his knowledge to good use.

Slowly the train ground to a halt, its driver timing things so that the passenger cars stopped in front of where the deputies stood. In addition, the conductor locked the end doors of the two cars, forcing the passengers to come out in the middle where Derringer's party could look them over conveniently.

"Howdy," greeted the gambler-deputy, blocking the path of a soberly-dressed, respectable-looking man who stepped from the forward car. "Can you tell me what *persona non grata* means?"

For a moment recognition flickered on the man's face, then it assumed a bland, puzzled expression. "I'm afraid I don't understand."

"It means 'No thanks, we've enough of our own.'," Derringer explained, thumbing open his jacket to expose the badge on his vest. "In other words, Mr. Ketter, this town doesn't need you."

"Kett—," the man began in a tone ringing with righteous indignation.

"You're blocking the other passengers," Derringer interrupted. "So just step aside, let them out and then get back aboard. Try going West, Ketter. Maybe they're short on gold-brick salesmen and card-sharks out there, but we've got all we want."

"I still don't know what you mean," the man stated, then shrugged. "But I'll do what you want and lodge a complaint with your bondsmen later."

With that he started to turn and his right hand disappeared from Derringer's sight in front of his body. The gambler did not hesitate. Catching Ketter by the left shoulder, Derringer swung him around and drove the other fist hard into his belly. A purist student of pugilism might have claimed that the punch went home a mite low for sportsmanship, but Derringer did not regard the affair in the nature of a sporting contest.

Nor did Ketter, judging by the way he gasped and started to fold over. On the heels of the blow, Derringer slashed his other hand from the shoulder to the side of Ketter's jaw and sent him sprawling at the feet of a tall nun just about to step down from the next car.

"If you wasn't reaching for that hid-out stingy gun, I'll think about apologising, Ketter," Derringer remarked, then looked at the nun and felt an explanation to be in order. "I'm sorry, ma'am. It was only a harmless bit of funning."

"So it seems," the nun replied, glancing down at the groaning Ketter. "I suppose Sister Bridget and I are *persona grata*?"

"Yes ma'am," Derringer agreed, seeing a second nun behind the speaker. "I reckon you are. Let me just help this gent out of your way."

Bending over Ketter, the deputy took hold of his jacket lapels and hauled him erect. Before the gasping man could shake the dizziness from his head and think about revenge, Derringer thrust him to one side. Then Derringer turned and watched the two nuns step down. Looking at the first of the pair, he wondered what had made such a beautiful woman renounce the world and take the veil.

Despite the habit which she wore hiding her figure, the woman conveyed an impression that what lay underneath would take seconds from none of her sex. Her face, framed severely, had beauty of a sultry kind that could not be hidden. She spoke with a refined New England accent and moved gracefully.

Behind her came a slenderly-built novice, walking with head

90

bowed and apparently conscious of the vow of silence imposed by her order.

"Can you direct me to the convent, deputy?" the beautiful nun asked. "I'm the new mother superior and Sister Bridget is a novice accompanying me there."

"Take the ladies along to the convent, will you, Waco," Derringer said and the youngster moved forward with no great show of enthusiasm.

"We couldn't think of interrupting you, or taking your assistant from his duty," the nun objected, glancing at the badge Waco wore. "Heaven only knows how many bad characters might get into town without you being here to stop them. I suppose you meet every train like this?"

"Trains and stagecoaches both, ma'am," Waco told her, relieved that he did not have to attend to such a minor chore when somebody interesting might come off the cars.

"How very thorough. I'll sleep more peacefully in my bed knowing that Mulrooney has such an efficient police force. Come Sister Bridget."

"I'll have somebody fetch your gear along, ma'am," Waco promised.

"Thank you, but I assure you that I can manage," the nun replied and walked across to where the usual bunch of loafers had gathered by the depot.

Body hunched in pain, breathing hard, Ketter glared at his assailant and snarled, "I'll not forget this, Derringer. One day—."

"Sure, I'll wait for the day to come," Derringer answered. "Could be I just saved your worthless life. Look—."

Following the direction indicated by the deputy, Ketter saw something that almost scared him out of a year's growth. Unnoticed until that moment the Ysabel Kid was lounging in the background, his rifle hanging negligently in his right hand. The negligence was more apparent than real, especially when taken with the position of his right forefinger. No man of the Kid's proven rifle-savvy curled that particular digit through the triggerguard unless prepared to start shooting. Cold sweat sent a shiver through Ketter at the sight. Recognising the Kid, he realised what his fate would have been had he drawn the Colt Cloverleaf revolver from its concealed holster.

"You're getting old and careless, *hombre*," commented the Kid amiably. "And you're not what I'd call welcome here."

"To hell with you and this whole stinking town!" Ketter spat back and turned to reboard the train.

Turning when he saw he would not be needed to deal with Ketter, Waco looked at the two nuns. They stood with one of the loafers, the novice silent and head bowed as before, the mother superior pointing with a white, elegant hand towards some baggage a Negro porter was bringing out of the second car. Something puzzled the youngster, a small thought nagging at the back of his mind but unable to break out in full. Before he could take time to mull over the matter, Derringer sent him to intercept a man and woman who the conductor suggested made a speciality of the old 'badger' game.

The couple, having seen Ketter's greeting, alighted on the other side of the car. Going over the platform, Waco jumped down and followed them.

"You won't like it here, even if we'd let you stop," he said.

Turning, the big, bulky man eyed the youngster from head to toe. Dressed in Eastern fashion, he did not wear a gun but looked a powerful bruiser with big, hard-knuckled hands.

"What's that?" the woman asked.

"The 'badger' game's mighty risky any place west of Chicago, ma'am," Waco replied. "Was I you, I'd head back to the Windy City."

"I don't get y—," the woman answered. She was a pretty thing, young and ideally suited for her part in the game.

"Gal in Hays was the last I knowed to try a 'badger' game," Waco told her. "Picked on a poor, half-smart Texas boy for it as her first one. Only when her husband come busting into the bedroom, he got his head blowed clean off—The feller they figured to 'badger' was John Wesley Hardin."

"Look, boy—," began the man, dropping their bags and advancing menacingly.

Then he came to a halt, staring in amazement at the Colt which flashed into Waco's hand. New out from the East, their knowledge of cowhands confined to one meeting in the comparatively civilized confines of Chicago, neither of the 'badger' pair had ever seen a real good Western gun-fighter draw. Like most folks who witnessed the phenomenon for the first time, the speed with which the gun appeared almost took their breath away.

"Mister, most cowhands're near on as fast as that and can hit what they aim at across the width of a bedroom," Waco warned, twirling away the Colt. "You take my advice and find some other town."

The man and woman exchanged worried glances. Operating the 'badger' game was simple. After the girl had lured a victim to her bedroom and disrobed, the man burst in on them. Claiming to be her husband, he accused the victim of alienating his wife's affections and demanded money to overlook the affair. While tough—he had fought in the prize-ring—the man realised that no amount of muscle could beat a heavy-calibre revolver. Smarter than her companion, the girl saw there would be little chance of operating in a town so efficiently policed, unless—

"You wouldn't—," she started.

"No, ma'am, I *wouldn't*," agreed Waco. "'Cause I'm a noble, true, honest lil Texas boy; and cause the marshal'd beat my pumpkin head shoulder-level if I let you bribe me to watch over you."

Deep rumbles came from the man, but the woman gave a philosophical shrug. "Thanks for the warning."

"Happen you don't take it, ma'am," Waco replied. "You'll wish you had."

Noting the underlying hardness in the youngster's voice, the woman nodded and told her companion to return to the train. While the man picked up his bags, Waco saw the two nuns and their helper come around the rear of the train. Holding the skirts of her habit up, the mother superior picked a dainty way over the rails on stylish shoes. As she saw Waco, she let the skirts drop with becoming modesty and flashed him a smile.

"Still doing your duty, deputy," she said.

"Yes, ma'am," he replied and then gave his attention to the 'badger' pair as they walked by him towards the train. By the time they had boarded the car, the nuns had passed out of sight between two buildings.

"And there's another good piece of work well done," Derringer commented as the train pulled out. "Even if I do say so myself."

"Let's take a look in on the Fair Lady as we go back," Waco suggested. "Maybe the gals'll be wearing their new outfits."

"And if they're not, you'll likely get a chance to talk to Babsy," the Kid grinned. "Chasing gals's all some of you fellers think about."

"Wasn't you ever young yourself, Lon?" asked Derringer as

they directed their feet towards the saloon.

"All them danged Injuns do for courting's steal hosses to give to the gal's pappy," Waco sniffed. "I reckon our way's a whole heap better."

"Stealing hosses's a whole mess of fun, boy," the Kid stated.

"Not as much fun as finding out that the gal's got no hair on her chest," Waco said without thinking and could have cheerfully bitten off his tongue.

"So *that's* what you did that night," Derringer gasped.

"For shame," the Kid went on. "And me thinking you'd learned some good ways since knowing me."

Waco's reply was blistering, profane and nothing to do with the subject of how he spent his night off watch. By the time he finished, they had reached the Fair Lady and he led the way inside.

If the deputies hoped to learn Freddie's plan to counter Buffalo Kate's attraction, they met disappointment. Being remarkably shrewd, the lady saloonkeeper did not intend to disclose her answer so early that her rival could defeat it. So the few girls present wore their normal dresses.

So far the only customers were a few townsmen and a quartet of younger visitors. The latter wore low-heeled, heavy boots and bib-overalls, which meant they did not belong to cowhand, buffalo-hunter or railroad trades. Looking at them, Waco concluded that they must be from the near-by sod-busting homesteads. Despite the fact that all they drank was beer, the quartet were entertaining all the girls.

"Hi," Waco greeted Vera, second of the barmaids. "Where's Babsy?"

"Trying on the new dress the boss'll have us wearing tonight, deputy," one of the girls called. "And is it something?"

"You'll get something if you blab your fool mouth off about it," Vera warned grimly. "What's it to be, gents?"

"You're buying, boy," Derringer stated.

"Am I?" Waco asked.

"You are happen you want me and Frank to forget about them hairs on the chest," the Kid told him.

"Damned if I shouldn't make you pair leave town!" Waco snorted. "Three beers and take something for yourself, Miss Vera."

"Just what's Miss Freddie fixing up back there, Vera gal?" the

Kid inquired after she served the drinks.

"Wait and see," the barmaid replied with a grin. "It'll make that Buffalo bunch sit back on their heels and wish they'd stopped back in Brownton."

Before any further attempt could be made by the interested trio to discover the secret, the Fair Lady received more customers. Half a dozen cowhands trooped in. From their fresh-bathed and barbered appearance, taken with the fact that all wore new clothes, they had only recently received their pay. No cowhand with money in his pocket ever wasted time in looking for a place to spend it. Nor did he want to spend it all on himself. The six cowhands came to the Fair Lady looking for drinks, fun and female company.

"Set up drinks, ma'am," ordered one of the party, hauling a wad of money from his pocket. "You gents from the marshal's office take something?"

"Just the one," Derringer replied. "The marshal'd slap a fine on us happen he caught us drinking."

"We wouldn't want to make lawmen bust the law," the cowhand grinned and looked along the bar. "Reckon you've any gals who'd take a drink with a bunch of thirsty Texas gents, ma'am?"

"Open up some wine if they do, ma'am," another cowhand went on. "They do say beer makes a gal fat."

"Let's keep it friendly, boys," Derringer said quietly, moving along the bar as one of the young farmers slammed down his beer schooner.

"You Texas boys seen the jail-house?" the Kid asked, facing the cowhands.

"Can't miss it, which same I've seen as good back to home," one of them answered.

"It's big and roomy," the Kid continued. "Trouble being they made the backhouse a mite small, so the marshal's having another built. He was just saying to me this morning how we ought to find somebody to dig the hole. Him and the judge allow to use the next bunch we bring in for making a fuss to dig it."

"The last thing we want's fuss," stated the leader of the cowhands.

However the girls drifted along the bar and joined the new-comers. Laughter rang out, along with squeals of pleasure as Vera decanted wine and other drinks that their previous companions could not afford.

"Blasted cowhands!" one of the young nesters spat out.

"You can't even buy a drink when they're here," another continued bitterly. "Let's try the Wooden Spoon, they don't have gals in there."

"It must be rough on the local kids," Derringer commented as the deputies watched the nesters stamp out of the saloon. "They come to town, but don't make the kind of money to compete with the cowhands, buffalo-hunters and railroad hands who drift in."

None of the trio had noticed Freddie enter from the rear. Coming up, she saw the nesters leave and heard Derringers' wry comment.

"What's the answer, Frank?" she asked.

"Huh?" he grunted, turning.

"To their problem. We have to keep our prices high to cover breakages and other overheads, like running through the winter when there're no trail-hands, buffalo-hunters or railroad construction gangs in. Or those who are have no money. So we go as high as the traffic will stand and the local boys are cut out because they can't afford it."

"Which must set in their craw something fierce at times," Derringer agreed. "Like just now."

"The girls shouldn't've walked away like they did," Freddie admitted. "But don't forget they're paid to entertain the customers, with bonuses for the amount spent. That means they go to those who can pay most. Mercenary, but understandable I suppose."

"Sure."

"Then what do I do, Frank?" Freddie insisted. "Stop the locals coming in during the trail season? That's not practical, or good business. They'll be around all through the winter. Let them pay less for their drinks than the visitors? Fine, until some visitor notices that I'm doing it. Have separate rooms, or a part of town, just for locals? It's been tried without much success in other places, or so I've heard. What *is* the answer, Frank?"

"You've got me," he admitted. "Human nature being what it is, whichever way you go, it'll be wrong for sure."

Freddie looked at the gambler with a smile. "You're either a cynic or a philosopher, Frank, but I don't know which."

"You tell me what they mean, and I'll right smart tell you which, ma'am," Waco put in. "Say, where-at's Babsy?"

"She'll be out when she's changed," Freddie promised and went on just a touch too innocently. "Have you been in the Buffalo today?"

"Nope," Derringer answered. "And if I had, I wouldn't say what I'd seen. One thing I'm not doing's getting mixed between you and Kate."

"You don't think I care what that fat trollop does, do you?" Freddie snorted, sounding as if she meant it.

"All I know is that coming between you two'd be worse than standing on a log between two bobcats," Derringer grinned.

"Which same you'll wish you was on that log happen Dusty has to come looking for us," the Kid remarked, setting down an empty glass. "Let's go and see what the boss man has for us to do."

"Knowing him," Waco replied. "It'll be something for certain sure."

II

It Goes with Wearing the Badge

"Well, what do you think?" Babsy asked, just a touch defiantly, as she twirled around in front of Waco to let him take in the full impact of the Fair Lady's answer to the Buffalo's challenge.

While aware that the rival saloon must be firmly put in its place, the little blonde felt a twinge of concern over how Waco might regard her appearance. The dress she wore ended just below the tops of her black stockings, exposing shapely legs to view, while the decollete was considerably more daring than anything so far achieved by the Buffalo's girls. Admiration flickered on the young deputy's face, for the dress set off Babsy's buxom figure to its best advantage.

"Whooee!" he said, reaching out and taking her by the arms. "Miss Kate'll have to go some to lick this, gal."

"Lay off!" Babsy ordered unconvincingly. "Give over."

They stood in a room at the rear of the Fair Lady, having met for a quick talk before starting their respective night's work.

97

Drawing Babsy to him, Waco bent and kissed her.

"If I wasn't on watch—," he breathed.

"And if I didn't have to work tonight, I'd say yes for sure," she replied. "Only Miss Freddie needs me to do some songs."

"It's surely hell," Waco said after kissing her again. "I'll have to get going, Babsy gal."

"You stay away from the Buffalo and that fat ginger-haired cow!" Babsy warned, opening the door to let him out.

"I wonder if she's got any hairs on her chest," Waco remarked.

"You just let me catch you trying to find out, that's all!" Babsy squealed and slammed the door in an attempt to hit him across the heels as he stepped into the night. Then she opened it again and peeked out. "Hey! Come back around ten and we'll take a walk."

"Why sure, honey. I'll take you to the livery barn to see the golden horse-shoe nail."

"Garn! A groom back home tried to show me it once."

"Maybe Ginger hasn't seen it," Waco grinned.

"She's old enough to have put it there," Babsy sniffed. "Ten o'clock."

"I'll be here, all being well," Waco promised and walked away as the door closed once more.

Still grinning, Waco strolled along the street. Take it any way, that Babsy was quite a gal. Then a frown wiped off the grin. Maybe Miss Freddie and Buffalo Kate were carrying their feud a mite too far with the abbreviations to their girls' costumes. While Freddie seemed to have gone the limit, Waco could not see Kate allowing the challenge to go unanswered. Waco wondered what further reductions the Buffalo girls could make to their clothing, if any, and whether the Fair Lady would be able to counter the measures.

Pleasant though the speculations might be, he shook them from his head and concentrated on the work for which the tax-paying citizens of Mulrooney had hired him. Derringer was supervising a high-stake poker game that night, while the Kid and Mark were keeping watch at the jail. As Dusty and Big Sarah both had other work, the youngster made the rounds alone. However, since handling the two hide-hunters at the Buffalo, he felt that he could cope with anything that came along.

Everything around town seemed peaceful enough, the newly-arrived cowhands enjoying themselves without running horse-races through the streets, or engaging in impromptu target practice. Maybe later things would liven up. Not that Waco cared if the pacific state continued. With almost a week's practical law-enforcement behind him, Waco had adopted the typical peace-officer's attitude. No longer did he hope for something exciting to happen, being content to stroll his rounds quietly and undisturbed.

As always the youngster did his work thoroughly. Passing Lily Gouch's establishment, he saw a few cow-horses standing hitched to the front fence, heard laughter and music from inside but did not enter. Lily ran a quiet, orderly disorderly house and the law saw no reason to interfere with it. So the youngster walked on, heading for the livery barn.

Always a tempting target for thieves, despite horse-stealing being a hanging offence, the barn received frequent visits by the patrolling deputies. So did the neighbouring freight outfit's warehouse, which also carried items to attract outlaws.

Coming towards the rear of the two buildings, Waco saw that a light was glowing in the freight outfit's first-floor office window. As usual the outside stairs up to the office were illuminated by a hanging lantern at their head. Walking between the two businesses' corrals, Waco saw a pair of men coming hurriedly down the stairs. Though the light, being behind them, threw their faces into deep shadow, he could see enough to realise they were neither clerks from the office, nor company drivers.

The one in the lead would be Waco's size and build, wearing a Stetson hat of some age and north-country style, a red and black check mackinaw jacket, levis pants hanging outside heavy, low-heeled boots, with a Ballard single-shot rifle in his right hand, the left gripping a bulging floursack. Shorter and slighter built, the second man wore a black wolf-skin coat that reached his knees, pants tucked into the same kind of boots as his companion's, a battered U.S. cavalry campaign hat without its insignia, and toted a long-barrelled, muzzle-loading shotgun.

Everything about the pair warned Waco that they meant trouble. So he moved forward ready to draw and shoot should the need arise. Even as he opened his mouth to yell out a challenge the two men saw him.

"Beat it!" hissed the taller and leapt for the darkness beyond the lamp's pool of light.

Without offering to raise the shotgun, fortunately for him,

the second man sprang with commendable speed after his companion.

"Hold it!" Waco yelled, right hand flowing down to draw its Colt as he lunged out from between the corrals. However the two men gave no sign of obeying the command.

One of the rules Dusty had emphasised from the start was that a gun must be used only as a last resort, not as a convenient means of halting a fleeing suspect. So Waco held his fire. If the pair had offered resistance, the youngster would have acted without hesitation; but he could not shoot down men who ran away.

Already the men were dashing through the shadows towards the end of the building. Colt in hand, Waco set off after them, running at an angle before the freight outfit's warehouse. Then he saw two figures appear at the office window, throwing up its lower section to look out. He recognised them as the outfit's clerk having met them both around town. With that thought in mind, he continued to run, ignoring the fact that each of the clerks held a revolver. Wanting to catch up with the fleeing pair, the youngster clean forgot that the darkness made him an indistinct, unidentifiable shape. He learned the mistake quickly enough.

"There he is, Willy!" screeched the chubby clerk Gus Schubert, pointing down at the running deputy.

Swinging up the Colt he held, Willy Wallenheim fired. Before Waco could realise his error of tactics and yell a warning, he heard the bullet cut through the air over his head. Glaring upwards, he saw Schubert also taking aim at him and wasted no time in trying to explain matters to the clerks. The previous Sunday, before Babsy and Ginger caused his return to the office, Waco had seen the two clerks shooting in a competition. Although they did not measure up to the exacting standards of a Western-trained gun-fighter, each had proved himself more than adequate at target shooting over sights. Enough for Waco to realise that he must take no chances with them.

Ahead rose the big horse-trough, filled with water and offering the kind of solid shelter his heart desired at that moment. With another bullet making its eerie 'splat!' sound as it winged by his head, Waco dived across the trough and landed in the welcome blackness beyond it. That he came down in an area left permanently wet and muddy did little to cool the anger he felt at the clerks' actions. From the darkness where the fleeing men had disappeared came the creaking of saddle leather as they mounted waiting horses.

"Hey!" yelled Waco, starting to rise.

Instantly Wallenheim's revolver cracked, water erupted from the surface of the trough and the bullet rapped on the side, its progress so slowed by the liquid contents that it could not break through. However the nearness of the bullet and the fact that Schubert had taken aim caused Waco to duck down faster than he came up. Under different conditions he could have dealt with the pair. Standing in front of the window, they offered a perfect target in its rectangle of light. Unfortunately they were on the side of the law and acting in ignorance. Otherwise Waco could have been throwing lead their way instead of taking cover. Flattened on the muddy ground, the fuming youngster heard the sound of hooves drumming away and knew the other two men had escaped. Then the sound of shouts reached his ears, followed by feet running in his direction.

Two familiar shapes appeared cautiously around the right hand corner of the building, while a third came into sight at the left.

"Law here!" yelled the Ysabel Kid. "Hold up on that shooting."

"One of 'em's behind the horse-trough!" Wallenheim shouted back in a voice pitched high with excitement.

Instantly Mark Counter and the Kid faced the required direction, Winchester and Colt aiming at the trough as they moved apart to offer a smaller target along with the problem of whom to shoot at first. At the other end of the building, Dusty Fog advanced watchfully to where he could see and shoot at the ear of the trough should that prove necessary.

"Come on out with your hands showing and empty!" Mark bellowed, wanting to hold their man's attention and keep him from noticing Dusty.

"I'm coming!" Waco shouted back. "Just make sure them two *loco boboes* up there don't shoot me in the head when I get up."

At any other time the youngster might have enjoyed the consternation his voice caused. He saw Mark and the Kid stiffen in their tracks and heard a startled gasp from the window. Looking up, he saw the clerks hurriedly jerk back into the room and started to rise.

"Is that you, boy?" Mark asked.

"You're expecting maybe the whole blasted Dick Dublin gang?" the furious youngster replied, standing erect. "God damn it. Them two son-of-a-bitching bastards were like to kill me and let the real owlhoots get clear away."

Before any more could be said, the office door flew open and the two clerks clattered down the stairs.

"Have you got him, Kid?" Schubert asking, brandishing his revolver in an alarming manner.

"We sure have," agreed the Kid. "And a right desperate villain he is."

Clearly the clerks had been hoping that their ears and eyes had played tricks on them from the window. Their eyes went to where Waco stood behind the trough and noticed Dusty coming up behind the youngster.

"It *is* you, Waco," Wallenheim gasped.

"I've knowed that all along," the youngster answered bitterly.

"We didn't know!" Wallenheim croaked, suddenly aware of how close he had come to making a terrible mistake. "You came running by just as we opened the window and we thought you must be one of the robbers."

"You ought to have yelled out who you were, boy," the Kid put in. "How'd these gents know who you might be?"

"Maybe you'd best tell us what happened," Mark said to the clerks, before Waco's spluttering fury could erupt into a reply.

"Two men came bursting in and robbed us!" Wallenheim answered, darting a nervous glance at the youngest deputy.

"One of them had a shotgun," Schubert went on. "There wasn't a thing we could do but open the safe and give them the money."

"They took three thousand dollars from the safe, our watches and wallets," Wallenheim continued. "Get after them."

"How?" the Kid asked quietly.

"How?" Schubert yelped. "They can't have gone far."

"They'd've gone a damned sight less if you hadn't—!" Waco started hotly, still standing by the trough and unaware that Dusty was coming towards him.

Stepping up behind the youngster, Dusty caught hold of his arm and chopped off the rest of his speech.

"Hush your mouth, boy," the small Texan ordered. "Let them do the talking."

"Damn it all, Dusty," Waco protested, "if they'd let me go

by, instead of throwing lead at me, I could've run them two down afore they reached their hosses."

"And likely got your fool head blowed off with the scatter," Dusty replied. "Could be they saved your life, boy."

"*They* saved *my* life!" the youngster spluttered. "All they did—."

"Was make a fool mistake," Dusty interrupted quietly. "Most folks do that once in a while. Even us Texans."

"They damned nigh killed me!"

"Don't you reckon they know that?"

"Huh?"

"Look at them, boy!" Dusty ordered. "They're both near on sick thinking what they might have done."

"I'm not dancing with joy myself," Waco growled.

"You've been shot at before, and likely will again if you keep on wearing a badge," Dusty told him. "Those boys've never before been in a tight like that. Standing on the wrong end of a scattergun for the first time's mighty unnerving and right likely to make a man think or act a mite foolish."

"Likely," the youngster agreed.

"It's certain, not just likely!" Dusty snapped. "I know how you feel, and'd probably feel the same had it happened to me. Only if you go in there, head down and pawing dirt, you'll make them forget every damned thing that'll help us hunt for those two yahoos."

"If they hadn't—."

"And if Babsy was a boy, you wouldn't give a damn whether she has hair on her chest or not."

"How the hell did you—."

"I'll tell you when you're older. Right now no amount of 'ifs' can change what's done. So we have to play the hand with the cards that're left. Wasting time thinking how you could've maybe run them down if you hadn't been stopped's no use. You did get stopped. So now we've got to work another way."

"So what do I do?" Waco asked.

"First thing is forget that they tossed lead at you," Dusty replied. "Mark it down to experience, boy. It goes with wearing the badge. Reckon you can do it?"

"I'll give it a whirl," the youngster promised, then grinned. "If I can go see Babsy later."

"Damned if you're not getting as bad as Lon and Mark,"

Dusty told him. "All right, do it and you can go off early."

"For a chance to see Babsy, I'd say I did all the shooting at myself," Waco stated. "Have you seen how Miss Freddie's got them gals dressed?"

"I've seen," Dusty answered. "Let's go talk to the clerks."

Something in the small Texan's voice and attitude warned Waco that he did not entirely approve of the Fair Lady's dress style. Waco wondered why, knowing that mere prudery was not the cause of the grim note in Dusty's voice. However he knew it was neither the time nor the place to raise the question.

Waco studied the two clerks' faces as he walked towards them with Dusty, reading the sick anxiety each showed. Taken with the distracted manner in which they glanced towards him while he spoke to Dusty, Waco began to understand his companion's insistence that he should overlook their actions. Worried by thoughts of what they might have done, the pair paid little attention to the Kid's questions. So Waco prepared to accept responsibility for their over-excited error.

"I—I'm real sorry that we shot at you, Waco," Wallenheim said.

"It was all my fault," the youngster replied. "I ought to have yelled out who I was when you opened the window."

"We could've killed you," Schubert continued.

"Shucks! I figured you was shooting to hold me down, not to hit me," Waco told him. "I didn't get hurt, so everything's fine."

In the face of the youngster's attitude, the clerks began to regain their confidence. The numb horror at discovering they had almost shot a peace officer wore off and they began to think rationally.

"Let's take a look in the office," Dusty said. "You come along, Waco. It's a slim chance, Lon, but get a lamp and see if there're any tracks. Mark, you'd best go back to the office. This could be a trick to get us away while they free Smith."

Going up to the office with the clerks and Waco, Dusty asked to be told all that happened.

"We were working on the books—," Schubert began.

"They came in through the door there—," Wallenheim started at the same moment.

"Suppose we let Gus tell it first," Dusty interrupted. "You listen, Willy, and see if you can think of anything he missed."

"Like I said," Schubert commenced. "We were working on the

books when the door opened. We thought it was the wrangler bringing up a can of beer. Only it was those two fellers. They'd got guns pointing at us, a shotgun and a rifle, and told us to hand over our wallets. We did it, marshal—."

"So would I, with a scattergun pointed at me," Dusty assured him. "You say they told you to hand over your wallets first?"

"Yeah. Then they took our watches and I thought they'd leave. Only the big one saw the safe door open—."

"You had the safe open?" Waco put in.

"Of course," Schubert answered. "How else could we check the money against the ledgers?"

"What'd they do then?" Dusty asked.

"The one with the shotgun kept us covered and the other picked up a flour-sack that we use for a door mat. He put the money from the safe in it, along with our wallets and watches. Then they made us lie face down on the floor and left. As soon as we thought it'd be safe, we got up, grabbed the guns from the desk and went over to the window."

"What'd they look like?" Dusty inquired before the clerks could start brooding on what had followed their opening the window.

"It's hard to say. They wore bandanas over their faces and their hats covered their hair."

"About how tall were they?"

"The one with the rifle was about Waco's size and the other closer to mine."

"Anything you can tell us that Gus missed, Willy?" Dusty asked.

"I don't think so."

"How'd they talk?" Waco put in, beating Dusty to the question.

"It's hard to tell, the bandanas muffled their voices," Wallenheim replied. "I couldn't even say to their accents. But I don't think they were Texans."

At that moment the Kid appeared at the door with word that he could find no tracks. Dusty shrugged, having expected no more, and told the clerks that he would let them know if anything happened.

"Some of the cowhands're getting mite festive," the Kid remarked as they left the office. "We'd best circulate a bit and let 'em know we're around."

"Do you want me, Dusty?" Waco asked.

"No. You go see Babsy; Lon and me can handle things for once."

"Was I you, I'd change my pants first," the Kid continued.

Not until that moment did Waco remember the damp, muddy state of his clothing. However he hesitated before taking the Kid's advice.

"About that hold-up, Dusty—," the youngster began.

"Think about it for a spell," Dusty answered. "There's nothing much we can do until day-break anyways. Before you go to meet Babsy, write down a description of those two jaspers and to-morrow we'll see about running them down."

Much as Waco hated the thought of the delay, he knew it to be unavoidable. Not even the Kid could read sign in the dark and the law did not know in which direction to start the hunt. Anger at the two clerks rose again, but the youngster fought it down. In doing so, he started to think about what they had said. Before any conclusion took definite form, Waco found himself alone. Still thinking, he made his way back to the marshal's office, then to the hotel to carry out the Kid's suggestion.

12

All in the Line of Duty

"What's up, luv?" Babsy asked, interrupting her comments as she became aware that they fell on deaf ears.

"Huh?" Waco grunted.

"You've not heard a word I said," she told him indignantly.

On his return to the hotel, Waco had cleaned his gunbelt and Colts before thinking of changing clothes or taking a bath. When he reached the Fair Lady to collect Babsy, he found her in a considerable temper because the Buffalo's staff had struck back far quicker than expected. On hearing how the opposition were dressing, Buffalo Kate had made each of the girls remove several inches from her dress hem and reduce its neckline still further. All through the walk to the hotel, where they intended to eat supper before taking a stroll around town, Babsy heatedly discussed the situation.

"Sure I have," Waco lied. "You was telling me how the girls thought they ought to go to the Buffalo and snatch them bald-headed."

"Only I'd finished telling you that and was asking what the shooting we heard was all about."

"Somebody robbed the Schubert freight outfit."

"Oo! Did anybody get hurt?"

"Nope."

"How much did they lose?"

"Something over four thousand dollars."

"And they got away?" she asked, eyes wide with interest.

"Yeah," Waco agreed, then told her the full story.

Indignation flashed across Babsy's expressive face. "Oo! Just wait until I see that Gus Schubert. I'll tell him a thing or two."

"Forget it, honey," Waco said. "They weren't to know who I was."

"You could've been hurt—."

"I wasn't. So we'll leave it lie."

"Cap'n Fog don't know who did it, does he?" Babsy asked after a pause during which Waco sank once more into the reverie which she had noticed since starting the meal.

"No," Waco admitted.

"But you reckon you do," she said. "That's what's on your mind, isn't it?"

"You're a real smart lil gal, Babsy honey," Waco told her with a wry grin. "There's something sets wrong about that hold-up. I think—hell, I don't know what to think for sure. Only I know that whole game was played wrong."

"Look, luv," Babsy said gently, reaching over to take his hand. "Why don't we leave that look at the golden horseshoe nail until later? Miss Freddie'd like me to do some more singing tonight and you'll not settle easy until you've thought this lot out."

"If that's what you want."

"It's not. But you've got a face like a wet week and you'll not rest until you've done what you have to do."

"You're too smart for a pretty lil gal," Waco said, gently squeezing her hand. "I reckon I'd be mighty poor company tonight."

"I'd already thought that out," Babsy smiled.

107

On returning to the Fair Lady, Babsy went to change from her street clothes into something more suitable. Before leaving, Waco crossed to the bar and asked Vera a question to which she gave a negative answer. Outside he paused for a moment and then directed his feet towards the Buffalo. At that place's batwing doors he paused and looked piously into the sky.

"Babsy honey," he said. "This's all in the line of duty, as Mark'd say."

With that he entered and, despite tending to support the Fair Lady, had to admit that Buffalo Kate had come up with a right smart answer to Miss Freddie's challenge. Ginger came towards him, wearing a skirt cut so high that white flesh twinkled attractively over the black of her stockings.

"Hey there," she greeted. "Where's that fat foreigner who's usually hanging on to your shirt-tail?"

"I should be so lucky," Waco grinned. "Babsy told me to say 'howdy' for her—And afore you ask, I'm working."

"I never did have any luck," Ginger pouted and walked away.

Crossing to the counter, Waco leaned against it for a moment until Wally, the head bartender, noticed him. Since Waco's smooth handling of the two drunken buffalo-hunters, Wally had come to regard him as a real deputy, not merely a kid wearing a badge. So the bartender passed paying customers to greet the youngster.

"Boss says your money's no good here, Waco," he said. "What'll it be?"

"Just a beer," Waco replied and jerked his head towards the tables. "A man can sure work up a thirst just looking in here."

"Better'n at the Fair Lady, huh?"

"You don't reckon I'd be loco enough to admit that—or deny it," Waco grinned. "Say, Wally. Have any of the sod-buster kids been in spending more than usual tonight?"

In another town, questioned by the usual run of Kansas lawmen, Wally would have given deep thought before answering and chosen his words with care. Such was the respect Dusty's office had built up that the bartender did not hesitate to answer immediately.

"Naw. Couple of 'em come in earlier, bought a beer each and left."

"What'd they look like and how'd they dress?"

"One was about your size, the other shorter, they wore

108

jackets, pants, blue shirts and ties, I think. Didn't pay them much mind."

"The big one didn't wear a mackinaw, did he?" Waco asked.

"No. A store-bought jacket, they both did," Wally replied. "What's up?"

"Nothing much."

"You thinking about the hold-up at Schubert's?" asked the bartender. "Hell, neither of 'em was packing a gun—I noticed that much."

That figured, a man without a gun being something of a novelty. Waco did not offer to enlighten Wally as to the arms the robbers carried.

"Likely I'm wrong then," the youngster said, taking the glass of beer Wally poured. "Don't say anything about this. I don't want folks thinking I'm blaming the nesters."

"You can count on me," Wally assured him.

"Why sure I can," Waco grinned. "Especially as I saw you and Vera from the Fair Lady last night down to the livery barn."

"That was only busi—," Wally began. "No, damn it, if that's not worse'n what we was doing."

"Shame on you, sir," Waco chuckled. "Anyways, I won't talk if you don't."

A broad smile creased Wally's face. "An I thought Cap'n Fog had chased all the sharks out of town. If I see anything, I'll let you know."

"Send word to the office, I've got some more walking to do. Say, I'm getting to like walking—it's worrying the hell out of me."

With that the youngster finished his beer and set the glass on the counter. As he turned to leave, Wally spoke in an urgent voice:

"One thing, Waco. Vera and me—."

"Yep?"

"We don't talk about business—if you know what I mean."

"I reckon I do," Waco answered soberly. "And I never thought you did. See you, Wally."

"I'll be here," the bartender promised.

Leaving the Buffalo, Waco went next to the Wooden Spoon. There the entertainment emphasis lay on gambling rather than girls, so he regarded it as a less likely choice for the men he sought. On his arrival, Dongelon told him that no young nesters had been in all night and asked no questions about the query.

That seemed to close the matter, for the theatre and other saloons had yet to find owners. While there had been some inquiries about vacant businesses, the interested parties had lost their desire to purchase on learning of the town's gambling ordnance.

Deciding to pass his theories on to Dusty and learn what the small Texan thought of them, Waco walked towards the jail. As he approached the Buffalo Saloon, he saw something not entirely unusual taking place. Two brawny bouncers half-carried, half-dragged a struggling cowhand through the batwing doors and dumped him on the sidewalk.

"Those gals in here's for looking at, not touching up, young feller," one of the pair stated. "Happen you got them sort of ideas, go around to Lily Gouch's place and she'll fit you up good."

"Damn it!" Waco breathed. "What've I been using for brains? All that walking must've addled 'em."

Then he started forward at a faster pace as the cowhand sat up, reaching for a gun.

"Why you dirty Yankees, you!" yelled the cowhand. "I'll—."

"Shooting bouncers's plumb again the law, friend," Waco warned, blocking the other's draw with his foot. "And going to jail for trying it's nowheres near as much fun as going to Lily Gouch's place."

"I'd go there for sure, if I knew where the son-of-a-bitching place is," the cowhand replied, forcing himself erect.

"Come on then, I'll show you," Waco offered.

"Friend, you surely is a friend indeed," the cowhand replied, then peered closer at the badge on the youngster's vest. "Well I swan! You're a John Law."

"Yep. Showing you's all part of the town service."

"Whooee! Those jaspers from the OD Connected we met going home sure called it right when they said this was a square town. I've been hauled out of a house by a deputy more'n once. But this's the first time one ever took me there."

"I'm not sure I should be doing it myself," Waco answered with a grin.

For all that he escorted the cowhand through the town's back streets and pointed out Lily Gouch's house.

"You coming in?" asked the cowhand. "I'll stand treat."

"Now there's an offer I'm not likely to have beat," Waco smiled.

"Trouble being I can't take you up on it. The marshal don't approve of us deputies going on his time."

"He sounds's ornery as a trail boss."

"You can say that again. You go on in, friend and maybe one day I'll take you up on that offer."

"Feel free any ole time," grinned the cowhand and ambled up the garden path with some speed.

Waco stood watching until the cowhand had entered the building, then went towards the fence. Set in a clump of trees, so as to attract as little unwanted attention to itself as possible, the house was well-lit. So well that Waco could see the horses tied to the picket fence clearly enough to believe at least two did not belong to cowhands.

An obvious Indian pony stood at the end of the line, its Cheyenne-roll saddle bearing a fine-looking Sharps buffalo rifle in the boot. Most likely it belonged to a hide-hunter celebrating the end of a successful trip. After one glance Waco ignored the pony and moved along to more likely prospects.

Even had there only been the night's light to guide him, the youngster would have known two of the horses had never worked half-wild longhorn cattle. Bigger and heavier than range stock, they looked suitable for light-draught work, but too slow and clumsy to ride herd on. Nesters used such horses, capable of hauling wagon or plough, but able to be saddle-ridden when necessary.

Further proof of ownership came from studying the saddles on the big horses. First, each saddle had but a single girth. Lesser men might dally one end to the saddle when roping, so it could be hurriedly released in case of an emergency. Figuring to hang on to whatever he caught, the Texan knotted his rope to the horn. Doing so threw such a strain on the square-skirted Texas saddle that two girths—a son of the Lone Star State scorned to use the word 'cinch'—were needed to hold it in place. While smaller than the dinner-plate style fancied by Mexicans, each saddle's horn was larger than any Texan used.

Speaking gently to avoid disturbing the horses, Waco moved closer. His eyes went to the saddle boot of the nearer animal and he felt a thrill of excitement run through him as he saw it held a Ballard single-shot rifle. From there he looked at the coat fastened lining outwards to the cantle. Fanning open the folds, he exposed the outer surface and found it to be a red and black check. The other nester horse carried a black wolf-skin coat on its cantle, while a long, old twin-barrel, muzzle-loading shotgun hung in a primitive boot. Neither saddle toted the floursack used to take away the loot, which did not surprise the youngster.

After completing his study of the horses, Waco withdrew and paused to decide on his next course of action. A certain amount of antipathy always existed between farmers and cowhands, due to a clashing of interests. In Kansas a furrow ploughed around one's holdings rated as a fence under law, giving the owner the right to prosecute for trespass against anyone crossing it. Such 'furrow fences' were sometimes cut on each side of cattle trails, to keep the trail-herds within certain bounds; this was regarded by some outfits as an infringement of personal liberty. So far little actual hostility had developed between the two factions around Mulrooney. However the nesters might regard his suspicions as unwarranted, or even persecution of their kind if he arrested the horses' owners. True everything pointed to the pair being the men he wanted; but it could be no more than coincidence.

Check mackinaw jackets of every hue could be bought in most towns. Possessing long-lasting qualities, wolf-skins were much sought after to make coats. Few nesters, particularly in areas safe from Indian attack, spent money on modern weapons if they owned something capable of bringing down pot-meat or for occasional defence. Selling for from twenty-five to thirty dollars, as against the Winchester's thirty-eight to sixty, depending on quality and fittings, the Ballard single-shot rifle found much favour among nesters.

"Which means that there're plenty of mackinaws that colour, wolf-skin coats, Ballards 'n' old scatterguns around. Only not all together in one place—Or could there be?"

A more cautious young man would have headed back to the office and asked his experienced friends for advice. Yet while he did so, the two suspects might come from the house, collect their horses and head for home. If they left town and disposed of the identifiable clothing, there would be little chance of locating them or proving their part in the hold-up. Sure Waco could point out the horses if he saw them again, but he doubted if such evidence would go far in court.

Once again Waco decided to act on his own. If he should prove wrong, his inexperience would offer Dusty an excuse when protesting friends of the accused came to call.

Opening the gate, Waco walked up to the house's front door and opened it. It was his first visit to Lily Gouch's establishment and he found that she had moved fast since her arrival. The main room, into which he stepped, had comfortable seats. Heavy curtains draped the windows, although they were left open so far. Seated at a piano, a Negro was playing a lively tune, while another coloured man stood behind a small combined bar and free-lunch counter. The few customers, all cowhands, and six or so girls looked curiously at the young deputy, but none offered to move in his direction. One of the girls darted to a side door, opened it and spoke to somebody on the other side.

Coming through the door, Lily Gouch showed some surprise at the sight of Waco. Then she crossed the room, a welcoming smile on her lips despite a wary glint in her eyes.

"Hey, deputy," she greeted. "Can I do something for you?"

"Yes, ma'am," he replied, then paused, not quite sure how to go on.

For a moment Lily's smile wavered and the suspicious gleam grew more intense. In other towns such a visit and comment usually heralded a request for some kind of funds, or the free services of one of the girls. So far there had ben no such demands made by either the peace officers or civic authorities in Mulrooney, but she could never shake off the uneasy feeling that it might start. So she waited to see how much, or for what reason, the bite would be put on her.

"You've got a couple of nester kids in here, ma'am," Waco said.

"Sure," Lily agreed and annoyance replaced the other emotions on her face. "Look, if their folks've been bitching about it, you tell them from me it's the first time they've been here and my gals didn't go out and drag 'em in with ropes."

"I don't reckon their folks know they're here, ma'am," Waco assured her, pleased that his theories had proved correct so far. "There's no need to get riled."

"Damn it, deputy, being treated fair's spoiling me," Lily said with a grin. "I was never this touchy when I had to hand over 'campaign funds' or pay up every time anybody felt they'd a grief against me. Have a drink?"

"A cup of Arbuckle's'd go down good, ma'am."

"Anything else? Lily inquired, darting a glance around the room.

"No offence, ma'am," Waco replied, "but all I want's to talk about them two nester kids. How long've they been in?"

"Look. I don't like talking about my visitors where anybody can see me. It's not good for business. Come into the office and have that cup of coffee while we talk."

Although not as plushly furnished as the main room, Lily's office offered a fair amount of comfort. Taking the comfortable chair she pointed out, Waco sank into it with a grin.

"You should try the chairs in our office," he told her. "Would you mind if we left the door open, so's I can see if those nesters come in?"

"Nobody'll tell them you're here——."

"You're getting touchy again, ma'am."

"Damned if I'm not! Sure, I'll open the door for you."

When sure he could see into the main room, Waco settled back in the chair and continued the questioning.

"When'd you say they came in, ma'am?"

"Maybe half an hour or so back. They're upstairs with two of the gals now."

"For the night?"

"At my prices?" Lily scoffed. "I was surprised to see 'em come in for a short time even."

"They didn't have much money then?" Waco asked, feeling a mixture of relief and disappointment.

"Do their kind ever?" Lily sniffed. "Their folks make eating-money at most and not much of that. Like I said, I was surprised to see 'em come in here. And I'll bet this's the first time they've been into a house, or paid for it."

"They shouldn't be long afore they're coming down then?"

"Not with a dollar 'short time'."

"Mind if I stay on in here and look them over when they do?"

A madam, even in a town like Mulrooney, could not easily refuse any request made by a peace officer. In addition to knowing that, Lily felt she owed the marshal's office consideration for their treatment since her arrival. While not sure just what Waco's interest in the two young nesters might be, she decided to help him all she could.

"Stay as long as you like,' she said. "I'll have some food sent in. Say, what've they done?"

114

"I don't know as they've done anything," Waco admitted. "That's what I want to find out."

"Huh huh. Do me a favour, will you?"

"If I can."

"Don't jump them in here. I wouldn't want the marks getting the idea I'd sic the law on 'em."

"I'll not make a move until they leave," Waco promised. "Is there another way out of here?"

"Through that door over there," Lily replied. "I'll keep 'em talking for long enough to let you get through the garden and over the fence."

"That'd do fine, ma'am," the youngster said.

Lily shook her head as she walked out of the office and left the door open enough for her guest to watch the room. Never had she met such an accommodating lawman. Most peace officers, even honest ones, would not have been so considerate even though she co-operated with them.

"Damned if I've ever been in such a town afore," she told herself in a mystified voice and went to order a meal for Waco.

13

Lord, What a Fool Mistake

Sitting in Lily Gouch's office, nursing a plate loaded with slices of ham, chicken and other choice items selected from the free-lunch counter, Waco again gave thought to his conclusions about the hold-up. He went through each item in its turn, examining it as he ate and watched the main room. All he knew increased the belief that he had called the play right.

No matter that the clerks at the freight office thought they were victims of the James brothers, or at least of Tricky Dick Cansole's gang, Waco felt certain that greenhorns had pulled the robbery.

Take the weapons the thieves used for a starter. While a double-barrelled ten-gauge shotgun might be unequalled as a pacifier, it could not be termed an ideal weapon for an outlaw. Nor did a single-shot rifle strike Waco as the kind of weapon an experienced owlhoot would carry. Neither the rifle nor the shotgun offered ease of concealment and both lacked the potential for sustained rapid fire in case of a fight.

Although successful and profitable, the hold-up had been carried out in a most amateurish manner. On entering the office, the thieves had taken the clerks' wallets and watches before going to the money-loaded safe. More than that, they had failed to bring along a container capable of toting off a large sum of money and had to use a floursack that chanced to be in the room. Men who knew their business would never have left the clerks free, even if face down on the floor, to endanger their escape. Nor would they have left the lamp illuminating the outside stairs lit while they went down, allowing themselves to be clearly seen by anyone passing by.

No, nothing in the way the two robbers had acted led him to believe they were experienced outlaws.

Before Waco had half finished his snack, he saw two young men coming down the stairs. Even without Lily going towards them, he would have known them to be the pair he wanted. Dressed in cheap, poorly-fitting town suits, they looked like any other young nesters in town for a celebration. They fitted the scanty descriptions of the robbers, although Waco could not state positively that he recognised them.

Thinking back, Waco remembered seeing the two young men in the Fair Lady and recalled their behavior when losing the girls to the more prosperous cowhands. Neither wore a revolver and he could see nothing to hint they carry a concealed weapon of any kind. One thing was for sure. The two nesters did not look or act like owlhoots.

"If I'm wrong—," Waco mused, rising and putting his plate on Lily's desk. "Damn it, a whole lot points to them. I'll take a chance."

With that he crossed to the rear door and let himself out of the building. Crossing the garden, he vaulted the picket fence and moved around to where the nesters' horses stood. From what he had seen, the taller of the pair looked the kind to take rash chances. So the youngster decided to nullify the risk. Quickly he slid the Ballard partly from its boot. Always eager to learn, he had taken the opportunity offered by being a deputy to study the various weapons on sale in town. Among them were several Ballard rifles, a popular item among folks who did not wish to pay a high price yet wanted a reliable weapon. So he knew how to operate the rifle's mechanism. Thrusting down the trigger guard opened the breech, but he had to work the sliding stud under the frame to extract the bullet. With the rifle rendered harmless, he replaced it and went to the shotgun. Disarming this proved easier, for all he needed to do was remove the percussion caps from the nipples and he did not even have to draw it from the boot to do so.

Light glowed as the front door opened. Waco drew back from the horses and crouched down, watching the nesters come along the path to the front gate. Laughing, shoving each other, they looked to be in excellent spirits.

"That was good, Vic," the smaller of the pair announced. "Say, that gal I went with told me she was a Russian countess—What's that?"

"A pack of lies, I'd say," Vic answered in a tone of worldly wisdom.

"We'll have to go in there again. For the whole night next time."

"Maybe, Tommy. Maybe."

"Aw, Vic. We can afford to now."

"Sure but we don't want folks noticing that, do we?" Vic replied, walking to his horse's head.

"Hold it right there!" Waco ordered, drawing and cocking his right hand Colt as he moved forward.

"Wha—!" Tommy began, spinning around.

"Do what he says, Tommy," Vic said, just a shade too calmly. "If you're looking to rob us, mister, you'll have mighty slim pickings."

With that he lunged forward, scooped the Ballard from the boot, lined it waist high in Waco's direction then squeezed the trigger. Only a dull, dry click rewarded his efforts and a startled curse broke from him.

"The scatter's got no caps on it either," Waco warned as Vic dropped the Ballard and swung towards Tommy's horse. "And I'm a deputy marshal, not an owlhoot."

Give Vic his due, he knew enough to yell 'calf-rope' and quit. Instead of trying to get around Tommy's mount to the useless shotgun, he stood fast.

"What's up, deputy?" Tommy asked in a worried voice.

117

"Let's take a walk down to the jail house and talk about it, shall we?" Waco replied.

"Why'd you want us?" Tommy began. "We don't know any—."

"Hush up, Tommy boy!" Vic interrupted, speaking in a mixture of urgent warning and reassurance. "Likely the deputy reckons he knows what he's doing. Just for the hell of it, though, what's up, deputy?"

"I figured you'd know that," Waco told him. "Let's go."

"Anything you say, you're pointing the gun. How about our hosses?"

"Take them along—from the right side."

Most white men mounted their horses from the left, so the animals became accustomed to it and showed a marked reluctance to letting a rider go up on the right side. Waco doubted if the nesters had taken the time to train their mounts in accepting them coming up to the saddle from the 'Indian side', so ordered them to lead from the right to lessen their chances of escape.

As he walked along behind the pair, placed so that he could observe them both and counter any hostile moves, Waco studied them. Watching and listening, he noticed that Vic did most of the talking. It almost seemed that the taller nester set out to jolly his companion on, or relieve the other's anxiety. At first the attempt met with no success. Tommy still continued to act nervous and scared.

"Ole Tommy's worried about what his pappy'll say," Vic remarked over his shoulder to Waco. "Him being arrested after just coming out of a goosing-ranch and all."

"Yeah," Tommy went on with the air of one suddenly presented with the answer to a problem. "Paw's not going to like it."

"Let's hope he doesn't have anything worse not to like," Waco answered dryly. "Only we all know he will."

"Hell, you can't arrest us for going into Lily's place," Vic replied. "At least I've never heard about it if you can. And the jails'd be full if you start."

Waco ignored the comment, but noticed that some of Tommy's nervousness appeared to be going. Possibly the smaller nester's worry did rise from the cause Vic suggested. Kansas dirt-farmers had a reputation among cowhands for being pious, church-going folk strong against all kinds of sin. So Tommy might feel concern, if not fear, at his father's reaction to learning where he had spent the evening.

Although the youngster could form no opinion as to the like-liness of their guilt or innocence, he felt sure that he had guessed correctly. Most likely Dusty knew of a way to reach the truth. It would be interesting to see how the small Texan handled the affair.

Once again Waco started to show his instinctive flair for law enforcement. He decided against taking his prisoners in through the front of the building. Doing so meant going along the main street, in full view of anybody who chanced to be on it. Possibly other nesters were in town and he wanted to keep the pair's arrest a secret until after Dusty had interviewed them. So he directed them to go to the rear of the building and leave their horses at the small civic pound corral.

As Waco escorted his prisoners towards the pole-walled pound, he saw a human shape drawing away from the rear of the office building. Having retained his Colt in hand while bringing in the two nesters, he did not need to draw it and tensed ready to meet any trouble that might start. It seemed highly unlikely that any other dirt-farmers knew of the pair's fate, or would try to take them from his custody by force, but he still watched the approaching shape. Drawing closer though it might be, he still could not say for sure whether it be man or woman. Whoever it was could have come through the alley from the street, or been at the rear of the building.

If it should be the latter, there might be some fuss. Waco knew the position of Smith's cell and remembered Dusty's comments about the Cansole gang attempting to contact the captured out-law. Should that figure be one of the gang, he might take exception to coming up against a deputy.

Then Waco realised that the approaching shape was a woman dressed in flowing clothes of a special kind. As she came closer, he recognised her as the new mother-superior from the convent. She slackened her pace on seeing the three young men, darting a glance around her.

"Howdy ma'am," Waco greeted. "I sure hope we didn't spook you too much."

"Oh! It's you, deputy," she answered, walking forward. "Good evening. I've been asked to come out and see one of our people who's taken sick."

"Can you find the place, ma'am?"

119

"Yes. I've been to see her before."

With that the woman passed by and Waco continued to head his prisoners in the direction of the pound. After fastening their horses to the central horizontal pole, the two young men went to the rear door. Watching them all the time, Waco reached around and knocked on it.

"Yeah?" came Pickle-Barrel's voice.

"Southrons hear your country call you," Waco replied, using the first line of General Samuel Pike's words to the tune 'Dixie'. During the War, the same line served as a password between Confederate spies.

When making plans to circumvent other escape efforts, Dusty had decided on the words as a sign to let the jailer know a friend requested admittance. So Pickle-Barrel did not hesitate to open the door. That he held his old Colt Dragoon showed no lack of faith, only a commendable sense of caution.

"Who're this pair?" the old-timer inquired, eyeing the nesters up and down.

"Couple of gents I reckon Dusty'll want to meet," Waco replied.

"Best make 'em welcome then," Pickle-Barrel declared, waving the nesters inside and re-locking the door after Waco had entered. "You gents don't mind if we'ns go through with the formalities, I reckon."

"You seem to know what it's all about," Vic answered calmly. "I'm damned if I do, but I'll go along with you."

"Thankee," grunted the old jailer, darting a long glance at Vic's face. Then he swung his attention to Waco. "You searched 'em yet?"

"Figured to wait until I could see what I was doing first," the youngster replied. "It's allus as well. Only let's do it in the back here."

"It's your game, young feller," Pickle-Barrel stated, although he could guess why Waco had made the request. "You watch the lil 'un while I tend to his pard."

Keeping guard while the jailer deftly searched first Vic, then Tommy, Waco felt a growing concern. The contents of their pockets proved to be nothing more nor less than one might expect; a jack-knife, some string, handkerchieves, not more than five dollars between them and a battered old watch which certainly did not belong to either of the robbed clerks.

Towards the end of the very thorough search, Dusty and the Kid walked into the office. They came through to the rear at Waco's call and listened to his reasons for bringing in the pair of nesters. However Dusty's reaction when told came as a complete surprise to Waco.

"You reckon *this* pair could've pulled the hold-up?" Dusty demanded in a disbelieving tone after studying the pitiful contents of their pockets.

"Sure I do!" the youngster answered.

"Lordy lord! Did you-all hear that, Lon?"

"I heard it, but I can't hardly believe it," the Kid replied. "Lord. What a fool mistake."

Annoyance and shock played on Waco's face at his friends' outspoken condemnation. Even if he had made a bad mistake, he did not expect such an open display of criticism. Malicious grins came to Vic and Tommy's faces, while they started to look more confident.

"I thought you'd learned better, boy," Dusty stated and Waco writhed at the use of a name normally only applied in private. "Damn it, that hold-up was pulled by two *men*, not by a couple of milk-cow churn-twisters."

"I told you we hadn't done nothing!" Tommy scoffed, but his lips remained in the tight line they had formed when Dusty used the cowhand's derogatory name for nesters. At his side, Vic stirred restlessly and scowled at the small Texan.

"And he told you right," Dusty went on, derision plain in voice and expression. "Whoever robbed the freight outfit had brains and guts."

"This pair of two-buckle boys couldn't find their mouths with a fork-load of food 'cept on a bright summer afternoon," the Kid went on. "Here's us been out hunting fellers slick enough to have pulled that stick-up and you waste time hauling in fool-hoemen."

Fury flickered on Vic's face at the words. "Hey!—." he began.

"Damn it, throw them out of here!" Dusty barked. "I haven't time to waste on sod-busters when I'm looking for the *men* who robbed that place."

"You've found 'em!" Tommy yelled, furious at the scornful dismissal.

"Shut it!" Vic shouted.

"Go on, get them the hell out of here!" Dusty snapped. "I—."

121

"I tell you we did rob the freight outfit!" Tommy insisted, wild with anger at the continued contemptuous rejection.

"Then where's the money?" Dusty barked.

"We hid it outs—."

"You stupid son-of-a-bitch!" Vic howled. "You've fixed our wagon now."

With that he flung himself through the door into the office and returned even faster, propelled by a thrust of Mark Counter's good arm. Knowing his presence would not be needed in the rear of the building, Mark had remained in the front and was in an ideal position to prevent the nester's attempt at escape. Fury showed on Vic's face as he returned. Screeching curses, he flung himself at his friend, laid hold of Tommy's lapels and slammed him against the wall. The Kid and Waco moved forward fast, catching Vic's arms and hauling him away from the scared Tommy. Even then the raging nester continued to struggle, but could not escape from their hold.

"Toss him in the cells," Dusty ordered and turned to Tommy. "I reckon you'd best tell me all about it."

Watching Pickle-Barrel spring to and open the door of a cell, then the two deputies thrust Vic inside, gave Tommy a chance to realise what his incautious words meant. Like most nester youths, Tommy resented the more affluent cowhands. Seeing them at the end of a drive, relaxed, with plenty of money to spend, he overlooked the way they earned their pay. Forgetting, or not knowing of the long hours worked, risks taken, dangers endured, while bringing the cattle north, he saw only men his own age who appeared to have advantages that never came his way.

It had long been Tommy's view that, given the same chance, he could lick anything done by a cowhand. So the thought that such an insignificant specimen of the cow-chasing breed regarded him with contempt spurred him to folly. The fact that none of the three Texans greatly exceeded him in age, with the tall blond kid even younger, drove all Vic's warning from his mind. So he blurted out that damning admission. Yet, having been granted time to think, he decided to bluff things out.

"I don't know what you mean," he said, swinging to face Dusty.

"Shucks, we've known all along you did it," the small Texan replied breezily. "All you did was tell us what we knew."

"So prove it."

Ever since they fled from the freight outfit's office, Vic had been telling Tommy that nothing could be proved against them. The older youngster's insistence originally filled his friend with confidence. While it had been badly shaken, the feeling returned as Tommy realised one vital piece of evidence was missing.

"That'll be easy enough," Dusty answered calmly. "The deputy who brought you in recognised you straight off—and the two clerks'll know your faces."

If Dusty hoped for a denial on the grounds that Vic and Tommy were wearing masks, the nester never gave it. Just in time Tommy bit down on the words as they rose to boil out in triumph.

"Maybe he figures the one they shot can't talk, Dusty," the Kid remarked.

"Sh—Shot?" Tommy gasped.

"We heard the shooting, that's what got us there so quick," Dusty told him. "And we'd've been after you a whole heap faster happen there hadn't been the shot clerk to tend to."

Standing back against the wall, where he had retired in the face of his two friends' attitude, Waco watched everything. Slowly the opinion formed that he had missed something. Yet he could not be sure what. So he followed some advice Dusty once gave him on the matter of what to do when unsure of the next move; he did nothing.

"Look, we never shot nobody!" Tommy gasped, looking from Dusty to the Kid.

"That's what they all say," Pickle-Barrel commented. "One feller told us we couldn't prove it 'cause nobody saw the bullet leave the gun."

"He'd a right smart legal point," drawled the Kid. "What'd you do?"

"Hung him for something we knowed he'd done."

"H—Hung—!" gulped Tommy, hands going almost automatically to his neck. "Y—You can't—."

"Not unless the feller dies," Dusty admitted. "Waco, go ask Mark if any word's come in yet."

"I tell you we never shot off our guns!" Tommy yelled. "Sure we robbed the freight office, but we didn't shoot anybody."

"Let's go into the office and hear what you've got to tell." Dusty said.

Seated before the marshal's desk, with the deputies forming a half-circle around him and Dusty on the other side holding pen to paper, Tommy hesitantly told his story. Coming to town, short of money as usual, the two young nesters had grown discontented at the sight of numerous pleasures beyond their slender purse. Everybody else seemed to have plenty to spend and they felt the deficit badly. A foolish attempt to increase their finances at a faro table ended in disaster and wiped out the little cash they owned.

One of the rules Freddie had brought in when she opened her place was 'broke-money'. Anybody who reached the blanket either drinking or trying to lick the house's percentage on the gambling games, could apply to one of the barmaids and receive five dollars. While collecting their 'broke-money', the nesters had overheard the freight outfit's swamper cursing the clerks for sending him to fetch a bucket of beer while they worked on the accounts.

Urging Tommy to leave, Vic put up the proposal that they should rob the clerks. Although Tommy had raised several objections, Vic produced answers for them all. Wearing the mackinaw and wolf-skin coat to hide their suits, and masked by their bandanas, they could not be recognised. Nor would Schubert and Wallenheim argue in the face of the shotgun. Robbing them would be too easy.

Raised to the point of bravado by the beer he had drunk before losing the rest of his money at faro, and smarting under the failure to attract a saloongirl, Tommy went along with the scheme. Neither expected such a windfall as came their way via the open safe, their first idea being merely to take the clerks' wallets; although Vic decided to take the watches and give the affair a professional flavour. Finding the safe open, they had made the most of the chance.

Although they had never heard of Tricky Dick Cansole's methods—Dusty kept the story of the stashed loot known only to his deputies—the nesters had hit on the same idea. Taking only enough money for a visit to Lily Gouch's house, they hid the rest outside town.

"I'll show you where," Tommy promised, looking and sounding close to tears as understanding of his position grew stronger on him.

"Go with him, Waco, Lon," Dusty ordered.

A somewhat indignant Waco accompanied the Kid to collect their horses. For a time he expected the Kid to make some comment, but none came. Unable to hold down his feelings any longer, the youngster let out an explosive snort.

"Damn it all, Lon!" he said hotly. "I sure never expected Dusty to roust me out like that. Especially when it comes out that I'm right."

Instead of giving any condolences, the Kid broke into a deep, hearty chuckle and slapped his companion on the back.

"Don't that beat all," the Kid finally got out.

"What's so funny, 'cepting you near on bust my back-bone?" Waco howled indignantly.

"For somebody who's acted real smart up 'til now, you're sure showing poor sense," the Kid replied.

"Huh?"

"You handled everything just right, boy. All the way."

Realisation struck the youngster, slamming him to a halt. Catching hold of the Kid's arm, Waco swung him around and thrust a wrathful face up close to the other's Indian-dark, grinning features.

"You mean that you'n' Dusty figured all along I'd got the right fellers?"

"I'd have to say 'yes' to that," the Kid admitted. "See, me 'n' ole Dusty maybe don't have half the gals in town running themselves ragged chasing us, but we can count to ten if we go slow and use all our fingers. We reckoned that hold-up hadn't been pulled by regular outlaws and's soon's things quietened down a mite we started asking questions. Then what do we find?"

"Try telling me."

"We find that our 'good-looking, young one's' already been 'round asking the same questions, only sooner."

"You couldn't miss guessing who they meant when they said 'the good-looking young one'," Waco said in a milder tone.

"Took us a while, but we figured it out," the Kid replied. "Anyways, we got to Lily Gouch's place in time to see you coming out stuffed to the craw with turkey and ham and all them other things we'd've had if you hadn't been so blasted nosy. Figured that seeing's you'd had the goodies, you might's well do the work and sat back to' let you. You handled it good, boy. Real good."

"So why'd you and Dusty start raw-hiding me?" Waco demanded, noting that the word 'boy' took on its old connotation; implying that he might be young, but he would grow from a boy into a real good man.

"Do I need to tell you?"

"Naw. He figured to rile them nesters into speaking up like lil Georgie Washingtons. 'I can't tell a lie, I chopped down that slippery elm' or something."

"Way I heard it, it was a chestnut tree he chopped down," grinned the Kid. "Anyways, there wasn't a son-of-a-bitching thing to prove they were the pair that snuck off with Pop Schubert's hard-earned wealth—We stood outside listening—So Dusty reckoned they might fall for an old trick—."

"Making out that you didn't reckon nesters, especially them two, was smart or brave enough to do it."

"Sure. Like I said. It's an old trick, but it still works when you pull it on wet-behind-the-ears buttons—on both sides of the fence."

"Yah!" Waco jeered. "I knowed all along what the game was, and that it'd work right."

"You should've told me which way it'd go then."

"Why?"

"I was betting that Vic jasper'd break first—unless you did."

"Gambling'll be your ruin for certain sure," Waco grinned. "Come on, stop holding me back. I want to wind up *my* arrest and go see Babsy."

"Yes sir, deputy," the Kid replied. "And you've sure earned it."

Escorted by the two Texans, Tommy rode from town and led the way to the hiding place of the loot. From the hollow trunk of an old oak tree the young nester drew the floursack and two hats. Using the same half-smart thinking that had led them to hide the proceeds of their robbery, the pair had also left the hats which might identify them. Then, like all beginners, they made a mistake by failing to dispose of their coats and weapons.

With the loot returned to the office and his prisoners bedded down for the night, Waco declared that he had done enough for one watch. Displaying an air of condescension his friends felt he deserved, the younster announced that such menial tasks as gathering up the crop of drunks was beneath his dignity. However he made sure that he stood at the open front door when he said it and departed before reprisals could be uttered against his person.

Going to the Fair Lady, he attracted Babsy's attention and quickly resumed the state of affairs that handling his first crime had caused to be interrupted. Later that night, with Babsy snuggled up to him, Waco went to sleep conscious of having done a real good job of work.

14

I Figure I owe Him that Much

"Waal, Smithy boy, ole Tricky Dick's not got 'round to hauling you out of here yet," Pickle-Barrel remarked cheerfully as he carried a food tray into the solo cell at noon on Friday.

Standing with his back to the far wall of the cell, Smith darted a glance past the old jailer. As always one of the deputies stood in the passage ready to back Pickle-Barrel up in case of trouble. Trying to escape under those conditions seemed almost certain to end in failure.

"There's time," Smith answered with a casual shrug. "If I knew Tricky Dick and needed him to get me out, that is."

"You'll have me believing it soon," Pickle-Barrel said dryly. "Now me, I'd say he'd found that money and don't give a whoop in hell what we do with you."

"Maybe one day you'll get somebody to tell me what you're yapping about," Smith replied. "Can I come get my chow now, or do you figure I'd be loco enough to jump you and get shot trying to escape?"

"It'd be quicker than waiting for Tricky Dick to come pry you loose," the old timer commented and backed out of the cell.

Despite figuring that Smith would wait for Cansole to rescue him, Dusty had ordered that no chances must be taken. At no time would Pickle-Barrel open the cell door, unless a deputy stood on hand to cover him and even then Smith must be made to back as far away as the cell walls allowed before the jailer entered. As a further precaution nobody went into the cell wearing a gun, but left all weapons with the man in the passage.

The comments on Tricky Dick's failure to effect a rescue were not made out of spite, or to goad Smith into a foolish attempt to escape, but with the intention of lessening his faith in his boss. After the first unsuccessful try Smith began to show signs of concern, which increased a little with each passing day. Yet there appeared to be a complete change in his attitude, as Pickle-Barrel remarked upon while leaving the cell.

"He's still not giving anything away," Waco commented.

"Nope. He was getting a leedle mite worried, but he's perked up considerable again," Pickle-Barrel answered, closing and locking the door.

"Here, take this fool cannon back," Waco ordered, holding out the jailer's highly-prized Dragoon Colt by gripping the top of its barrel between the tips of thumb and forefinger. "I thought only a danged Injun'd be mean enough to tote a rusted-up relic like this."

"Injuns is smart on some things," Pickle-Barrel replied as they walked towards the front office.

"What's up with us Injuns now?" demanded the Kid, seated at the desk and having heard enough to be alert for an attack on himself.

"You got two-three hours to spare?" Waco wanted to know.

"We was just talking about my handgun," Pickle-Barrel went on!

Being a stout advocate of Colt's thum-busting four pound, nine ounce predecessor to the streamlined, light-weight—comparatively speaking—1860 Army Model revolver, the Kid often found himself called upon to defend its virtues against attacks by supporters of the later gun.

"It's the only thing you showed any sense in since I've knowed you," he told the jailer.

"How's Smith this morning?" Dusty asked before the wrangling could start.

"Right chirpy, Cap'n," Pickle-Barrel replied.

Before any more could be said, a small, dirty, sly-looking man wearing worn range clothes entered the office. While he dressed cowhand style, he did not have the appearance of one who worked the long hours needed to handle cattle.

"Is the marshal here?" he asked, darting nervous glances around him.

128

"That's me," Dusty replied. "What can I do for you?"

"I'd like to speak to you—in private like."

Taking in the man's nervous attitude, Dusty guessed what kind of mission brought him to the office. The small Texan knew also that the visitor would not talk in the presence of witnesses.

"Don't you bunch have work to do?" he growled, looking at the deputies.

"Why sure," agreed the Kid. "Let's go around town and see what's doing, boy."

"I'll teach you how to catch owlhoots while we're out," Waco promised, heading for the door.

"Time I looked in on the other prisoners," Pickle-Barrel continued. "Mind if I shut the door behind me, Cap'n?"

"Not this time," Dusty answered.

Left alone with Dusty, the man darted another worried look around, with particular emphasis on the street outside the windows. Then he turned to face the small Texan and said, "I got something mighty important to tell you, marshal."

"What?"

"It's been a long, hard ride here and I'm losing money all the time I'm away from my spread—."

"So?"

"What I've got's worth something."

"Try telling me and *I'll* be the judge of that."

"How much is it worth?" demanded the man, studying Dusty's insignificant, young appearance and making a mistake.

"Try me first," Dusty countered.

"But—!" the man began.

"I'm busy, *hombre*," Dusty growled, pushing back his chair. "You've got until I reach the door and put my hat on to let me know what's brought you here."

"There's a bunch of Texas owlhoots in town!" the man said hurriedly.

Sitting down again, Dusty took out his wallet and extracted a five dollar bill. "Here," he said, dropping it on the desk.

"Is that all?" the man squawked, reaching for the money.

"You've not told me anything worth even that much yet," Dusty snapped, catching the scrawny hand before it closed on the five dollar bill.

Surprise and pain twisted the man's face at the unexpected

strength with which Dusty gripped him. At that moment he stopped regarding the grim-faced Texan as insignificant, young or small and realised that he faced a big, tough, experienced peace officer with whom it would not pay to trifle.

"They're at Lily Gouch's place right now, waiting to meet up with one of Tricky Dick Cansole's boys," he yelped.

"You're sure?" Dusty demanded, thrusting the other's hand from him.

"I'd swear to it on a stack of Bibles shoulder high," the man replied.

"Now that *would* convince me," Dusty assured him dryly. "Who is it down there, Dick Dublin, Alf Marlow, Bill Brooken—."

"It's Smokey Hill Thompson and three of his boys," the man interrupted.

Only with an effort did Dusty prevent his surprise showing. Looking at his cold, grim face, the man never realised just how big a shock he had handed the small Texan. When Dusty did not speak, the man decided to strengthen his case.

"They're wanted down in Texas—."

"But there's no warrant out for them here in Kansas," Dusty pointed out. "If you figure on using me to collect a reward, mister, you've come to the wrong man."

"I'm only doing my right 'n' civic duty," the man said sullenly. "Ain't you going to do nothing about it?"

"Sure. I'm going to see H—Thompson, if it's him, and tell him to ride out of Edwards County. Thanking you right kindly for doing your civic duty, of course."

"Five dollars ain't a whole heap for the time I've lost," whined the man.

"It's plenty for something I don't know's true or not," Dusty pointed out. "After I get back from Lily's, I'll see if it's worth more."

"Aw, the five'll do," the man sighed. "I'll take it and be on my w—."

"Pickles!" Dusty called and the jailer ambled in.

"Yeah, Cap'n?"

"Keep this jasper entertained until I come back—and see he stays here until then."

"I'll do just that," promised the old timer, waving the man into a chair. "Set, friend. I sure hopes you like a good game of

130

cribbage, ain't none of the fellers in the cells can play a lick."

As he left the office, Dusty saw Mark coming along the street. Aware that the man's information might be a trick to clear the building for another escape bid, Dusty halted and told the blond giant to keep guard until he returned.

"Let me fetch Frank along to do that, Dusty," Mark suggested after hearing what news the man brought. "Then I'll go with you."

"I'm going alone, Mark," Dusty replied. "If we both go, there might be trouble."

"And there'll be two of us to handle it," Mark answered. "You know Hill's had some hard cusses riding with him."

"Sure. And I know we've been good friends for a lot of years. I figure I owe him that much, Mark."

"If you're set on it—."

"Real set. If Hill's only here for a meeting, there'll be no fuss. And if it's a smart move to clear the jail, I'd as soon not fall for it."

"Likely you'll be right," Mark said with a faint grin. "Like always. Only Dusty—."

"Yeah?"

"Don't get your hands too far from your guns."

Concern gnawed at Mark as he watched Dusty walk away. While Smokey Hill Thompson used to be a cheerful, amiable jasper and a spirited companion on a spree in town, life as a wanted outlaw might have changed him. Yet Mark knew why Dusty insisted on going alone to the meeting.

Turning, Mark collided with Big Sarah as she and Derringer approached the office door.

"Hey—!" the female deputy began.

"Sarah, you're lovely," Mark told her, gripping her shoulders and planting a kiss on her hung-open mouth. "And so're you, Frank. Stay put in the office until we get back."

Before either of the amazed pair could ask questions, Mark strode off along the street at a fast pace. Blushing just a mite, Sarah scratched her head and turned a baffled face to the grinning, if puzzled, gambler.

"What in hell—?" she began.

"Damned if I know, Sarah," Derringer admitted frankly. "I'll never understand cowhands."

Not knowing that Dusty had gone alone to face four outlaws,

131

Waco and the Kid strolled leasurely through the better section of town. Their route took them by the convent and they studied it with the curiosity most men feel at the sight of women who voluntarily cut themselves off from the normal pleasures of life.

"They're not doing much work outside today," Waco commented, seeing only three nuns in the grounds.

"Maybe the new mother superior wants the inside fixed first," the Kid replied. "She's some looker, for a nun."

"She's a looker for any kind of gal," Waco corrected, seeing the woman in question stood by the front door, then came walking across the garden as they drew nearer.

The same novice was still working at painting the fence. On hearing the deputies drawing nearer, she looked around. For a moment she seemed to be on the verge of speaking, but the mother superior reached her side.

"Good afternoon, gentlemen," the beautiful woman greeted. "There's nothing wrong, I hope."

"No, ma'am. Just making the rounds," the Kid replied.

"Go to the house, Sister Teresa," the woman ordered and, after a moment's hesitation, the novice obeyed. Then the woman looked at the deputies. "I must ask you not to come around here any more than is absolutely necessary."

"How's that, ma'am?" asked the Kid.

"You must understand that our order places a great strain upon us. Living under a vow of silence is far from easy for a woman, without further diversions."

"I reckon it must be, ma'am," the Kid agreed.

"It is especially hard upon a novice such as Sister Teresa," the mother superior went on. "Seeing two good-looking young men like yourself adds greatly to the strain. I'm sure neither of you wish to make her task any harder."

"No, ma'am," Waco said.

"I haven't seen Sister Bridget around since you came, ma'am," the Kid remarked, watching the novice enter the building.

For a moment some emotion flickered across the mother superior's face, coming and going too fast for the Texans to identify it. Then she replied, "With my arrival Sister Bridget is once more under the vow of silence. It is such a trial that she is segregating herself until learning to accept it again. You won't forget what I asked, will you?"

"No, ma'am," the Kid replied and, seeing that the woman clearly wanted to bring the meeting to an end, went on. "Let's get going, Waco."

"Sure," the youngster replied. "We'll bear what you said in mind, ma'am."

With that the deputies turned and walked away. The mother superior stood watching them go for a time and then returned to the door of the convent but did not enter. Instead she remained outside, watching the remaining nuns work.

15

I'll Stop You if I Have To

Walking towards the brothel's front door, Dusty thought out the variety of tasks a lawman faced during his day's work. That morning he had seen the fathers of the two nesters and, after some patient argument, convinced them that their sons came to be under arrest for committing a crime, not out of cowhand-farmer spite. Then he arranged with the judge for the pair to be let out on bail until their trial, and saw the current gathering over over-night offenders fined and released. After that he had hoped to be able to call Freddie Woods and Cattle Kate together to request an end to the way the feud developed, but the informer arrived before he could do so. Now he went to face an old friend turned outlaw, meaning to make the other leave Mulrooney and Edwards County before attempting a robbery.

Silence dropped on the room as Dusty walked in. Only four girls were present, gathered around the table seating the house's four customers. Dressed in cowhand clothes that showed signs of hard travelling, not even the low hanging guns set the quartet apart in appearance from a freshly-arrived trail crew. Two were of middle-age, tough, durable, experienced long-riders with alert watchful ways. The third, more of a dandy than his companions, had fewer years behind him and showed a raw brashness that spelled trouble to Dusty's knowing eyes.

However Dusty's main attention went to the man he remembered as a very brave, capable cavalry officer and competent rancher. In some way Smokey Hill Thompson did not appear changed from their last meeting. Tall, tanned, good looking in a rugged way, dressed as neatly as possible under the conditions, that was the same. Yet his face carried hard lines, the mouth no longer grin-quirked and merry, an alert wolf-caution replacing the humour.

If the girls did not know their guests' identity, they guessed at the nature of the men's employment. While Dusty crossed the floor, Lily's employees withdrew from the table. All three of Thompson's companions studied Dusty, but the older pair clearly waited for instructions.

"Howdy, Hill," Dusty greeted, halting at the table's edge across from his one-time friend.

"You wanting something with us, badge?" demanded the youngest of the four.

"Afore you start something that you can't finish, Joey," Thompson put in. "This here's Dusty Fog and he's my *amigo*. Howdy, Dusty. I haven't seen you in a coon's age."

"I tried to get to you, Hill, but it was too late."

"Sure, I heard. Thanks for trying anyways, *amigo*."

"This's my town, Hill," Dusty said quietly. "And I'm sworn in as a deputy sheriff of Edwards County."

No comments came from the two middle-aged outlaws, and Dusty expected none. Their kind lacked the intelligence to organise, or the ability to lead. Recognising their failings, they were content to take orders from a smarter man. Not so Joey. Young, ambitious, regarding himself as uncurried below the knees, he sought for ways to prove it.

"So?" he asked truculently.

"So I'll stop anything that starts, no matter who starts it and help run down anybody I have to," Dusty replied.

"You!" Joey spat out, shoving back his chair and reaching gun-wards as he started to rise. "Why you short-growed r—."

Swiftly Dusty estimated Joey's potential and decided on how to handle him. Fresh to the outlaw life, with a head full of ideas about his own toughness, the young man lacked experience. That showed in the way he acted. No man who knew the score would have taken such a chance when dealing with the almost legendary Rio Hondo gun wizard.

Before Joey could complete rising or draw his gun, Dusty

134

backhanded him savagely. Caught with the full force of a swing from a real powerful arm, Joey pitched backwards. His chair disintegrated under him and he sprawled heavily to the floor. Even so he still retained a grip of his gun and, despite being winded by the landing, jerked it from leather. Going around the table in a bound, Dusty sprang forward to lash out his foot. A howl of pain broke from Joey as the toe of Dusty's boot connected with his hand, sending the gun spinning from it. Bending down, Dusty laid hold of Joey's vest and almost ripped it from him while jerking the youngster erect.

"Sit fast!" Thompson ordered his men. "Maybe the kid'll get some sense knocked into his fool head."

Slamming the dazed youngster on his feet, Dusty released him. As Joey began to stagger, the small Texan smashed a punch into his belly. Up whipped Dusty's other hand, colliding with Joey's jaw as he folded over from the other blow. The youngster straightened once more, spun around and landed limply on the floor. Turning fast, Dusty faced the table with hands held ready to deal with any kind of attack. One glance told him that the rest of the party did not intend taking up the play for their companion.

"Keep him out of my way, Hill," he warned.

"Sure, Dusty. You boys take him out and wake him up, then make sure he doesn't come back."

"Sure, boss," replied one of the men. "Will you be needing us?"

"If I do, I'll shout," Thompson promised and watched his orders obeyed. Then he turned back to Dusty and grinned, "See you're as fast as ever."

"When I have to be," Dusty agreed.

At that moment a very nervous-looking Lily made her appearance. Coming across to the table, she prepared to make excuses and wondered how Dusty would regard finding outlaws in her place.

"The lady didn't know who we are, Dusty," Thompson stated, before she could speak. "I don't reckon she goes to her visitors and asks for references."

"She'd not have much trade if she did," Dusty replied. "That chair'll have to be paid for, Hill."

"I'll see to it," the outlaw promised.

"And I'd like to talk to him in private, Miss Lily," Dusty went on.

"My office's as private as you can get around here, Cap'n," Lily answered.

"Let's go, Hill," Dusty ordered.

"Like you said. It's your town."

Going into the madam's office, the two Texans sat at her desk. After offering to supply free drinks or food, Lily withdrew. At the door she paused, then, unable to decide what to do next, went out. Her bouncer came over and asked for orders.

"Go get some rest for tonight," she replied. "I figure the marshal knows what he's doing and don't need any help to do it."

"How's it going, Hill?" Dusty asked as the door closed behind Lily.

"I can't complain."

"Why not give yourself up? Davis' carpetbaggers aren't in office any more, so you'll get a fair trial."

"And go to jail for maybe ten or more years," Thompson answered. "I'd sooner live and die an owlhoot, Dusty."

"Then don't try anything in Mulrooney, or Edwards County," Dusty warned. "Like I said, I'll stop you if I have to. So don't make me do it."

"I didn't know who held the badge here," Thompson assured him. "And, as far as I know, I'm not up here to pull anything local."

"You don't know why you're here?"

"That's the living truth. All I heard was that Tricky Dick Cansole wanted for me to come up here to meet him."

"Cansole, huh?" Dusty repeated.

"Yeah," Thompson agreed. "You've likely heard of him, wearing a badge in a Kansas town, although he's not too well known in Texas. He passed word to me that he'd got something big coming up and needed extra help. Offered me five hundred just to come up and talk it over. I heard tell he's sent for Dick Dublin and Alf Marlow to come up. Word has it that he's calling down some north country hands as well."

"He must have something big on."

"Big enough to offer waiting money for them who stick around until he needs 'em," Thompson answered. "At least that's the word that came with the five hundred."

"You figuring on taking him up on whatever it is?" Dusty asked.

"I don't know until I've learned what the play is. Anyways, I reckon I'll take some waiting money for a spell. Texas's a mite too lively since the Rangers were brought back. You and your Hooded Riders sure spoiled things back to home, Dusty. If it hadn't been for them, we'd still only have the State Police to worry about. Which wasn't any worry at all."

A faint frown came to Dusty's face at the words. Despite the fact that he had played an important part in bringing a decent, elected government back to Texas, he still hated to be reminded of how it came about. Learning of a plot, hatched by certain members of the corrupt Davis administration, to ruin Texas' economy by wrecking the State's major industry, ranching, Dusty knew he must fight back. Yet to be caught, or even recognised, doing so would compromise his Uncle Ole Devil and other influential Texans who were working to regain the franchise for the people of the State. So, reluctantly, Dusty and the rest of the floating outfit had organised the Hooded Riders as a means of fighting the State Police. To a pure-dyed Texas fighting man like Dusty hiding his identity under a hood held no appeal. However he did so, achieved his goal, then tried to forget the means employed to do it.*

Then a thought struck him and he looked hard at Thompson. "How'd you know I ran them, Hill?"

"It wasn't hard. Those Hooded Riders worked like you did with Company 'C' in the War, fast and unexpected. Who else could it've been?"

"I hoped nobody knew," Dusty said quietly.

"Nobody does know, for sure. You must've had some mighty slick help to keep you so well informed about what the Yankees aimed to do next."

"You might say that."

"Anybody I'd know?"

"That's one thing I don't aim to tell," Dusty stated flatly.

With the War over, Belle Boyd had accepted an offer to join the Yankee Secret Service. One of her contacts had gained the information which led to the forming of the Hooded Riders and she passed on much news they used. The future safety of the

*Told in THE HOODED RIDERS.

137

Rebel Spy depended too much on secrecy for Dusty to mention her part in the affair.

Not wishing for further discussion of what he regarded as a tasteless, unpleasant, if necessary, business, Dusty changed the subject.

"I'll only be here for another couple of weeks, Hill. Until Kale Beauregard comes up from the Indian Nations to take over. Don't pull anything while I'm here. I'd hate like hell to have to bring you in."

"But you'd do it," Thompson said, more as a statement than a question.

"I took an oath with the badge and I'll not break it."

"Which same I'd hate to put you where you might have to," Thompson said. "So me 'n' the boys'll ride back to the hideout and let Tricky come there to us." He grinned. "Don't suppose it's any use asking who told you I was here?"

"You're right," Dusty agreed. "It's not. *Adios*, Hill."

"*Hasta la vista*," Thompson replied. "Only not up here."

Just as Dusty prepared to leave, a thought struck him. "Say, Hill, how'd you know to meet Cansole in Mulrooney?"

"He sent word to the hideout for us to come up here instead of waiting for him," Thompson answered. "Said for us to stop at the house and he'd be in touch with us afore night."

Knowing that he would learn no more, and in fact knew more than he had a right to expect even from an old friend like Thompson, Dusty walked out of the house. Moving away without a backwards glance, Dusty thought over what Thompson told him. As he entered the trees, he saw Mark Counter leaning against the trunk of a large flowering dogwood.

"What the—!" Dusty began wrathfully.

"Sarah and Frank come in just after you left and allowed to want to be alone. So I thought I'd take a walk, not wanting to get the name for being a spoil-sport," Mark replied. "I just happened to be passing and leaned on the tree to rest my poor aching shoulder."

"I believe in fairies," Dusty growled. "Damn it, Mark. I said that I'd come here alone—."

"That's what you said," Mark interrupted. "Only who'd it be who had to go home to tell Ole Devil and Betty happen you got shot? Me, that's who."

"You've got a right smart point there," Dusty said in a milder tone, his anger tempered by the knowledge that Mark's disobedience stemmed from concern over his safety and well-being. "If that shoulder's better now, we'll find some place where we can keep watch from."

"Are you expecting trouble?"

"Nope. Just wanting to see who comes calling."

"Was it Hill Thompson there?" Mark inquired as they found a place which allowed them to see front and rear of the house.

"Sure. He'll be pulling out soon."

"Did he say why he's here?"

"Tricky Dick Cansole sent for him."

A low whistle broke from Mark's lips and he asked, "Why?"

"To help pull something big," Dusty replied. "You know that we've been wondering why Cansole tried to get Smith out; or if he'd try again after losing those two men?"

"Sure," Mark agreed. "I'm starting to think that he's forgot Smith and's set to take a loss on the hidden money."

"I'd've gone along with you this morning," Dusty admitted. "Only now I reckon he's got to free Smith and lay hands on it."

"What'd Hill tell you?" Mark asked, guessing the source of Dusty's changed opinion.

"That Cansole's calling in a slew of high-price help for whatever he plans. And offering to pay them to stick around until the right time for it. That'd run into big money."

"Which he can't raise from more hold-ups after losing Stayley and that other pair," Mark mused. "Say, if Hill came here, Cansole must be in town or close by."

"That's why we're waiting," Dusty answered. "Even if it's not Cansole who comes to meet Hill, whoever it is might lead us to him."

Settling down with the patience acquired performing more than one such task, the two Texans waited and watched. After about half an hour Thompson and his men left, Joey supported by the other two and offering no objections to the departure. Time dragged by with no callers arriving. A couple of girls emerged, passing the hidden lawmen and returned later carrying baskets of laundry. In another town Dusty might have suspected them, but he figured Lily had too much to lose to chance siding with outlaws.

On their return to the office, the Kid and Waco listened as Pickle-Barrel told what he—with Dusty's unspoken consent—

had overheard during the interview with the informer. Guessing what must have happened, the Kid told the others that he would go and lend a hand. Although Waco wanted to go along, the Kid stated his turn would come later.

When the Kid joined them, Dusty told Mark to return to the office, pay the informer another ten dollars and order him out of town. In case of objections, Mark was to hint that Smokey Hill Thompson might like to know who told Dusty of his presence. On hearing that, the informer left in a hurry and did not return.

At sundown Waco joined the watchers, sent by Mark to relieve Dusty. However by that time the evening's business had started to build up. Dusty decided that the man they wanted would not come. Or if he did, they had no way of knowing him. Figuring there would be plenty of other work to do, Dusty called off the surveillance and walked with his companions back towards the main business section of the town.

Passing the Fair Lady, Dusty glanced through the window. What he saw brought him to a halt. At his side Waco and the Kid also stopped and stared. While they all realised that the staff of the saloon regarded the feud with the Buffalo as a deadly serious affair, none expected it to be carried to such extremes.

The girl who first caught Dusty's eye wore a skirt that trailed to the floor—at the back. In front the material ended at the waist and was cut down almost to the nipples of her unsupported bosom. Although the Kid and Waco looked in frank approval, Dusty clearly found the sight less pleasing.

"Damn it!" he growled. "What in hell's Freddie reckon she's doing?"

Much as the Kid appreciated the female form so attractively displayed, he knew what Dusty meant. "Let's go look at what the Buffalo gals're wearing," he said.

On arrival, they found that Kate offered girls in outfits little more than bodices; ending at the level of frilly, brief drawers and with only one layer of cloth above the waist.

"I'll be damned if I'll ever credit a woman again with having good sense!" Dusty barked, stamping off along the sidewalk.

"What's riling him?" Waco asked. "Those gals look mighty good to me."

"And to them," the Kid replied, nodding to a group of goggle-eyed cowhands who came from the direction of the Fair Lady.

"There'll be trouble tonight, boy."

Before half past eight that evening Waco knew what riled Dusty and understood the Kid's cryptic utterance. By then they had quelled a near riot between gandy-dancers and the Buffalo's male staff, stopped a buffalo hunter attempting to drag a towns-woman into a dark alley and prevented three cowhands chasing girls along the street.

At which point Dusty decided to put an end to one aspect of the feud. Sending for Freddie and Kate, he interviewed them in private. For the first time since they met Freddie was not treated as a lady and received a tongue-lashing she never forgot. Finally Dusty delivered an ultimatum: each saloon must get its girls back into suitable clothing before half an hour passed, or be closed down. Realising they had asked for all they received, and probably more, the women obeyed. However Dusty knew that the feud had not ended, nor would until they knew who was boss between them.

16

He Walked Right By Us into Town

The full story of how the rivalry between Freddie Woods and Buffalo Kate Gilgore came to its explosive head has been told elsewhere.* Briefly, a group of prominent Brownton citizens, finding their town did not render the expected financial success hoped for, planned to use the feud as a means to help them rob the Mulrooney bank. In addition to offering them a better than fair profit, it would also ruin the other town. By a trick the Brownton crowd brought Freddie and Kate together in a boxing ring, relying on the noisy approval of the audience to drown the noise as they blew the safe. This failed due to Wally and Vera, acting as seconds to their respective employers, drugging both contestants in an attempt to keep them from inflicting too much damage on each other. The collapse of Freddie and Kate came just as the explosion sounded, and the lawmen heard it in

*Told in THE TROUBLE BUSTERS.

the shocked hush following the abrupt end of the fight.

Although Dusty feared the fight might be a trick on Cansole's part, he took all the deputies to the Buffalo Saloon; leaving Pickle-Barrel locked in the jail with orders not to open up to anybody but himself. So he had the means on hand to break up the hold-up, although the task of halting the riot which started among the disappointed and angry crowd fell upon Big Sarah.

Learning the identity of the robbery's organisers from one of the men who attempted it and was captured, Dusty received a warrant for their arrest. Although it was then Sunday, he intended to head for Brownton and serve it. Then word came that Kate meant to force a showdown with Freddie that morning. Once again Dusty faced a problem of what to do. At last he decided that the Brownton bunch must be brought in. Sarah claimed she could confine the trouble between Freddie and Kate to the Fair Lady, so once more Pickle-Barrel received his orders to remain in the locked building and admit nobody. While Dusty and the male deputies rode out, the female staff of the two saloons came together in a clash which finally brought an end to the feud.

In the middle of the afternoon Dusty's party returned. As they approached Mulrooney, bringing two wounded Brownton citizens in a buggy, they saw a couple of rifle-armed riders galloping their way.

"What's up?" Dusty asked, recognising the men as a gandy-dancer and cowhand who had each spent a night in the jail for being drunk on the streets.

"There's been trouble down at the pokey, Cap'n," the cowhand replied. "M—!"

Dusty waited to hear no more. Setting his spurs to the huge paint, he sent it racing towards the town. Leaving Derringer to continue driving the buggy and bring in its occupants, only one of whom was a prisoner, the floating outfit went hot-foot after their leader.

Ignoring the men gathered before the office, although they came from every section of the community and visitors, Dusty brought his paint to a halt. He hit the ground before the huge animal stopped, leaving it free as he crossed the sidewalk to enter the building. Inside he found two trail bosses, the head of the railroad division based on Mulrooney and a pair of prominent buffalo hunters. Slumped in a chair, dressed in her town

142

clothes, cleaned up but showing signs of what had been one hell of a fight, Freddie raised a face lined with remorse and anxiety to look at the new arrival.

"What happened?" Dusty asked, speaking to Sarah who stood at Freddie's side.

"It was near on noon when I got here, what with one thing and another," the big female deputy answered in a husky, grief-ladened voice. "I found Pickles—dead on the floor and Smith gone."

"God damn it!" Dusty blazed, swinging in sudden fury to face Freddie. "If you and Kate hadn't—."

"You don't have to tell me about that," Freddie answered in a sick voice.

Not since the day outside Dodge City, when Bat Masterson told Dusty that the wrangler of the Rocking H trail herd had been killed in mistake for him, had Mark and the Kid seen him so angry.* Freddie sank into herself and seemed almost on the verge of tears, all her calm self-possession gone before his fury. It was Big Sarah who spoke first.

"Leave her be, Cap'n. Miss Freddie's near on crazy with sorrowing now. Only as soon as she heard what'd happened, hurt like she is, she come down here to do what she could. And she's done plenty."

"That's true, Captain Fog," the railroad supervisor went on. "Freddie's got every trail crew's scout cutting for sign around town, had groups of men searching every empty house, or un-occupied place in town. Few men could have organised things better."

"You've no call to rawhide her, Cap'n," one of the buffalo-hunters went on.

"When I want you t—!" Dusty began; then the others could see him make a visible effort to control his temper. "You're right, friend. I'm sorry, Freddie."

"It *was* all my fault," Freddie replied and extended her arms. "Lord! I'd have cut my hands off at the wrists rather than have—."

"It's done with, Freddie," Dusty said in a gentle tone. Then he became cold and business-like. "How'd they get in, Sarah?"

"Now there you've got me, Cap'n," she replied, putting aside her annoyance at him for his treatment of Freddie. "The place

*Told in TRAIL BOSS.

143

was locked up tight when I came down. I used the key you gave me to get in."

"Unless you took it with you, they went out of the back door, locked it from the outside and took the key along," Freddie put in. "I checked on it."

"Thanks, Freddie. Did you—How long'd Pickles been dead when you found him, Sarah?"

"Not long," the woman replied and her face showed emotion. "He was still warm when I—I—."

"You did good," Dusty assured her quietly. "Only don't go woman on me now."

"He couldn't've been dead for more than half an hour," Sarah stated. "I wasn't sure what to do, so I headed for the Fair Lady and told Miss Freddie. She did the rest."

Which, if her present condition meant anything, must have put her through hell. However Dusty held back his comments and thoughts of gratitude until a more suitable time. At that moment his sole concern was to learn all he could.

"No fresh hoss or any other kind of tracks leaving town, Dusty," one of the trail bosses announced. "And I sent men on speed-hosses along every trail to see if they could learn anything. I'd swear they never left town by hoss or wagon."

"There've been neither stage nor trains leave," the supervisor went on. "So they must be here someplace."

"Not in any empty place, we've looked in 'em all," stated the buffalo-hunter. "Which means, unless they've done gone off in one of them balloons the Yankees used in the War, they must be hid in town."

While listening to every word said, Waco could not help noticing the way the different factions of the town worked together and how they gave Dusty their willing co-operation. Faced with a crisis, the careful, fair, honest effort put into enforcing the law in Mulrooney had paid off. Few other trail-end town marshals holding office in Kansas could have claimed such a response.

After thinking on that for a moment, Waco turned his attention to other, more important issues. Ever since Freddie held out her soft, well-cared for hands, something had gnawed at the youngster. Then memory flooded back.

"And I reckon I know where they're hid out," the youngster

144

said, wishing only the other members of the office stood listening.

"Where?" Dusty demanded.

"It's only a guess, mind. But I reckon they're at that convent."

"Go on, boy," Dusty encouraged.

"There's something about that new mother superior never rode right with me, Dusty," Waco continued. "Now I know what it was."

"What?"

"It's her hands. Soft, white, with long nails, like she'd never done a lick of work in her life. All the other nuns work too hard to have hands like that—or the ones I saw around the place did—."

"A nun, even a mother superior, with soft white hands and long nails would be unusual," Freddie remarked.

"And she sure wears fancy shoes," the youngster went on, grateful for the confirmation. "I got a peek at 'em as she crossed the railer—Hell's fire! That nun with her must've been Tricky Dick Cansole. He walked right by us into town!"

"You're making good sense," Dusty told him.

"There's another thing," Waco replied. "When I was fetching them two nesters in I met her, the mother superior, out back there. She allowed to be going to see some sick folks. If it'd've been anybody but a nun, I'd've fetched 'em in to tell you about it. But it being her, I took her word. She could've been talking to Smith. The morning after he started to perk up again instead of acting a mite edgy and worried."

"Ole Pickles wouldn't've opened up to anybody—," the Kid growled. "Except somebody like a nun."

"Just like the Bad Bunch!" Mark breathed.

"Just like it," Dusty agreed, thinking back to the notorious gang which had plagued Texas, and brought him and Mark close to death before being broken up.* "And likely they're still hid out in the convent, waiting for the hunt to die off."

"Oh my god!" Freddie suddenly gasped, stiffening in her chair. "The convent—!"

"What's wrong with it?" Dusty asked.

"Every Sunday since it opened I've sent two baskets of food around, some delicacies they wouldn't have otherwise—."

"So?"

*Told in THE BAD BUNCH.

145

"So Babsy took them today. Ginger went along, I think to prove that she was as tough as Babsy—."

"Babsy!" Waco spat out and started to turn. "Then she might be—."

Dusty caught his hand in a tight, firm grip. "Hold hard there, boy. We don't know there's anything wrong."

"Dammit, she might be—."

"And if she is, one sight of you charging out there waving your guns could see her dead, or used as a hostage, which'd wind up the same."

Despite his concern for the little girl's safety, Waco realised that Dusty spoke the truth. He saw that his original plan—or intention, for no planned thought prompted his actions— would not do.

"We've got to do something!" the youngster insisted.

"And we'll make a start at doing it right now," Dusty answered. "Lon, get over to the convent, only don't let them know you're watching it—."

"Let me go," Waco requested.

"I want you with me," Dusty replied.

"Don't you trust me?"

"If I didn't, you'd not've started to wear that badge. I want you to go in there with me when the right time comes."

Even discounting the youngster's personal stake in the affair, Dusty knew him to be the best choice. With Mark still unable to make full use of his left hand, Waco stood next in revolver-shooting ability. Up close, as they must be inside the building, a handgun licked a rifle even in the Kid's highly-skilled grip.

"Sure, Dusty," Waco said contritely. "Times I talk too much."

"If it wasn't for the company you keep, I'd say you'd grow out of it," Dusty answered. "Sarah, head for the Fair Lady and see if the gals're back."

"Yo!" she replied, dropping into the old cavalry assent almost automatically. Then she and the Kid left the room.

"Get some of those fellers to help Frank Derringer, Gil," Dusty said to one of the trail bosses as the buggy halted outside.

"It's done," came the reply and the man went to obey.

"What do we do, Dusty?" asked Waco.

"Just about the hardest thing, boy—Wait."

Any slight hope the party held for the two girls' safety died when Sarah returned with word that they had not come back to the Fair Lady.

"What now, Dusty?" asked the railroad supervisor. "Do we smoke 'em out?"

"Only by doing it my way," the small Texan replied. "I want every man you can lay hands on strung around town so tight that a gopher couldn't crawl through even in the dark. Only keep them out of sight of the convent. Mark'll show you where to go."

"Let's make a start," Mark ordered.

"If that's all you want—," the supervisor replied.

"The rest's up to us," Dusty told him. "Make sure those fellers know not to come closer, Mark."

Leaving the office, Mark started the organisation. While the supervisor had expected objections from the gandy-dancers to taking orders from a deputy who was also a cowhand, none came. O'Sullivan, Voigt and Rastignac collectively promised to half-kill any railroad man who failed to obey; and their threats carried weight.

"This's how I figure we'll play it," Dusty told Waco, Freddie and Sarah, Derringer being occupied with the Brownton prisoner.

"I'm the one to help you, Dusty," Freddie stated after hearing the plan. "It's my fault this happ—."

"Which doesn't worry me right now," Dusty interrupted. "I'm taking you because I reckon you can handle it best. Can you get what you'll need?"

"Easily," she assured him. "How about you?"

"We've got all but one thing. Moccasins, our guns."

"What else do you need?" Freddie inquired.

"Lon's knife," Dusty replied and something in his voice made her shudder. "Clean your guns, boy."

"But—."

"We can't move until after dark—And you can't chance having a misfire through not taking care of your Colts," Dusty said quietly. "Get to it, and I'll do mine."

Hearing a knocking at the front door, Tricky Dick Cansole and Stella Castle looked at each other. The outlaw fitted Sheriff Bracker's description, being stylishly dressed, medium-sized and almost effeminate in appearance. However the two Webley

Bulldog revolvers thrust into his waist band were deadly weapons in his long-fingered hands.

"I'll see who it is and get rid of them," Stella promised, adjusting her nun's headdress. "And you three stay in here with the door closed. If that fool Triblet hadn't been wandering around, we wouldn't have this pair of calico cats on our hands."

They stood in the large room which would be the chapel, although as yet it was uncompleted. Behind them, roped to chairs and gagged, sat Babsy, Ginger, each sporting signs of their fight, and Sister Bridget. Smith came to join Cansole and Stella while the tall, gaunt owlhoot named Triblet turned from the window where he had been watching the land behind the building.

"Go to it," Cansole ordered. "Nobody suspects that we're here."

On stepping into the entrance hall, Stella saw Sister Teresa emerge from the lower floor room where the nuns had been ordered to stay.

"You make one sound, or fancy move, and they'll kill Sister Bridget," Stella hissed, wondering how the girl had got out of the locked room.

Before taking the veil, Sister Teresa had been a criminal and had learned to pick locks from her father. While she had failed to open the nailed-to shutters at the window, she had dealt with the lock, but too slowly to reach the door and give a warning. Stella thought of ordering the girl back into the room, but decided Sister Teresa admired the big Irish nun too much to endanger her life. Having the girl in plain sight would serve to hold down any suspicions should it be men searching for the escaped prisoner.

Going along to the front door, Stella darted a glance behind her. Sister Teresa stood silent, watching, but the door to the chapel remained closed. Then Stella looked through the window beside the door. Despite her belief that nobody suspected anything, she felt just a twinge of concern at seeing law badges reflected in the light of the lamp outside.

Standing just outside, the marshal and that damned blond kid supported a dancehall girl who appeared to be in pain. Dressed in the garish clothing of her kind, black hair untidy and bare shoulders mottled with bruises, she hung in their arms, head drooping and body sagging as she held her ribs with her hands. Behind them stood the woman deputy. As Stella opened the door, she heard the end of a conversation specially carried out for her benefit.

"Damn this slut!" Dusty was growling. "I should be out on the range with a posse, not foo—Howdy, ma'am."

"What is it?" Stella inquired, holding down a smile at the change in tone.

"This cali—gal got hurt in the fight this morning," Dusty replied and Freddie accompanied the words with a sobbing moan that sounded genuine. "It was worse than they figured and she needs caring for."

"But the doctor—."

"He's had to go out to a farm, ma'am. And seeing's how this gal's one of your folk, I reckoned you'd tend to her."

"She was asking to come here and won't rest easy any other place," Sarah put in.

"But I—We aren't a nursing order," Stella said hesitantly, unsure of just what kind of order the nuns might be. "Surely—."

"Folks'll reckon it's mighty un-Christian happen you turn her away, ma'am," Dusty remarked.

True enough, but far worse to Stella's way of thinking was that a refusal might arouse the small Texan's suspicions. From what Triblet told them, Dusty Fog packed considerable savvy at his work and could not be underestimated in the thinking line. Already he had caused every building which did not have occupants searched, even before Smith's rescue, so he must suspect their presence in town. Give him reason to doubt her *bona fides* and she did not doubt that Dusty would come up with the right answers.

"If you don't want the fellers inside, I'll help you tote her," Sarah offered, darting a glance at Sister Teresa who was hovering in the background.

"It may be best," Stella agreed. "Once she's in, we can manage her."

From the look and sound of the 'injured' Freddie, Stella did not doubt she could prevent the other raising any outcry on learning the true state of affairs. So she stepped outside, doing what Dusty gambled she would. He saw the other occupant of the hall was a woman, guessed she did not belong to the gang and figured Stella had her there to quiet any suspicions, relying on the vow of silence or threats to keep her quiet.

Just an instant too late Stella realised her mistake. Even before she reached the trio, the men released the woman. Opening her mouth to scream a warning, Stella tried to halt her forward progress. Like a flash Freddie moved, ripping her clenched fist with all her power full into the pit of the other woman's stomach. Stella's scream finished before it started as agony knotted her body and the breath burst from her lungs.

Moving fast, Dusty shot out his hand, caught Stella and prevented her from stumbling back into the hall. With a surging heave he swung her around and backed her into the wall. Holding her erect with one hand, he reached out to take the Kid's bowie knife—borrowed on their arrival—from Sarah who had kept it concealed until the appropriate moment.

"Make one lil sound and I'll mark you so bad you'll never dare face folk again!" he snarled, holding the knife's razor sharp blade close to Stella's face.

Probably no other threat could have ensured the woman's complete silence. Hurt and winded though she might be, without the menace to her beautiful features she would have chanced giving the warning and relied on Cansole to save her. Yet she believed that Dusty aimed to do what he said and so stood as if frozen.

"Let me have her, Cap'n," Sarah said.

"Sure," Dusty answered and waited until the big woman took hold before releasing her. "Let's go, boy."

Without speaking Sister Teresa pointed out the door behind which Cansole held the hostages, then she stood watching the Texans approach it on silent feet.

Holding their guns, Dusty and Waco halted on either side of the door. Quietly Dusty stepped around in front of it, satisfied the men inside did not know they were there. Then he braced himself ready to perform a technique learned from Tommy Okasi. While Dusty could not equal his teacher's *tameshiwari* ability in breaking wood or stone with the bare hands and feet, he felt adequate for the work to hand.

Inhaling deeply through the nose, Dusty composed himself for the effort. A glance at Waco told him the youngster stood waiting. So Dusty gave the traditional spiritual cry of "Kiai!" and drove his right foot with all his power into the door. As it burst inwards, Waco plunged through, going across to the left. A moment later Dusty entered the chapel headed the other way.

For once Tricky Dick Cansole had been over-confident. Satisfied that the local law did not know of his presence in town, he had taken no other precautions than preventing the three prisoners from making any noise. While Cansole held one of his Webleys, he did not line it at Babsy although standing at her side. Gripping a Colt, Triblet held it to Sister Bridget's head. Smith contented himself with using his good hand to cover Ginger's gagged mouth.

When the door burst open Cansole and Triblet swung their weapons towards it and Smith belatedly started to draw. However the way the Texans entered threw the outlaws off balance. Fast as a striking diamondback, Cansole fired at Dusty but missed. Almost as swiftly Triblet threw down on Waco while the youngster prepared to shoot Cansole, the menacer of Babsy.

Unlike Waco and Dusty—due to the small Texan's forethought —Triblet did not take trouble to care for his gun. Its hammer fell on a percussion cap so long on the nipple as to become inoperative. Only a click sounded. Before Triblet could recock the gun, Dusty drove a bullet into his head.

Showing the same speed as when shooting, Cansole hurled himself backwards. He missed death by inches as Waco's bullet fanned by his head. Recognising the quality of the opposition, Cansole knew better than make a fight. Twisting around, he raced across the room and dived head-first through the window before Waco had a chance to fire again. Already having tasted the Texans' deadly brand of gun-play, Smith jerked his hand away from the weapon and yelled that he gave up.

"He's mine, Dusty!" Waco yelled, running across the room. Yet even at such a moment he remembered to take a basic precaution. "Lon! Don't shoot. I'm coming out!"

And, warning the Kid that a friend would be the next to appear, the youngster sprang into the darkness to give chase to the fleeing Tricky Dick Cansole.

That was Real Smart Advice

When Cansole burst through the window, the Kid snapped off a quick shot. In the poor light the deadly Winchester missed, although not by much. The bullet passed the outlaw close enough to hand him a nasty shock, but only caused him to run the faster. Before the Kid could take sight again, he heard Waco's shout, saw the youngster follow Cansole out of the building and held his fire. Nor did he follow as Waco gave chase to the fleeing Cansole. A skilled night-fighter, the Kid knew his presence would be a liability to Waco. The youngster stood a better chance alone and free from the danger of shooting at a friend instead of the enemy.

Thinking back to a comment made by himself earlier, the Kid grinned. "Yes sir," he thought, walking towards the convent. "*This's* sure one place that won't cause us any trouble."

Racing along, Cansole looked back over his shoulder. From the speed the young deputy followed, he wore something more suitable for running than the usual high-heeled cowhand boots. So he must be killed if the outlaw hoped to escape. The problem being how to bring this off without taking a .44 Colt bullet in return.

Suddenly Cansole skidded to a turning halt, threw up his right hand Webley and fired. At the same moment Waco swerved, ducked down and flame licked out from his Colt. Cansole's bullet missed and he heard the sound of Waco's lead passing his head. Fast taken, while on the move, the youngster's bullet failed to connect by such a narrow margin that it served as a grim warning. It confirmed Cansole's judgement of his ability. The outlaw knew that he must take no chances when dealing with so efficient a gun-fighter. However trickery might prevail where skill failed.

Close by stood an empty house and Cansole headed towards it. Finding the door unfastened, he jerked it open. Turning, he threw another shot in Waco's direction. Then he entered the building, closed the door behind him and backed off across the room. Halting at the opposite wall, he glanced at the square of the unfinished window. The sound of approaching feet jerked his attention back to the door. Hearing the sound of the deputy trying the handle, he fired three shots, angling them to fan across the entrance. An agony-filled cry rang out from beyond the door, followed by the thud of a falling body. Satisfied that he had dealt with the deputy, Cansole walked across to the window and kicked aside a plank blocking his way through it. Once outside, providing no other lawmen were close at hand, he could make his way into town, steal a horse and escape.

Following Cansole, Waco approached the door with the intention of crashing through it. Then he remembered what Dusty told him and slowed down, stepping silently to the left. From there he reached around, gripping the handle as if meaning to thrust the door open.

"That was real smart advice, Dusty," he breathed as the bullets burst outwards throwing splinters before them. If he had been stood in the normal position to open the door, one or more of them would have torn into his body.

Only the youngster did not waste time in idle self-congratulation. Letting out a screech like a man caught by a bullet, he flung himself backwards and lit down with a thud. That ought to convince Cansole there was no further danger, the youngster assumed and braced himself ready to charge into the building. The sound of the knocked-aside plank reached his ears and he darted along the front of the building and turned the corner. Ahead of him Cansole had already climbed through the window.

"Cansole!" Waco yelled, sliding to a halt.

The outlaw turned fast, gun bellowing as he came around. However he moved too fast. Waco felt as if a hot iron sliced over his ribs, but did not let it prevent him cutting loose with both Colts, having drawn the left hand gun while rounding the building. Left, right, left, right, the long-barrelled Army Colts spat. Caught by the bullets, Cansole reeled and hurtled backwards. The Webleys dropped from his hands as he crashed to the ground. Any one of the four bullets would have killed him.

"You all right, boy?" came the Kid's voice.

"He nicked me, but I'm still on my feet," Waco called back.

Coming up, the Kid looked anxiously at Waco, then to where Cansole lay unmoving on the ground.

"You've done good. Go tell Dusty what's happened. I reckon I can tend to him now."

"Yeah," Waco replied and managed a faint grin. "I reckon you can."

An hour later, the graze on his ribs stitched up and bandaged, Waco sat in the marshal's office with the other deputies and listened to Stella Castle talk. Thoroughly scared and wanting to save her neck, the woman insisted on making a full confession.

On hearing of Smith's capture, Cansole guessed that his orders regarding the loot had been carried out. Needing the money to pay the outlaws gathered for his big scheme, Cansole knew he must try to rescue the prisoner. When the first try failed, he decided to handle the affair himself, particularly in the face of his men's opposition to making the next attempt.

Although Stella insisted she did not know where Cansole had obtained the nuns' clothing, Dusty believed she lied. It would never be proved that the man murdered the original mother superior and a novice. Their bodies, buried outside Newton, were never found.

On arrival in Mulrooney, they went to the convent and took its occupants prisoner before being suspected. Using the well-liked Sister Bridget as a hostage, they prevented the other nuns from trying to escape and managed to keep up appearances by having a few of them working outside. Triblet came in to town on the buggy of a contact, hiding at the convent except when needed to meet somebody. It had been him who should have met Hill Thompson, but saw the outlaws leaving, smelled a rat and kept away from the brothel.

Fearing that Smith might feel neglected, Stella visited him and passed word through the bars of his cell window that Cansole was in town, preparing to free him. She directed a venomous glare at Waco while commenting on the scare he gave her.

Due to various reasons, Cansole failed to take advantage of the Saturday night diversion created by the Brownton men. Instead of telling his boss about the proposed fight, Triblet stayed at the Buffalo Saloon to watch, then became involved in the after-fight riot. By the time he returned to the convent, it was too late for them to make a move.

That morning when Triblet brought word that Dusty and the male deputies were out of town, with Big Sarah fully occupied in supervising the brawl at the Fair Lady, Cansole saw his chance. Dressed as a nun, he gained access to the marshal's office and killed Pickle-Barrel, then freed Smith and brought him back to the convent. Although they planned to leave as soon as possible, Freddie's quick action prevented them from doing so. After seeing the searching of the empty buildings and noting that nobody gave the convent a second glance, Cansole decided to lie low there until an opportunity to escape presented itself.

While delivering the baskets of food, Babsy and Ginger saw Triblet in the building. So they had to be taken captive and held. The rest the listening men all knew.

"If that bastard Triblet had told us about Saturday!" she spat out. "Or come back earlier today instead of hanging around hoping to see those lousy bitches fighting—."

"Only he didn't," Dusty told her. "Put her in a cell, Sarah."

"Sister Bridget suggested that seeing's how she was all set at at looking like a nun, she ought to learn to act like one, Cap'n," the woman deputy replied. "You know, like digging the garden they've had to neglect, painting, scrubbing floors."

"Let her start in the morning," Dusty answered.

"It'll be a pleasure," Sarah grinned. "Come on, girlie and just give me one itsy-bitsy chance to stop you misbehaving."

"Smith's ready to talk, Dusty," Mark said as the women left the room.

"Leave the Wells Fargo boys to handle that part of it," Dusty replied. "I wonder what that big job was to be?"

"Reckon that gal didn't know?" asked the Kid, for Stella disclaimed all knowledge of it when questioned.

"I'm not sure," Dusty admitted. "Maybe after she's had Sister Bridget and Sarah looking to her for a spell, she'll change her mind."

The hope did not materialise. Whatever big robbery Cansole planned, his death prevented it happening.

"Sure is quiet and peaceful tonight," Mark commented, opening the front door. "I reckon I'll be getting to bed."

"I've got to go down and see Freddie," Dusty went on, for

the lady saloon-keeper had gone to the Fair Lady as soon as she knew Waco was all right.

Coming to his feet, Waco yawned as openly as he could. "Seeing's how I've done *all* the work tonight," he said. "I allow I can go off—Reckon you boys can manage without me?"

"We'll make sure you're close to hand," Derringer assured him.

Before the youngster could object, his friends descended on him, picked him up and carried him into the rear of the building. There they dumped him in an empty cell and locked him inside.

"Maybe comes morning you'll've learned to keep quiet," the Kid said.

"Anyways," Dusty went on. "Stopping to sleep in the cell's something else a lawman has to learn."

Left alone, the youngster settled on the bunk and grinned up at the roof. They were sure a great bunch of fellers to have for friends and they had taught him much of what it took to make a lawman.

Interested readers can read about the work of a present day sheriff's office in THE PROFESSIONAL KILLERS *by J. T. Edson, the first of his new series of Rockabye County stories. Mr. Edson will also continue to write new books about the adventures of Dusty Fog, Mark Counter, The Ysabel Kid, Waco and the others he has made famous.*

Waco's Debt

CHAPTER ONE

OLE DEVIL GIVES THE WORD

It was a man's room. The furniture was good and comfortable but without any of the softer frills a woman would give to it. Over the big open-fronted fireplace hung the battleflag of the Confederate States of America, the Stars and Bars. Flanking the bullet-scarred flag hung two cavalry pennants, each also marked by bullets. Beneath them, obviously in a place of honour, was a shining, polished oak box, the lid open, the red felt caressing and holding two magnificently chased, pearl-butted and gold inlaid Colt Cavalry Peacemakers. On the lid of the box was a brass plate with the inscription:

COCHISE COUNTY FAIR PISTOL SHOOT
WINNER
CAPTAIN DUSTY FOG

Fanning out from the flags, hung on pegs, were revolvers and pistols. The line of Colt revolvers, from the first Paterson model, up through the Walker, the Dragoons, the Navies, the Wells Fargo, the conversion of the 1860 Army cap and ball by Richardson or by Thuer, the Peacemaker and the Lightning. Beyond them were other handguns, single-shot Remington cartridge guns, deadly pistols of a bygone age. There, mixed among the others, looking like a sawed-off Winchester rifle with a pistol butt, was a Volcanic; next to it a European-made ten-shot, pinfire revolver, smuggled through the Yankee blockade to aid the arms-starved Confederacy.

The man who sat in the wheelchair fitted well into this martial setting. He was tall, spare and hard looking. Not even the years he'd spent in the wheelchair had bowed his shoulders or relaxed the ramrod straight back in the coat of a Confederate Army General. His lean, tanned, fighting man's face, the eyes black and piercing, the hooked nose and the tight, firm mouth with the tiniest hint of a grin at the corners, showed nothing of self-pity. He sat his chair as he'd always sat his horse, straight, and with the air of a man long used to command. He was Ole Devil Hardin, owner of the biggest ranch in this section of Texas, if not the biggest in the whole of the Lone Star State.

Right now he was relaxing, frosty eyes looking down unseeing at the book on his lap, mate to the many on the shelves at the far end of the room. He was, perhaps, thinking of the days when he commanded the Texas Light Cavalry in the War Between The States. Whatever the reason for his reverie, he paid no attention when the door opened behind him.

'Is there any word from Dusty yet, sir?'

The voice, an easy and even Texas drawl, came from behind him, and brought him swinging the chair around to look at the speaker. The black eyes showed nothing of his thoughts, but his lips broke in a rare smile at the words. It was so like young Waco to ask this. He'd asked it nearly every day since the Rio Hondo gun wizard, Dusty Fog, left with a herd for Texas John Slaughter over to Cochise County, Arizona. Waco gave to Dusty Fog the loyalty, devotion and hero-worship which would have gone to his father, had not Waco Indians left him an orphan almost from birth.

'I heard from him when the mail came in this morning, boy. The Kid's not fit enough to ride just yet, about another week and they'll be on their way back home.'

Waco grinned at this. He was still hoping for a chance to saddle his big paint stallion and head for Escopeta County, New Mexico, and help Dusty Fog and Mark Counter find the men who shot down the Ysabel Kid. Now there was going to be no excuse for it and he would have to carry on his work with the floating outfit here at the O.D. Connected.

He was a tall, young man, over six foot, with wide shoulders and a lean, trim waist. His face was tanned by the elements, handsome and young looking, his blond hair curly and taken straight back. In dress he could be mistaken for nothing but

6

what he was; a Texas cowhand and a good one at that. He'd hung his low-crowned, wide-brimmed J. B. Stetson on the peg behind the door and was now hanging up the buscadero gun-belt on the hook, the matched, staghorn-butted Colt Artillery Peacemakers in the holsters. Around his throat was a tight-rolled, long, blue silk bandana, the ends falling down over his dark blue shirt and calfskin vest. His brown levis hung outside his high-heeled, fancy-stitched and costly boots. The boots themselves had Kelly spurs at the heels and were real, genuine Justins.

After his query into Dusty Fog's welfare, Waco crossed the room and sat at a side table, taking up the deck of cards which lay on the table ready for use. Two more men followed him into the room and were hanging their hats on the hooks.

The first was as tall as Waco, just as well built, though not so trimmed down towards the hips. His hair was a violent red, curly, rumpled and untidy as if it rarely felt the mercies of comb and brush. His face was freckled, tanned and handsome, a happy untroubled face. His clothes showed him to be as much a Texas cowhand as Waco and, unless the sign read wrong, one of the top water. The bandana around his throat was of silk and brilliantly coloured. He stripped the heavy gunbelt with the twin, walnut-handled Colt Cavalry Peace-makers butt forward in the holsters, and put it under his hat.

The last of the trio was also tall, though not as tall as Waco or Red Blaze. He was slimmer, his face studious, pallid with a tan-resisting pallor, mild almost. Yet for all of that he wore the dress of a tophand cowboy and the gunbelt around his waist, with the ivory-butted Colt Civilian Peacemaker at his right side spelled only one thing. Here was a fast man with a gun. The only difference between this man, Doc Leroy and the other two was that he invariably wore a brown coat, the right side stitched back to leave him clear and fast access to his gun.

These three young men, Waco, Red Blaze and Doc Leroy were members of the elite of the O.D. Connected Ole Devil's floating outfit. They, along with Dusty Fog, Mark Counter and the Ysabel Kid, were the floating outfit, picked men, skilled

7

with cattle and all branches of the cattle industry, but also skilled in the use of their guns. They alone of the ranch crew had access to this room here, Ole Devil's library. Here Waco spent much of his spare time, improving his education from the books in the library, cleaning or just examining the guns, or playing poker with Doc Leroy, practising the skills of a crooked gambler.

Right now, poker was in the offing and Waco gave the cards a fast riffle stack then said, 'You playing, Red?'

'Not me, boy. I like to play fair when I play.'

Waco chuckled and gave the cards a fast riffle again, passing them to Doc to cut. Doc was no mean hand with the pasteboards himself and their games were not so much poker playing as a battle of wits as each tried to outcheat the other.

Red Blaze joined his uncle, answering questions about the work they'd done on the range that day. Then he took up a newspaper which lay on the table and opened it out. The front page was typical of the day, nothing out of the ordinary on it. He looked down the columns where the news was recorded and an editorial damned Sam Bass's efforts at train robbery. Then another item caught his eye.

'You hail from the Ranse country, don't you, Waco?'

'That where I started out from,' Waco agreed as he flipped a desired card from the centre of the deck for the first time without Doc detecting him.

'There's a rancher been murdered up there. Him and his two sons. Name of Sunshine Sam Catlan——'

The cards fell from Waco's hands. He thrust back his chair and came to his feet. His usually expressionless face was hard and set and his voice brittle and cold. 'What did you say, Red?'

Crossing the room Waco took the paper and looked down the columns of print until he saw what Red was talking about. His hands were not as steady as they usually were as he read the item:

PROMINENT RANCHER MURDERED

Today in Hood City, County Seat of Ranse River County, a

verdict of murder by person or persons unknown was brought by coroner's jury investigating the murder of rancher Sunshine Sam Catlan and his two sons, Race and Matthew. Sunshine Sam was noted for ...

Waco read on through the article, his face losing colour and turning pale under the tan. He crushed the paper in his powerful hands without even knowing what he was doing as he stood still, swaying slightly. Red caught the youngster's arm, steadying him and easing him into a chair.

'What is it, boy?' Ole Devil's voice cut in gently.

Waco's head was bowed for a moment then he got a grip of himself and looked up, face drawn. 'Sunshine Sam and his family raised me after the Indians got my folks. They'd nine kids of their own, but they still took me in. Lost all the kids 'cepting Race, Matt and Mary Anne. They lost all the others, Indians, illness, accidents. Yet they always treated me just like I was their own. Mary Anne, she was eighteen months older'n me and she looked after me. Used to call me her baby brother. Sam had him some bad luck, lost the kids, then just after I pulled out on my own he made him a killing in a poker game, started to build up the S.S.C. Made it real big, made it by hard work. I always aimed to go back up there and see them again but I never did.'

Red smoothed out the paper, cursing himself for being all kinds of a fool. It must have hit Waco hard, being told that the man who raised him was murdered. He read the article and said, 'Says here that Mary Anne's in school back in St. Louis and they've sent for her to come back. This paper's a week old and the killing took place three days afore that. She'll be nearly on home, not more than a couple of days off it at most.'

'You'd best go along, boy. She's going to need some help.'

Waco hardly understood Ole Devil's quiet spoken words. He was shocked more than ever before in his life. Since he was thirteen he'd ridden with death as a constant companion but never before did it strike so close to him. Sunshine Sam was the only kin he'd ever known. He'd taken him in and made

9

him one of the family; he and his wife couldn't have treated Waco better had he been one of their own. Now out of all his family only Mary Anne was left. Sunshine Sam's wife went the year before, according to the paper. Now Mary Anne his little Rusty gal, was alone in the world, going back to the S.S.C. She was going to need a lot of help now her father was dead, murdered by person or persons unknown. Then slowly the meaning of what Ole Devil said came through his jumbled thoughts. Ole Devil was giving him permission to go off; at this time when they were all needed here at the ranch he was allowing a tophand to go off on a mission which might take any length of time. He started to stammer out his thanks, the words coming awkwardly from his usually glib tongue.

Ole Devil waved the thanks aside and snapped, 'Red, tell Kiowa he'll take over as *segundo* and handle your work for a piece. Doc, check over your gear and see if there's anything you need. If there's anything at all you want go collect it from town. You'll be riding from here at sunup tomorrow.'

Waco could hardly believe his ears. It was now, more than ever before, that he realised why the men of the O.D. Connected would gladly have died for this hard-faced man who ruled them with a rod of iron. Not only was Ole Devil allowing him to go to Ranse River County, but he was also sending along two men who would be of the greatest use in case the murderers of Sunshine Sam Catlan wanted to get the rest of the Catlan family.

'I—er, I——' Waco began again, trying to show his gratitude to Ole Devil. Red and Doc were his friends and they were the ones he would want along with him in this, with Dusty Fog, Mark Counter and the Ysabel Kid not being here.

'You've got some riding to do, Doc,' Ole Devil Hardin cut in before Waco could finish. 'Go make your check. Red, head down right now and see Kiowa.' The two turned and left the room and Ole Devil gave his full attention to Waco who was still seated in the chair and staring, without really seeing, at the paper before him. 'All right now, boy. You stay here and tell me all about Sunshine Sam Catlan.'

CHAPTER TWO

MARY ANNE COMES HOME...

'I'LL give five to one she sells, boys!'

Doctor Henry J. Smethers, sole medico for Ranse River County, glared at the speaker, his usually mild, sun-reddened face showing some anger. The woman who was shouting this speech stopped, studied the doctor for a moment, then came forward with her hand held out in a warm and friendly greeting.

'Why Doc,' she said winningly, 'We don't often see you in here.'

Della Christine was a beautiful woman and knew it. It showed in the arrogant way her blonde hair was piled up on top of her head, in the beautiful, almost flawless contours of the face with the pouting, sulky lips. It showed in the skin-tight, figure-showing red dress, a dress which was slit to the hip on one side showing her black stockinged shapely legs to anyone who wished to look at them. She wanted them to look, for Della Christine lived only for the admiring glances of men.

Doc Smethers was one man who did not admire her. He was a small, cheery, bald man, fat and passing middle-age. His town clothes were rumpled, his shirt open at the neck and tieless. His admiration for Della was not so large as other men's for he was not fooled by her. She was something he'd seen from New Orleans to San Francisco and back the long way, a woman preying on the woman-hungry men. It was the way she made her living, and Della Christine was good at it.

The saloon here, Della's Tavern, was not what one would expect in a small Texas cattle town. There hardly appeared to be sufficient trade for so garish a place. Smethers thought that when the place was built a few months before. It was bigger than most every other place in town, a two storey construction which dwarfed the surrounding buildings on Whittle Town's Front Street. The saloon inside kept up with the pretentious appearance of the outside, the gaming tables as good or better than could be found even in Hood City, the county seat. The bar was long and of shining mahogany; behind it an array of bottles and a long mirror which showed the whole of the room. It was surprising that such a place should be here in this small town, for there did not appear to be any use or need for it.

'I see you're betting that Mary Anne Catlan sells the S.S.C.' Doc ignored the hand, his voice mild compared with Della's strident tones.

'Sure, Doc,' Della threw back her head and laughed. 'What would a milk-faced dude like her want with a ranch?'

Smethers held down a smile. Mary Anne Catlan was far from a milk-faced dude. She'd been as wild and reckless a tomboy as could be found in the West. The Catlan family were proud of her prowess on the back of a horse or in a hair-yanking battle with some other girl. She'd been sent to the Eastern school in the hope it would teach her the social graces which Sunshine Sam thought she needed. Today she was due back; would be coming in on the stage which would soon arrive.

Doc studied Della for a moment, then said, 'I'll lay fifty dollars on that, with you.'

'It's a real foolish chance, Doc,' Della answered.

'I doubt it. Besides I make enough when Brarsand's guns shoot each other up.'

Della frowned. She did not like Smethers' attitude. She was used to respect from men and the old doctor never showed her any. She did not care for anyone talking in such a manner about her boss, Carl Brarsand. Her fingers drummed on the bar as she frowned at Doc, then she said something which under normal circumstances she would not have thought of saying:

'All right then, Doc. If you're so sure I'll make another bet with you. If she stays I'll drag her out of town by the hair.'

Smethers was turning to leave the bar but he came around with a grin on his face. 'I'll have another fifty on that. Let me know when you aim to try and I'll get ready to do some work.'

'On her when I've finished with her?'

'On you. If you try a thing like that with Mary Anne Catlan she'll whip you so fast you'll think the hawgs have jumped you.' Saying this, Smethers raised his hat to the woman and walked from the saloon with a swagger in his stride.

Della scowled after him. Somehow every time she tried to out-talk the old man she was left standing and wondering what went wrong. Then she felt a hand grip her arm and turned. Her boss, Carl Brarsand, stood by her side, annoyance plain on his face. He was a big man, tall, heavy and handsome. His clothes were cut to the latest Eastern style, but under his arm there was a bulge which spelled shoulder holster to eyes which could see the signs.

'What's going on here, Della?' he asked.

'Just a little bit of fun for the boys,' Della answered, her voice whining and frightened. 'Betting she sells out. You know we need some money towards running this place.'

His fingers bit hard into the firm flesh of her arm. 'You stupid cow. We don't need money that bad. Look, we've built this place so we're ready when the town booms open. We don't want folks talking about us.'

'All right,' Della sounded scared and she had need to be for Brarsand was a vile-tempered man when crossed. 'Did you see Doc Pilsener in Chicago?'

'Yeah. He did it for us. I sent the letter off as soon as it was done. It should be here either today or tomorrow, then I'll go and see O'Rea, and make him an offer.'

'How about Doc, will he talk?' Della watched the big man's face.

'No, he won't talk.' Brarsand instinctively patted the bulge under his left shoulder.

Smethers stamped along the street towards the smaller and not so pretentious bar of the Hood City Saloon. He pushed open the batwing doors and entered the small, dark and cool bar-room. Only two men were in here at the moment. One was Jabe Spencer, the owner, a short, and cheerful man. The other was tall and lean, wore range clothes and belted a low-tied Leech and Rigdon percussion-fired revolver which had seen some use. He was Lafe Sanger, once town marshal, now reduced by the arrival of a younger man, to jailer.

'A glass of your Old Scalp Raiser, Jabe!' Doc bellowed as he came across the room. 'I've just made us some money.'

'Man can always use it, Doc,' Spencer answered.

'What's up, Doc?' Sanger went on.

'I was just in Brarsand's place to collect a bill, him having been away for a few days. Della's betting Mary Anne Catlan sells out. Then she bet that she'll run Mary Anne out of town personal if she don't sell and go.'

Two startled faces looked at Doc, faces in which delight started to show. It was Sanger who spoke first, 'I surely hopes you lay some on for us two.'

'Thirty dollars each.'

Thirty dollars was a lot of money to the two men, but they did not appear to be worried by it. They knew Mary Anne Catlan and were willing to take more than just that much on her in a matter of this kind.

'Them bunch there allows they're some slick,' Spencer whooped. 'They don't know ole Mary Anne.'

'Remember the bay Jack Wilmont bought?' Sanger went on. 'His Molly and Mary Anne tried to ride it. I reckon it piled them both five times, but every time one of them was throwed the other got on it. They licked that hoss between them.'

'The only thing they couldn't lick was each other and they sure tried often enough,' Smethers remarked. 'Now Molly's in Chicago and letting ole Whit Dwyer run the ranch for her. I wish she'd come back now, what with Mary Anne coming home and Sunshine Sam getting killed out there on the Ranse.'

'I wonder who killed Sam and his boys,' Sangster spoke gently. 'It wasn't one of them nester families on the other side of the river. You handled the inquest, didn't you, Doc?'

'Sure.' Doc appeared to be wanting to change the subject.

14

'The gal needs help. There ain't nobody she could turn to now except maybe you two and Colonel O'Dea. But the ranch crew needs them a leader and she can't give them that.'

Pulling his watch out Sanger glanced at it and grunted. 'Stage's just about due in, let's go and see it.'

'Sure, let's show ole Mary Anne she ain't alone.'

The three men finished their drinks and walked out of the saloon, back along the street to where, facing Della's Tavern, the Wells Fargo stageline office stood. A crowd was gathering to greet the westbound stage, the event of the day. Sanger noticed that the saloon crowd were on the sidewalk in front of Della's Tavern, Della with them. So was Brarsand, the old-timer noted and wondered where the handsome man had been for the last few days. He'd left soon after the death of Catlan, Sanger recalled and only returned this day or early yesterday. He lounged by the door of the saloon, around him seven or eight hard-looking, gunhung men who worked on the payroll of his saloon.

Sanger's thoughts on the owner of Della's Tavern were distracted by the arrival of the stagecoach. It came hurtling along the street and halted in front of the office. The door opened, a flashily-dressed whisky drummer jumped out, turned and held out his hand to the young woman who came to the door. The watching men were amazed at the charge in her for they recognised Mary Anne Catlan.

She'd gone away a tanned, happy-go-lucky tomboy and come back a lady. Mary Anne Catlan stood on the sidewalk, her cheeks were no longer tanned by the elements, but soft and delicate. She was a tall mature girl, as tall as Della Christine and with a figure, which, while not being so openly displayed, was just as rich and full. She wore a small, eastern-style hat on her elegantly cared for rusty red hair, her face was innocent of makeup and her black dress plain yet stylish. In her right had she held a vanity bag which she toyed with as she looked around at the familiar sights of her home. There was a twinkle in her eye as she saw the three men converging on her.

'Good to see you, Mary Anne gal,' Sanger said, moving

forward and holding out his big hand to her. The coach was moving now, making its way around the side of the building to off-load mail and luggage.

Mary Anne sighed. 'The ride completely fatigued me. I cannot imagine how anyone could stand to travel further in such a bumpy vehicle. It really was too much for me.'

The three men exchanged looks. This from a girl who'd ridden many miles on the back of a half-wild cowhorse. Sanger gulped, then went on. 'We've got that old dun hoss of your'n down at the saloon. Had him brought in from the spread for you, thought you'd want to ride him back.'

'Goodness me!' Marry Anne sounded horrified. 'Ride a dangerous creature like that. I will hire a buckboard and a gentle team, then get a driver to take me home.'

Brarsand and Della could hear every word being said and the blonde sniggered. 'I could go over there right now and win both them bets.'

'You stand here and keep your mouth shut,' Brarsand snapped back. 'We'll handle it the way I fixed it.' With this he nodded to a man who lounged against the wall at the end of the saloon.

The man lurched forward from the porch, moving like he'd taken on too much bravemaker and was set to have him some fun. He crossed the street by the waterbutt which stood, full and ready for use on the dirt street, just in front of the Wells Fargo office. Swinging up on to the porch he halted and looked owlishly at Mary Anne, then grinned. 'A redhead. I likes redheads. Going to have me a kiss.'

Sanger was about to lunge forward and intervene as the man came at Mary Anne with his arms held out to enfold and hug her. Suddenly the sedate mildness left Mary Anne and her eyes flashed with the fire of sudden anger. She swung her arm, bringing the bag around to smash into the side of the man's head. For a blow with a vanity bag it looked to pack unseemly power. The man staggered backwards and from the pain and the way his head spun he knew there was more than just ladylike trifles in that bag. His suspicions were proved when Mary Anne's other hand shot into the bag and emerged with an item that should not have been in the possession of a milk-faced dude girl. He snarled out a curse, but his lunge forward came to an abrupt halt as Mary Anne gave an order.

'Stop right where you are.' Her voice was changed from the bored elegant tones to a hard, clipped-down Texas drawl that brooked no argument.

The man stayed where he was. He always did as requested. The Merwin and Hulbert gun in Mary Anne's grip was pointed right at him, pointed and held by a hand which was used to doing such things, the .45 bore of the short barrel was lined right at his stomach. Short barrelled or not it would make a hell of a mess of him if the girl was anything like a shot and she gave the impression she was.

'Sorry lady,' the man's voice was sober now, sober and worried. 'I was only funning——'

'Drift and *pronto*!'

The man gulped. From the way the girl talked now she knew the range country well. He turned on his heel and shambled away, followed by the laughter and jeers of the crowd. Mary Anne let him go, throwing back her head and roaring with unladylike laughter as she pushed the gun back into her bag again. She turned to Sanger who was shoving his old gun back into leather after drawing it ready to put a .36 ball where it would have done the most good.

It was the old Mary Anne Catlan who looked at them; 'Lordy me, your faces when I started talking to you,' she finally gasped out. 'I thought I'd play it that way and see how you acted.'

'You surely had us fooled, gal,' Spencer grinned back. 'I thought you'd gone all eastern dude.'

The smile faded for a moment. 'Where did you bury pappy and the boys, Lafe?'

'In that grove with the others,' Sanger answered. 'I——'

'That's all right. I'm over the worst of it now. Pappy wouldn't want me to start sniffing.'

Brarsand was crossing the street now with Della following on his heels, a disturbed look in her eyes. He came to a stop in front of Mary Anne, swept off his hat and said, 'Welcome home, Miss Catlan. May I congratulate you on the way you handled that drunken cowhand.' He shot a look at the three men. 'I would like to see you alone.'

'I've known Lafe, Jabe and Doc for more years than I can count. If they can't hear what you've got to say to me, I don't want to.' Mary Anne took an instant and completely inexplicable dislike to the man. It was the western girl's natural aversion to a fancy-dressed dude.

'I would much rather speak to you alone.'

'And I'd rather you didn't.' Mary Anne saw the saloon woman's face redden. The crowd was dispersing now, seeing there was nothing more dramtic likely to be happening. 'Tell it, mister. I want to be on the way to the S.S.C. in time to get there before dark.'

'All right then.' Brarsand held down his anger. 'I would like to make you an offer for the S.S.C.'

'It's not for sale.'

'I'll make you a good offer for it, Miss Catlan. You know, a young woman cannot run a large ranch like the S.S.C.'

Mary Anne shrugged. 'I can make a try. I didn't do too bad with that gunny of yours, did I?'

'My gunny?' Brarsand frowned, looking puzzled. 'I'm not sure what you mean. He was just a drunken cowhand.'

'He wasn't drunk and he wasn't a cowhand,' Mary Anne contradicted. 'I saw you wigwag to him just before he came across here.'

'You saw too damned much!' Della hissed. She was fast losing her temper, for she could see she was costing Brarsand money. The ranch girl was not going to give things up.

Mary Anne looked the blonde up and down with a cold and contemptuous gaze, then, as if dismissing her as of no consequence, turned to the man again. 'You must have thought I was green, pulling a play like that. What was he supposed to do, make me think the wild, wild West was too wild and woolly for me.'

'Listen you——!' Della hissed, seeing Smethers watching her with a grin on his face.

'Ask your mother to keep out of this,' Mary Anne remarked.

Della snarled out a curse, pushing by Brarsand and lunging forward at the girl, hands reaching for her hair. Mary Anne's eyes flickered with the light of battle. She moved and acted in a manner which caught Della by surprise. Mary Anne's hands shot out and pulled with a strength that was out of all proportion to her size. Della shot forward and hit the hitching rail hard. She went right over the rail and fell head first into the water-butt. Della's angry squeal sounded as she went over, then died away as her head went under the greenish and stagnant water.

Mary Anne stood back with hands on hips and roared with laughter as she watched Della's legs waving. The laughter was echoed by every man in the street and it was some seconds before three of Brarsand's men came to pull her out. They had to help the winded, half-drowned, soaking and dishevelled woman across the street. Mary Anne watched them and then gave her attention to Brarsand again.

'Still think I can't run the S.S.C.?'

'It could be awkward and lonely out there. I hear your crew aren't too happy about working for a woman.' Brarsand could see this girl was going to be more trouble than he first expected.

'I'll chance it.'

'Why bother. With the money I'll pay, you could go east and live the life a young lady should. There is no reason why you should tie yourself to a place like that ranch.'

'Mister,' Mary Anne's voice was grim. 'My pappy took the S.S.C. back in the old days. He fought Kiowas, Comanches and rustlers. He rode trail-drives, worked twelve or fifteen hours a day to build the S.S.C. up. He built it for the family and I'm not letting his work go for nothing.'

'I approve of your determination.' Brarsand made a change in his stand. 'If I can send a man to help run your spread, I will do so. If I can help you in any other way, just let me know.'

'Thanks. After I've looked the spread over I'll maybe take you up on it.'

Brarsand raised his hat again and was about to go when

Smethers coughed and remarked. 'I made a couple of bets with Della.'

The big man turned back. His face working angrily, but he knew better than quarrel with a gambling debt. 'All right, Doc. How much did you put on?'

'One hundred. At five to one.'

Brarsand scowled, but he took out his wallet and peeled off six one hundred dollar bills, passing them over. Then he turned and crossed the street, entering the saloon. Mary Anne watched him go then turned back to her three friends. 'What was all that about, and who was he?'

'Name's Brarsand, owns the saloon there. Bought out the old Shannon Ranch in the back country early on, but he sold it again. What you going to do, gal?' Sanger asked.

'Head down to see Colonel O'Dea, then go to the ranch,' Mary Anne replied. 'Where's that old dun of mine?'

'Down at the O'Dea place. Took him there when we heard you'd be coming in today,' Sanger explained.

On the walk to the O'Dea house at the back of town Mary Anne tried to learn as much as she could about the death of her father. There was not much to tell. Sunshine Sam had been fishing on the bank of the Ranse River, after a big old bass. His sons, as usual, went along with him, and there they were, found shot in the back, all three of them.

The county sheriff made a thorough investigation of the matter but could find nothing to help him in the search. Sunshine Sam was a man liked by all who knew him.

The ranch crew were still working the spread, but they were uncertain as to their future and might not stay on now. Mary Anne knew full well the difficulties which were coming to her. She also knew a strong hand was needed to control them. She thought of the many friends her father made. One of them was a curly-haired, smiling young man called Sam Bass. He might come and help her, but he was being hunted for some train robberies.

It was then she remembered Waco. It was all of five years since he'd left home to see something of the world. She'd heard little enough of him in the time which followed, although

Sunshine Sam passed the word for his adoped son to come home when he'd got the ranch going again. If Waco heard he'd never shown up, although word had it he was riding for Clay Allison's C.A. outfit. The thought did not make her happy, for she knew something about the hardcase crew who rode for Allison. They were not the best sort of company a boy would get into. His men were noted for ability with cattle but more so for ability with a gun. One thing she did know, if Waco heard of her father's death, he would return and give her all the help he could. She only hoped her little brother would return to help her now. The three old men here were her loyal friends and there were other people in town who would stand by her. They were not cowhands, however, or if they were once, were now too old and stove-up to be of use to her. With the ranch crew she would need a young man to lead them. She wondered how she could get in touch with Waco.

CHAPTER THREE

A VOICE FROM THE PAST

MARY ANNE CATLAN rode towards the old ranch house with misgiving filling her. She'd found Colonel O'Dea, the lawyer in town, was along at the County Seat attending to business and his two daughters along with him. So, leaving her luggage at the O'Dea house, she'd changed into a tartan shirt and old jeans, then with her stetson on her head and high-heeled, fancy stitched boots on her feet, she got her dun horse and headed for home. She thrilled to the rapid beat of hooves and the feeling of the horse moving under her. Yet for all of that she was worried. There was a lump in her throat as she rode towards the long, low white house. From the right, its lighted front showing people were in, was the bunk-house. She could hear the sounds which told her the ranch crew were having fun in the usual rowdy cowhand manner.

Swinging from her horse she took it down to the corral and attended to it. Then with the dun looked after she returned to the house. A small, fat Chinese man looked out of the door, his eyes drawing even more narrow, then a grin split his face and her threw the door wide open. 'Miss Mary Anne.' There was pleasure and affection on his face which did not go with the meat cleaver he held in his hand. 'I thought you would be back today.'

'Why sure, Lee.' Mary Anne gripped the man's hand in her own, knowing she'd got one friend here who would stand by her. 'I came as soon as I heard.'

'Is bad business, Missy. Hands all scared, ready to give up if you not got good man to lead them.'

Mary Anne bit down the flood of tears which welled up

inside her as she entered the hall of the house. She stood for a moment just inside, then made her decision. She was going to show the men that a woman could handle the ranch here. Turning on her heel she stepped back out into the night, pausing to speak to Lee Chan, her cook.

'You got any chow yet, Lee?'

'Got plenty, knew you'd want it. You always did, Missy.'

The girl managed a smile. Good old Lee Chan. He would stand by her no matter what. She hoped the other men would be the same. Walking across the open space to the bunkhouse she tried to decide what course to adopt. All too well she knew cowhands, knew their ways and habits. This first meeting was vital, for it could make or ruin her chances with the men. She felt the weight of the Merwin & Hulbert revolver thrust in her waistband and wondered if she should take it to the house before going to see the men. She decided against it and walked to the door, listening for a moment to some of the choicer expressions being used inside, smiling, not blushing for she'd used the same expressions herself. She knew better than to open the door and walk in for there was no telling what embarrassing state of undress some of the men might be in.

'Come in, Lee,' a voice yelled in answer to her knock. 'We done got ole Larry tied down.'

Mary Anne knocked again and the door was thrown open. A tall, lithe-looking young man with an untidy thatch of hair glared out. 'What the hell, Lee——!' The words died off as he looked at the girl. 'Gee, I'm sorry, ma'am. I thought it was——' He paused again and turned to yell a warning to the others to keep their talk clean as there was a lady at the door. 'I tell you there's a sure enough lady at the door. So hush down will you. Sorry, ma'am, they don't mean nothing about it. The house is up there, if you want it, ma'am.'

'Yeah, I know,' Mary Anne liked the look of the young man. He was obviously a good cowhand and might make a loyal friend. 'Likely I knowed it afore you did. I'm Mary Anne Catlan. Your new boss.'

'You're Miss Catlan?' The cowhand's face showed surprise as he looked at her.

'So they tell me. My pappy sure spent some money raising the wrong gal if I'm not. Reckon I could talk to the rest of the boys?'

'Sure, ma'am, just hold it for a minute.' Stepping back the cowhand yelled a warning that Miss Catlan was here and coming to see them. Waiting until all the other of the eight hands were respectably attired, he opened the door. Entering the bunkhouse Mary Anne found the men all standing around. She studied them with a quick glance. They were all newcomers; not one could she remember from her last time at home. Yet they all looked like they knew the cattle business and they did not look the sort either to panic or be scared off. All they needed was a leader. Then they would stand by her, fight for her if they needed to do so. They were not a hardcase fighting crew, proddy and ready to hunt trouble though.

The bunkhouse showed the usual untidy state, clothes, boots and other gear scattered about in profusion. The table in the centre of the room was littered with old Police Gazettes and mail order catalogues. She shoved them into the centre and sat on the edge, legs swinging as she watched the men. They were giving her some attention and she guessed they liked what they saw.

'I'm your new boss. The name's Mary Anne. Who's been acting as *segundo*?'

'I have, ma'am.'

'Mary Anne,' the girl corrected the tall young man who'd answered the door and let her in.

'I am, I reckon, Mary Anne,' the cowhand answered. 'I'm Larry Beaumont.'

'Pleased to meet you, Larry. I'll get acquainted with the rest of you boys as soon as I've fed. Then tomorrow you can take me out to see the range, Larry.'

The young man opened his mouth to say something, then closed it again. He did not show the eagerness she'd expected. Yet he did not look as if he were a slacker, nor could she see any sign of the range work having been neglected since her father's death. She looked at the other men. Their faces showed the same thing. There was bad trouble coming on the

24

range and they did not want to be led by a young woman fresh from the East.

The room was silent now and from outside came a sound which took Mary Anne's attention. The men heard it and exchanged glances, but none of them said a word. Mary Anne ran the tip of her tongue across her lips and wondered what four horses were doing coming to the ranch at this time of the night. She went to the window and tried to pierce the dark and see who was coming.

'Who is it, Larry?'

'I don't know, ma'am. We don't get many callers out here. There's been some night riding done, up at Wilmont's.'

'All right!' Mary Anne knew few men would travel at night unless they had a definite purpose. It could not be a good purpose either, not in the present state of affairs.

'Get your guns! We'll show 'em.' Mary Anne gave the order in a whoop, but the men did not make a move. She read the indecision on each face and knew what was holding them back. They needed a man to lead them. Anger flooded over her and Mary Anne Catlan could work up quite a temper when she was riled. Drawing the revolver from her waistband she hissed, 'If you're all scared, I'm not.'

With that she turned and flung herself to the bunkhouse door, tore it open and ran out into the night. Tears were filling her eyes as she ran from the bunkhouse. Through the mist of them she saw three riders, one leading a packhorse, approaching. She brought up the gun and fired a wild shot. The three riders brought their horses to a halt and left the saddles with a speed which showed they were not exactly unused to being shot at. One of them flung himself behind the water-trough while the other two disappeared into the shelter of the blacksmith's forge. Mary Anne suddenly realised she was exposed to their return fire, standing out in the open.

Inside the bunkhouse the men looked at each other. They heard the shot and Larry yelled, 'Come on, that gal's worth fighting for.' He dived forward, right over his single bunk, collecting the revolver from where it hung holstered on his gunbelt. Landing on his feet he went for the door with the gun in his hand. With a fresh look in their eyes the other men grabbed up their guns and ran for the door, following him.

Mary Anne stood in the dark. She was scared but did not give way to the fear. So far no bullet had been thrown her way but she knew the men were likely to start any time now. Then a voice from the past came floating to her, a voice she could barely recognise for it was both familiar and strange to her.

'Hey, Rusty gal. You never could shoot wuth a cuss so put up the gun or I'll get Molly Wilmont to come and take it from you.'

Mary Anne did not hear the bunkhouse door thrown open behind her. She could not believe what she was hearing either. Only the family ever called her Rusty and only one living person ever called her Rusty gal. The gun fell from her hand as she saw a tall man rise from behind the water-trough. For an instant she stood without moving, then ran forward to throw herself at the man.

It was at this moment the ranch crew ran from the bunkhouse ready to defend the girl. They saw Mary Anne running forward and throwing herself at one of the men, bringing him crashing to the ground. One of the cowhands was carrying a lantern and they dashed forward until the scene was lit by it. At the same moment a voice said, 'Hold it up, gents.'

The cowhands stopped in their tracks. They'd acted without thinking and now were in trouble. A tall, grinning young man came from the shadows of the forge, a Spencer carbine held hip high. Behind him stood a second tall young man holding a Colt. He gave his approval to the course of action his friend laid down.

'Sure, hold it up, she's doing all right.'

The cowhands could see what the slim man meant. Mary Anne was kneeling astride the man, shoving his expensive black stetson hat into his face and gasping out incoherent words. Then with a heave he threw her from him, came up and lifted her as if she were a baby. Turning, he walked towards the water-trough and held her over it.

'No—Waco—no!' Mary Anne screamed as she saw where she was. 'Don't you dare drop me in the——'

The rest ended in a wild shriek and splash as the tall man

let the girl fall into the water. The ranch crew prepared to hurl themselves at this man even in the face of the guns the others held. Before they could make a move they saw the girl was sitting up in the water and laughing. The tall, handsome young man who'd thrown her in stepped forward and helped her out again.

'Rusty gal, you haven't changed one lil bit,' he said, then glanced at the other two. 'All right, put them away. They ain't going to hurt you none.'

The red-headed cowhand laughed, lowered the hammer of his Spencer carbine and walked to where his horse stood. The big claybank stallion snorted and he avoided the nipping teeth, then slid the carbine into his saddleboot. The lantern light showed the brand the horse carried to the interested gaze of the watching cowhands. It was made of two letters, an O and a D, the straight edge of the D touching the side of the O. The cowhands read the brand correctly and eyed this redhead with more interest.

Mary Anne climbed from the water-trough and, laughing still, threw her arms around the man who had put her there, kissing him. She held on to him for a moment then he gently moved her back, smiling down at her and looking her over.

'Rusty gal,' he finally said. 'I'm sorry I couldn't get here afore this. These are my pards, Red Blaze and Doc Leroy.'

Talk rumbled up among the cowhands at the names for both were well-known. Red Blaze was known as a tophand with cattle, as a better than fair hossbuster and as wild a yahoo as ever helped tree a trailend town at the end of a drive. Doc Leroy's name was also known as a tophand. People also spoke of his medical skill; of how he treated the gunshot wounds, set the broken bones and pulled the teeth of the cowhands of the Wedge trail-drive crew, and how he removed a man's appendix with the aid of that most scientific of surgical instruments, a bowie knife, by the light of a lantern, out in the open air just north of the Salt Fork of the Brazos River.

Waco himself was not so well known to the cowhands, although in the time he'd been riding for Ole Devil's floating outfit he'd become known as a good man with cattle, or a gun.

27

Right now Waco was holding the girl's shoulders gently in his powerful hands, looking down at her face. 'I'm sorry I wasn't here when Pappy got his. I came as soon as I heard.'

'I know, boy.' Mary Anne winced as the fingers tightened on her shoulders. Then he released her and a mischievous grin flickered across her face. She moved back slightly, walking around him, looking him all over and halting so he stood between her and the water trough. 'I do declare you haven't growed a single inch. Just stand there and let me take a good look.'

Waco stood, his face impassive and showing nothing of his thoughts as the girl moved closer as if to make her comparison. Then suddenly she lunged forward with hands shooting out to push hard. At the last instant, Waco swayed aside and carried by her impetus she shot by him. She felt his hand catch the seat of her pants and gave a howl of rage as she was dumped head first into the water once more. She came out of it using some choice expressions which would have shocked Mrs. Dupre, principal of the school for young ladies she'd so recently attended.

'You tried that fool trick on me afore this,' Waco reminded her.

Climbing out Mary Anne laughed, standing hands on hips and throwing back her head. She could see the cowhands watching her and saw the difference in their faces now. Then she turned and held out a hand to Red and Doc, shaking with a firm grip. 'Thanks for coming and taking care of the boy. Thanks for coming out to help me, boys. Now I'm going up to the house to get changed. You got me all wet, Waco.'

'You always was, Rusty gal.' Waco gripped the girl's arm and they headed for the house.

Lee Chan stood at the door of the house staring at the girl as she came on to the porch, dripping water at every step. 'What happened, Missy Mary Anne?'

'I fell in the water-trough,' Mary Anne replied, grinning. 'Get a meal going at the chucksack, I'll be down when I'm changed. Make up three more beds here, Waco and his pards will be living at the house.'

'We can bunk down at the hawgpen with the crew if you

like,' Waco told the girl.

'I *don't* like. You'll stay here at the house, all three of you. Where are you going now?'

'Put up the hosses.'

'Pleased to see me again?'

'Sure, real pleased, gal.'

'Pleased enough to hay down my dun for me?' Mary Anne asked innocently.

'That pleased I'll never be,' Waco answered grinning. 'All right, I'll do it. But I won't like it.'

'I never knew you to like anything that spelled work.' Mary Anne headed for the bedroom before Waco had a chance to answer this last remark.

By the time Waco returned with his two friends and their duffle, the girl was changed into dry clothes and a pair of Kiowa moccasins.

She showed them to their rooms and then escorted them to the bunkhouse. The ranch crew were at the table when the girl came in with Waco, Red and Doc. Larry Beaumont pushed back his chair and went to the girl, drawing the chair at the head of the table back for her. She took her seat and looked at the men. Larry resumed his seat again and glanced at the three newcomers.

'You staying on here, Waco?'

'For a spell. If Rusty gal here'll have me.'

Mary Anne looked up, grinning. 'I've got enough trouble on my hands right now without that. Looks like I'm stuck with you though so I'll have to put up with it.'

'Why thank you most to death,' Waco replied. 'I can surely see you haven't changed a little mite.'

'You'll take over as *segundo* for a spell, Red,' Mary Anne ignored Waco. 'The boy's too young yet.'

The ranch crew, even Larry agreed with the girl's choice of foreman. Red knew the cattle business well, knew how to handle men. If it came to trouble he would be best able to deal with it. The atmosphere at the table was different now, laughter rose and talk welled up in the way it always did with a happy crew led by a strong man. There was a new light in every face, and Mary Anne felt better.

With the meal over, Waco and the rest sat around smoking and talking. The girl watched this young man she'd always regarded as her little brother, seeing how he'd matured. She liked what she saw. Here was no proddy rider for a hard outfit but a man wise in the ways of the west, a fighting man yet not one who would start a fight. There was a look about him now that she liked. She was proud to see her little brother in such good company.

Waco found himself by Larry and asked, 'Where did it happen?'

'You know that deep hole down on the Ranse?' Larry was not sure just how this tough young man figured, but guessed he knew Mary Anne more than just casually. 'It was there. Sunshine Sam and the boys went up to try and catch the big old bass there. You know the one I mean, Mary Anne?'

'Sure, ole Mossyhorn. He was there when you left home, boy. Biggest bass I ever saw.'

'Yeah, I remember him. He wasn't so big.'

'Bet you've never seen his beat,' Larry remarked, his eyes on Mary Anne all the time.

'Caught one bigger,' Waco replied, spreading his hands about a foot apart. 'He was that big.'

'That's not big for a bass,' Mary Anne snorted.

'That was the width between his eyes.'

There was a laugh at this from the men. They were looking at Waco with fresh respect now. They'd thought he was a fast gun and now they could see he was also a real friendly young gent. Red Blaze was also watching Mary Anne and guessed she was not wanting to talk about her father's death just at the moment. He decided it was time to change the subject and this sounded like a good time to do it.

'Ole Waco here got caught one time. We was in Langtry visiting Uncle Roy and we saw this hombre sitting fishing. Looking real unusual.'

'What's unusual about a man fishing?' Mary Anne asked without thinking and knew she'd let herself in a trap.

'He was fishing in a wooden bucket. So ole Waco here goes up and says, "Caught any?" and the feller says——'

'You're the fourth.' Mary Anne finished for him.

'Wrong, he said you're the fifth.'

Waco grinned amiably and started to spin a windy about catching a walleye the length of his arm. Others of the crew took it up, vying with each to spin the biggest fishing lie. The room sounded as it always used to in the old days when Sunshine Sam sat at the head of the board and kept the hands amused with his stories. Laughter rang out and the ranch crew looked more like cowhands.

Sitting back Waco watched the men. He approved of Mary Anne putting Red in command as *segundo*. That would leave him more free to make his investigation into the death of his adopted father and brothers. Right now though, there was no need for talk about it. There would be time to start in the morning.

Red suddenly stopped telling what amounted to the best biggest lie of the evening. He frowned and listened. The others also fell silent wondering what brought about this change in him. He came to his feet and went to the window. 'Douse the lights!' His voice showed the urgency of the matter. 'We got callers coming.'

The cowhands heard the sound then. Faintly, but growing louder at every minute, came the rumble of many hooves. Not one of the cowhands spoke but there was a difference in their silence now. They'd been worried and uncertain, now they were ready, willing and only waiting for orders. Mary Anne blew out the lamp on the table and Larry, hands slapping his gunless side, doused the other light.

The cookshack as they called it was actually a room in the back of the main house. The men were not armed, coming to a meal rarely called for it. Now they could hear the rumble of hooves they all wished they were carrying weapons. Yet there was no panic among them, just waiting for orders.

Red took charge of the situation, once more proving that while he was a hot-tempered, reckless young man who was likely to pitch into any fight he came across without much thought of consequences, he was cool and capable when the chips were down.

'Get to the bunkhouse, boys. Go the back way, run for it and get your guns. Then stay in, if you have to shoot do it from the windows.'

The cowhands made a rush for the door. Red, Waco and Doc went for the house door and ran along the passage towards the front door and the gunbelts hanging on the hooks. The hooves were very near now and Red doubted if they would be in time. He pulled one of his guns out, cocking it as he jerked the door open and lunged out. The porch was in the shadow, something he was grateful for. The moon was just gone the half and gave out enough light for him to see what he was doing.

There were nine or ten riders coming towards the ranch, riding fast, their identity covered by the hoods they wore over their heads. The leader of the group swung a blazing torch as he rode. Red and the other men on the porch watched this rider. He kept grabbing at the saddlehorn to keep his uncertain seat, riding awkwardly and without the unconscious grace even a bad drunk cowhand retained. There was something unusual about him, apart from his awkward way of riding. He did not appear to be wearing range clothes and was not wearing a gunbelt. There was a fancy, white-handled gun thrust into the waistband of his pants, but he did not make any attempt to draw it.

Red heard a gasp and twisted his head to see Mary Anne by his side watching the approaching party. He growled deep in his throat. 'Get back in there, gal. This's no place for you.'

Mary Anne did not reply or move, she was staring at the torch-waving man. He sent his horse forward at a better speed, swinging the torch around his head wildly. She licked her lips and was about to speak when she heard Red hiss, 'Just a little mite nearer, friend, and I'll bring you down like a coon off a log.'

The rider was coming just that little bit nearer, the other men crowding up behind him and encouraging him with wild yells. Then from the riders behind this first one sounded a shot. The man's back arched as lead hit him. He bowed his back in the sudden agony which welled up over him. Another rider was alongside, shooting out an arm to grab the torch and push the shot man from his saddle.

CHAPTER FOUR

A PROFESSIONAL'S GUN

THE shooting down of the man by a member of his own group made Red hold his fire for an instant. He could not see just what the attacking group were doing. The rider swinging the torch did not appear to be making any serious attempt to attack the ranch. The others hung back, the torch lighting up the scene and their horses fiddlefooting nervously as the hooded men milled around the man on the ground. Then one gave a rebel yell and sent his horse leaping forward. He swung back his torch ready to throw it.

'Drop it!' Red shouted a warning.

Flame spurted from behind the man, the bullet slapping into the wall of the house near Red. That was all the young Texan needed. His right hand Colt boomed loud, throwing flame at the leading man. The torch flew off at a tangent as the rider took lead, reeling in his saddle. From the other hooded men sounded fast shots, flame stabbing the dark and lacing at the ranch. Red was a wise hand at night fighting and knew better than to be where he'd been when he fired his shot. He slid to one side, crouching and hoping the porch furniture broke up his outline and made him a poorer target. He knew Doc was going to the other side and could guess just what Waco was doing.

Mary Anne stood by the open door. She was unable to tell what was happening and Red's shot made her start back. She felt a hand catch her arm and shove her roughly back into the house, hearing Waco snap, 'Keep in there, Rusty gal.'

With the girl taken care of Waco flung himself from the porch, landing on the ground with a gun in either hand, and saw the spurt of shots coming in a roaring answer to Red's Colt greeting. In the light of the torch he saw a stocky man directing operations. Waco knew the best way to handle any group was to down the leader. His Colt came up and lined, crashing, and as it crashed so Waco rolled sideways. He saw the man he'd aimed at clutch his right shoulder, swing his horse and yell an order.

Red's victim was down and from all around sounded the sporadic crash of shots as the men took a hand. They were shooting fast but with little effect that Red could see. The hooded men were turning now but the swaying, wounded man shouted something and they brought their horses around, shooting fast. Two of their number swung down from their horses while the rest kept up a fast covering fire. They dragged Red's victim up and shoved him across the saddle of a horse. As they ran by the man one of their party shot to their own horses and mounted again, riding off into the blackness.

'Anybody hit?' Waco called, liking the way the ranch crew held their fire until Red opened the ball. It showed they could be relied on not to spook if it came to trouble.

From the various places where they'd taken up fighting positions the answers came back. Everyone appeared to be all right. Red Blaze was moving forward, gun in hand as he stepped from the porch. He could see other shapes moving and called, 'Stop down, all of you. One target's enough at a time. More'n enough if I'm the target.'

For all the levity in his tones Red was moving like a trained lawman. The first thing he did was kick the ivory-butted Colt from where it lay by the fallen man, having slid out of his waistband. That gun was a deadly danger to Red. It was a simple precaution to remove it and the temptation it offered if the man were shamming. Then Red saw the hole in the centre of the man's back and knew there was no trickery here. That man was dead, dead as he could be when two hundred and fifty-five grains of .45 lead smashed through his spine and into his body. There was little or no blood seeping through the hole and on to the coat as yet, but Red knew this man was dead.

'Doc, come over here.' Red straightened up and thrust his gun into his waistband.

Doc advanced fast, gun in hand and ready for action. He joined Red, looking down at the body, then shoved his gun into Red's hand, bent down and rolled the body over. The clothes were not the sort a cowhand would be wearing: an old, crumpled, sober black suit, a collarless shirt, white and not too clean, and fastened at the neck by an inexpensive stud. His boots were heavy, square-toed and low-heeled; no cowhand would ever wear such boots for he would never willingly perform any task which did not entail sitting the back of a horse.

Waco turned back into the house and returned his guns to the holsters then gave Mary Anne his attention. Lee Chan came out of the kitchen with a lamp in his hand, illuminating the scene. The girl was standing flattened back against the wall but there was both anger and annoyance in her face.

'Had fun?' There was a grim note in her voice.

'Why sure,' Waco agreed, grinning.

'Good. Listen to me now, lil brother. I'm the big one in this family. Next time there's some shooting don't you go shoving me back into the house like I was some twittering, blushing Eastern biddy. You long ...'

'Sure honey.' Waco grinned still. Ole Rusty gal hadn't changed one little bit. She was still pawing the ground and bellowing if she wasn't allowed to take her full share in anything that came up. 'Let me have the lamp, Lee. I want to go out there.'

Taking the lamp, Waco left the room, the girl following and telling him just what she thought of him, his friends, their friends and anyone who was even distantly associated with him. They crossed to where the cowhands were gathered around the body. Waco forced by them and held the lamp, looking down. Mary Anne was by his side, her face just a shade pallid as she looked at the first man she'd ever seen dead by violence.

'Did you kill him, Red?' she asked.

'Not unless my bullet went round the back and in him,' Red replied. 'It was one of his bunkies shot him.'

'Why'd he do that?' Mary Anne asked, then realised she'd let her tongue slip again.

'Maybe they play it different up this way,' Red replied, winking at Waco. 'Each side shoots their own men, saves bullets that way.'

Waco was not in the mood for levity right now. His brain was working fast, turning over every detail of what he'd seen out there. He was never willing to accept anything at its face value but always delved deeper, seeking out the inner whys and wherefores. He bent forward and pulled the hood from the dead man's head. In the light of the lamp a thin face showed. It was a face twisted in agony and Waco looked up at the surrounding men. 'Any of you know him?'

Larry leaned forward, examining the face closer. 'Sure I know him. It's Ben Silver. His paw's one of the nesters across the river. Kind of a preacher. But what's his boy doing riding with a bunch like that. I never even saw him pack a gun.'

'He was this time,' Red remarked, picking up the Colt Silver dropped when he came off the horse.

'Tote the body down to the barn for the night, Larry.' Waco spoke up. 'He been drinking, Doc?'

'Why sure. Smells like a moonshine still.' Doc straightened up. 'You on to something, boy?'

'Just thinking.' Waco lifted one of the dead hands, looking at it in the light of the lamp. He let the hand fall loose and nodded to Larry who, with three more of the cowhands, lifted the body and carried it off towards the barn.

They gathered in the cookshack again and Waco laid the revolver on the table and the hood by it. The rest of the ranch crew came in soon after he'd done it. Waco was looking thoughtful. He gripped the girl's hand in his and shoved her gently into a chair. Lee Chan brought coffee in, pouring Mary Anne a cup then standing back.

'You ever had trouble with the nesters before, Larry?' Waco asked.

'Nope, not more'n the occasional fist fight in town. Don't get on bad with them most times. Never see much of Ben Silver. He don't go to the saloon like the others do. Told you, his paw's a kind of preacher. Real strong against sin of all kinds.'

'Only thing not being sin is breathing, way he sees it,' another cowhand put in. 'Always on about saloons. Never thought to see his boy there drunk.'

'Or with a gun. Never thought his pappy gave him enough money to buy one.'

'He didn't buy this gun.'

All eyes went to Waco. The young man was holding the gun, turning the chamber and emptying it. Mary Anne sniffed. 'I suppose he told you?'

'Doesn't have to.' Waco held the revolver in his palm, hefting it and feeling the balance. 'This here's a real fast man's gun.'

'Are you just guessing, boy?' There was pride in Mary Anne's voice. She was satisfied with the way her little brother was growing up.

'Nope. The inside of the gun's been worked on. The safety notches on the hammer filed out. Look at the hammer spur here, the checking's been filed smooth. The gun's been used by a real fast man and that *hombre* in the barn isn't a fast gun. I looked at his hands, they've seen too much rough work for them to belong to a fast gun. This isn't his gun at all.'

Mary Anne looked at the Colt. To her eyes it was no different from any other. Waco held the smooth, hand-fitting butt in his grip and held it out to her. The ivory grips were smooth and the gun itself was made in the deep blued, best citizen's finish. She could see it was a gun which cost money and which had been well cared for. Then she saw the rough checking which usually tipped the hammer spur was filed down smooth. It was a trick she'd heard her brothers talk of, allowing for faster firing of the gun. It was not a thing a man did unless he was good with a gun. She watched as Waco drew the hammer back under his thumb. She could see the ease with which it worked, ease which made all the difference between life and death in a down grab and shoot affair.

'You seem real sure, boy.'

'I'm sure enough. I'd say this was one of a brace, could be wrong though.' With that he held the gun close to the lamp, turning it over and looking at the ivory grip. 'Man's worn it at his left side most all the time. The left grip shows just a shade more weathering than the right. You have to look real close to make it out. But it's there if you look.'

Mary Anne accepted the gun and looked down at the grips. In the light of the lamp she could make out, faintly but there all the same, that the left-side grip showed the faintest darkening. Waco asked Doc to fetch along his gun and when the slim man returned held out the ivory-handled Peacemaker for her to look at. She saw the darkening on the right side and knew Waco was right. The gun Silver had carried must have been regularly in the holster at the left side. Doc thrust his own gun away and the girl asked, 'Know anything more about it?'

'Don't know a thing about it at all. Just guessing.'

'Guess some more then,' she went on.

'Waal, I'd say it was one of a brace. It's been worked on, grip altered. I'll bet that some place there's a gun that's the mate to this one. Some place real close.'

The girl was silent for a moment, thinking over what he'd said. Red Blaze was whistling, watching Waco with the tolerant air of an elder brother watching a creditable performance by a younger. He asked, 'Are there many two-gun toting gents hereabouts, Larry?'

'A few. Two more rode in tonight.'

'Apart from us,' Red answered.

'There's a few hang around town, work for Brarsand as either table men or dealers. He's got Cholla Jocelyn, allows to be real good with a gun. Then there's Dave Tull, he *is* good. You heard of him?'

'Some,' Waco agreed. 'They say he's tolerable fast.'

'Well, he works for Brarsand, boss dealer. There's a few more of them all fair to good.'

'How many of them have a brace of ivory-handled guns though?' Red inquired.

'Tull, two or three of the others.'

'You know, this Brarsand sounds like a real important man,' Waco remarked. 'He a rancher?'

'Runs a saloon in Whittle and hires him good guns like Tull

to handle the tables. Or has Whittle grown up some since I was last there?'

'Sure it's grown. There's three more houses at least now.'

'And this gent runs a saloon there, gets him enough trade to keep all them many men going?' Waco sounded puzzled.

'Shucks, there's our crew, Wilmont's and the other two spreads. Then there's the nester families on the other side of the river,' Larry objected. 'They must take in a fair piece of money.'

'Not enough to pay for a big staff, for the likker and the upkeep of the place, if it's anything like.'

'Anything like.' Larry's pride in Whittle rose to the fore. 'I tell you, Waco, that place is as good as the best I've ever seen. Why I bet there ain't another small town like Whittle got such a place.'

'That's what I mean. Whittle isn't a big place at all. Now you allow there's a real fine saloon in town. You've got me all interested now, Larry.'

Mary Anne chuckled. She'd been thinking the same thing all the time, wondering how Brarsand managed to make a big, fine-looking saloon pay in such a small place. Even if all the cowhands spent all their pay over the bar every month it would hardly do more than meet the payroll of the saloon's hired help and cover the cost of upkeep. She couldn't see how the place could pay or, with bigger, more prosperous towns growing up all over Texas, why Brarsand chose Whittle to build.

'Did you get any of them?' Larry asked. 'I thought I saw one go down when you started shooting.'

'Red got one and I put a bullet into another's shoulder,' Waco replied. 'But they toted him off with them.'

'Pity. We might have recognised him.'

'That's why they toted him off.' Larry made the obvious remark.

'Then why did they leave the other one?'

Once more all attention came to Waco as he spoke. Red could see the young man was thinking out the reasons behind the actions again. Waco was like that; he was never content

39

unless he was delving into anything which was a little out of the ordinary.

'Maybe didn't have time to tote him along with them.' Larry and the other cowhands were more willing to go for the obvious and easy answer. 'Them nesters are . . .'

'There was only one nester riding and they left him dead. The rest of them, even if they weren't cowhands, rode better'n most any nester I ever saw,' Waco answered. 'They knew at least some of you boys would recognise Ben Silver and they still left him. Yet they toted off the other man we downed. In fact they went by Silver's body to get that one and under fire at that.'

'What do you make of it then?' Mary Anne wanted to know.

'You told me about what happened in town. Looks like somebody wants you out of the way, Rusty gal. This try tonight was aimed to scare you off, or stir up trouble between you and the nesters. Either way you'd likely give up the spread. The boy's wouldn't want to follow a woman and with a range war brewing they'd likely want to be getting out of it. You'd be left without a crew, Rusty gal. Then you'd have to sell out.'

'That means Brarsand!' Mary Anne snapped the words.

'He's one, could be any of a dozen others. Don't you go pawing earth, gal. Who's town law now?'

It was Larry who answered. 'Mean cuss called Talbot. Got him elected on the last time. Reckon the nester vote swung him in, there being some talk going round that Lafe Sanger was too old for the job.'

'Lafe's the best Town Marshal Whittle ever had,' Mary Anne snorted. 'Too old for the job indeed!'

'Thing being how's Talbot stand with you boys,' Waco interrupted Mary Anne's angry speech.

'Mean cuss, like I said. Don't take to cowhands at all. Real nester lover.'

Waco grinned. He knew that Larry, as a cowhand, disliked the man for some reason. It could be a valid one or it could be that Talbot's ideas of fun did not run to cowhand rowdiness.

This matter here at the ranch did not come under the province of the town marshal for it happened well beyond city limits. However, Waco always tried to stay friendly and do things right by the town law. The killing of the nester was a matter for the county sheriff's office and they should be informed unless there was a deputy sheriff in town. The town marshal's duties were concerned with the town itself and out beyond the town limits he held no jurisdiction.

'Who's County Sheriff?' he inquired.

'Vince Cole. Real nice gent from all I've seen. Don't come down this way often.' Larry was acting as spokesman for the ranch crew.

'He got a deputy in town?'

'Ole Lafe Sanger does most of the deputising for him up this end of the county. Ain't often much to do though.'

'Then it's old Lafe who'll be doing the investigation here.' Waco was relieved. Sanger was an old friend and would be fair in his judgment of the situation. There was more, far more, to this raid than first met the eye.

He laid the gun on the table and came to his feet. 'Bring a lamp along, Red. I want to go and take a look out there.'

Red knew full well Waco's skill in the reading of sign. The Ysabel Kid was a masterhand at the reading and following of sign and in Waco the Kid found an apt pupil. If there was any sign at all out there Waco would find it.

The rest of the ranch crew followed Waco and Red out, staying by the side of the house and watching as the two young men went to where the burned-out torches lay, showing the exact place of the raid. By light of the lamp Waco examined the churned ground, going over it with care. He was nearly sure that there would be no chance at all of finding anything to help him. The ground was too hard, too churned up by the hooves of not only the raiders' mounts but by the remuda of the ranch too. He knew his guessing was correct for all of that. The men who'd ridden this way were not nesters. He knew some nesters could ride well, but not with the easy grace those men showed. Ben Silver was drunk, that was plain to see. The other men were not. Waco was almost sure he could lay down the full idea behind this raid but he did not aim to show his suspicions until he was sure of them.

'Rusty gal,' he said, as he and Red walked back to the others, 'We'll tote that *hombre* into town tomorrow. I want the hood put back on again. We'll make like we did not look to see who it was. I'm going to see Doc Smethers when we hit town.'

'Why?'

'Red wounded one. He's going to need some treatment. If he goes to the doctor we'll know who he is. Doc Smethers wouldn't be scared of any cheap gunny and he'll tell us. Then we can start to make a move.'

'All right. I'll let you handle it. See what sort of a mess you get us in.' Mary Anne ruffled Waco's hair. 'What do you want us to do?'

'We'll all go in to town tomorrow. All the crew. I want to show whoever's causing the trouble you've got a crew that'll stand by you.'

The girl nodded. She could see Waco was capable of handling her affairs. She wondered at the change in him. When he'd left home she was sure he'd end up as another Wes Hardin. The finished product pleased her. It would have amazed her if she'd seen him in the days when he rode for Clay Allison. Then Waco was a sullen, truculent youngster with an edgy temper and readiness to fight in his heart. The change in him since joining up with the Rio Hondo gun wizard, Dusty Fog, was amazing. His intimate friends noticed it far more than did the girl.

'Say, Mary Anne.' The girl turned and found Larry standing by her side. 'We're sorry about the way we acted when you first came in the bunkhouse. We're cowhands, not gunfighters but we're ready to stick by you now.'

'I know that.' The girl smiled back at the young cowhand. She made sure Waco was not near enough to hear, or his two friends. 'Waco's a real good man to follow and the other two are almost as good. We'll make out.'

'Why sure.' Larry went into consultation with the others then turned to the girl. 'Ole Waco ought to be talked out of dumping you in the water-trough. We have to wash in that water.'

Mary Anne was not slow on the uptake, she smiled back at the circle of faces around her. 'Yeah, he should at that.'

Waco, all unsuspecting, was standing discussing the plans for the ride into town on the following day with Red and Doc. He paid no attention to the ranch crew and the girl as they gathered around him. Then the girl gave a yell and they hurled forward. Waco was hit by a flying wedge of bodies. There was a wild and hectic struggle in which Red and Doc lent a willing hand. Bucking, struggling, held by arms and legs Waco was lifted and carried to the water-trough. The splash as he went in was like music to Mary Anne's ears.

CHAPTER FIVE

A NEAR FATAL MISTAKE

THE five men pitching horseshoes behind the livery barn turned as they heard the sound of hooves. They studied the rider, seeing a tall, slim and studious looking young man, who sat his limping black stallion with easy grace. They also noted that he wore an ivory-butted gun in a fast man's rig, trigger-guard left clear for the easy insertion of the trigger-finger. He brought the horse to a halt, swung down and lashed the pigging thong of his holster, then bent and lifted the black horse's foot and looked at the loose shoe on it.

One of the horseshoe pitchers grinned at the others and winked. He was a tall man, handsome and dressed in the style of a range dandy, buckskin shirt with long fringes, tight-legged trousers carefully tucked into his shining boots. Around his waist was a gunbelt supporting a brace of pearl-handled Colts, their butts flaring handily to his grip. His eyes took in this studious-looking young man, who was acting, or trying to act, like a big, fierce gunman. Swinging from the others this big man stepped forward towards the newcomer.

'You looking for somebody, bub?'

Doc Leroy turned and looked the gunman over with cool contempt, every working cowhand held for a man who lived by selling his guns to the highest bidder.

'Man'd say you were right.'

'Who?'

'The gent who owns the forge there. Likely it's not you though.'

'You working hereabouts, bub?'

One of the other men stood waiting for the dandy to take

his throw with the horseshoes. 'Leave him be, Cholla. Come over here and take your toss.'

Cholla Jocelyn grinned and shook his head. He was an arrant bully with gunspeed to back it up, and picking on a mild-looking pale-faced dude like this was always good fun. 'I said who do you work for?' Jocelyn held his voice hard.

'S.S.C.,' Doc answered mildly.

There was an instant change among the men. They let the horseshoes fall and moved forward to flank their friend. Doc knew he'd made him a mistake but it was one he could soon correct.

'Work for the S.S.C. do you?' Jocelyn sneered the words out. 'Now that's a real unlucky spread to work for. Man'd do better if he just got on his hoss and rode out, got clear of it.'

'That the truth?' Doc sounded interested in a polite way.

'The living truth, boy. So you can just start in by handing me that fancy-looking gun.'

'This gun?' Doc's attitude suggested he was not even sure if he was wearing a gun or not. 'Why, I couldn't rightly do that, suh. See, I'm buying it on time and it still isn't paid for.'

Cholla Jocelyn grinned and winked at the other men who stood by him. They were standing here more with the expectation of having a good laugh than with any thought of their assistance being needed. That was the rig of a real fast gunman, but this pallid-faced youngster could not be one. Only one of them was in the least worried. He was thinking of another pallid, inoffensive-looking man who talked like this one, with a sleepy southern drawl. That one was Doctor John H. Holliday, the deadly dentist of Dodge City.

Jocelyn did not know the notorious Doc Holliday and would not have taken this young man for him anyway. He held out a hand and snapped out: 'All right, hand it over.'

'If I don't?' There was a slightly different sound in Doc's voice now, and a slight difference in the way he stood.

'I'll just take it from you, bub.'

'Oh!' Doc answered gently.

Jocelyn moved forward, hand reaching out. Doc Leroy's thin, almost boneless-looking hand made a sight-defying flip

45

and the sun caught the glint on the four and three quarter inch blue barrel of his Colt. The gun was clear, lined, the hammer drawn back under a skilled thumb. The gunmen froze, all of them. Jocelyn halted with his right foot raised from the ground and hands still half reaching out, looking like a rabbit mesmerised by a snake. The dandy gulped. That draw was as fast as he'd ever seen and he'd seen fast men. Here was no pasty-faced dude dressed up in range clothes. This was the real, full growed and ready for stud thing.

'You going to take it right now?' Doc's voice was still the same but there was mocking irony in it. 'The name, *bub*, if you're interested, is Marvin Elldridge Leroy. Better known under the sobriquet of Doc.'

'Doc Leroy of the Wedge?' Jocelyn gulped the words out.

'Once, now permanently riding for the O.D. Connected and temporarily on loan to the S.S.C.' Doc watched the men, knowing they were well aware of his reputation. 'Although you seem all fired set to have me leave the S.S.C. You still wanting my gun, *bub*?'

Jocelyn gulped. The gun was back in leather again, gone back in that same flickering, lightning-fast move. The thin hand lifted and once more he looked as he did when he first rode in. There was one slight difference though. They knew how good with a gun he was. Jocelyn stood very still. He knew the other men would back his play to the last bullet, that gave him no comfort at all. There were fast men here, one at least he would say was faster than himself. But not one of them, nor any other man Brarsand hired, could face Doc Leroy's speed and walk away from the fight. There were five of them here, more than any one man could handle and live to boast of it. If they called the play that way Doc Leroy was a dead man, but before he died he would get at least two of them and probably three. They would kill Doc but the chances of survival were no more than two to one. In Jocelyn's case the odds were even lower. He knew when Doc Leroy drew, the first shot would end Cholla Jocelyn's life.

'Doc, can't you go no place without getting into trouble?'

The voice was an easy southern drawl, a cheerful sounding

46

voice. Cholla Jocelyn looked at the side of the building and knew war was long out of the question. There were two young men standing out from the side of the building and by the wall three of the S.S.C. hands. It was the first two who gave pause to Jocelyn. He could read the signs right then showing as well as the two cowhands showed them. He noted the two guns each wore and knew that here was just as real a thing as Doc Leroy. The big, handsome blond boy might look young, but so did William Bonney.

Red Blaze and Waco studied the scene before them. They'd been waiting for Doc to return to them and come to see what was delaying him. They'd observed most of what happened and took a hand to prevent killing for *they* knew without needing proof how good Doc Leroy was.

'They abusing you, Doc?' Red inquired.

'Gent here wants to take my gun and warned me how unlucky it was to work for S.S.C.,' Doc answered.

'Didn't you tell him you still owed for it?' Red watched the gunmen all the time, hoping for a fight.

'Nope. You can just bet he didn't,' Waco said as he watched the owner of the livery barn and the blacksmith who were standing and studying all this with obvious pleasure. 'Now why'd it be unlucky to work for the S.S.C. friend?'

'Hell, we were just funning,' Jocelyn replied. He knew he was licked and the feeling hurt.

'Man could die doing just that.' Waco's voice was grim. 'I work for S.S.C., so does Red here. You all aiming to take my guns?'

'Hell friend, we was only funning. We——'

'We're not stopping you from doing anything, are we?'

Cholla Jocelyn took the hint. He did not need a yard high sign to tell him that stopping on would be both dangerous and asking for bad trouble. He turned on his heel and walked away, his men following him. They did not resume their half done game of horseshoes but walked away, headed for the saloon. Brarsand was going to need to know that S.S.C. was led by three real fast men with guns. It would clear the air about a few things which were bothering the saloon keeper.

Doc watched the gunmen walking away and grunted in disgust. 'You pair's always spoiling things for a man, now aren't you?'

The owner of the barn and the blacksmith came ambling over. They were much alike, being twin brothers. Seamus and Mike Reagan looked only a little different from when Waco last saw them. They'd been big, grey haired and hard looking then. They weren't much different now, just a little more wrinkled. Seamus looked hard at Waco, studying him.

'I should know you, friend. Never forget a face. You working for Mary Anne out at the S.S.C.?'

'Only when she's looking. Rest of the time we're sleeping for the S.S.C. The name's Waco.'

'Waco?' Seamus rubbed his jaw, then his eyes bulged out. 'You mean you're——'

'Yeah. I'm the one. How's things——?'

'Red!' Larry came around the corner fast, skidding to a halt. 'The great siezer's coming up fast. Shotgun and all.'

'Sorry I can't stop, Seamus. Let's go.' Waco turned on his heel and walked away followed by Red.

'Tend to my hoss, Colonel, will you?' Doc jerked his head to the big black stallion. 'Needs shoeing.'

Without waiting for confirmation of his request, Doc joined the other two and headed for the street where Mary Anne was waiting for them with the wagon. The S.S.C. hands, all except a couple who were on guard at the ranch, were forming a protective circle around the girl. They were sitting their horses and facing a man who walked towards them. The man was tall, thin and looked as lean and vicious as a weasel. His face was pointed, the nose looking sharp enough to plough with. His narrow-set eyes were black and glittered. His mouth was tight as a rat trap and looked like it was permanently set in a sneer. He wore a cutaway coat with a marshal's badge on it and around his waist was a gunbelt with a Colt butt forward in the holster at his right side. In his hand he held a ten-gauge shotgun which he hefted as he came to a halt in front of the wagon.

'You bunch in town to hooraw it?'

48

'Not yet.' Waco's voice was flat and even as a crowd started to gather. 'We brought a body in.'

'Body?' The marshal's narrow eyes appeared to get even more so. 'What body's that?'

'Under the tarp in the back.' Red jerked his hand towards the wagon where Mary sat by Lee Chan. 'Take a look at him.'

'Just who might you be?' The marshal made no move to go and see the body, but stood looking them over. He could read the signs and knew that here was a real hard trio, gunhardy and dangerous to tangle with.

'We ride for the S.S.C.' Red's quick temper started to pop up at this breach of Western etiquette. 'Miss Catlan's ranch. Who are *you*?'

'Name's Talbot. Lyge Talbot. Town Marshal here.' Shoving back the side of his coat, Talbot showed his badge more plainly. 'Like I just——'

'You don't seem interested in the body back there, mister. You know who he is, or something?'

Talbot stiffened as Waco spoke. There was a fair-sized crowd gathering now, townspeople and nesters from the look of them. Waco was looking at the crowd. He saw a white-haired, thin and miserable looking old man wearing a sober black suit standing with a smaller, plump and cheery-looking nester. His eyes next went to the tall, tow-haired youngster who was standing by these two. There was worry and fear in this young man's eyes. Next his eyes went to three men who stood just clear of the crowd. Three hard-faced, hard-eyed men wearing range clothes, two of them with low-tied guns. The kid, a stocky man of medium size, better dressed than the other two, was not wearing a gunbelt. Instead, an ivory-handled Colt was thrust into his waistband, pointing towards the left. The reason for this was plain, his right arm was held in a sling.

Talbot was watching Waco, reading the signs right. It was something he'd not seen since he worked with the Earps in Dodge City as one of the noble, fearless Kansas law and order group. There he'd seen men like this youngster. Texas men, men whose names were legends. Clay Allison, Dusty Fog, Ben Thompson, King Fisher, Wes Hardin, all of them had the

49

same look as this soft-talking boy. It was the look of a man supremely confident in his skill with a gun. Since taking over as town law here Talbot gained a reputation for being tough. He wore the halo of the Kansas trailend town law proudly. The young cowhands here were not gunfighters and he'd never been called on to prove himself. Now he knew there were three men in town who were no respecters of Kansas lawmen.

With this in mind he walked to the rear of the wagon and pulled the tarpaulin from the shape which lay beneath it, looked down and then up at Waco. 'He's got a hood on.'

'Now me, I thought it was a beard,' Red scoffed.

'You make another remark like that and I'll bend a gun-barrel over your head.'

For a threat or a bluff this remark fell singularly flat. Red Balze grinned savagely, his hands stayed at his sides, the palms turned slightly out, fingers spread and ready to lift his guns clear of leather. 'That so?' he asked. 'Any time you think you can, whup ahead and start into doing it.'

Talbot backed down, climbed down faster than he liked doing. He knew that his ten-gauge shotgun did not scare this freckle-faced heller any more than it scared the blond boy. He knew he must act fast, get this over with before he lost any more face. He reached out a hand, drawing the hood from the head.

'My son?' The thin old nester came forward, his gnarled hands gripping the edge of the wagon. 'It's my son.'

The small nester moved forward also, looking down, his face losing its happy look and paling. He turned his eyes to Waco again and began to speak, 'What——?'

'My son. My son. You killed him.' The white-haired man stared up at Waco. 'You killed him.'

'No sir.' Waco's voice was gentle. 'Last night he was with a bunch of masked men who hit at the S.S.C. One of his pards shot him down, put a bullet in his back. They left him out there. I got one and wounded another before they went.'

The old man did not appear to be listening. He was standing rigid and staring at the body. Doc Leroy had laid it out for burial and the stiffening shape looked peaceful in death. It lay face up and there was no sign of the wound. Ezra Silver licked his lips, swaying as he stood there. The other man caught his arm and supported him. Waco's eyes went first to the tow-headed boy then the three hard-faced men. He caught the glance which passed between them and saw the one with the sling shake his head and tap the butt of his gun. Waco's attention was drawn to the knot of the sling and his eyes narrowed, then dropped to the ivory-butted gun in the man's waistband.

'You reckon he was with that bunch that hit the S.S.C. and they shot him?' Talbot asked. 'Why'd they do a thing like that, if he was with them?'

'Because they wanted him dead and where we could find him,' Waco went on. 'The one I shot they toted off with them. Reckon they knew we'd recognise him.'

'They left this one and knew you'd recognise *him*,' Talbot pointed out. 'Yet they took the other one——'

'Sure. They wanted us to recognise this one. That way we start blaming the nesters. If we see the other man we know it's not the nesters, but, waal, whoever it was.'

Ezra Silver's face lifted and his voice was cracked as he said, 'My son is dead. Struck down in his prime and without a chance. He never even carried a gun.'

'He carried one last night,' Red held down his usually quick temper for he knew the man was feeling the loss of his son. 'That one.'

'Real fine-looking gun for a poor nester to be carrying.' Talbot picked the gun up and examined it with exaggerated attention. 'Your boy buy that gun, Ezra?'

'He never owned a gun at all.' Silver's face was haggard and the other nester supported him.

'That's right, he didn't own the gun.' Waco spoke evenly. 'Red said he was carrying one. He carried the gun but he didn't own it. He'd been drinking some, too.'

'That's a lie!' Silver straightened, shaking a fist in front of Waco's eyes. 'My boy never touched the drink of the devil. You must have taken him out to your ranch, poured whisky on him and shot him.'

Red caught Waco's arm, holding him as the young man

51

started forward. 'Easy boy!'

The cowhands growled out angrily and Talbot hefted his shotgun in a threatening manner. Lafe Sanger's voice cut through as he forced his way through the crowd. 'Hold hard now, Ezra. Mary Anne Catlan wouldn't back no play like that. Anyways, I'm deputy sheriff and this comes under my balliwick, not Talbot's.'

Talbot snarled something under his breath. He'd hoped for the richer pickings of deputy sheriff but the County Sheriff was adamant in his decision to leave Lafe Sanger as deputy for the Whittle area.

'All right, Lafe. Only wanted to make sure these cowhands don't start hoorawing the town. We ain't having that sort of thing here and I don't aim to.'

'Mister, this isn't Kansas. You aren't Wyatt Earp and we're not a trailcrew just paid off.' Waco spoke in a flat even tone. 'We came to town to bring this gent's son and to report that raid to the County Law. We brought the crew because we didn't know if the same bunch would be waiting for us. Another thing you might remember as Town Marshal, it's cowhands who bring the money into town, we pay your salary, friend. You're a public servant. Wouldn't you say that was right, Lafe?'

Lafe Sanger nodded. 'Why sure.'

'Then you go get me a glass of water, friend.'

Talbot opened his mouth to make some angry statement but there was something in Waco's eyes which made him pause. The young Texan was throwing out a warning in those mocking words. If Talbot pushed this matter any more there would be shooting and that shotgun was not so fast or good in a tight spot against a real fast gun. That Texas boy was a real fast gun, it showed in every line of his lithe, powerful frame.

'Now hold it all of you.' Lafe Sanger pushed forward, hand resting on the butt of his old Leech and Rigdon revolver. 'Ezra we all respects your loss but there ain't no call for you accusing Mary Anne's crew of what you did. Was your boy in town last night?'

'He came to town,' the old man's face was working. 'But he

never took a drink in his life, nor did he ever wear a gun.'

Once more Waco's attention was taken by the three gun-hung men and the nester boy. The boy's face was pale and he appeared to be troubled by something. Then once more Waco's eyes went to the knot of the sling and he remembered something Doc Leroy taught him about the way to put on a sling. Waco knew that there was something between the three gunmen and that boy. He was never one to let a chance slip by. The three men were turning to walk away and Waco stepped forward from the others, jerking his head in a signal which brought Doc and Red after him. They did not know what was wrong here but they were ready to back his play.

'Hurt your arm, friend?' Waco's voice, soft and caressing as it brought the men to a halt.

All three men turned, fanning out slightly, the one with the sling nodded his head. 'Fell off my hoss, landed on it.'

'That's real unlucky, falling off your horse,' Waco answered; the two men turned as if to walk away. 'Don't go yet, friend. You want to take care of things like that. Has Doctor Smethers seen it?'

'Why sure. He fixed it up for me.' The man did not turn fully round although the other two did.

'Might be as well let Lafe there take a look, too.'

'Meaning?' The man's voice dropped slightly.

'I wounded one man last night. Hit him in the right shoulder.'

'You're asking for trouble, boy.' The gunman at the right spoke up, hand lifting over his gunbutt. 'You tend to your own business or you'll be buying a tolerable heap of grief.'

The lethargy left Waco now, his voice suddenly that of a suspicious lawman questioning a suspect. 'I want to see that wound.'

'All right, boy. All right. Not any trouble at all.' The man lifted his left hand towards the knot of the sling.

'Take 'em!' The man at the right hand dipped down towards the butt of his gun.

Doc Leroy's right hand flickered and the gun was in it, ahead of the other man. The gun rocked back in his hand,

53

throwing a shot into the body of the man, knocking him off his feet before his gun was even clear of leather. Waco's hands were going down as Doc made his move. Two shots sounded as one. He felt the hot breath of the bullet as it passed his cheek. The bullet missed and in no way put Waco off his shot. He'd made a near fatal mistake in his judgment of the man, meaning to wing him. Now there was no time, this was a real fast gun and a man could not take chances with such. His gun roared and the bullet kicked into the centre of the man's chest, staggering him, and he went down after Doc Leroy's victim.

Red Blaze never thought of himself as being a fast man with a gun. It took him all of a second to draw and shoot. The man he was up against was not good either and must have panicked at the way his two friends died. His gun was lifting clear when Red's hand twisted palm out, lifting the long-barrelled Cavalry Colt from the holster a fast done cavalry twist. The seven and a half inch barrel kicked up as flame tore from the muzzle and the man reeled under the impact of the bullet which caught him high in his shoulder. He went backwards, hit the hitching rail and hung there trying to raise the gun. Talbot yelled out something and brought up the shotgun, firing. The gunman was slammed backwards, caught by nine buckshot, his gun dropped and he followed it down.

'What the hell?' Red swung around, his face angry.

'Don't you know more'n stop shooting when a man's got a gun in his hand?' Talbot answered. 'He could have killed you.'

'Yeah.' Red's growl was deep. Talbot was right in one way. It was a prime rule for a lawman to keep on shooting when a man he'd wounded still had a gun and was willing to use it. Talbot might have been acting in good faith or there might have been a more sinister motive. The man was now dead. He might have been taken alive and able to talk.

Waco went forward with his gun held ready and rolled his victim over on to his back. There was no need for caution now. The man was dead but it was close, very close. There'd been no time for fancy shooting when dealing with a man like that. He was one of the topguns, the speed he brought the gun

54

from his waistband and with his left hand showed it. For once in his life Waco had made the near fatal mistake in judging another man's gunspeed.

He bent down, holstering his gun and taking out a knife. Cutting away the sling below the knot he slit open the shirt and opened up the bandaging around the man's shoulder. He straightened up and pointed down to the hole.

'This's one of the men who rode on the raid last night. The other two must have been with him. What's his name?'

'That's Dave Tull. Works for Mr. Brarsand,' Sanger answered.

Waco swung around and saw both Brarsand and Della Christine in the crowd although he did not know them. 'Where do I find this Mr. Brarsand?' he asked grimly.

CHAPTER SIX

A LETTER FROM MOLLY

'YOU'RE looking at him, boy.' Brarsand stepped forward, his eyes taking in every detail of Waco's dress and appearance.

'He your man?'

'He worked for me. I fired him a couple of days back. Della found he was rigging the roulette wheel.'

Waco glanced at the saloon girl, noting the swollen, blackened eye and the fact that lipstick could not hide the swollen mouth. He wondered how she'd gained the battle-marks. Della did not give him a chance to find out, she nodded in agreement to what Brarsand said. 'Sure, we caught him and the boss fired him.'

'What's he been doing since then?' Waco asked.

'Hanging around town. What's he been doing?'

'He led a raid on the S.S.C., Mr. Brarsand. Killed the old gent's boy, either him or one of the other of the bunch did.'

'You're sure he was one of them?' Brarsand asked, never taking his eyes from Waco's face.

'Near enough sure. I hit one in the shoulder, just like he's been hit. Then he allowed he'd seen the doctor and had the wound fitted up but I knew he was lying. No doctor put that sling on.'

'How'd you know that?' Talbot growled. 'Looks like an ordinary sling, to me.'

'Sure look real ordinary. 'Cepting that a doctor allus fastens a reef knot. They're taught to do it that way, makes the knot ride easier on the shoulder. Ask Doc Leroy here, he'll tell you.'

''Sides Doctor Smethers went out to the Jones' place to see Mrs. Jones having a baby.' Lafe Sanger spoke up. 'Went yesterday and hasn't been back yet.'

Waco remembered what he'd heard about Dave Tull and picked up the gun which lay by the man's side. It was a real fine Colt, costly and showed sign of having had the mechanism worked on for extra speed. It was the sort of gun a real good man would tote. Then Waco looked down at the grips, holding them to the light. The right side grip showed just that slight discolouring which told him why he was still alive. That gun was slightly different in grip from the other. It was only the slightest variation, but in the hands of a master would make all the difference.

It was that slight difference, undetectable except to the man who owned the gun, which saved Waco's life. Tull was used to handling the gun in his right hand, changing it to the left threw him off that vital split-second. His using that gun meant only one thing. Waco took up the gun which Ben Silver had carried, hefting it and the other in his palm. Although he was not used to the guns he could tell they'd been balanced one against the other. This was the second of Tull's guns, the one he'd always used in his left hand.

'This's Tull's other gun. He left off his gunbelt because he'd look real strange walking around town with an empty holster at his left side. He must have given the boy the other gun when they got near to the S.S.C.'

'It happened for the best then. I think you might be right about them.' Brarsand saved Talbot answering this for which the town marshal was pleased. He owed his post here in town to the good offices of Brarsand and did not want to jeopardise his chances by taking the wrong sort of attitude. Brarsand stepped to the old man and patted his shoulder. 'I'm sorry about this, Ezra. Your boy came in the saloon last night but I made him leave. I didn't want to offend you any by serving him. I don't know where he went after that. It might have been to the Hood City Saloon.'

'It warn't,' Lafe answered. 'I was there all night. Saw him once but he never came in. He was with your boy, Wilben.'

57

'Not me, Mr. Sanger,' the tow-headed boy spoke hurriedly, his face pale as he stared down at the three bodies. 'I left him early on. I didn't see him at all after——'

'After what?' Waco snapped.

'Nothing.' The boy looked even more frightened. Turning he walked away before another word could be said to him.

Wilben watched his son with worried eyes, then gave his attention to the old man. Ezra Silver was standing with his hands still gripping the edge of the wagon, his face drawn. He still could hardly bring himself to believe his son was mixed up in such doings. Yet the boy was dead, and so were three other men.

'My boy, drinking. Riding about in a hood,' the old man's voice sounded strangled with grief. 'What devil's work was it he was about?'

'A man in likker does strange things, mister. Especially a man growed taking if for the first time. It was a real smart idea somebody had. Bring a nester along with them, leave him dead and stir up trouble between the ranchers on this side of the Ranse and the nesters on the other.' Waco's voice was gentle. 'I'm sorry it came to killing.'

Mary Anne climbed down from the wagon with Lee by her side. She was pale-faced like most of the crowd, for the town of Whittle was not used to the savage sudden death which struck on the streets from the guns of those three young Texas men. She moved alongside Waco and her voice was steady as she said, 'Leave it, boy. Mr. Silver I can't express in words how sorry we all are about your loss. Take the wagon and carry your boy home.'

Silver looked up. He did not appear to know what the girl was talking about. Wilben gripped the other man's arm gently and led him to the side of the wagon and helped him in. Climbing up into the wagon he reached for the reins and looked down at the girl. 'Thank you, Miss Catlan. I'll return the wagon as soon as I can after taking care of Ben's burying and getting Ezra settled down.'

'Stay by him, there's no rush for the wagon,' Mary Anne replied.

Wilben started the wagon forward, headed along the street. His son came from the sidewalk and climbed alongside him while Silver sat on the edge, rigid and with eyes staring ahead of him. The crowd started to break up now. Talbot and Lafe Sanger told some of the watchers to help carry the bodies to the undertaker's shop and followed them. On the street, Mary Anne stood by Waco and glanced at Della, wondering how the woman's face came to be marked up. Della was glaring her hate at the ranch girl who caused her to get a beating from Brarsand after losing him five hundred dollars. Though she hated Mary Anne, Della did not intend to resume hostilities. Brarsand was definite in his orders about it.

'You figured all that out well, young man,' Brarsand remarked. 'Bring your crew down to the Tavern and have a drink.'

'Not now, thanks. The boys are headed back to the spread right now. I'll be going with Mary Anne as soon as we've seen Colonel O'Dea.'

'Have you decided to take my offer, Miss Catlan?' Brarsand went on as the S.S.C. men followed Red back to where he'd left his horse. 'Although, with things happening as they are I wish I hadn't made it.'

'It doesn't need any thinking about. I'm not selling the S.S.C. and nothing's going to make me. Not riders or any other thing.'

'What makes you think there's someone trying to scare you out?' Brarsand was still smiling and friendly as he looked the girl over.

'What makes you think somebody isn't?' Mary Anne was just as friendly sounding. 'That try last night was aimed at scaring either me or the ranch crew. It didn't come off.'

'I can see that,' Brarsand replied truthfully.

'Mister,' Waco's voice cut in bringing the other man's attention to him. 'There's two real good reasons why Mary Anne here won't be scared out of her spread.' His hands brushed the butts of his matched Colts guns. 'I'm wearing them.'

Brarsand's eyes strayed down to the staghorn-butted guns, noting how they were worn. He knew how fast Dave Tull was with a gun and this boy beat him to the shot. 'They're real strong reasons.'

'Sure. The next man who tries making a play at the S.S.C.'s going to find out how strong. We'll be seeing you, Mr. Brarsand.'

Brarsand did not reply as Waco and Mary Anne walked along the street. Then he turned and took Della's arm under his own, walking her back to the Tavern. 'That's a shrewd, smart young man. He'll take some watching. I wonder who he is. He isn't a hired gun, I'm sure of that. I thought she was the last Catlan.'

'She was.' Della was sullen and resentful still. 'Them two boys were the last of the brothers. There was a button they adopted, I've heard Sam talk about him. Boy they just called Waco, didn't know who he was or anything. Went off and rode for Clay Allison for a spell. That might be him. He's good with a gun.'

'Tell me something I don't know. Dave was better than most and two of them drew faster than he could. That pale-faced man, he's the one Jocelyn tangled with. Doc Leroy of the Wedge.'

'They're a bad bunch to tangle with. The redhead's another of them. What're we going to do now, Carl?'

'Nothing for a couple of days. O'Dea must have the letter by now. Then we can make our move and without risk, or without half the risk of trying to get rid of the S.S.C. by violent means.'

Colonel O'Dea received Mary Anne and Waco in his study. He was a tall, spare man, white haired and aristocratic looking. His face was tanned and keen, his eyes frank and honest, meeting a man without flinching. His clothes were still of the style worn by the deep south planter before the war and he looked as if he'd just stepped from a riverboat in New Orleans after a successful cotton selling trip.

'It's good to have you back, Mary Anne,' he greeted warmly, holding out a hand. 'I appear to remember you, young man.'

'This's my lil brother, Waco,' Mary Anne introduced.

'Waco?' O'Dea was puzzled for a moment, then he remembered the boy who'd ridden off at fourteen years old to see the West. 'Now I remember. You rode for Clay Allison, didn't you?'

'Sure, sir.' Waco noted the disapproval in O'Dea's voice and knew why. Clay Allison's crew were noted for their wild and rowdy behaviour and for skill with a gun. 'I'm riding for the O.D. Connected right now.'

'I see.' There was something like admiration in O'Dea's eyes for the O.D. Connected was known to be discriminating in their choice of hands. 'Sit down, sit down. Both of you. I hoped you would come in to see me today, Mary Anne. What was all that shooting I heard?'

Mary Anne explained as she sat down at the table. The Colonel did not speak, listening to all the girl told him. His eyes kept flickering towards Waco as he listened. At the end he nodded in approval. 'Not enough evidence to take to a court of law, but it was not needed the way things turned out. Now we'll get down to the other business. The S.S.C. is solvent, Mary Anne: and has never been more so. Under the terms of your father's will you as sole surviving kin inherit it——'

'But Waco's my brother,' Mary Anne objected.

'Only adopted as you both know. Not even legally adopted. I'm sorry. Mary Anne but that is how it stands. To carry on, you don't owe anyone a red cent, except for the time due to the hands. If that was all you wouldn't have a thing to worry about.'

'Is there more then?'

'Not so far, but there could be. Your water supply might be curtailed, which would ruin your land.'

'How?' Mary Anne asked. 'The Ranse River forms our main supply and from what I saw there is plenty of water in it.'

'The headwaters are on the Lazy W property.'

'They always have been. Molly Wilmont and her pappy would never interfere with them. They never have.'

O'Dea nodded, taking out a box of cigars and offering it to Waco. The young man accepted, lit the smokes and sat back, listening, knowing there was more than just casual conversation behind the Colonel's words.

'I agree with you. *They* have never interfered with the running of the water. You know of course, that since her father died last year, Molly has been living in Chicago and leaving the ranch running to her foreman, Whit Dwyer, with myself acting with power of attorney for her interests in matters which Whit could not manage?'

'I didn't know, but that figgers.' Mary Anne sounded puzzled..

'Well, she wrote and asked me to sell the ranch.'

'She did *what*?' Mary Anne came to her feet, leaning forward with both hands resting on the table top and looking down at the man.

'I received this letter only this morning.' O'Dea reached inside his coat and pulled out a letter holding it to Mary Anne.

Mary Anne took the letter, glancing at the sprawling, not over elegant writing and recognising it for what it was. She'd seen enough of Molly Wilmont's writing to recognise this now. Taking out the sheet of paper she read the short, concise and businesslike note asking Colonel O'Dea to sell the Lazy W and act in all matters dealing with the disposal of it as soon as possible. She examined the notepaper. It was from the Reed-Astoria, one of the best hotels in Chicago.

'Are you sure she wrote this letter?'

'How do you mean, girl. Am I sure?'

Mary Anne handed the letter back to O'Dea before she replied. 'I know Molly, she's been like a sister to me. Put a pen in her hand and she's away like the devil after a yearling. Molly would never write a short note like this. You'd have had five or six sheets with news and asking about folks with the business of selling the spread mixed in with it. She'd never write anything as clear and concise as this.'

O'Dea scowled at the letter, then rose and went to the door to yell for his daughter, Susan Mae. The girl came, a slender, pretty blonde about Mary Anne's age. She smiled a delighted greeting to the ranch girl but did not get a chance to greet her. O'Dea asked Susan Mae to go to her room and fetch any letters she might have from Molly Wilmont and the girl knew better than waste time when he used that tone of voice. She left and soon after came back, carrying three envelopes. The Colonel extracted the letter from the first, checking on the handwriting, then glancing at the way Molly wrote. There was eight pages of the sprawling writing and the Colonel saw straight off what made Mary Anne suspicious. Molly wrote slower than she thought, apparently. Her letter was disjointed, one moment asking about the welfare of her pet horse, then going right on to describe a dance she'd attended, then on to something of more interest.

'This looks like the same handwriting for all that.'

'Mind if I look, sir?' Waco inquired and took the letters. He crossed to the window and held them both to the light, studying the writing with care. 'I'm no expert on things like this, but I'd say it was two different hands that did this.'

'A forgery?' O'Dea's face reddened. 'By cracky, boy, if I thought it was I'd——'

'Why'd anybody want to forge a letter like this though, Colonel?' Waco cut through the hot-tempered threats.

'Well, I've power of attorney as I just told you and can handle *any* business she wishes me to. With this letter I would take up any reasonable offer which came my way.'

'Without consulting her?'

'That depends. Her letter says take the best offer I can and sell as quickly as possible. If the price was right I'd sell without worrying her any. That's the idea of having an attorney.'

Waco laid down the cigar, his face showing nothing of the way his thoughts were whirling, sorting and debating the reason for this letter. 'Unless I recollect wrong, Rusty gal, there was two watercourses to the Ranse, the one it follows and a drywash that only fills when there's a real high fall of rain in the hills. But dam the top of the Ranse and that other cut would get the water, run the Ranse dry and leave you out. If the Lazy W wanted to make the dam, that is.'

'Molly wouldn't do a thing like that.'

'It wouldn't be legal, either,' O'Dea pointed out.

'Sure, but a rock slide could do it and who could tell if that same slide was accidental or caused by dynamite?'

63

'I tell you Molly wouldn't pull any play like that, boy,' Mary Anne snapped, watching Waco's face. 'You always was slow at picking things up unless they was for eating.'

'Sure Molly wouldn't do it,' Waco agreed. 'But what if she sells out and the next owners aren't so friendly?'

'It would have complications, bad complications if the next owner was wanting to be awkward and make trouble,' O'Dea remarked. He saw his daughter was standing listening and waved her from the room. 'Is that what might be behind the letter, if it is a forgery?'

'It could be. That letter is to make you sell out when somebody comes along with a real good offer. They can afford to pay high for the Lazy W, they'll control all the water and with the Ranse run dry they can buy out the S.S.C. and the nester land cheap.'

Mary Anne paced the room. She halted by the table and her face was grim. 'I tell you Molly wouldn't sell out the Lazy W without making sure Whit and her crew were well taken care of first. It just doesn't fit Molly at all.'

'I thought that myself when I first received the letter. I checked the postmark on the letter. It was posted in Chicago all right. I wish there was some way I could talk with her.'

'That might be the answer, Colonel. I'd like to take this letter along with me when Rusty and I head for Chicago,' Waco put in.

'Well, I'm not sure it would be correct for me—head for Chicago. What do you mean, boy?'

'Molly's in Chicago, I figger she'll hear us better if we go to her than if we stand out in the street here and holler. Rusty and I'll go overland by hoss to the railhead, then take a train East. We can make better time than going by stage, night over at a couple of places along the way.'

'Hm! It might be possible, except for one small matter. Two young people like you travelling together might excite some curiosity, especially when one is a pretty and unmarried girl, the other a man.'

'Why Colonel,' Mary Anne sounded far more shocked than she felt. 'Waco's my lil brother. Anyways I think it's the best thing we can do. If Molly isn't selling and didn't write that letter we can get to her long before a letter could. If she is thinking of selling I'll bring her back here if I have to yank her all the way by the hair.'

O'Dea belonged to a more leisurely age when a young lady did not casually talk of going off on a long jaunt with a man, even if he was her adopted brother. This modern youth was beyond him and he was not at all sure he approved of it. One thing he did know, there was no stopping Mary Anne Catlan once she made up her mind. She was like her mother in that.

'I'd surely like the letter to take along, Colonel. And when you get the offer for the ranch you can safely and truthfully say you don't have a letter from her. It won't be a real, outright lie if you say it that way. You won't have the letter.'

'You've got a real law wrangler's mind, boy,' Mary Anne scoffed. 'All filled up with tricks——' Then she stopped and her face reddened. She'd forgotten that Colonel O'Dea was also a law wrangler.

O'Dea laughed. He was used to having range people regarding his profession with suspicion. He handed over the letter with a smile playing on his lips. 'Mary Anne's nearly correct at that. You've got the right sort of mind to make a lawyer. You've got more on your mind than just easing my conscience over this.'

'I'll tell you the truth, sir. I have. Know a man in Chicago who might be able to help us. Like you say the letter was posted there, I reckon it was written there, too. If it is a forgery, it's a good one and done by a tophand. He'll likely be able to point us to a few likely ones.'

'What is he, this friend of yours. A bank robber?' Mary Anne inquired. Her little brother seemed to know the strangest people.

'Not quite. He's a Detective-Lieutenant of the Chicago Police. I met him a piece back. Helped him some and he'll likely do the same for me. I'll get a telegraph message off to him as soon as we know when our train leaves for the East, he'll meet up with us at the depot.'

'You think he can help?'

'Why sure, Ed's been a policeman in Chicago all his adult life and knows them all. Like I said, this kind of work here's not been done by a yearling, it's tophand stuff. There can't be more than two or three men in Chicago capable of it. If it can be done Ed'll point us to the men who wrote it. Then I'll find out why.'

'When will you leave?' O'Dea asked.

'Today, as soon as we get back to the S.S.C. I'll leave my paint with Doc and Red. He don't take to strangers and I wouldn't want to leave him in the livery barn at the railhead. We'll take a couple of speed horses and light out on them.'

'Won't be able to take much luggage, travelling like that,' Mary Anne pointed out.

'Never thought we could. We'll take just enough to last us to the railroad and then buy some more when we get there.'

'That's all right for you, boy. But I like to travel neat.'

'You always did,' Waco laughed and ruffled her hair. 'Like when you went coon hunting and lost the seat of your pants. Come on, you can pack a dress or two and tote them along in a warbag.'

Mary Anne chuckled. Her little brother might be able to think things out and figure the whys and wherefores, but he surely did not know much at all about women's clothes. Not if he thought a stylish city dress could be bundled up and wrapped in a warbag.

CHAPTER SEVEN

MARY ANNE PAYS A CALL

CHICAGO in 1879 was almost over the Great Fire which gutted and decimated most of it in '71. It was also trying to establish itself as a prosperous eastern metropolis and live down the era of rowdiness. Down by the stock yards a man could still find western style clothes. In the badlands, the slum areas which surrounded most of the business sections life was much the same, but up in the North-East, in the area they called Streeterville, the new rich made their homes, built their high-class hotels, and lived a life well clear of the rougher element of town, striving to lift their cultural level to that of New York or San Francisco.

It was into the depot of the westbound railroad that Mary Anne and Waco arrived. They'd bought clothes more suitable in the railhead town, the best money could buy for them, but Mary Anne knew she was hopelessly outmoded. Waco still retained his Stetson and high-heeled boots but wore store suit, white shirt and black string tie. From under the bottom of his coat showed the tips of his holsters, the pigging thongs fastened to his legs. He stood by the girl and looked at the milling crowd around him.

'Man, oh man. Just look at all the folks,' he said. 'Looks like ole Dodge City in the train season.'

A man came through the crowd, a man as big as Waco, and older. He wore a curly brimmed derby and brown suit, with town shoes on his feet shining as he walked. He was not a good-looking man, yet there was a rugged attraction about his face, his teeth were rather prominent and gave him a look of furtive amusement. He held out a powerful hand which Waco gripped eagerly. 'Howdy Ed,' he greeted. 'Glad to see you again.'

'Same applies, boy. I thought you might be in on the train so I came down to greet you.'

There was genuine pleasure about the meeting. Lieutenant Ed Ballinger owed Waco his life. That was in the days when he chased a gang of big city criminals down to the Rio Hondo country of Texas. It was in the Rio Hondo country Ballinger learned that Western lawmen were far from country hicks and Waco was one of the men who had shown him.

Ballinger's eyes dropped to where the tips of Waco's holster showed and a grin broke across his face. 'I knew you'd come wearing all that armament, boy. Here, you'll need this.'

Waco accepted the sheet of paper held out to him. 'What is it?'

'A firearms permit.'

'A *what*?' Waco almost shouted the last word, bringing several people to a halt.

'Firearms permit. You need one to tote a gun around here. And we don't even like folks doing it. I had the hell of a time getting it for you, even you are still a Deputy Sheriff of Rio Hondo County, so don't go shooting out the street lights.'

'Lord, what'll they think of next?' Waco sounded shocked. 'Hell, just think how we'd be if we had to get one of these things every time we wanted to go to town.'

'This isn't the West, boy. We're civilised here. So they tell me!' Ballinger glanced inquiringly at Mary Anne.

Tucking the permit into his notecase Waco introduced the girl, but did not offer to explain his business any. 'Come along to the Reed-Astoria, Ed. I'll tell you all about it when we get there.'

'All right. I've got nothing but time. Took me a day or so off when I heard you were coming. Reckoned we'd make a round of the town. I owe it to you. Don't know about it now, though. Chicago's a town full of evil temptations.'

'And I bet you was going to introduce him to most of them,' Mary Anne remarked, eyeing Ballinger grimly. 'Can't say I approve of my lil brother doing things like that. But I don't reckon that's going to stop either of you any.'

Ballinger led the way to the stand where Victorias stood ready for hire. He opened the door of one and helped the girl in, then climbed into sit next to her. Waco swung up and joined them, facing them and waiting until the coloured porter brought their one small bag. He tossed the grinning man a coin as the bag was passed to him, then the driver started his horse forward.

There was little talking done on the trip for Waco was absorbed by the sights of this, the biggest city he'd ever seen. They left the poorer section and came towards Streeterville, the streets widening and the buildings becoming more imposing all the time. Waco's attention was held by the stores, then they came to a halt before a large, stone-built establishment. Over the awning, in large black letters was the sign 'Reed-Astoria Hotel'. It was the best, most elegant place in Chicago and Waco felt a momentary panic. He knew the social graces, having learned them at the O.D. Connected, but the chances to use them were sadly lacking in the West. Yet he'd never even thought of staying at such a place as this.

'Wowee?' The words came from him as he looked at the building. 'There's nothing like this in Dodge City. I bet they make you shave before they'll have you in the barbershop.'

Mary Anne and Ballinger laughed at this. They were both watching the young man and comparing Waco in the city to Waco on the range. There he was the master of every situation, knowing the land and at home in it. Here he was a stranger, out of his depth almost. Ballinger could appreciate Waco's feelings. He'd felt the same way when the stagecoach carried him over the miles of open range into an unknown land. Then he'd been the one who was lost and Waco helped him out, Waco and the members of Ole Devil's floating outfit.

Mary Anne was used to buildings like the Reed-Astoria and led the way into the hotel. Inside she saw people looking her over and was conscious that she was not as well dressed as she would like to be, when entering a place like this. The fat desk-clerk studied her and Waco with a frown as they walked to the desk, then glanced at Ed Ballinger, nodded a greeting and turned a frigid face to the girl.

'I want two adjoining rooms.'

'You wish a room *here*, madam?'

'Miss. And I want two rooms, *here*, right now.'

The clerk gulped. He'd seen some of these Texas people before. They were inclined to get rowdy if they did not receive attention and firm handling. He hoped they would not cause a scene for there were the other guests to consider, including the Earl of Hawksden and his wife. In fact the Earl was coming now, striding along the hall, his monocle gleaming in his eye. He stopped and looked at the tall young man. The clerk gulped, hoping this rough-looking young man did not offend the Earl's susceptibilities for the British aristocrats were known for their dislike of democratic ways. The Earl was advancing now, screwing his monocle more firmly in his eye.

'Waco, you damned old hell twister. Gad! It's good to see you.'

Waco turned. For a moment he did not recognise this elegant and stylishly attired young man, then he grinned and gripped hands with a whoop of: 'Brit! What the hell are you doing in that get-up?'

The two men shook hands and Mary Anne stared at them, then at the clerk whose eyes were bulging out like two balloons. She did not know this elegant-talking dude, but apparently the clerk did, so did Ballinger from the look on his face.

'Say Mary Anne, this's Brit. We met down in Azul Rio Country when we was helping Mark's cousin.'

'Pleased to meet you.' Brit held out his hand to the girl. 'Are you Mrs. Waco?'

'Not under any circumstances. I'm his big sister.' Mary Anne turned to the clerk again. 'About those rooms?'

'There is the suite, next to mine, Jules,' Brit remarked. He could guess what was going on.

'Yes sir, my lord.' Jules grabbed up the pen and turned the register. 'Of course, sir. Front!' A page darted forward. 'Take this lady's bags to her room.'

'Shucks, ain't no call for that.' Waco scooped up the bag. 'I'll take it.'

'This *is* annoying.' Brit sounded exasperated. 'Gloria and I have to leave on the train tonight. If I'd known you were coming I'd have stayed on a few days. You'll have to come and see Gloria before we leave, Waco. She'd never forgive me if you didn't.'

Jules looked at the book after Mary Anne filled it in, noting the address was a Texas ranch. His eyes met Ballinger's inquiringly as the Earl of Hawksden talked to Mary Anne and Waco, Ballinger leaned forward across the desk and dropped his voice in a confidential whisper. 'You're lucky, Jules. If you'd offended them you'd have been looking for a new job. He'd likely have bought the hotel and tossed you out of it.'

Jules gulped and held his voice down. 'Are they rich, then?'

'Just about the richest in Texas. The chief asked me personally to take care of them.'

Jules' face showed his worry now. Ballinger was head of the Chicago murder division of the police and an important man in his own right. For so important a man to have been given the task of shepherding this couple must mean they were important also. Of course, many of the Texas-new-rich people were likely to turn up dressed below themselves. It was just their democratic way of doing things. They were good natured, if a trifle rowdy. The Reed-Astoria was used to a certain amount of rowdiness, the amount depending on the bankroll of the person involved. The Texans were the worst, boisterous, inclined to shoot out the fittings. They were also more generous in their repayment for any damage they might cause and would give out large sums on leaving.

He handed the girl the key to the suite and waved the page forward to take them to their rooms. Mary Anne turned to the man again. 'Is Miss Molly Wilmont here?'

'No madam.' There was a respectful note in Jules' voice now. Miss Wilmont was a respected customer. 'She is attending a music afternoon at the home of her fiancé.'

'Who might he be?'

'Mr. Keith Wellington. Of the Streeterville Wellingtons.'

71

'Thanks.' Mary Anne followed the others.

There was not time to discuss the urgent business which brought them to Chicago yet. Brit fetched his wife, Gloria, and there was a happy reunion with inquiries about old friends. They lunched in Brit's suite and afterwards they left the Earl and his wife to get on with their packing. Gloria and Brit would have liked to stay on with Waco for a few days but business was calling them back home to New Mexico and their reservations were booked on the train. Mary Anne was more amazed at her little brother than ever. He knew the most remarkable people and appeared to have a range of friends which extended from gunfighters and Chicago policemen to a scion of the British aristocracy.

In the dining-room of their suite, which Waco described as being bigger than one hotel he'd used in Texas, they settled down to talk.

Waco was making a study of his surroundings. He grinned at the other two and took a seat in the comfortable chair. 'Man, this is really living. Ole Red Blaze never had it this good, he just wouldn't appreciate it none. Beats all I've ever seen. Even the one in El Paso. That was some place in its way. I was in bed the first night and there was a knock on the door, a voice shouted, "This is the manager, have you got a woman in there?" I said, "No," so they opened the door and threw one in.'

Ballinger laughed. 'You didn't come all the way to Chicago just to tell me windies like that, did you?'

'Nope. This here's what brought me.' Waco extracted the letter which O'Dea received and which was reputed to have been sent by Molly Wilmont, then added to it one Mary Anne produced also from Molly.

Taking the two letters Ballinger glanced at them, read both, then looked up. 'Well?'

'Real nice, aren't they?'

'Sure, lady writes a good letter. What's so interesting?'

'She only wrote one of them.'

Ballinger took up the letters again. He went to the window and held them to the light. There was no change in his facial expression at first, then he turned and there was a glint in his eyes. He was more interested in this than he let on.

'I'd near on swear they were written by the same hand. If one's a forgery, it's real good.'

'Thought that. It's why I asked you to come and meet me. I'd say no year-old beef handled the pen on that. It was written by a mossyhorn at the game, a real tophand. How many men in Chicago could handle a thing as good as this?'

Ballinger frowned. 'Right now not more than two. And I doubt if they could handle it well enough. Not this much writing. Sure, they'd do your signature so that nobody could tell the difference, but not write as much as this and address the envelope. There's not a man in all Chicago who's that good. Not now.'

Something the way Ballinger said this made Waco suspicious. The Detective Lieutenant was more than just casually interested in this forgery. There was more to it than first met the eye. Ballinger knew criminals, knew them as Waco knew the cattle business, as only a tophand could know them. He knew who'd done the writing of this letter, but there was more to it than just that.

'How about when the letter was written?' Waco asked. 'Which was afore that date there on the postmark stamp.'

'There was one man who could handle it. He was the best of them all. I never heard of a forger who could touch him. His name was Doc Pilsener.'

'Where at's this here said Doc Pilsener now?'

'That's a real good question, boy. There's only one of two places he could be and I wouldn't want to guess which he's at right now.'

'Try real hard, just for me,' Waco prompted.

'It could be heaven, although knowing old Doc's tastes on this earth I doubt it. We found him the day after this letter was posted. He was laying down in the stockyards.'

'Dead?' Mary Anne asked innocently.

'Never seen anybody deader. Shot three times in the back with a heavy calibre gun. Poor old Doc, must have mortified him being found dead down there. He was always fond of the elegant life and never went into the badlands if he could help it. Then gets killed down there, shot with a heavy calibre handgun.'

'That'll be a lot of help. There can't be more'n a couple of million .44 revolvers in the country and maybe not more'n three or four million .45's of different sorts. Unless there was more to it than that!'

'There was. We got the bullets out of him. All three of them and holding their shape. They were interesting, real interesting. I don't know if you hick lawmen know it but we've been making strides in this scientific crime detection. Got us systems of identification which are real good. We've also got a collection of bullets fired from Colt, Remington, Smith & Wesson, Merwin & Hulbert, Forehand & Wadsworth revolvers. We can compare most kinds of bullets we get with those in our files.'

'And this one was?' Waco asked, knowing there was something out of the ordinary. He was so interested that he did not make any comment on the subject of Eastern lawmen when confronted by an ordinary, everyday task which a Western lawman was accustomed.

'It wasn't any of them. So we asked around the place after we measured up the bullet. It was .450 calibre and that helped Kitteridge, the firearms dealers; helped us in the end. The gun they reckon it was fired from is made in England, a Webley R.I.C., stands for Royal Irish Constabulary. They'd one in stock and we got a bullet from it. Now all we've got to do is find a man who's got him a Webley R.I.C. revolver, was in Chicago, knew Doc Pilsener and had a good reason to kill him. It's as easy as that.'

'Like to see one of those Webley guns. I haven't ever seen one,' Waco remarked. 'Reckon we could go to that place and take a look at the gun they've got?'

'Sure, I'll take you as soon as you're ready.'

Waco paced the room for a time. Then he halted and said, 'Look, Ed. This letter here,' he indicated the forgery. 'It was written on paper from this hotel. Who can get that paper?'

'I don't know. Reckon anybody could if they wanted. Hold it for a minute and we'll find out.' Ballinger left the room and returned soon after with Jules, the desk clerk. 'Jules, who can get hold of the hotel notepaper, any of the staff?'

'No sir.' Jules sounded horrified at the thought. 'The hotel stationery is not for use by any of the staff.'

'Could the hired help get hold of it, happen they wanted?' Waco inquired.

'Hardly, sir. We take care that they do not. It leads to abuses. There is no paper in the writing room downstairs. If anyone wishes to use the hotel paper they send to me and I personally deliver it. I or one of the other desk clerks, whoever is on duty. I hope nothing is wrong, Lieutenant.'

'Nothing at all, thanks, Jules. I want to have a look at the register on my way out.'

'Register?' Jules gulped. 'I trust that there is nothing wrong which might reflect on the high standard of the hotel.'

'Nothing at all, Jules. I just like reading hotel registers. It's surprising how many Smiths there are in the world.'

Jules sniffed pompously. 'Not at the Reed-Astoria.'

Waco closed the door on the slightly offended, little fat man and grinned. 'Reckon he's telling the truth. His kind live for the place they work for. I bet he counts out each sheet, just to make sure they don't fall into the wrong hands. You know what that means, Ed, don't you?'

'Sure. It means the man who got the paper stayed here.'

'Could it be Doc Pilsener?' Mary Anne asked, then shook her head. 'No, of course it couldn't. He was a crook.'

'You'd never have known it to see him. He always dressed to the height of fashion, was a real gentleman. His kind has to be. Can you see a bank clerk handing money over to a man who looks like he's fresh from cow-prodding on a cattle-train?'

'I suppose not,' the girl answered. 'It could have been him then!'

'I doubt it. Jules there knows nearly every big-timer criminal in Chicago. He wouldn't entertain the idea of having Doc Pilsener even in here.'

'Let's work the range this ways, then,' Waco spoke up. 'The man who killed Pilsener is the one who paid for this letter to be written. That means he's the one who I want as well as you,

75

Ed. He's a man who's been in Chicago and stayed on here as a guest. Likely not be under the name we know him, if we do. Is there any chance of my getting one of the bullets that killed Doc Pilsener to take back with me?'

'I reckon we could fix it. The Chief's being chased by the papers because of Pilsener's killing. It came just at a time when the Chief was saying we'd cleaned up the town. He wants the man who did the killing. I'll be able to get you one of the bullets if I tell him you're still working as a deputy sheriff. Are you?'

'Still hold the badge, although I haven't done any work for the sheriff for a piece. I want to check the bullet against a man's gun.'

'Whose gun, boy?' Mary Anne asked.

'I'm not saying yet, big sister. Hondo Fog always told me never to name a name until I was real sure. When I am, I'll name him. It might even come out I'm wrong.'

'You usually are.' Mary Anne smiled as she watched Waco.

'You think Doc Pilsener's killing is tied in with whatever brought you here, boy?' Ballinger asked. 'It's a real long shot. Doc made him some enemies in his life.'

'Sure, but it's too much of a coincidence to think one of them killed him just after he'd finished a job like this. Was there any money on him when you found him?'

'Pockets were empty, everything gone from them. I've got some pictures of his body at Headquarters. That's another way we have of working out here now. Photograph the body so we've got proof of how it lay and everything.'

'Did you search his room?' Waco asked.

'Sure. It'd been gone over real careful before we got there and there was a pile of charred-up paper in the fireplace. We didn't find anything to help us except some blood. Looks like Doc was shot there and took out to the stockyards to be dumped.'

'Looks like I'm right, too. Call it this way, Ed.' Waco's eyes were glowing with eagerness. 'This man who killed Doc hired him to write this letter. He wrote it, then tried to blackmail the other man, or get more money out of him. That was why

76

he was killed. Would that fit in with what you know of Pilsener?'

'Sure it would.' Ballinger could see the country boy in the city air was falling from Waco now there was a serious job on hand, a job the youngster was as good at as was Ballinger himself. 'Doc was always a greedy cuss.'

'Then the man killed him, he'd got what he wanted. Searched the room to make sure there was nothing to point to him. Destroyed all the papers. Then took Doc out to the stockyards and dumped him. But what I don't know is how the man would know to contact Doc in the first place.'

'I don't follow you, boy,' Mary Anne put in.

'A man like Pilsener doesn't put a note in a paper saying, "Doc Pilsener, Expert Forger, available for work",' Waco answered. 'But this man knew how to find him. Let's go take a look at the register, go to Kitteridge's and see the revolver, then along and see Molly.'

They left the room and went to the desk. Ed Ballinger turned the register, flipping the pages until he came to the date of the letter. In the three days immediately before, during and after the killing only five people had left the Reed-Astoria. A man and his wife from New York, a Mr. Bannister whom Ballinger knew, a titled Englishman going west on a hunting trip and a Mr. Jackson who was marked as a businessman from Denver. Ballinger closed the book and handed it back to Jules, then turned to Waco. 'Satisfied?'

'What's this here Mr. Jackson look like?' Waco inquired.

'Big, always well dressed. A gentleman.'

'So's Cole Younger,' Waco answered. 'Can't you do better than that, friend?'

'A rather distinguished-looking gentleman if I remember. I'm afraid I see so many people I rarely take much notice of them. He was acquainted with several members of the Streeterville Sporting Club.'

There was nothing more to be found out here so they left the hotel and took a Victoria to Kitteridge's Hardware and Sporting store. The manager of the gun department greeted Ballinger as a friend and took them to the gun showroom.

They were passing through the fishing department when Waco found something which brought him to a halt. He went to a counter and looked down at the thing which lay there. 'What's this?' he asked.

It looked like a flattened out fish, was made of two pieces of rubber shaped like the wings of a grasshopper, a metal set of fins and swivel at front and three triangle hooks attached to it. 'It's an English fishing lure called a phantom. We received a consignment of them a few months ago. They're deadly for bass fishing. We're the sole suppliers in this country.'

Waco thought of the big old bass on the Ranse River and the time people spent in trying to catch him. 'I'll take one of them,' he said.

With his purchase in his pocket he went on to the gun showroom. Here he was at home, among the smells of gun oil and fine woodwork. He was shown the Webley Royal Irish Constabulary revolver. It looked a good enough gun but the butt was not as well made as that of the Colt Peacemaker, that was the finest grip ever used on a handgun. 'Sell many of them?' he asked.

'Not too many. They're hard to get ammunition for. Don't take the normal .45 bullet, it's too long for the R.I.C.'s cylinder. We're not the sole agents, but I've given the Lieutenant a list of all we've sold.'

Waco was turning to leave when he saw a rifle on a rack. It was like a Winchester Model of '73 but looked heavier and longer. Always interested in weapons he went to the rifle. The manager followed him and, salesman at heart, said, 'This is the latest model Winchester lever action. Centennial model of 1876. Calibre .45·75. Chamber capacity is cut down to twelve shots, but the range is greatly increased.'

Waco took the rifle from the rack hefting it. It was heavier than the Model of 1873 which he was used to. However it also possessed several advantages: it was heavier and took a better bullet. His own rifle was in need of renewing and this would be just the answer. 'How much are they?'

'This model sells for forty-eight dollars.'

'I'll take it. Box of a hundred shells for it and a reloading outfit.' Waco turned to Mary Anne as he finished making his order. 'Sure wish I'd known about that bet Della was going to make about you and her. I'd have won enough to take me another hundred hulls.'

Ballinger laid down the short-barrelled Colt Lightning revolver he was looking at and came over. 'Did you say Della?'

'Sure, why?'

'Doc Pilsener used to go around with a girl called Della. A blonde, real good looking, about your size, Mary Anne.'

Waco rested the rifle on the counter again and swung to face Ballinger, his face showing his eagerness. 'What was her other name?'

'Who, Della?' Ballinger frowned for a moment. 'I'm not sure. I think it was Della Christine.'

CHAPTER EIGHT

THE S.S.C. LOSES CATTLE

RED BLAZE took command of the S.S.C. ranch without any great worry as to his ability to handle things. He'd acted as segundo of his brothers' ranch back home and helped Dusty Fog out enough to know how to handle things here. He and Doc were skilled cowhands, they'd got the backing of a good crew and even though there was a chance of trouble they were not worried.

For two days they handled the chores of the ranch, keeping the men close in and doing the chores around. Then on the third Red slung his double-girthed Texas saddle on his big claybank stallion. He called Larry and Doc and they rode out over the range looking for odd chores the other hands could take care of. It was a rule that the ranch buildings were never left unattended, there were always two of the crew to stay behind, their orders, in case of attack, or needing Red back in a hurry were to light the fire in the house sitting-room, heap it with wet grass and make plenty of smoke. The ranch crew who were on the range had their orders to return as fast as possible if the signal was sent up.

A mile from the ranch they came on a herd of some two hundred head grazing quietly down at the foot of a long slope. The cattle were in a great fold of land. There was plenty of food and water for them.

'Stock herd, in case we ever need them in a hurry. They don't move about much. Stay down there most times, the food's good and plenty of water. The boys come out this way every other day or so just to check on them and make sure they're all right.'

Red nodded. He understood this. The O.D. Connected and many another ranch held the nucleus of a herd like that for use in case of a fast market being found. The herd down there, with good water and grazing were not likely to stray far. The cattle were not longhorns but whitefaces, the cattle which were fast replacing the old, ornery longhorn. It was the march of progress. The longhorn was ideally suited to open range grazing for it was half wild and could live off the land like a wild animal. The only trouble was the longhorn's beef was not up to the same high standard of the whiteface's. The whiteface cattle were easier to handle, less likely to raise hell when being shipped by rail. Their arrival was a marking of the end of the old, open-range days when a man's cattle roamed at will, were gathered in the great round-ups which often covered many hundreds of miles and involved many separate ranches.

Red was never one for dreaming of the days gone by. He lived for the day, lived full, wild and reckless like a true cowhand. Never one to be hampered by self-restraint, Red was regarded, by the people he came into contact with as the *enfant terrible*. He lived under the shadow of his more illustrious cousin, Dusty Fog. Even in the War he'd been under Dusty's shadow, as his second in command. Folks tended to treat Red as an amiable but reckless young heller. Only one man really knew his full capabilities. That man was Dusty Fog. Dusty knew that Red might act in a wild and reckless way, that he could and often did jump feet first into any fight that was going. He also knew that when once in the fight Red became as cool and capable as he usually was wild and reckless.

Right now Red was accepting his responsibilities. He was cool and would not let himself be swayed from his duties, nor would he fail in them. He turned the big claybank and rode across the range again with the other two men by his side.

'Buzzard, Red,' Doc pointed ahead. 'He's circling like he's over something and calling the rest of the boys up.'

They rode across the range making for where the buzzard was spiralling and saw what was wrong. A lone bull stood there moaning dolefully and making no attempt to avoid them as they rode nearer.

'Looks sick to me,' Larry remarked.

Red unstrapped his rope and rode nearer the bull, swinging the loop gently. He watched the big animal carefully and rode around it to flip the loop out in a hooleyann throw which landed the rope around the head and drew tight.

'He's all swelled up here, Red,' Doc announced as he rode behind the bull and looked down. He'd been almost sure of what the trouble was and this was proof.

'He's one of our best bulls. A mite old but he's still the best we've got. Going to shoot him?'

'Nope. Goodnight him.'

'Do what?' Larry looked puzzled.

'Goodnight him. Something I've learned from Uncle Charlie Goodnight. He always put bulls in his early trail-drives and found he was losing a lot of them. They got bruised up and swelled like this one's. Head back for the house and get me some grassrope, real thin, Larry.'

Larry swung his horse. He did not hesitate as he sent his horse leaping forward headed back for the ranch. He made a fast ride, collected the thin grass rope from the store and headed back. He found that Red and Doc had thrown the bull, hogtied its forelegs and were waiting for his return. Doc held a sharp knife in his hand. He took the grassrope, stripped off a strand or two then nodded to Red. Bending, the young man forced the bull's seeds up into the skin of the belly then cut off the loosened bag of flesh. Red held down the bull's off hind leg and kept the near hind held up while watching Doc work. Red could have done this as well, or nearly as well as Doc, but the slim young man was better at the next and most important part. The wound left must be stitched up so it would not open again, if it did, the operation was a failure for the seeds would come down again but without the protective bag.

Doc moved fast, punching holes in the flesh and carefully winding the grassrope fibre through the holes made, then drawing the edges up together. When he finished the job he nodded to Red and let clear, swinging back on to his black horse. Red released the legs of the moaning, struggling animal and leapt for his saddle. The bull came up with a bellow and Red swung afork his horse.

'What good's that done?' Larry asked. 'You castrated him.'

'Nope, just cut off the bag. Give him a week and he'll be back out there chasing the little gal cows ragged again and bellowing coarse as he ever did,' Red answered. 'We'll take him back to the spread and leave him in the corral where we can keep an eye on him.'

'You mean he'll be all right?'

'Why sure. Colonel Charlie always does it to his bulls when they start showing age. He allows it might not make a young bull out of an old'n, but it does keep an old'n going a piece longer,' Red Blaze replied. 'Lead him back, boy.'

'That's what they call Goodnighting a bull,' Doc remarked. 'I've been thinking of setting up as a doctor and do the same on old gents.'

The three young men headed back to the ranch, leading the bull with them and leaving it in one of the two corrals which were at the back of the house. Larry was dubious about the success of the operation although he had to admit the bull did not look any the worse for the Goodnighting.

A week later it was still all right, bellowing as coarse as ever and Larry admitted that the two cowhands knew what they were talking about. He was explaining this to one of the other hands, then turned as Red called him over.

'Saddle up, Larry, and you, Song. We'll head out and see how the stock herd is.'

The other two did as they were told, collecting their horses in a rush which showed how they liked to be out and about with Red Blaze. The three of them made good time across the range, headed for where the stock herd were grazing. The valley was just the same: the stream flowed along the bottom and the grass grew just as green and lush. There was only one thing wrong. The herd of cattle was gone.

Spurring their horses down the slope the three young cowhands brought their horses to a halt and looked down. 'Not more'n two hours back,' Red snapped, indicating the sign.

'Rustlers?' Larry asked.

'Unless you think maybe the cattle just took a yen to go off by themselves, which ain't likely,' Red answered. 'Song, head back for the spread and bring the ranch crew. Tell Doc what's happened and bring them along. Wish we'd brought our rifles along with us.'

'You reckon you could hit anything with that relic of your'n?' Larry replied, for Red always boasted he was a poor shot with his old Spencer carbine.

'Nope. It's just nice to tote it along. It likes to go out for a ride now and then. Let's go.'

Song grunted. He did not like the idea of leaving when there was the chance of a fight, but he knew better than waste time arguing at a time like this. Swinging his horse he lit out for the ranch, riding as fast as the horse would run. There would be several men with the cattle and a rustler would always fight. With a rope or a long stretch in the State Penitentiary waiting for them rustlers would always fight. Red and Larry were going after the gang right now. Two men would not be enough to handle them.

Larry and Red rode side by side. They did not speak for a time. Red was concentrating on the sign, trying to estimate how many men were handling the herd. Larry was thinking of what would happen when they caught up. He wore a revolver and was a reasonable shot with it but he'd never used the Colt on a man before. He knew that he was not even as good with a gun as was Red, who insisted that he was the veriest beginner when it came to weapons. Not that Larry or the other members of the ranch crew believed him, they'd seen him use his guns and knew that he was good.

'Say Red,' Larry spoke up. 'They're headed for the Ranse from the look of the sign. That means they use Dead Horse Ford, it's the only place where they could move cattle across in a hurry and they'll be in a hurry.'

'That figgers,' Red agreed. He did not know the country as well as the other man and was going along with Larry's thinking. The rustlers would not know how long they'd be un-pursued and would not want to waste any time in trying to swim the herd across a difficult stretch of water if they could find a reasonable ford.

'We can head for the ford and get after them.'

There was a problem facing them right now. The herd might be taken across the Ranse River and if it was, by taking the shortest and most direct route for the ford, they would save time. If the rustlers were not headed for the river, they would be wasting time for they were going to have to search for the tracks again. It was an even gamble, one way or the other. Red gave the matter some thought as they rode along the line. The rustlers would have to drive across S.S.C. and Lazy W land if they were not going to cross the river. They would be risking detection from any of the crew of either ranch who might be about. Most likely they were taking the herd over the river.

'All right, Larry.' Red made his decision. 'Head for the ford by the fastest way you know. If we miss out we'll have to come back this way and follow them.'

Larry turned his horse and headed across the range, going by a route which would have been impossible for men handling a herd of cattle. Red followed the other man's lead, trusting Larry's knowledge of the range. They rode at a fast trot yet held the horses in, for speed might be necessary later. Red was wishing he was afork his claybank for he was riding one of his string today and giving the stallion a well deserved rest. The horse he rode was all right, trained for cattlework, but did not have the speed of the claybank stallion.

They came to the Ranse River and rode the short distance along the banks, making for the ford. Red brought his horse to a halt and pointed down into the shallows. The body of a big bass lay on its side in the water, a real big bass, weighing perhaps ten or more pounds.

'Old Mossyhorn,' Larry remarked. 'I've seen him more than once in his hole. What's that thing in his jaws?'

Red swung down from the saddle, tossing the reins to Larry and then sliding down the bank. He stood in the ankle-deep water and picked up the dead bass by the thing which hung from its mouth. The weight of the dead fish dragged it loose and Red looked down at what appeared to be a grasshopper shape thing made or rubber and with three triangle hooks in it.

'Looks like Sunshine Sam got into the big feller after all,' Larry remarked. 'I remember he brought that thing back with him from town on the day before he was killed. Called it a phantom.'

Red took his handkerchief out and wrapped the phantom in it. 'Where'd he get it, I've never seen anything like it.'

'Nor me, didn't say. He just showed it us and told us that it was going to win him some money. Went out, him and the boys, they didn't come back again. We went out and found their bodies.'

Thrusting the phantom, wrapped in his handkerchief into his levis pocket Red climbed back up the slope and mounted his horse. 'Let's get on to that ford, we've wasted time enough now.'

Riding on again they came to the ford and Larry gave a sigh of relief. The sign was plain, the herd was driven across the stream here. The water was still muddy and the hoof sign made Red bring his horse to a halt and examine it more closely. The herd was not far in front of them and from the look of things did not cross easily. The rustlers appeared to have had trouble in taking the herd across although it should not have taken them any effort at all. The water here was not deep enough to give the cattle any concern, the sun was, if anything, behind them. No driven beef liked to enter water with the sun in its eyes so it could not see the other side. There was not even this cause of trouble here.

'Good work, Larry. You called it right. Let's go across and see where they're headed.'

They sent their horses into the muddy water, it was not even deep enough to wet their boots as they rode across. On the other side they allowed their horses to make better time for the tracks were fresh and easy to follow. Ahead they heard, faintly, but growing louder all the time, the sound of cattle moving.

Topping a rim the two men looked down on the herd, it was

below them and being hazed along by nine men, too big a bunch for so small a herd if it was being driven legitimately. The men, for all their number, seemed to be having trouble in handling the cattle. Far more trouble than experienced rustlers would have. One thing which could always be said for a rustler was that he was a tophand with cattle. He needed to be, for fast handling was of vital importance to him.

'They're not nesters riding the herd,' Larry remarked. 'But they're headed right for Wilben's place. It's just over that rim there.'

Red was watching the cattle and hardly heard what the other cowhand was saying. Then the import of the words struck him. He lifted his eyes from the herd to the rim ahead of them, on the other side of it smoke curled into the air. He saw that although the herd was down below them and headed away the men at the point were swinging it to line on the house. In that instant he saw it all.

'Let's go!' Red barked the order and swung his horse in a direct line towards the slope, not at the herd.

'Herd's down there, Red!' Larry yelled as he sent his horse after Red's. 'What're you going this way for?'

'They're going to stampede that herd over the Wilben place,' Red shouted back. 'They're not rustlers, can't handle cattle well enough for them to be.'

There was no time for more talk. The two horses were hitting the best speed they could manage. Down the slope the two men raced, sitting their horses with that ease which every cowhand showed in the saddle. They were both well mounted, Larry on his favourite, go-to-town horse, a leggy and fast bay and Red afork a powerful bay coyote which was generally conceded too fast for cattlework. They were riding these horses as what they were on amounted to a *pasear* rather than a working trip. Right now speed was of far more importance than good handling qualities. Red, a light rider, despite his size, handled his horse like the master he was, sending it at a far better pace, bounding and reaching out down the slope.

Racing his bay, Larry followed Red, riding in close in the mad race. Excitement tingled his cheeks, wild excitement like

87

he'd never known before. The route they were taking would bring them to the rim in front of the herd, after that he was willing to follow any lead Red Blaze cared to make. Then he heard a scattered volley of shots and the steers were running in a wild stampede, the nine men hazing them and encouraging them to run faster than trying to halt them. Larry knew for certain Red was calling the play right, the men were not rustlers at all and they were trying to stampede it across the nesters' cultivated land.

Three of the wild riding men around the herd turned their horses from the line and came hurtling towards the two cowhands, guns in their hands. Larry watched them although Red did not appear to be giving them any attention at all. His eyes flickered in their direction just once, then were back on the route they were riding. It was then Larry saw the men were all masked. Real rustlers would not be, not while travelling with the herd off the ranch land from where they stole it. Masked men would attract attention and no rustler wanted to do that. Larry's gun was in his hand, but he held his fire. He saw a flame flicker from the Colt of one of the riders, but did not hear the bullet. This was not unexpected for it would have taken a lucky shot to hit at that range when riding a fast running horse. Larry lifted his own Colt but Red snapped, 'Don't waste lead yet.'

The two parties swept together, converging with each raking stride of the horses. Red's right hand twisted palm out and lifted the long-barrelled gun from leather and lined it, firing once. The nearest man gave a hoarse cry and rocked back in his saddle, then slowly crumpled sideways from the horse. Larry lined and fired twice. He saw the second of the men clutch at his shoulder and bring his horse to a one-handed halt, sliding it on to its rump to avoid the next shot which might be coming his way. The last man brought his horse to a halt also, swinging down from the saddle and tossing the reins over the horse's head, then pulling the rifle from the saddle-boot.

'Yeeah!' Red's wild rebel yell shattered the air. His horse left the ground in a bound and lit down making better speed, while Larry's bay flung itself out in a desperate attempt to keep up. 'Flatten down over the horn, Larry!' Red followed his yell with this warning. 'Rifle!'

Larry did not understand for a moment, then he heard the flat slapping sound made by a close-passing bullet. He fanned the horse's ears with his hat and the bay responded with a fresh burst of speed. He caught alongside Red and saw the other grinning. Red whirled the Colt on his finger, twisted it around and holstered it. 'Just like home!' he whooped. 'We're gaining on them, boy.'

The two horses were gaining on the herd, for a whiteface could not make the sort of speed a Texas longhorn could. The men urging the herd fired a few wild shots after the fast-riding cowhands but the range was too great. It was also getting too great for the man with the rifle for he was not shooting. He'd taken Larry's hat off with one shot but that was the nearest he'd come to making a hit.

Topping the rim Red and Larry saw Wilben and his two oldest sons standing staring up at them. The nester and his boys were working at cutting hay and lines of it were ready for collecting in the wagon which stood without a team but nearly full, on a level piece of ground halfway down the slope.

There was no time for much at all. Red gave a yell of 'Stampede, get to your house!'

Wilben might be plump but he was neither slow moving, nor slow thinking. He knew what that ominous rumbling was well enough and only needed the yelled warning to galvanise him into action. He snapped out an order and his sons started down the slope at a run with him following.

Red and Larry came down the slope and swung from their horses. Red bent and laid a hand on the hay. 'Bone dry, Larry. Lay a pile of it along here and watch for the herd.'

Larry grabbed up a pitchfork and with Red working by his side made a long wall of hay. Wilben saw what was happening and guessed what Red was thinking of. He turned and came back, his oldest son, the one who'd been with him in town and who'd attracted Waco's attention, followed him. They grabbed up their pitchforks and went to work. The lead steers of the herd came into sight over the rim top and Red barked, 'Run for it all of you.'

There was no arguing now. The men started down the slope at a run. Larry suddenly realised Red was not with him. Then Sandy Wilben spun around, clutching his shoulder and stumbling. Larry grabbed the young nester by the arm, got him across his shoulders and went off as fast as he could.

Reaching into his pocket, Red took out a match and rasped it on his pants. He bent and applied the tiny tongue of flame to the hay, watching the fire leap from strand to strand. He ignored the shots which were now being thrown at him as the wind caught the flames, fanning them along the line of hay. He saw the half-crazed cattle boiling down the slope towards the leaping flames, still being hazed on by the masked men. He knew that nothing but fire would stop stampeding cattle and it needed to be a fair-sized fire at that. He did not know if the small fire would do the trick. There was no time to do anything more right now except hope. He turned and saw Wilben; Larry and the other boy were almost at the house.

The bay coyote horse was standing with reins hanging as it was trained to do but its ears were flattened back and it fiddle-footed as it felt the intense heat of the fire. He ran back to the horse, caught the saddlehorn and vaulted afork, catching up the reins and setting his Kelly petmakers to work. The horse left the ground and headed down the slope. He was halfway down the slope when the horse took lead and started to go down. Red kicked his feet free of the stirrup irons and landed running even as the horse hit the ground. He felt the wind of other shots as he raced down the slope, covering the ground with raking strides in spite of his high-heeled cowhand boots. The others were all in the house by now, Wilben holding the door open. Red dived the last few feet, right through the door and with perfect timing Wilben slammed the heavy wood closed. He heard the thuds as bullets struck the door but they could not pierce the thick timber. Then he turned and watched Red Blaze getting to his feet.

It took a lot to put Red off his stride and he grinned cheerily at Wilben's plump, happy wife and his two daughters. The woman's face was not cheerful now as she worked on her son's shoulder.

'What happened?' Wilben asked as Red went to the window.

'It turned them,' Red replied. 'I was scared they might not turn at the fire.'

'What happened? How did the stampede start?'

'It was our stock herd. Run off. Larry and me trailed the men who did it. They came this way.'

'Rustlers?'

'Nope, they took it to stampede it over your place.'

'How do you figure that out?' Wilben studied the young man now.

'Easy, they drove it right at your place. Had they been rustlers they'd have stayed clear of anywhere they could be seen.'

Wilben was not looking from the window and watching the remnants of the herd scattering away. 'Why would they do a thing like that?'

'To start up trouble between the cowhands and you. The same sort of way they tried when they raided the S.S.C. and killed young Silver.'

Sandy Wilben looked up. His face was scared and worried again. He opened his mouth, then closed it again and sat still as his mother did what she could with his wound.

The masked men were coming down the slope now, most of them holding rifles. They started to take up cover behind stumps, rocks and one landed behind the dead horse. Wilben watched this and said, 'Looks like they want a fight.'

'All right, we'll make a try at giving them one,' Red replied.

CHAPTER NINE

THE FIGHT AT WILBEN'S

THE Wilben house was built on the same lines as most other such places. The front of the house was one big room which served as dining and sitting-room. Behind this was a passage and on the other side of this, kitchen and bedrooms. Red did not need to be shown the rest of the house. One could guess what it was like. In his run down the slope he'd seen enough to know that only from the front, on the slope could any serious attack develop. The land at the back and the sides was too open and did not offer any cover for the attacking men.

The next thing to occupy Red's attention was the state of defence the place was in. He saw they were not as well off as they might be. Wilben was holding a Henry rifle and his wife laid a box of .44 rimfire bullets out for him. This appeared to be his only weapon, apart from a long, old but beautifully chased, Kentucky rifle which hung on pegs over the fire. A powder horn scraped so thin that the level of the powder could be seen through the sides, and with a measure fitted to the top; and a bullet bag, hung over the gun. Red gave the old muzzle-loading gun little attention; he was thinking of cartridge weapons. He and Larry only carried their revolvers with them. Red cursed the inspiration which made him leave his old Spencer carbine behind. He was a good enough shot with either hand to make his Colts dangerous to the men if they came into anything like pistol range. They were armed with rifles and knowing the kind of men they were Red did not think they would take a single chance unless they were forced to do so.

A bullet slapped into the wall and Red flattened himself to

look out of the window. The gunmen were settling down with their rifles at about sixty yards which was beyond anything like the range of their Colt guns. It was also beyond the range at which the old Henry would be anything like accurate. The Henry was a fairly reliable repeating weapon and in its day was the best money could buy. However, even its most ardent supporters could not claim it was accurate over any range. The combination of the flat-nosed, two hundred and sixteen grain bullet and the weak, twenty-six grain powder charge made accuracy at ranges of over fifty yards uncertain to say the least.

The men on the slope were not much better off for most of them appeared to be armed with Winchester Model 73's. These were a better all-round rifle than their grandfather, the Henry, but still did not have enough power to drive a ball through the thick log walls of the house.

'Get your lady into the back of the house. Send your boy. He's hurt and can't help us any,' Red said to Wilben, watching the slope all the time.

A man slid in behind a rock and Red knew straight off he was going to make trouble. That man was holding a Sharps Old Reliable rifle. The Sharps might be a singleshot weapon but it could be reloaded fast enough by a man who knew what he was doing. It would hold true at half a mile or more and would retain enough power to knock down a full grown buffalo bull at the end. The rifle roared and smoke rolled from behind the rock; the heavy .50 bullet came through the wall like it was tarpaper and gouged a splinter-throwing groove in the top of the oak table top.

'Quick, ma'am!' Red checked the woman's objection to leaving her husband. 'He'll shoot this place plumb full of holes and with all of us here he'll connect with some of it. The less here the less chance he has of doing any harm.'

'Do as the young man says, Martha,' Wilben said mildly. 'He's acting for the best.'

Another bullet from the Sharps hit the wall and burst clear through, kicking up splinters near Sandy Wilben's feet. The young man was pale from the shock of his wound and from something more which was worrying him. His mother came forward and helped him leave the room, then ushered the rest of the family out after. She came back to lay a hand on Larry's shoulder. 'That was a brave thing you did out there young man. Thank you for saving my son.'

Larry blushed. He smiled at the woman. 'Shucks, ma'am. I only did what he'd done for me. You best get out of here, ma'am.'

The window frame smashed as a bullet from the Sharps struck it, sending glass flying. Red ducked back instinctively, then growled, 'We got to get that Sharps gun and get him fast.'

Larry took Mrs. Wilben, led her to the door of the room and opened it. He gave her a reassuring smile and said, 'Don't you go fretting, we'll get you out of this and we'll take care of your man for you. Ole Red there rode as a Lieutenant in the Texas Light Cavalry. He can handle any bunch like them.'

Closing the door on the woman Larry took his place by the other window and looked out. He took time to reload the empty chamber of his Colt and push a bullet into the usually empty sixth chamber. This was a safety precaution, for no man liked to carry a revolver loaded with six bullets when riding a horse. Red watched him with approval, Larry was growing up fast. He'd make a good foreman for the spread if Waco did not stay on at the end of the trouble.

Once more the Sharps rifle boomed and a hole appeared in the wall. Wilben gave a startled curse and ducked back, holding his face.

'They get you?' Red asked.

'Splinters is all. We've got to stop him, Red.'

'Mister, you've never been more right than now.' Red turned and looked at the Kentucky rifle again. 'The old gun work?'

'Sure. Sandy bought it when we came out here. He's kept it clean and uses it to bark squirrels with.'

'Mind if I use it?' Red darted across the room and lifted rifle, powder flask and bullet bag down. He hefted the bag and was relieved to find it was full of ready-moulded balls. Returning to the window he knelt down. 'This old gun's got the range over that Henry.'

'What do you want me to do?' Wilben was willing to let Red run the fight.

'Keep their heads down. Don't let them get in too close. Larry, you let a few shots off, not too many, we've only got the loads in our bullet loops to fall back on.'

Leaving the other two men to get on with their tasks Red started to load the old gun, working with a speed which showed he knew what he was doing. First he poured a measure of powder into the barrel from the flask. Opening the patch-box he took out a well-greased felt patch from the pile of them which filled the box. He put the patch in the muzzle of the rifle, took the roundest ball he could find, placed this on the patch and rammed both home. There was neither flurry nor nervousness in the way he acted. He primed the frizzen pan, checked the flint was held firmly. He hefted the rifle with appreciation, knowing it to be as fine an example of the gun-maker's art as was ever made. He'd handled these fine, long, old rifles before and knew their secrets.

'How's she fire?' he asked.

'About three inch high and just a mite to the left at seventy-five yards.' Wilben could see that here was a man who knew well how to shoot, a man who could handle the old Kentucky even better than he himself could.

Red brought the rifle up, lining through the window. He felt the smooth curve of the butt nestle into his shoulder and the balance the forty-inch barrel gave. He focused the V notch of the backsight and pinhead sight at the tip of the barrel. His aim was not at the man but the small rock in front of where the Sharps user was hidden. The old rifle cracked. For an instant smoke obscured Red's vision but it quickly dispersed and he saw a dark blotch on the rock right where it should be if Wilben called the sights right. Red was ready to take the Sharps user right now. Even as he primed and reloaded the Kentucky he marvelled at the way it held its accuracy. The gun held as true as the day, which was not just a couple of years back, when some gunsmith along the banks of the Ohio

River made it in his small shop. It was still accurate enough to bring off the honoured, old time trick of barking a squirrel. Barking squirrels was a trick attributed to Daniel Boone and required a steady aim, also an accurate rifle. It came about in the old days. A man could only take one weapon along with him, mostly only possessed one, when he went hunting, bad whites and hostile Indians, a man took along his .45 calibre Kentucky rifle when he went out. A squirrel was a delicacy but when shot with a rifle like the Kentucky was messy. A man did not need to skin it out, the bullet spread the squirrel. So barking was discovered. To do it a man aimed, not at the squirrel but at the branch just under the animal. If the shot was made correctly the bark splinters flying up, killed it as well and more cleanly than a direct hit.

Waiting his chance Red lined the rifle. The man with the Sharps was getting over-confident through the lask of opposition to his long shooting rifle. He sent another bullet through the wall and watched the other members of his bunch moving closer in, soon they would be at a range where their Winchesters could also throw lead through the walls. He came up more leisurely and lined his gun carefully. One of the logs of the cabin looked as if it might be splitting and a couple more shots would speed the process.

Bringing the Kentucky up Red lined and fired, holding as steady as a rock even though bullets were coming through the window. The heavy boom of the Sharps was answered by the flatter bark of the Kentucky. The old muzzle loader kicked up and smoke hid Red's man from him but, with the instinct of a good shot, Red knew he'd made a meat-pie-in-the-pot hit.

'Yowee!' Larry hooped. 'You got him, Red!'

'Clean through the chest, friend,' Wilben went on, just as enthusiastic at the shooting.

Red looked through the window and could see no sign of the man, although the Sharps rifle lay on this side of the rock. The gunmen on the slope certainly aimed to try and get the Sharps back. While the others poured lead down the slope and at the house, three darted for the rock. Wilben's Henry beat a tattoo as fast as he could work the lever and fire it. One of the running men stopped in his tracks, then crumpled down, rolling over. The other two hurled themselves the last few feet and were behind the rock.

The barrel of a Winchester came into view around the side of the rock, trying to hook the Sharps and drag it in. Red tipped the bullet-pouch and spilled the balls into his hand. He examined them carefully and picked the most perfect. There was only going to be time for one shot and it needed to be accurate. That Sharps must not be allowed to fall into the hands of the gunmen again. Realising the value of the Sharps to their plans the men up the slope fired fast, sending their bullets through the windows in an attempt to hold the defenders down. It prevented any chance of the Kentucky being rested on the windowsill and for a shot like this a steadier rest than human arms was required.

Fast action was needed for the man was drawing the rifle slowly to a position where it could be grabbed by a quick, snatching arm. Red did not hesitate for a moment. 'Larry, come over here and kneel down.'

Larry obeyed fast. He also knew the urgency of the situation and moved back into the room, kneeling in front of Red and allowing the barrel of the Kentucky to rest on his shoulder Red bent and lined the rifle, aiming up the slope to where he could see the rifle sliding along slowly, inching to where the men waited for it. The room reverberated to the crack of Wilben's Henry as he recklessly exposed himself, trying to draw the fire from Red's window and allow the Texan an uninterruped shot at the Sharps.

Calmly Red issued orders, his voice steadying Larry. 'Down a mite, little more. Up a touch, now down. Hold it there!'

The sights lined, moving along the barrel of the Sharps, towards the breech, knowing this was the only place where a hit might permanently damage the rifle. Allowing for the slight cavagry of the sights Red squeezed the trigger. The sear released, the hammer fell, propelling flint down, kicking a spark into a frizzen and the priming powder. There was a faint hiss as the powder fired and ignited the charge in the barrel and sent the bullet winding up, patch catching in the rifling and turning it. The Kentucky rifle cracked and even through the smoke Red saw the Sharps kick but whether from his shot or the pull of the other rifle he could not tell. The men behind the rock must have guessed what was wrong for one shot out an arm and grabbed the Sharps, pulling it in.

Larry straightened up, grinning broadly. Old Red was a ringtailed ripper with a rifle and that was for sure. He might try and say he was no sort of shot but when the chips were down he showed he could call his shots with skill.

Up on the slope, hidden behind a stump, a voice called, 'You got that Sharps, Hal?'

'Sure, but they hit the breech and bust it to hell. Jack is dead!'

The big man kneeling behind the rock made a wry face behind his mask, not at the death of the gunman, but at the loss of the rifle. His original nine men were reduced to six and one of them wounded. If they were going to get that bunch in the house they were going to need some real fast thinking and action. His five friends were good fighting men but those two cowhands were also good, especially that damned red-haired Tejano. Fighting from the cover of the house he would do plenty of damage before they got at him.

A man darted forward joining the one who'd called out for information about the gun. 'They got Jack, Cholla.' Not even the mask could hide the rage this man was showing.

'Sure Ted, they got Jack.' Cholla Jocelyn was not as interested in the death of the Sharps user as the big man. After all, Jack Kell was the man's brother and as close as only a hardcase Kentucky hill farmer could get. 'We have got to get them out of there and real fast. Those two from the S.S.C. might be missed and the rest of the crew will be coming out to look for them.'

Ted Kell was not worrying over that. His brother was dead and he would never rest until the men who did it also lay dead. 'We're going to get them out, all right.'

There was hatred in the man's snarl, yet there was also a fight-wise caution in him which would not allow anything foolish. Kell was born and raised in the feud country of the Kentucky hills. He knew hate of an enemy must be controlled. Any wild charging attack on that house would end in disaster from the very start. The men inside were all able to handle their weapons. There was another and easier way of doing this. Kell's eyes went to the hay-wagon.

'I'll start the boys moving in again.'

Kell turned as Cholla Jocelyn spoke. 'Ain't no need to risk us losing men. That hay wagon'll roll right down there and smash into the house front. All we need to do is light a match, put it to the hay and let her go. It'll burn them clear out.'

Jocelyn grinned. He was wondering why he hadn't thought of this himself. The hay was dry and would flare up just as well as when that red-headed cowhand used it to stop the stampeding cattle. It would be even worse, for the great pile would flare up just as readily and the wind would fan it higher as the wagon raced down the slope. It would be a roaring, unquenchable mass by the time it smashed into the front of the tinder dry house. There would be no holding the fire then for the house would go up, becoming a funeral pyre for the defenders.

'Get the boys here!' Jocelyn snapped. 'It'll take all of us to turn that wagon and get it started.'

In the house Red watched the slope with the other men. He saw the gunmen making for the hay-wagon. Larry turned towards him and grinned. 'Looks like General Meade exhorting his veterans.'

Red did not smile, he snapped, 'You got a cellar to the house?'

'Sure, a small one. Trapdoor's in here, under the table.'

'Get your wife and family down it then, and go yourself.'

Wilben wondered at the note of urgency in Red's voice. Since the Sharps rifle stopped barking he'd felt that the worst was over; that the men on the slope would spend some more time in long distance shooting then pull out. He was not even wasting any more ammunition on the men as they gathered behind the—

'Lord. You think they'd——?'

'I don't *think*, mister. I *know*. Move!'

Wilben moved fast. He'd heard that note in a voice before. It was the voice of a martinet officer. Pulling open the door he went through and out of sight. Red wasted no time; he jerked a hand towards the table and told Larry to move the table then lift the trapdoor ready.

'What're we going to do, Red?'

'*You're* going down the cellar.'

Larry caught the emphasis on the first word and got just what Red meant. 'Like hell I am. You're not sending me down there with those folks while you go outside and—— What the hell do you think I am, Red?'

Red grinned at the other young man. 'A damned fool. All right, you stay on up here.'

Wilben came in followed by his family. The woman stopped and looked at Red who was checking the loads of his revolvers and Larry who stood by the door.

'What're you going to do?' she asked.

'Nothing, ma'am. You go down there and stay down. Take *all* your family with you.'

Sandy Wilben stood with his arm in a sling. He darted to the window and looked up the slope. The gunmen were trying to turn the wagon and he knew what they were doing it for. He also realised what Red meant to do. 'I'm not going down there when that bunch are planning to——'

Red did not argue, or hesitate, his right fist came round to crash into Sandy's jaw. Larry caught the young nester and pulled him across the floor. 'Sorry, ma'am. He fainted. Get him down there.'

Red swung back to the window again. He did not know what the Wilben family thought of his actions in knocking Sandy out but he was not even going to waste time finding out. The gunmen up the slope were swinging the hay-wagon slowly around. It was hard work for men on foot and none of them thought of getting their horses. Red looked at the old Kentucky rifle and wondered if he could get one or two of the men with it. The range was even greater than when he'd used it on the Sharps user, at least a hundred yards, and that was a long shot for a Kentucky. There would not be time to load the old rifle fast enough to do any good with it.

Wilben licked his lips. He'd seen his family safe down into

the cellar and came across the room, picking up the Henry rifle and levering a bullet into the chamber. 'Get down the cellar, friend,' Red said gently.

'No. I'm going out there with you.'

Up on the slope the gunmen strained and heaved on the wagon as they swung it around to point down the slope. Cholla Jocelyn snarled out a curse as a thought struck him. 'Hold it!'

The straining men relaxed and waited to hear what was worrying Jocelyn. Kell snarled out, a match in his hand. 'What's wrong now, Cholla?'

'Get the hosses here. If any of them get out they'll be coming through that door at the back. We want to get around there ready for them and we can't do it on foot. Besides there'll be some smoke and folks'll be coming on the run. We've got to load Jack and Frank on their hosses ready to take them with us. You know the boss don't want any bodies leaving behind.'

Three of the men darted off to get the horses and returned fast, riding down the slope and slinging the two bodies across the saddles of two riderless mounts. Then they returned to the wagon and Kell growled impatiently at the delay. He was like a savage, his eyes flaring as he reached for the match again and rasped it on his pants, then set the hay alight, watching the flames leap and spread. Then he moved back to his horse and jerked the rifle from the saddleboot. He knew the men in the house could see what was going on. He also knew they would not tamely stand by and let it happen. They would be coming out of the building and up the slope in an attempt to get within range so they could use their handguns. He was going to make sure they did not get the chance to do it. Without a word to the others he slipped down the slope and flopped down behind a rock, his Spencer rifle cuddled into his shoulder and lifted the sights.

Red Blaze hefted his right-hand gun. He saw Larry's face was just a trifle pale but the young man looked steady enough. 'Let's go!' Red said, 'You open the door, mister.'

Wilben did it without suspecting a thing. Red jerked his head to the cellar and Larry went to lift the trapdoor again.

Then Red's pistol lifted to land on Wilben's head and knock him down. The man was dazed and before he could recover Red was pulling him to the trapdoor. Larry helped lower Wilben down then heard Red say, 'Never trust anybody, boy.'

Red's shoulder came round and thrust Larry into the cellar after Wilben, his foot kicked down the door and he ran across the room. Opening the house door Red drew a breath. Jerking the door open he leapt out, running for the foot of the slope.

Kell's breath let out a savage snarl as his eyes lined the sights of his rifle on the weaving, fast-running man while above him the other gunmen inched the wagon towards the edge of the incline.

CHAPTER TEN

MOLLY BREAKS HER ENGAGEMENT

MOLLY WILMONT was bored. The wailing screech of the string quartet got on her nerves. The thin-faced leader annoyed her by the way he screwed up his face in what he fondly imagined was a look of rapture but which resembled someone who'd been sucking on a lump of alum. She stood by the double doors of the sitting-room of the Wellington house and tried to look as if she were enjoying herself. Glancing sideways at the mirror on the wall she half approved, half hated, what she saw: a tall, slim, black-haired and beautiful young woman dressed to the height of fashion. The frock, leaving her shoulders bare, was tight and constraining to someone who'd been used to more casual clothes. Her face was losing its tan now and taking on the socially acceptable pallor which she so disliked.

Across the room Laverne and Alvine Wellington were tittering and whispering behind their fans. She watched them and felt disgusted. They were something she hated, simpering flirts who lived for two things only, gossip and flirtations. They and the others of their kind in the room did not interest her; they'd nothing in common. By the punchbowl Mrs. Wellington stood erect, her thin, pointed face showing disapproval at something or other. Molly did not like Mrs. Wellington any more than her two daughters, nor did Mrs. Wellington particularly like her.

Looking around the room Molly hoped that her fiancé, Keith Wellington, had arrived. There was no sign of him, or his father, the bluff, hearty Sam, a man she could like and admire. The old man was rich now, very rich, but he'd earned his money the hard way though he was reputed to be one of the richest men in Chicago. Money would not change him but his wife had done so. Mrs. Wellington was an arrant snob, a sourfaced arbiter of what she thought was good taste.

The piece of music ended to polite applause and Molly wished she could find an excuse to leave. There was no hope of that. Mrs. Wellington's plans for the day included this musical afternoon, then a visit to a theatre. There was no avoiding either. She must sit through the agony of the music all afternoon, then attend the dry as dust play that evening. She wished Keith were here. Keith was some boy and she loved him but she wished he would relax more. He'd taken her around with him to the usual social round, visits to the Streeterville Sporting Club where the bloods of upper-class Chicago foregathered. He'd taken her riding and proved to be good on a horse, though not as good as the youngest cowhand working on the Lazy W, but that was to be expected. Molly, knew that riding for a living was different to riding for sport. He'd taken her to a meeting of the Streeterville Rifle Club and displayed skill with a rifle although she was amused at the way he and his friends handled revolvers. They could shoot good groups on a target at twenty-five yards but she'd seen men who could do better. For all of that she loved Keith and knew that, given a chance, and away from his mother, he would be all man.

'Miss Wilmont.' Molly turned at the disapproving voice of Limbkin the butler. 'There are two persons asking for you at the front door.'

'Who are they?' Molly knew Limbkin did not approve of her and she didn't like him.

'I did not inquire. They are not the sort of people madam would encourage to come visiting.'

'What is it, Molly dear?' Mrs. Wellington was by Molly's elbow, frowning. 'Monsieur le Beaufort is just going to perform again.'

'Somebody's asking for me at the door,' Molly answered, seeing the leader of the quartet lifting his bow.

'Dear me. I do hope they are not like the last ones.'

Molly bit down an angry retort. Early in her acquaintance with the Wellington family a cowhand and his wife came to visit her while on a trip to Chicago. Mrs. Wellington arrived in time to hear Molly entertaining her guests, Mr. and Keith Wellington and a prominent railway president to a rowdy and slightly bawdy cowhand song. There'd been some unpleasant scenes over that and Mrs. Wellington never gave Molly a chance to forget it. It was only because of Sam Wellington's intervention that the engagement did not end then. He swore that he'd never heard the song done better.

Turning on her heel Molly went towards the door. She could not think who would be visiting her here. There were few enough people in Chicago who knew her, outside the circle of the Wellington family. Whoever they were they did not meet with Limbkin's approval. Then, nobody apart from Mrs. Wellington did. She opened the doors before Limbkin could arrive and forestall her. It always annoyed him. She went to the front door and a liveried footman drew it open for her. She didn't know what to expect and stared, hardly believing her eyes. She gave a most unladylike whoop. 'Rusty!'

'Hi Molly.' Mary Anne stepped forward and the two girls hugged each other.

'Say what're you doing here?' Molly asked, her pleasure at seeing her old friend making her forget where she was. Behind her the doors were open and the music came to a stop as everyone turned to see what the noise was about.

'Came to see you, gal.' Mary Anne grinned delightedly. 'Say, you remember my lil brother, Waco.'

Before Molly could answer there was an interruption. Mrs. Wellington was standing there, a vinegar sour scowl on her face. 'Molly!'

'I'd like you to meet——' Molly began.

Mrs. Wellington ignored the girl, looking Mary Anne and Waco up and down. They were still wearing the clothes they'd bought at the Texas railhead and these were not to the best of fashion. She sniffed then said, 'Tell your friends to go round the back to the kitchen if they want a meal. And I would like to see you immediately in the library.'

Molly's face turned red, wild anger in her eyes. She swung to Mary Anne. 'You come in a Victoria?'

'Sure,' Mary Anne was annoyed. She knew she was not well dressed, but there was no call for such impoliteness.

'Wait for me in it. This won't take long.'

Mary Anne and Waco watched the girl following the sour-faced woman into a side room. The annoyance at once left Mary Anne. She turned and grinned at Waco. 'Man, there'll be some fur flying soon. I haven't seen ole Molly so wild since she caught Susan Mae O'Dea with the boy who'd brought her to the quilting party. Come on.'

Molly went into the library with fire in her eyes. Mrs. Wellington was waiting for her and the Wellington girls, tittering behind their fans, were also in the room. Mrs. Wellington looked at Molly with the scowl she usually saved for her social inferiors.

'I have asked you repeatedly not to associate with those low people, Molly. After all, when you are married to a Wellington you——'

The door opened and Keith Wellington came in. He was a tall, fair, handsome and well built young man, his well-cut suit emphasizing his powerful figure. He came forward, face worried for he'd seen that look on his mother's face before and knew what it meant. 'What's wrong, Molly?'

Molly ignored him. Her temper was up now and when that happened she was wild as a longhorned Texas steer. '*If* I marry a Wellington the first thing I'll do is get him as far away from you as I can. That girl out there is my best friend. She's more like a sister to me. She happens to own a ranch as big, if not bigger, than the Lazy W. Not that that bothers me. She could still come to visit me even if she was as poor as a Texas sharecropper and she'd be welcome. Friendship doesn't mean how much money a person has in the bank. Not to me. She was my friend and came to see me, not to be insulted.'

Laverne Wellington gave a shriek and her mother sat rigid at the girl's effrontery. Then her voice lashed out in the tone which cowed unruly business people and servants. 'Listen to me, young woman. I've never been in favour of you marrying my son. You are not the kind of person a Wellington should marry.'

'Is that right?' Molly's eyes flickered to Keith. 'What do you say to that, Keith boy?'

Keith's mouth opened and then closed. He was in an awkward spot now, torn between loyalty to his mother and love for this fiery Texas girl. He tried to smooth things over. 'Look, Molly——'

'No, you look. I'm not good enough for your family, it looks like. All right, that suits me. I didn't intend marrying all your family. If I marry you it looks as if I'd have to marry the family.' She pulled the engagement ring from her finger and threw it on to the table top. 'There, give it to some tittering, simpering flirt like these two. There's a whole lot of them out there who'd just be ready to let your mother wipe her feet on them to become a Wellington. Give that ring to one of them. You don't want a woman.'

'Don't you dare speak to my brother like that?' Laverne shouted, determined to show this girl her dislike. 'I'll——'

The words ended abruptly as Molly gripped the front of Laverne's dress and pulled the girl forward, holding a folded, hard-looking fist under her nose. 'You'll do nothing. You dumb little sheep, you couldn't walk the width of the room without a guide. It's a pity you didn't see the man who was with my friend. He'd really have set you going after some of the things I've seen you flirting with.'

Molly gave Laverne a contemptuous push which staggered her back across the room. Mrs. Wellington gave a cry and flopped back in her chair with arms hanging limp and mouth open. Molly looked at Keith. 'I'm going back to Texas. Goodbye.'

Keith was about to speak but the Wellington girls were by their mother and shrieking that she was having one of her turns. Once more he was caught in that mess. It was either the girl he loved or his mother. He'd seen enough of her turns to know how dangerous they were. Yet for all that he could not just walk away and leave her, it might be serious. Also sense told him that in her present mood Molly would not listen to any reason. Turning, Keith bent over his mother, hearing the door of the room slam behind Molly. He thought there was a flickering smile of triumph across his mother's lips.

Stamping down the passage towards the door Molly ignored the sea of faces which watched her. She knew everyone here was interested in what was going on. It would give them something to talk about for days she guessed. Limbkin was opening the door for her, a supercilious sneer on his face. There was a look of delight about him that annoyed her as he said, 'The persons are waiting in the Victoria, Miss Wilmont.'

'Why thank you most to death, Limbkin.' Molly's voice dripped with poison loaded honey. 'You remind me of a pet packrat I once had, only he was better looking, smelling and tempered. Don't drink too much of Mr. Wellington's best whisky. He'll catch you one of these days.'

With this she swept proudly through the front door, for all her poise giving the footman a broad wink and seeing an eyelid droop in the impassive face. Limbkin watched her go, frowing, shocked out of his usual blank expression by the fact that his secret incursions into Wellington's best bonded whisky were noted. He was pleased the girl was going but knew she'd left him the loser.

Mrs. Wellington was recovering when the door of the library burst open. Sam Wellington came in, his usually red face redder as he pulled open his collar and slammed the door with a bang which jarred the pictures on the wall.

'What the hell's going on?' he roared.

Laverne sniffed. 'That horrible girl said nasty things to Mama. I thought she would strike me.'

'It's a pity she didn't. Might have knocked some sense into you,' Wellington growled, then looked at his wife. 'Stop your fooling, Clara, them turns of yours don't fool me. You never had them when we lived in the badlands, down Clancy Street.'

Mrs. Wellington sat up again, her turn ending even quicker than it began. Her husband, like the few others so privileged, usually called her Clarissa, rather than by her given name of Clara. She also knew that her husband was usually mild and compliant but when he took that tone it was time to step carefully.

'Samuel——'

'Where's she now?' Wellington growled, ignoring his wife's words.

'She's left.' Keith stood looking at the ring on the table.

'So you finally did it, did you?' Wellington roared at his wife. 'You finally drove off that little girl. Before I made my pile you'd have been proud to have a gal like Molly marry our boy. You're getting so high toned and snooty you've forgot how we started out.' He turned his attention and anger on his son. 'And you. For once in your life you pick a decent gal, the sort who'll make you a good wife and make a man out of you. So what do you do, you let her get away. I'd have hoped you would show more damned sense than lose her and by hell you're not going to lose her. You're going out of this house and you don't come back until you bring her with a wedding ring on her finger. Understand?'

Keith drew himself erect. 'I understand.'

'All right, get going.'

Walking from the library Keith was aware that all eyes were on him. He turned and went to his room. Inside he began to pack his bag with a change of clothes. He knew Molly and knew that the only way to get her back was to go to Texas and win her. He knew little of the West, except what he'd read in the blood and thunder stories of Ned Buntline and what Molly told him. He could ride and hoped to get work as a cowhand until he could win her back. The door of his room opened as he packed his small bag with a change of underclothes, that was all he would be taking with him. He did not turn around or even look up as his father's voice came to him.

'You going all the way after her, boy?'

'It's the only way.'

Sam Wellington took out his wallet, extracted a sheaf of money, dropping it by his son's hand. 'You'll likely need some of this, then. Good luck.'

Leaving his son's room Wellington went downstairs. He glared at the crowd in the room. Every eye was on him, every one giving him their attention. He'd never realised how much he disliked most of his wife's circle of friends before. The time was on hand for a revolution and Sam Wellington was the man to make it.

'Limbkin,' Wellington yelled. 'Send down to Pat O'Leary's shebeen down on Clancy Street and get a couple of bottles of his whisky.' Then turning to the pained-looking quartet leader he went on. 'Say, Horace, do you know Finnigan's Wake?'

Keith Wellington packed his bag and left, making for the Texas and Chicago Depot. He made a reservation on the night westbound train, left his grip and went to the Reed-Astoria. Entering the hall he went to the desk. 'Hello, Jules. Is Miss Wilmont in?'

'No sir. She returned and left with Mr. and Miss Catlan.'

'When will she be back?'

Jules sniffed. 'She didn't say, sir.'

Keith got it. Jules was under orders not to give anything away. He must have seen the missing engagement ring and drawn his own conclusions. Jules was a smart gent, besides, knowing Molly she'd probably given orders for her whereabouts not to be mentioned. Turning on his heel Keith left the hotel and went to the Streeterville Sporting Club to spend a miserable afternoon.

Molly was also spending a miserable afternoon. Her temper was still at boiling point when she got to the hotel. Mary Anne knew there was nothing they could do but wait for the storm to blow over. She worked on the principle that the best way to cool a woman's temper was to get her to spend some money.

'Damn all men!' Molly slung her bag on the bed. 'There's not a good one any place, they're all the same.'

'Sure are,' Marry Anne agreed, winking at Waco who was standing back and keeping quiet, showing wisdom. 'Ain't none of them worth the keeping. Let's go shopping.'

'I'm going home tonight.'

'Thought you was selling the Lazy W,' Mary Anne asnswered.

'You thought what?'

Mary Anne held out the letter and Molly took it. She read

110

the letter and her face got even more red. 'What the hell?' Molly's voice was hard. 'I never wrote this.'

'I never thought you did. Look at the spelling, it's too good for you,' Mary Anne answered. 'But it got to Colonel O'Dea.'

'Got to Colnel O'Dea.'

'Got to Colonel O'Dea?' Molly felt stupid repeating the words but her mind was not working properly.

'Sure, got to him. Look, you're not thinking properly yet. Let's go shopping and I'll explain it all to you.'

Molly agreed to this but she just could not get up enough energy yet. She looked at the letter again and shook her head. Waco came forward and Mary Anne jerked a hand to him. 'Didn't get time to introduce you to my lil brother before. This here's Waco.'

Molly grinned, holding out her hand. 'Hi, boy. Some lil brother. You growed up, boy.'

'So'd you. Who'd you write to down in Texas, Molly?'

'Colonel O'Dea, his gals. I wrote to White, a couple of the other gals, telling them about getting engaged.'

'Short letters?' Waco went on.

Mary Anne laughed. 'Short letters. She wouldn't know how.'

Molly eyed her friend. 'Listen Fatty——'

'Fatty is it?' Mary Anne answered. 'Why you——'

'Simmer down, both of you.' Waco pushed Mary Anne on to the bed and Molly into a chair. 'This's more serious than having a hair yanking. Didn't you meet anybody from Texas in the past month or so?'

'Nope, nor was I likely to. Mrs. Wellington thinks all Texans, including me, are uncouth savages, just one stage further advanced than the Indians. Mind,' Molly eyed Mary Anne and Waco, 'I'm not saying she was far wrong where some of us are concerned.'

'Sure, you Lazy W bunch were always the same, wild, woolly, full of fleas and never seen a currying below the knees. Come on, let's go shopping and make reservations on the night train. I never thought you would sell the Lazy W.' Mary Anne grinned at her friend. 'You aren't smart but you're too smart for that.'

'Yeah,' Molly snorted. 'I'm not sure with neighbours like you I'd show sense if I did sell out.' She paused and picked up her hat from where she'd thrown it. 'Why'd you pair come here anyway?'

'To show you this letter,' Waco explained. 'Lootenant Ballinger allows a Doc Pilener wrote it, Doc being found dead the day after it was posted. That means the man who did it is an Eastern man, but one that knows the Ranse River country. He wants both Lazy W and S.S.C. and with this letter he'd likely come to get them both. Colonel O'Dea would have sold him the Lazy W. and then with control of the water he could run S.S.C. off.'

'You got somebody in mind, boy?' Molly asked, watching this handsome youngster and wondering where he'd learned to act like this.

'Mebbee, mebbee not. Man never can tell and I sure don't aim to.'

Mary Anne could see that Waco did not wish to say any more on the subject and pressed that they went shopping before they pulled out of the big city. Molly took the hint and Waco was evicted while she put on a dress which, while not being so stylish was at least comfortable.

Jules studied the three as they came to the desk, noting Molly was not wearing her engagement ring now. 'If anyone comes asking for me you don't know how long I'll be gone, Jules,' Molly said grimly.

'I understand, Miss Wilmont.' In his frigid way Jules liked the Texas girl and he did not intend doing anything she would not wish him to do. 'I hope your suite is satisfactory, Miss Catlan?'

'Sure. We'll be checking out tonight.'

They'd left only a few moments when Keith arrived. That night found them all on the westbound train, headed for Texas. Molly did not even suspect Keith was on the train, nor did Keith guess the girl he loved was in a sleeper in the compartment next to his own. He sat moodily in the room for a time then rose and made his way to the smoker.

The smoker was almost deserted as he sat at one of the

tables and called for a beer. Two beefy, flashily-dressed men sat by the bar and nodded to the other. They rose, coming along to the table. 'Can we join you, friend?'

'Sure, take a seat.' Keith looked up. These men were not the sort he would have chosen to associate with in Chicago but things were done differently out west.

'Going west?' the bigger of the pair asked, offering a cigarcase.

'Texas. And you?'

'Texas, too. A fine country.' The man was heavily moustached, his face reddened from either sun or long exposure to the full glare of a whisky glass. He wore a loud check suit which clashed with his salmon pink shirt and big bow tie. 'I'm Joe. Sell razors, bayrum and stuff for a barbershop. This's Lou. You might not believe it but he sells ladies' corsets.'

Lou was bearded, dressed as glaringly as his friend and grinned amiably. He did not appear to be at all worried by his friend telling what he sold. 'Good things to sell. The gals are always going to wear them. Have a drink.'

The train was moving now, rattling along the rails. Keith sat back laughing at the stories the men told, stories of their adventures while travelling. They appeared to be a pair of cheery, rough diamonds and were just what he wanted now to relieve the monotony of the journey.

'Say, how about a game of poker to pass the time?' Joe asked. 'Lou here owes me a dollar fifty from our last game and I sure hate to see him win.'

Keith was just a little suspicious. He'd heard of cardsharps on trians before. His first inclination was to decline the offer but Lou shook his head. 'I don't know, Joe. We don't know this young feller. I know he looks all right but——'

Keith frowned. The man did not trust him. The feeling hurt. Here he was, a member of the Streeterville Sporting Club and this overdressed drummer did not trust him. He sat back, his mouth a tight, grim line and Joe snorted. 'You've hurt the young feller's feelings. You can't take him any place twice, they won't even have him back to apologise for the first time. I'm not playing unless our friend plays, Lou.'

Lou looked contrite. 'All right, all right. No offence, friend. It's just that there gets to be a lot of sharps on these trains. I wasn't making out that you are one. Say, to show you there's nothing in it you go get the deck of cards from the bar.'

Keith was mollified by this. He'd been doubtful but now he felt ashamed of himself. Here were two perfectly decent men and he'd thought they were crooked gamblers. Now they were going to let him get the cards showing they trusted him. He was a good poker player. The play at the Streeterville Sporting Club was often high and he'd held his own there. He might win or lose a few dollars in this game but that would not matter for his wallet was bulging and he could afford a small loss.

Taking the cards back to the table Keith sat down facing the two men. He was seated with his back to the leather seat while they were facing him across the table, yet they were well apart. Nothing could be wrong.

'What's the stakes?' Lou asked.

'Whatever you fancy.' Keith felt expansive.

'Man, we'll have to watch him, Lou,' Joe chuckled. 'He's got a gleam in his eye. Let's us set down real small and try him out. Say five cents to twenty-five.'

Keith chuckled, giving the cards a riffle. The stakes would not break him, he was going to enjoy a friendly game.

CHAPTER ELEVEN

A TOPHAND FROM CHICAGO

'HE's not there!' Molly withdrew her head from the open window.

'Isn't he?' Mary Anne sat back on the bunk of their sleeper compartment. 'Did you think he would be?'

'Me?' Molly snorted. 'I'm not in the least worried about Mr. Keith Wellington. I wouldn't speak to him if he was the last man alive.'

'Was he the last man alive I don't reckon he'd have time to worry,' Waco remarked.

'That's the sort of remark I could expect from a man.' Molly was in no mood for jollity. She'd been hoping Keith would at least come to the train and try to stop her leaving. 'Men! There's no good in any of them. The whole lot are stupid, conceited, boasting, tied to their mothers' apron strings. Where'd they be without a woman to look after them and to sew their buttons on for them?'

'If there were no women we wouldn't need the buttons.' Waco felt called on to defend the male sex in this den of womanhood.

'Very funny,' Mary Anne snorted. 'Don't worry, Molly, you'll never be troubled by him again.'

'I know.' Molly suddenly gave a sniff and flung herself on to the bunk, sobbing. 'If only he'd stood up against his mother just once.'

Waco grinned, taking up his hat and making for the door of the compartment. This was no place for a man and the sooner he got out of it the better. 'I'll go and see to my bunk,' he told Mary Anne. 'Likely see you in the diner later on.'

Waco went along two doors, opening the sleeper reserved

for him. His bag lay on the bed and the new rifle by its side. He took it up and turned it over in his hands. This was a weapon a man could be proud of, more range than a '73 and just as reliable. The Ysabel Kid would be green with envy when he saw it, might even trade in that 'One of a Thousand '73' for this kind. He cleaned the rifle and his twin Colts, then got to his feet and unbuckled the gunbelt. There did not appear to be much point in wearing it tonight. It was too far east for there to be any danger of a hold-up and a brace of matched guns weighed heavy on a man. He thrust his right-hand gun into his waistband so that his coat hid it then picked up the rifle, gunbelt and second Colt, taking them to Mary Anne's sleeper and knocking. He was let in by Molly who was over her tears now and looking annoyed at her lapse. 'Lock these away for me, Rusty gal,' he said. 'Then let's go eat.'

The meal was not a success for Molly was about as cheerful as an undertaker with a toothache. After it was over the girls were all for going to bed but Waco decided he would go along to the smoker in the hope he would meet some fellow spirits to pass the night. He walked along the swaying aisles and across the platforms between the train's carriages. The city was gone from sight now and they were lulling out into open country again. He breathed in the air and grinned. If that was a big city he hoped such would never come to the West, and that he never need go to another.

Entering the smoker he found it still almost empty and his attention was drawn to the poker game. He moved forward and halted by the empty seat, looking down. Lou was dealing and Waco grinned as he noted the way the man held the cards, three fingers gripping the long edge, fourth around the front and holding square the short edge. Next Waco's eye went to the young man who sat alone. The two drummers were fleecing him, that was for sure. It was the sort of game a prudent young man would steer clear of; nothing but trouble and loss faced one sitting in on such a game.

'Room for players, gents?'

Lou looked up from dealing, taking in every detail of Waco's dress and his apparent youth. He read Waco as a cow-

116

hand returning from the big city, a young one and easy meat. His eyes, unused to looking for such things, did not see the bulge made by the gun. Waving a hand he cheerily said, 'Sure, friend. Set and play a few.'

Waco took the seat next to Keith Wellington with no idea who the young man was. Lou introduced himself, Keith and Joe just by their christian names and Waco told them the only name he'd ever known. He did not remember Molly's ex-fiancé's name or connect this young dude with him. He noted Keith was flushed and worried looking and could guess why.

Keith felt relieved when Waco sat in. The game was getting out of his depth and he was losing heavily. It was the opposite of the early stages when the stakes were low and his luck very good. Hand after hand came to him and brought in pot after pot. Then Lou asked if they could raise the stakes. From a friendly and harmless five to tenty-five cent limit it was now fifty cents to five dollars and Keith's luck had changed for the worse. Now he could rarely do anything right and was losing heavily. His suspicions were aroused but he could not get over the fact that he chose the cards.

Waco accepted the cards after Lou's deal and gave them an awkward overhand stack, the way the veriest amateur would handle cards. He offered the cards to Lou to cut, then dealt in a clumsy way which brought grins to Lou and Joe's face. He'd laid his money on the table and they were eager to add it to Keith's pile. It shouldn't be hard; a man who dealt in such a manner would not cause them any trouble.

In that casual stack Waco checked the cards and could see no sign of their being marked. That meant the two men were using other methods to take Keith's roll from him. He knew his awkward handling of the cards was lulling the suspicions of the two men. They did not guess he knew how to handle cards and knew more than a little of the ways of crooked gamblers. His eyes were alert. Without appearing to, he saw everything. He saw Joe make what appeared to be a nervous gesture, gently and quickly pull the second of his five cards out. Just an apparently casual pull but it told Lou, and Waco, Joe held a pair.

The betting went the rounds and Waco discarded his hand right off while watching him and in a casual move he extracted three jacks, laying them on the top of the deck. The move was done fast and unseen by any of the others. He waited for betting to end then asked, 'Cards gents?' hoping Keith held a pair and took three cards.

'Take three,' Keith answered.

Picking up the three cards Keith almost dropped them again. He was in the game with a pair of queens, now he held a full house, jacks and queens. Keeping his face impassive he managed to hold down his excitement as Joe took three cards and Lou two.

Joe grinned savagely. 'I've got them this time, boys. So run for the hills.'

'I never was any good at climbing,' Keith replied and opened the betting eagerly.

Joe's grin of triumph died an uneasy death as his three kings went under to the full house. He knew the chances of filling a full house from a three card draw were high. His eyes flickered to Waco but on the youngster's face was nothing but mild interest. Joe decided it was pure bad luck which cost him this sizeable pot.

The game went on. Keith took the next pot and Lou reached for the cards and dealt. There was nothing wrong with the deal that Waco could see but he noticed that Keith showed the signs of having a good hand. Waco wondered where this young man learned to play poker. He wouldn't last in a real rough game like this even without cheating. Waco once more discarded and Joe made a joking reference to it. At the same moment Lou fanned his cards out, tapped the top edge once in an apparently nervous move, then moved the third card up and down twice. Waco read the signal that Lou held three aces and caught Joe's almost imperceptible agreement that he held the fourth. Waco knew what was coming now; it was called the spread and an old gambling trick.

The betting in the game was brisk for Keith held a flush dealt pat and felt he had a better than fair chance of winning. He shoved up the betting cheerily and the other two went along with it. Joe folded his cards and grunted.

'This's too rich for my blood.'

Waco watched the cards falling in a pile and knew that only four were there, the fifth, the desired ace was palmed by Joe ready for use. Lou was holding his cards bunched together but he fanned them out as a man would when the betting was steep. When he folded them together once more he'd got one card palmed. His left hand dropped out of sight behind the table in a casual move and slid the card between his knees, holding it. Now he only held four cards and needed the extra ace his partner was holding out.

Lou took one card on the draw, laying his four in a neat pile before him. He grinned knowingly as Keith declined to draw and pushed his draw card on to the others. Keith pushed the betting some more then called. This was what Waco was waiting for, the moment of the spread. Lou turned his cards, still in one pile and said, 'Four aces.'

In a casual appearing move Joe reached across the table as if to spread the cards out, the palmed ace ready to drop into place. Waco moved fast, one hand shoving Lou's cards to one side, the other reaching for Joe's wrist. Fingers like steel clamps closed on the man's wrist and turned it, exposing the ace laying in his palm. Then Waco's other hand shoved the cards, showing four, not five laying there.

Joe jerked his hand free, dipping it into his pocket. The light of the smoker glinted on the shining steel of his razor as it licked out at Waco's face. The young Texan pitched sideways from his seat, the razor lashing over his head and ripping open the seat. Even as he fell Waco's right hand went across his body and brought out his Colt. The crash of the shot sounded louder than a cannon in the confines of the smoker. Joe rocked backwards, hit under the armpit by the heavy bullet and thrown back on to the seat again.

There was a thud and Lou crashed from his seat, a small light calibre Smith & Wesson revolver caught half out of his pocket. Waco came to his feet and grinned his thanks to Keith, whose help, via a well placed left fist, saved him from what could have been a ticklish position.

'Hold it!' Waco gave a warning as he lined his Colt on Lou who was clawing for his gun again. 'Let loose or I'll drop you and I've got me a permit to do it.'

Lou licked his lips. He still thought this was an easy mark cowhand here, one who'd made a lucky guess. He'd never seen a real fast man with a gun and did not have any idea how fast and deadly one could be. He still kept his hand on his gun, snarling, 'I'll get——!'

'Pouch it or I'll let you join your friend,' Waco answered, blue eyes never leaving the man ignoring Joe who was laying back with an arm which would never be of use to him again. 'You must think we were real easy, friend, trying to pull the spread on us.'

It was in that moment Lou realised that he was up against something more than just a dressed up cowhand. Here was a man who was a master with a gun. Then it hit Lou. A man who knew enough about the cheating trick called the spread, knew more than a little about cards. He knew far more than a man who gave a clumsy, overhand stack should know.

The few occupants of the smoker were on their feet now and the conductor forced his way through them. He came up, a big, burly man well capable ot taking care of himself. 'All right, all right. What's it all about then?'

Waco did not take his eyes from Lou, who still held his revolver, as he answered. 'These two tinhorns tried to take Chicago and me in a brace game. I caught them trying to use the spread on us. That gent there took his razor but I allow it's some too late for shaving. If the other don't let go of his gun I'll help him to. Me'n ole Colonel Sam.'

'Well, if it ain't Joe and Lou.' The conductor knew these two men from way back. 'Haven't I told you two not to use the train I'm conducting?' He put his hand under his coat and took out a revolver. 'Come on, both of you. Get down to the caboose. You're getting off at the next whistlestop.'

For a moment Waco thought Lou was going to argue the matter but the man was no gunfighter and knew the conductor was capable of either shooting him down or felling him with the barrel of the gun. He rose and helped Joe up. Then his eyes turned to Waco, full of hate. 'You should be throwing him off the train as well. He's a damn cardshark.'

'Me?' Waco grinned, it made him look about sixteen. 'I'm just a lil ole Texas boy who got lucky.'

'Yeah,' the conductor's voice was heavily sarcastic. 'You sure look it.'

The conductor herded Lou and Joe from the smoker with a warning that he would be back. Waco shoved the Colt back under his coat again and waved to the money on the table. 'There enough there to cover all you lost, Chicago?'

Keith counted the money and nodded. 'Enough and more. Do you mean they were cheating all the time?'

'Why sure. They weren't real good at it though.' Waco picked up the remaining money and made it into two equal piles. He took five dollars from each pile and scooped his share into his pocket, leaving the ten dollars and Keith's pile on the table.

The conductor returned and found the two young men seated at the table. 'You playing cards again?' he asked.

'Not me,' Waco answered. 'I only sat in to lend Chicago here a hand when the wolves were fleecing him. It was a real rough school you got tied in with, Chicago.'

Keith's face reddened slightly. His Streeterville Sporting Club training did not appear to be so good after all when a chance passing stranger could spot he was being fleeced. He kept his mouth shut for this young man saved his bankroll for him and prevented him from making a complete fool of himself. He could imagine what Molly would say if she'd met him and he confessed a couple of cheap crooks took all his money in an easily spotted card game.

The conductor grinned, eyeing Waco warily. 'Good, I wouldn't want a boy as smart as you taking up where Joe and Lou left off. They're good but you must be better, you caught them out.'

Waco took up the ten dollars, handing them to the conductor. He waved a hand to the roof of the smoker car where his bullet, after passing through Joe's shoulder was now buried. 'This'll pay for the hole I put in the roof.'

The conductor accepted the money, folded it and put it in his pocket, then turned and walked away. Keith turned to the tall, young man who'd come so suddenly into his life and did not know how to express his thanks. 'I don't know how to thank you,' he began.

'Don't try. I sat in for the laughs and made some money out of it. You headed west?'

'Yes, to the Ranse River country in Texas. I want to be a cowhand.'

Waco was naturally suspicious, more so when things were in the state that they were in Ranse River country. He wondered why, out of all the many miles of Texas this young dude was headed for the Ranse River country. He did not ask the obvious question for that would be against the etiquette of the land.

'You thinking of settling down there?' That much was permitted.

'Maybe. I'd like to be a cowhand. I can ride a horse and shoot.'

'There's just a bit more to being a cowhand than riding and shooting. You got any place in mind down there to work?'

'No.' Keith could hardly explain his true reasons for going to Ranse River, not even to this youngster who'd saved his bankroll. 'I decided to try and learn the cowhand business, maybe settle down out there and buy a ranch. I saw the Ranse River on the map and liked the sound of it. That's why I'm going there.'

Waco did not speak for a moment but his mind was working. He was suspicious of the other's motives. Of course the young man might be going innocently to Texas but there might be a more sinister motive. Waco was nearly sure he could lay a hand on the man who was behind the killing of his adopted father and the trouble in Ranse River Country. He could be wrong, this young dude might be the one. He made his decision right away and said:

'I work in the Ranse River country myself. Just been to Chicago with my boss. Come along and happen Rusty'll give you a riding chore.'

Keith thought this was a remarkable coincidence, meeting a man who was from the Ranse River Country. The offer of work was attractive. It might make Molly change her mind about him if she met him in Whittle while he was actually working for another ranch in the area. He did not connect the name Rusty with Molly. She'd talked about Mary Anne Catlan but Keith did not remember it. Nor did he guess Waco's real reason for offering him work was to keep an eye on him and have him where his movements could be watched. He gave his agreement to going along and seeing Waco's boss, expecting to meet a lethery cowhand.

The two young men made their way to the sleepers and Waco knocked on a door. A most unmasculine voice called out to know who was knocking.

'Waco and a friend.'

The door opened and Mary Anne looked out, her Merwin & Hulbert gun in her hand. 'Hey, lil brother,' she greeted. 'We were just set to go to bed. Who's your friend?'

'A tophand from Chicago, headed west and looking for a riding chore. I told him we'd likely be able to take on another hand.'

Mary Anne smiled, suspecting a typical cowhand joke. Waco looked serious about it, but he would even if it was a joke. Of course the other young man might be headed west and looking for work but the Ranse River country was not the best place for a dude to come in and start learning to earn his pay. The young man was well dressed and did not look as if he was coming west because he could not find work in the East. She decided Waco must have some reason for bringing the young man here. Of course, this might be one of his friends wearing dude clothes.

'All right, I reckon we could take you on, Chicago. I'm Mary Anne Catlan, the boss of the S.S.C.' She heard Molly getting up and coming towards the door. 'This is my friend and neighbour, Molly Wilmont.'

'I believe we've met.' Keith managed to retain control of his senses as he found himself facing his ex-fiancée. 'I think she dropped this the last time we met.'

Molly looked down at the engagement ring he held out and snorted angrily. 'What're you doing here?'

'Going west,' Keith replied.

Mary Anne smiled. She did not know if Waco guessed who the young man was. There was nothing to be gained in standing here talking. 'Come in, both of you.'

Keith entered the room, followed by Waco. Molly made no attempt to take the ring. Her eyes flickered at Keith's face and she asked, 'Just what's the game?'

'No game. I'm coming west to find work. Miss Catlan just hired me to work on her ranch.'

'She did, did she?' Molly growled. 'Well you're not working for any fat mantrap.'

'Fat is it, you scraggy hen!' Mary Anne yelled. 'Why for two cents I'd——'

'You'd what?' Molly was so mixed up emotionally that she did not know what to do or say.

'Come on, Chicago,' Waco said, grinning at the girls who were glaring at each other. 'This ain't going to be no safe place for a couple of innocent boys like us.'

Keith followed Waco from the room, was pulled rather, for he wanted to stop and talk with Molly. He did not realise until he was standing in front of the sleeper compartment Waco had reserved that he'd left the ring on Molly's bunk.

The two girls were now examining it and Molly smiled, her face showing her delight. 'He's coming with me, Rusty, he's coming with me.'

For all of that Molly was cool towards Keith the next morning and remained so until they reached the railhead in Texas. In the thriving, booming trailend town Molly decided that Keith must look like a cowhand, even if he would never make one. So Keith and Waco went along to a general store.

'You want a Stetson for a start, Chicago,' Waco stated and they made their way to the counter where such were on display. 'Buy the best you can afford, you'll never regret it.'

Keith bought the expensive and genuine Stetson Waco chose for him and allowed the young Texan to shape it for him. He put it on and tried to get it at the right jack-deuce angle over his eye. Then he chose a tartan shirt, Levis trousers and high-heeled boots. Waco was adamant on one point, the boots must be replaced by made-to-measures as soon as they got settled in Whittle. No cowhand worth his salt would wear ready-made boots. Spurs, the real, genuine Kelly spurs of Texas came next, bought from the store which could sell a man all he would need in clothing and gear. A saddle, bridle, reins, horse-blanket, tarp and warbag came next but one purchase Keith wished to make did not come off. Waco watched him buy a brand new, ivory-handled Colt Cavalry Peacemaker but drew the line at a ready-to-wear gunbelt.

'I'd like a gunbelt,' Keith remarked as they sat at the campfire on the first night of their trip to Whittle, after leaving the railroad and travelling with the girls in the rig they hired and the two men riding the horses which brought Waco and Mary Anne to the railhead. 'One like yours.'

Mary Anne laughed. 'That's a Gayline belt, Chicago.'

'Couldn't I buy one?'

'Not from Joe Gayline. He'll sell you a saddle, or a pair of his boots, if you'd got enough money to buy them. But he won't sell his gunbelts to anyone. He chooses the men whom he makes them for. I bet there aren't more than thirty of them in the West.'

Keith could read the pride in Mary Anne's voice as she told of the gunbelt her little brother wore. She was proud that he owned, wore and was a member of that élite group who carried the Gayline gunbelts. 'I could buy another,' he finally said.

'Sure, but get one made in Whittle. You might go all your life and never need a gun,' Waco told him. 'But if you need one, lord, you need it fast. A ready-made's the best way I know of getting you killed. Can you use a Colt?'

Keith rose, smiling. He was the best shot in the Streeterville Sporting Club and held the club record for pistol shooting. True, he'd been using a target-sighted Smith & Wesson .32 revolver then but he did not expect any trouble in shooting the .45 Colt. He asked for Waco to suggest a target.

'How about that tree?' Waco inquired, grinning, a grin

which was mirrored by the two girls.

Keith looked at the tree and smiled, Waco was picking a big enough target. It was probably the best he could do at a range of about twenty feet. Keith opened the loading gate and slid six fat cartridges into the chambers. Then he stood with his left hand on his hip, sideways to the target, feet placed correctly, right pointing to the target, left at right angles. He started to lift his right hand.

From his side came four rapid crashes, so fast that they sounded almost as one. Flame lanced from the gun which Waco held waist high, locked tight against his side while his right hand fanned the hammer. Keith gulped. He saw splinters kicking from the tree and then gazed down at the gun Waco held.

'See, Chicago,' Waco said, friendship in his voice, not mocking in any way. 'With a gun you've got to be fast.'

'Fast!' Keith gulped. 'I've never seen anything so fast in all my life.'

'Yeah, the boy's fast,' Mary Anne chuckled. 'There aren't many faster, are there, Molly?'

'I've never see faster.'

'There's three,' Waco said seriously.

'Who are they?' Keith wanted to know all he could about the West.

'Dusty Fog, Mark Counter and Doc Leroy.' Waco replied. 'Come on, settle down by the fire and clean your gun.'

They came into Whittle City in the early morning and rode slowly along the main street. Keith looked the part of a Texas cowhand, even sat his horse like one. He brought his horse to a halt and pushed back his hat. A man was coming along the street towards him. Keith stopped talking to the others and studied the man. Then he rode forward and halted the horse, looking down at Brarsand.

'Why, it's Mr. Jackson. I thought you were in Denver.'

Brarsand stopped in his tracks, his face, long schooled in frontier poker games, showing nothing of his thoughts. Then he looked up at Keith with the right expression for a man mistaken for some other person. 'Sorry, friend. You've got the wrong man. The name's Brarsand, I've never been to Chicago in my life.'

Keith frowned. He'd worked in his father's business and developed an ability to remember faces and names. It annoyed him that he'd made a mistake and of course it must be a mistake. Jackson was a gentleman, the Streeterville Sporting Club was exclusive and kept a high standard of its guests. This man here wore what Keith had seen to be the dress of a frontier gambler. He inclined his head politely. 'I'm sorry, sir. The resemblance is remarkable but I must have made a mistake.'

Waco was pleased that Keith said this. It saved him cutting in helping out. His eyes were cold as he watched Brarsand and the man looked back at him, then at the two girls.

'Haven't seen you around yet, Waco,' Brarsand remarked. 'I thought you'd be in to take that drink with me.'

'Would have, but I've been away. Took Mary Anne here over to the big city.' Waco gave the information to see how Brarsand took it. He was forced to concede the man held his emotions in perfect control. 'We went to fetch Molly here back home. Figgered she might be needed to look after things.'

Brarsand nodded in agreement. 'It's always as well to have the owner living on the property. Well, I've got work to do. Ladies.'

Raising his hat politely Brarsand walked on without looking back and entered the tavern. Waco watched the man go, noting that Brarsand stood at the door to watch them. Keith was still frowning. He shook his head at last.

'I could have sworn he was the man I met at the Sporting Club.'

'Who'd you think he was, Chicago?' Mary Anne inquired.

'A man called Jackson. I was introduced to him but Jackson came from Denver,' Keith replied as they started to move forward. 'Where are we going now?'

'To the livery barn. Molly and I want to borrow a couple of horses from Uncle Seamus and arrange for him to send this buggy back to the railead. Then we'll head for the S.S.C.'

Brarsand entered the saloon and looked around. There were

only three hard-faced gunhung men and his regular workers here. Jerking his head to one of the men, Brarsand gave orders as he came over. 'Get down to the livery barn, Ed. You'll find two men and two girls there. You'll know who I mean, one of them's that Tejano who shot Dave Tull. I want the other killed. Get both if you can but get the one wearing the tartan shirt first.'

The gunman turned and walked away and Brarsand called another over. 'Hank, head for the ranch. If Cholla is back bring his bunch into town. If he isn't bring every other man who's there.'

Della Christine joined Brarsand now, watching the men leave, curious. 'Where's Ed going?' she asked.

'There's a man in town who met me in Chicago,' Brarsand answered, then his face darkened. 'I made a bad slip. Said I'd never been in Chicago and neither of the men even mentioned they'd been to, or come from, Chicago.'

'They'll never notice it.'

'I've told you before, that Texas boy is smart, real smart. He knows I've made a slip. He's no fool and can think things out. I asked around town about him since he first came. Thought at first he was just a hired gun brought in to help the girl. He's more than that, he's Catlan's adopted son.' His face clouded for a moment. 'That letter, it means O'Dea or Waco was suspicious. Do you think they knew it was a forgery, Della?'

'I told you Doc Pilsener's the best of them all.'

'Yet they knew. I saw O'Dea and hinted I'd like to buy a ranch around here but he never mentioned the Lazy W. Thought the letter was delayed, or maybe lost. So I told him to let me know if he heard of one going around here. They must have been suspicious and Waco took the Catlan girl to Chicago to bring Molly Wilmont home.'

Della gulped. She was worried now. 'Do you think they found out who wrote the letter?'

'How could they. And if they did Pilsener's dead. Besides how could they find out about him. In the West Waco could, likely. But not in a big city like Chicago. I couldn't have found him without your help. No, they didn't know about Pilsener.'

Before Della could reply they heard shots and stopped talking, looking at the door and awaiting the report from their man when he returned.

Waco and Keith were standing by the corrals and watching the horses while the two girls made arrangements for mounts and the return of the buggy. To Keith's eyes the horses here were good and he said so.

'Sure, they're all right for what they're used for. They aren't cowhorses though. Say, who did you say you thought Brarsand was?'

'Jackson. I met him at the Sporting Club.'

'Who was he with?'

'Theo Benedict. The head of the Chicago–Texas Railroad. But it can't be the same man.'

'Jackson?' Waco rubbed his jaw. There was something worrying him, something he should know but could not just remember.

'Yes, but he came from Denver.'

Then Waco's tenacious memory got it. The register at the Reed-Astoria and a man called Jackson, from Denver who'd checked out the day the forger, Doc Pilsener died. He got something more, something Brarsand said there in the street. Mr. Brarsand was going to be needing to answer questions real soon. For all that Waco was cautious for he knew he could not handle all Brarsand's men alone. The best plan was head for the ranch, ole Red Blaze would—

Waco thrust out his hand, sending Keith staggering violently behind the water-trough. At the same moment Waco flung himself backwards, landing on his back, gun in his right hand as he rolled over. From behind them a gun roared and the bullet hissed between them. Waco was right out in the open and a clear target for the man who was flattened behind the wall of the livery barn. Waco expected to feel lead slamming into him and threw two fast shots which kicked splinters from the wall by the man's head.

Keith was shaken up by the push and his landing, but he saw where Waco was and knew his danger. Drawing his Colt he cocked it and came up, firing fast. Since Waco's showing him how to handle a gun Keith had made practice with his Colt. His bullet, fast taken, missed the man and he went down as lead slashed at him, sending water erupting from the trough as he lit down.

Lunging up Waco fanned off three fast shots, throwing the lead at the edge of the building. The gunman backed off, turned and ran for it. 'Keep down, Chicago!' Waco called, drawing his left-hand gun as he darted forward to the edge of the building, then leapt around ready to shoot. The alley between the livery barn and the next building was empty and the street was ahead. Waco went forward to look along the street but could see no one who might either be the gunman, or have seen him. The ground was too hard to allow him to read any sign from it.

Keith came up, gun out and ready. 'What was it?' he asked.

'Somebody tried to kill one of us,' Waco replied.

'You?'

Waco shook his head, turned on his heel and headed back to the corral. 'No, you!'

CHAPTER TWELVE

WACO MAKES FRIENDS

THE two girls, Seamus Reagan and Lafe Sanger came running up. Molly came straight to Keith and asked. 'What happened?'

It was Waco who replied. 'Somebody tried to kill Chicago. Get the hosses and let's get out of here. The sooner we're out of town the happier I'll be.'

'But what about the police when they come to investigate the shooting?' Keith, full of ideas about how things would be done in Chicago, asked, 'Shouldn't we wait to explain?'

'Nope. Lafe here's county deputy sheriff. He'll handle it for us!' Waco jerked his head to the corral. 'Pick two that can move, Rusty gal.'

'What was it, boy?' Sanger growled as the girls went to work, picking two horses and saddling them.

'Like I say, somebody tried to gun Chicago down.'

'Who?'

'You can call it as well as I can. If Talbot comes tell him we were having home target practice.'

Sanger grunted, looking Keith over. 'He's a greener, ain't he?'

'Sure.'

'Man'd say he makes him a tolerable amount of enemies, real fast. You sure it wasn't somebody after you?'

Waco's grin was mocking and sardonic as he replied, 'Could have been, 'cept I was laying right out there in the open and without cover, the man didn't try for me. He did for Chicago.'

The horses were saddled now and the girls mounted. Sanger scratched the side of his bristly jaw. 'Like to see you real soon, Waco. This wants some talking out.'

'Sure, I'd like to see you and Colonel O'Dea both. Where's

the Colonel at now?'

'Over to one of the nesters, holding a meeting.'

'We'll likely be back tonight, then I'll have something to tell you.' Waco swung afork his horse. 'See you later, Lafe.'

They were riding out of town before Keith spoke again. 'I think we ought to have stayed on and seen the sheriff or some other peace officer, Waco.'

'There's only Talbot, the marshal, and he's no use to us.' Waco answered. 'Besides I don't want you killing just yet.'

'That man must have been shooting at you, not me, I haven't been out here and don't know anybody——'

'You *thought* you knew somebody,' Waco pointed out.

Keith opened his mouth, then closed it again. The girls were now both looking hard at Waco and Molly snapped, 'Do you mean that man tried to kill Chicago?'

'Me?' Waco's eyes were flickering at the range around them, watchful and alert to locate anything which could spell hidden men. 'I don't think, not like you three smart folks. All I know is that if that hombre was after me he'd got a damned funny way of showing it. I was out in the open and a clear shot and it was still Chicago he went for.'

Keith frowned. He was not used to accepting being shot at. He thought the law should do something and said so vehemently. Mary Anne laughed and remarked, 'You listen to my lil brother, Chicago. He won't lead you more'n a couple of miles wrong. That damned Kansas sheep, Talbot, wouldn't do a damned thing.'

'But if he's a peace officer——'

'He's one of Earp's dirty crowd,' Waco growled.

'But Wyatt Earp is known as a great lawman,' Keith pointed out.

'Earp?' Waco spat the word out. 'He's nothing but a lying, bribe-taking, pious hypocrite. Him and all his bunch.'

Keith could see that Wyatt Earp was neither liked nor respected in Texas. Waco's view was typical of any cowhand who'd come into contact with the Kansas law and order crowd. He changed the subject again. 'Are you just going to forget it?'

'Nope, Lafe'll ask around and when we get back tonight he might know something for us.'

'What're you going back for?' Mary Anne asked grimly.

'To ask some questions.'

'Like which?' Molly wanted to know.

'For one like how Brarsand knew where Chicago came from without even asking. For another, what sort of gun Brarsand carries.'

'Then you think it was Brarsand who killed that man in Chicago?' Mary Anne said, her eyes on Waco's face. 'And killed pappy?'

'Yes, honey. That's what I think.' Waco reached over and gripped the girl by the shoulder. 'That's just what I think. Tonight Red, Doc, me and the boys are coming in to find out.'

'Not without the Lazy W boys,' Molly snapped. 'This's their fight, too.'

Before Waco could reply Keith said, 'Funny the way the smoke over there is acting.'

Looking up Waco saw the puffs of smoke rising into the air. It was not going up as normal smoke should but rising in separate, irregular clouds. Mary Anne noted where it was coming from and gasped. 'It's from the house.'

'Yeah, putting up smoke. It's an old trick we use at the O.D. Connected to call the hands in fast,' Waco answered, then set his Kelly petmakers to work sending his horse leaping forward. 'Let's go!'

The horses sprang forward in a racing gallop, each rider urging speed from their racing animal. Keith was a good rider, he'd always ridden, or all the time from when his father could afford it. He'd ridden in races but never before ridden with such urgency as now. He saw the set faces of his three companions and knew there was something badly wrong here. He was charging into another wild adventure, that he was sure of.

Doc Leroy was throwing a saddle on to his black and yelling to the other hands to saddle up when he heard the thunder of hooves and turned to see who was coming, for all the ranch crew were here now. He felt some relief when he recognised his friend, Waco. At a time like this Waco was worth three other men. 'Song,' he yelled. 'Throw a rope on Waco's paint.'

By the time Waco brought his sweating horse to a halt by the corral Song was holding the big paint stallion roped ready for him to slap a saddle on it. Waco made good time in saddling the big horse, then he slid the new rifle out and threw a bullet into the chamber. Keith was standing by the girls and Waco called, 'Take care of them, Chicago. Ride out.'

'Rustlers, took the stock herd. Red and Larry went after them,' Doc called back.

'Willie!' Molly yelled to a cowhand she knew. 'Give Chicago your hoss, I want you to go and fetch my crew here.'

Willie swung down from his horse. He did not like the idea of missing a fight but knew better than to disobey an order. Keith swung into the saddle of the horse and sent it after the rest of the party as they rode across the range. He thought how the West was just like in Ned Buntline books. He'd been shot at and now he was riding after rustlers with a posses of cowhands. This was the life and sure beat Chicago.

'Sorry about this, Willie,' Mary Anne told the cowhand. 'I'll get Lee to bake you a special apple pie and you'll get your chance tonight unless I'm wrong.'

Willie, a trencherman of note amongst the hearty eating cow-hands, was somewhat mollified by this promise of pie. He caught another horse from the remuda and was soon headed across country, making for Lazy W.

Waco brought his horse to a sliding stop and looked at the direction the tracks were leading. 'They're headed for the ford on the Ranse likely, Doc. We'd best make for it.'

'It's a big risk, boy. We might miss them, they might not have headed there.'

'We'll have to chance it. Let's go.' Waco swung his horse from the broader line of the herd and headed it in a direct line for the ford of the Ranse River.

Red Blaze left the Wilben house and raced for the foot of the slope, then up it, swerving as he ran. Above him the gunmen strained as they shoved against the weight of the wagon, trying to get it over the lip of the incline and rolling down to smash it into the front of the house. To their side Kell's eyes glowed murder as he sighted his Spencer rifle on the fast-running man. His rifle cracked loud, sounding even over the curses of the straining men and the crackle of flames as the hay at the front of the wagon blazed up.

It was close, very close. The shirt was ripped from Red's side as the bullet tore between his arm and side. Red did not halt. He kept on with his fast swerving run and heard the angry slap of another bullet passing close to him. Then he flung himself forward and landed behind a rock. Gripping both hands around the butt of his Colt, Red rested them on the rock and sighted up the slope. He'd seen Dusty Fog, Mark Counter and Waco do creditable shooting at ranges of up to a hundred yards by this method and made practice himself, but knew he was not good. He fired and saw the dirt kick up from the slope well below the wagon. The man with the Spencer sent another bullet down. Red swore after he felt the wind of it passing and knew he would get the next. For once in his life Red was cursing Christopher M. Spencer for devising such an efficient weapon. That .52 calibre rifle was not going to do him any good at all if it hit him.

He lined the gun again and from the corner of his eye saw the man standing, resting one foot on the rock and lining the rifle. Still Red would not allow himself to swerve from his attempt at stopping the men pushing the wagon. His Colt bellowed again and the bullet struck above the men. He saw them suddenly break away from the wagon and run for their horses, then heard the thunder of hooves. The man with the rifle suddenly spun around, his rifle fell from his hands and he toppled forward over the rock. Red came to his feet, recognising the men who came hurling over the top of the rim. His wild rebel war yell was echoed by Waco whose rifle saved his life.

One of the attackers went down before he even made his horse; a second crumpled over the saddle and slid down. The remainder headed off fast. Cholla Jocelyn did not worry about leaving bodies behind; he was only concerned with saving his life. His horse was running fast now and he knew he would soon be out of range of the Winchesters the cowhands always carried. He heard the slap of a bullet passing his head and urged his horse on at a better speed.

Waco swung down from his horse. It, like the rest of the cowhands' mounts was hard run and could not hope to catch up on the fast-riding men. One thing was for sure though. He knew that man who was headed out in the lead. There was one sure way to find out and seeing the wagon, guessing what it meant, Waco did not feel any scruples in shooting the man down. He brought up the rifle, lining it and firing fast, working the lever. That was where Jocelyn made the final mistake of his mis-spent life. He heard the bullet whistle by and thought one of the cowhands must be using either a Sharps or Remington singleshot. He was wrong. The rifle Waco was using had almost the range of the two old singleshots but with the magazine capacity neither possessed. Four times he fired, flipping open the lever each time to throw another bullet into the breech. On the fourth shot the man stiffened in his saddle and came off the horse to crash into the grass.

Doc Leroy gave a yell. The wagon was inching towards the edge of the slope now. Waco dropped his rifle and flung himself forward, bracing himself. He saw Keith and two of the cowhands leap to his side and even in that moment was pleased to see Keith was the first to move. The boy was going to make a hand, he'd make Molly a real good husband, the Lazy W a good boss.

The heat bit at the men as they strained to force the wagon back. Straggles of burning hay fell. But slowly, as more of the hands came up, the wagon was moved back to safety and Doc Leroy slid a rock under the wheel then watched the others step back. Waco wiped the sweat from his face and turned with a grin to grip Red Blaze's hand as the redhead reached them. It took a lot to put Red down for long and, despite his narrow escape, he was grinning broadly. 'Howdy boy, you came back just in time. Everything all right?'

'Sure, where's Larry.'

'I shoved him and the folks from the house down into the cellar. Reckon he'll be some riled when he gets out. But I couldn't let him come out here, one target was enough for them at one time.'

The cowhands crowded around Red; their jeering comments hiding their relief at finding both Red and Larry safe. They admired the redhead all the more for shoving Larry to safety before going out to almost certain death.

On the way down the slope Keith was introduced to the others, introduced in a far less formal manner than he'd been used to. He was given just the one name, Chicago, and no attempt was made to explain his presence. He did not know but none was needed; he was introduced by a friend and would be treated as an equal unless he gave cause for the cowhands to change their opinions. They'd noted the way he was the first to leap and help Waco hold the wagon and that was a point in his favour, that he'd ridden with them was another. He was accepted by the time they'd walked down the slope and reached the house. Then they heard hooves and fanned out fast, guns ready.

Colonel O'Dea, Smethers and several nesters came riding up. They all held rifles or shotguns and eyed the cowhands suspiciously. Waco lowered his rifle and stepped forward, 'Howdy Colonel.'

O'Dea looked first at the cowhands, most of them still holding their rifles ready, then glanced up at the burning wagon. 'What's all this, boy?' he asked.

'A bunch of guns attacked Wilbens.' It was Red who answered for the others. 'Waco and the crew came just in time to stop them rolling that wagon down there.'

'Now you're going in to ask Wilben for a drink?' a nester, a tall angry-looking young man, asked.

'We're surely hoping he'll get one for us,' Waco agreed knowing this man would be trouble unless handled correctly. 'Got to get him and his family out of the cellar first.'

There was danger in the air. The nesters were suspicious at finding the cowhands in such a position. The cowhands were angry. They'd ridden here, found two of their friends helping to defend the house, and stopped the blazing hay-wagon. Now these nesters were coming here and looking for trouble. The cowhand was for the most part an amiable, friendly soul, but not when met with ingratitude such as this. There were angry mumbles on both sides.

Swinging down from his horse Colonel O'Dea walked forward and tried the Wilbens' door It opened and he looked back at the nesters. 'I take it as trusting, leaving the door open when they're fighting off an attack.'

The trapdoor lifted carefully and Larry, gun in hand, looked out. He grinned and called down, 'It's all right, folks. We can come up now.'

Wilben came out, rubbing his head. He walked across the room and gripped Red's hand in his own, shaking it. 'I'm riled with you, Red, so's Larry, what's the idea, shoving us down there while you go out and near get killed.'

'He wants to hog all the honours,' Larry scoffed, then as they reached the door they found the rest of the party standing around. 'You came back just in time, Waco.'

'Unless they were here all the time,' the nester who'd been doing all the talking growled.

Wilben stepped forward. He saw the anger on the faces of the cowhands and the suspicion of the nesters. 'Hello Charlie, how'd you lot get here?' he asked.

'The Colonel was seeing us over at my place. We heard the shooting and saw the smoke from that wagon of yours and came over in time to see the bunch making for the house.'

'The S.S.C. had a herd rustled, brought over here.' Wilben knew the young farmer, Charlie Hedge, did not like cowhands and knew why. He also wanted to end the suspicion between the cowhands and the nesters. 'The men who stole the herd stampeded it right at us. Red there, and Larry beat them here, turned the herd and helped me defend the house. If they hadn't been here I wouldn't have had a chance.'

'Why'd anybody steal a herd just to stampede it over your place?' Hedge asked, eyeing the Texans truculently.

'To cause trouble between the nesters and us,' Waco remarked. 'They knew some damned fool would want to make trouble if it happened. And they were right.'

'What's that mean?' Hedge snapped.

'Some damned fool's doing just that.'

'Charlie!' Wilben's snapped out word brought the others to a halt as Hedge realised what Waco meant. 'I know why you're against these men and I've told you I believe what they told us about Ben Silver. Red and Larry came here, risked getting killed to help us. Red stayed up on that slope until the right time to light the hay which turned the herd, Larry carried my Sandy down here when he was shot. Then when the men were going to send that burning wagon down here Red shoved all of us down into the cellar where we'd be safe. Then he went out alone and tried to stop them doing it.'

The other nesters listened to Wilben for they accepted his wisdom in anything. Waco watched them, then said, 'Talk's getting us no place. Let's get those bodies in here and take a look at their faces.'

The cowhands mounted their horses and headed to bring all the bodies in, laying them in a row along the side of the house. Waco went along, removing the masks. The first man was the one Red killed with the Kentucky rifle.

'That's one of the Kell boys,' Hedge growled. 'Bought that small spread from Brarsand. They've allus been friendly when I met them in town.'

'Was real friendly out there, too.' Red's tones were mocking. 'Where's the one who was trying to down me?'

They went along the line and then, as they reached the last, Waco pulled down the mask and nodded. 'Cholla Jocelyn. I thought it was him.'

'Brarsand's men. All of them, they were all hired by Brarsand.'

Waco looked at Hedge. 'Yeah, mister. Brarsand's men, all of them. We'd best talk this out.'

The men gathered round in a half circle. Waco stood facing them, one of the youngest here. Yet there was something about him which made the others listen to what he had to say. Before he started to speak he saw Sandy Wilben standing at the door of the cabin. The youngster's face was showing the same worry as it had that day in Whittle when Dave Tull died.

'First,' Waco said, 'I'm Sunshine Sam Catlan's boy. You know he was gunned down and I came to get the men who did it. I know why he was killed, or some of it. I know who ordered the killing.' Then he remembered something Keith said to him. 'Chicago, who was that *hombre* Jackson was with when you met him?'

'Benedict of the Chicago and Texas Railroad. They're thinking of running a spur line down to Whittle. He was after my father to invest in it.' Keith realised he was betraying a confidence, but knew that the betrayal was necessary.

'That's the reason. Look at the lay of the land. The railroad would come down here, through your land, across the Ranse and along the S.S.C., Lazy W line.'

Talk welled up among the nesters. This was news of vital importance to them, far more so than to the cowhands. Hedge spoke up, 'What do you make of it, then?'

'I've got it all now. Molly was in Chicago, my pappy killed. They thought either to scare Mary Anne out, or break her.' Waco went on to explain about the forged letter and what its consequences would have been. The men here knew the lay of the land and did not need it explained in detail. Then he told of his suspicions and the trip to Chicago to find proof. He finished off, 'That raid on the S.S.C. when the young nester was killed, that was to scare off Mary Anne or stir up trouble which would make her even more willing to sell. Who'd have known that pappy was going fishing that day?'

'Nearly everybody who was in the tavern that night,' O'Dea replied. 'We'd been spinning windies about shooting and fishing and I bet Sam he couldn't take Old Mossyhorn. He said he'd be going out next morning. Brarsand was stakeholder for us. He said he'd go out and see how Sam went on.'

'Brarsand, did he go alone?'

'He said he never went. I went out and looked over the ground, there'd been four men there,' O'Dea replied.

'How'd one man take all three of them?' Waco shook his head. 'Pappy wasn't good with a gun, but him and the boys would be too much for one man.'

'Not if they were watching your pappy playing a big bass,' Red put in, pulling out his handkerchief and unrolling the phantom lure. 'I found a real big bass and took this out of his mouth.'

'And Sam's line was bust when we found him,' O'Dea said thoughtfully. 'Brarsand faded out of sight just after the shooting. Della told us he'd gone east on business.'

'Then Brarsand killed my pappy,' Waco took the phantom from Red. 'They'd all be watching the bass, not one of them would give him any attention. That was how he got them.' He faced Sandy Wilben, eyes hard and voice dropping grimly. 'All right, what happened the night Ben Silver was killed?'

Sandy gulped. His eyes went to his father but Wilben ordered him to tell anything he could. 'Ben and me went into the back room of the tavern. Dave Tull and the rest were there. They started to get us drunk, asked us if we wanted to go with them and have some fun. They were going to the S.S.C. to hooraw the hands. Ben was drunk, real drunk. I wasn't so bad and I got scared. Said I was going out back and just as I was going I saw Tull give Ben one of his guns. I lit out for home and left Ben with them.'

Hedge's eyes were hard. He turned to Waco and held out his hand. 'Looks like I owe you an apology, friend. It *was* just like you told it. What's Brarsand expect to gain by all this?'

'The railroad'll pay good prices for the right of way they want. That land of your'n be worth more'n it was solid gold. The man who owned it all and the two ranches would make him a fortune. That was what Brarsand would be aiming for. Same as the saloon he built. It wouldn't pay any in a small town like Whittle. But when Whittle boomed open with the railroad he'd be ready. He'd have the first and biggest saloon in town, he'd pile money up before the others could be built.'

'What're we going to do, friend?' Hedge asked for the other nesters. 'Ben Silver was kin even though I never saw eye to eye with his old man and I don't take to him being killed.'

'I'm going to town after Brarsand. There's one way to prove he killed the man in Chicago, look at his gun. I've never seen it, have any of you?'

There was a chorus of noes to this and O'Dea stepped up to stand by Waco. 'You haven't enough proof to take him into court, boy.'

'That's right. But I'll get it one way or the other.'

'We're with you,' Wilben spoke for the nesters.

'All right. We'll ride by the S.S.C., pick up more shells, then head into town. It'll be morning before we can do anything at all. Comes sun-up we'll go for a showdown.'

Mrs. Wilben came out. 'Coffee's on the boil, you'll have time for a drink before you leave.'

O'Dea came to Waco's side as the other men gathered to gether, talking. 'What're you going to do, boy?'

'What I came here for, get the man who shot down my pappy.'

CHAPTER THIRTEEN

MARY ANNE GETS HER CHANCE

BRARSAND got the news of the failure of the stampede from one of the men who'd escaped. He got it in the back room of his saloon early in the evening. 'Where's Cholla?' he asked.

'Dead and the Kell boys.'

'You get their bodies clear?'

'No boss. There wasn't time. The cowhands were on to us foot, hoss and artillery. We was lucky to get clear alive.'

'Were you?' Brarsand snarled. 'You damned, loco fool. I told you not to leave any bodies.' There was no time for re-crimination now, the young man called Waco would be coming here. Brarsand licked his lips. He thought fast. 'Get the place cleared of all but our men, then lock it up. I want all the boys ready for a fight. They'll be on us come sun-up at the latest.'

The occupants of the saloon were considerably surprised to be told it was closing down. Brarsand's men did not give them a chance to object but evicted them. Then the gunmen set to work to prepare the place for a fight that they knew must come. Della and the girls were set to work by Brarsand and within half an hour the place was silent, locked. Behind the walls the gunmen loaded their rifles and put out boxes of bullets ready for use.

At the Hood City saloon Lafe Sanger and Jabe Spencer were both surprised and pleased by the sudden influx of customers who'd been evicted from the tavern. Sanger was worried when he listened to a cowhand's voluble discussion on the fate which caused him to be turned out just when he'd hit him a lucky break. Picking up his hat the old-timer left the saloon and walked along the street towards the jail. He saw a man come out and recognised the angular shape of Talbot, the town marshal. Sanger was about to call out for, although he disliked the man, he always tried to co-operate with Talbot in any law matters. Then he shut his mouth for two more men left the jail, each loaded down with rifles, shotguns and ammunition. It was the supply held in the jail and Talbot should not be moving them at night. Sanger trailed the men around the back of the saloon. He saw a door open and Della Christine look out. The woman beckoned the other three men to enter and closed the door once more. Sanger went forward fast, his old Leech and Rigdon gun in his hand. He heard the click of the key turning in the lock and moved in closer to try and hear what was being said. All he could hear was a low muttering and drew back. Lafe Sanger was a wily old cuss and knew there was something afoot here, something concerned with Brarsand and that soft-talking young feller out at the S.S.C.

Della Christine locked the door and dropped the key into her bag along with the Remingtom Double Derringer which lay there. 'That all the weapons, Talbot?' she asked.

'Sure.' Talbot held down his anger at this woman talking to him in such a manner.

'Did anybody see you?'

'No.' Talbot would not admit that he clean forgot to see what was going on in town and did not know if he'd been followed. 'What's goin on?'

'We've got trouble,' Della was mocking. 'You're going to start earning some of your pay right now.'

Sanger withdrew, made his way home and collected his horse. He rode out for the S.S.C. and found a large party gathered there. All Mary Anne's crew, the nesters and the Lazy W hands were there, eating a hearty meal, checking their weapons and stuffing boxes of bullets into their pockets. It took Sanger only a few minutes listening to give his approval to the capture of Brarsand although he gave a grave warning about the state the saloon was in.

'They'll take some getting, boy,' he finished.

'I know, but we're going to get them.'

Mary Anne and Molly came over as the men mounted. Waco gripped the girl by the arms and kissed her. 'You stay on here, Rusty gal. We can handle this one without your help.'

Mary Anne nodded with surprising mildness. Waco was expecting violent objections from both girls at being left out of things but they were not raised. Molly kissed Keith, the engagement ring once more on her hand. 'Take care of yourself,' she said.

'I'll do just that.' Keith held her tight to him.

The men mounted and Waco gave his last orders. 'Remember, we'll get all round the place in the dark. Don't start in to shooting until it's light enough to see who you're shooting at. If any of them come out try and rope them. But don't take chances, you're up against trained gunhands. Shoot if you have to and shoot to kill.'

Mary Anne and Molly watched the men riding out and waited until the hooves faded into the distance. They stood side by side and finally Mary Anne spoke. 'Lil brother said we'd got to stay out here out of the way, didn't he?'

'Sure, and Chicago. We wouldn't want to do anything they didn't want us to, now would we?'

'We sure wouldn't.' There was a light in Mary Anne's eyes. 'A woman should always do what the menfolks tell her.'

'Sure.' Molly took a rope from the corral side. She went over to the corral and deftly built a loop, sending it snaking out over the head of a horse. 'Now isn't that strange, I caught a horse.'

Mary Anne was also building up a noose and caught her dun. They worked fast, throwing saddles on the horses. 'I bet Susan Mae's scared to death. We're her friends and should go and comfort her.'

'Why sure,' Molly agreed. 'One must stick to one's friends, mustn't one.'

With this kind thought in mind the girls rode for town, keeping well behind the men, and on reaching it sneaked around the back of the O'Dea place where a handful of pebbles thrown at the window woke Susan Mae O'Dea up. She came down, opened the door and allowed her friends to enter;

they went to her room without waking the rest of the house. Then Molly and Mary Anne told why they were here. Susan Mae offered to let them stay here in her room from where they should have a fair view of the fight.

Unsuspecting that the girls were in town, Waco put his men out around the saloon, moving them in under the cover of darkness and the waiting with the patience of an Indian for the morning. The sun came up, the shadows of the night faded back and in the cold grey light of the dawn Waco called, 'Brarsand! Brarsand. We got your men.'

'So?' Brarsand called back.

'Are you coming out or do we have to come in and get you?'

'Come and get me!' Brarsand was scanning the street. He could not locate any of the attackers.

Red Blaze, Spencer carbine in hand, darted forward to the side of a house and dropped behind the porch along with the two cowhands who were already there. Larry Beaumont grinned at Song. 'They sent us a loader, Song. Hope he don't get in the way.'

Song eased himself up to reply. The side window of the tavern broke and a rifle roared. Song slid down again, a hole through his shoulder. Red's carbine lifted and roared back, then from every side, every window of the tavern, came the thunder of shots. Larry pulled Song to one side and was about to say something when Song yelled, 'Up there!'

Turning, Larry saw a man with a rifle at one of the upper windows of the saloon. The young cowhand whirled fully around with his rifle raising and crashing as fast as he could work the lever. On the fifth shot he saw the man stagger backwards holding his face. 'Got him!' he whooped.

'Throw enough lead at them and some of it's bound to,' Red scoffed, levering another bullet into the chamber of his Spencer, then drawing the side hammer back. He sighted carefully on the lower window and promised he'd make anyone using it sorry. Then he remembered something. 'Watch the upstairs windows, Larry. How's Song?'

'Needs some help. Where's Doc?'

'Him and Waco are up there, between the Wells Fargo office and the store.' Red swung around as he heard someone coming. It was the Reagan brothers, each carrying a Springfield carbine. 'Howdy gents!' Red ducked as a bullet from the lower window narrowly missed his head. 'One of you help Song there?'

'Sure boy,' Seamus Reagan agreed.

'Good!' Red came up fast, his old Spencer roared just as the man at the window appeared for another try.

'Bet you missed,' Song muttered. The pain of his shoulder was intense but he held down any sign of it.

'I ain't you,' Red scoffed. 'His rifle's out there and——'

The rest of the words were cut off by the spat of a bullet near his head and the deep boom of Reagan's Springfield. A hole was in the wood of the porch about three inches in front of Red. He looked down at it then asked. 'What did that?'

'Mice,' Larry answered.

Waco and Doc were in a safe location, by the side of the Wells Fargo office. They knelt there with their rifles and watched Red further along. The saloon was surrounded now and from all sides came the flat crack of rifles and the deeper roar of Colts. The barking of the cowhand Winchester was backed by the deeper roar as Colonel O'Dea cut loose with his double-barrelled Colt rifle, and the heavy boom as Sanger brought his Sharps Old Reliable into the game. Word passed around the town in the night, alerted every citizen and they were all here, fighting along with the cowhands and the nesters against this man who'd tried to take over their town. From the saloon windows rifles, revolvers and shotguns answered the fire of the cowhands. Lead slashed the street and tore through the air, whining ricochets went off and occasionally men were hit.

'Reckon we can get them out, boy?' Doc asked.

'Sure, might take us some time. Depends how they are for food and water.' Waco lined his new rifle at a man who was showing too much of himself. The rifle crashed and the man spun around, out of sight. 'We can't rush them, that's for sure.'

'Yeah, that's for sure. Could try their own game on them if we can find a hay-wagon.'

'We're not that kind,' Waco answered. 'Besides, there is no way we could get one up there. Those guns won't stand by and fight if things go wrong. They'll want out of it.'

In the saloon Brarsand was thinking the same thing. His men were hired guns and they would not stand by him if things were going really bad. He turned to where Della and her girls were hidden behind the bar.

'Della, get those girls out of here. The Texans'll let them go through. You go with them, I've got something for you to do.'

'What?' Della was relieved to be getting out of the saloon for bullets were flying freely inside.

'You'll all go right across to the Wells Fargo office. Take some money with you and slip out the back. Go to the post office, you'll have to go round the back, by the livery barn, and send a message to the sheriff in Hood City. Tell him to come here.'

'What good will that do?' Della ducked as a bullet came through the window and smashed the bar mirror.

'It'll take him two hours at most to get here with a posse. I'll give myself up to him. There's nothing they can prove on me, nothing that a good lawyer can't break for me. I'll let him take me in.'

'Will that help?'

'Sure. That Texas boy, Waco, he'd kill me out of hand, but not if the sheriff's here. That way I'll get a trial, I wouldn't if they got in here.'

Della picked up her bag and opened it. She went behind the bar to take money from out of the cash drawer, then picked up the Remington Double Derringer and placed it on top. She turned and called the girls to her, then nodded to Brarsand.

Waco saw the handkerchief waving at the end of a rifle barrel and poked through the window. He yelled for the other men to stop shooting and as the noise died down went on:

'Giving up, Brarsand?'

'No, sending the girls out. I wouldn't want them killed by

your bullets.'

'Good enough, send ahead!' Waco gave his consent for he did not want any of the women hurt.

The batwing doors opened and the saloon girls came out, one after the other. Waco watched them, suspicious of Brarsand's feelings for the welfare of the girls. They crossed the road and entered the stage office, Della last, closing the door behind her.

'How about you, Brarsand?' Waco called. 'You giving up?'

From the window where the flag of truce came a rifle barked in reply and once more the gunfire shattered the silence of Whittle's streets.

Della Christine ignored the other girls as they clustered at the windows of the office, looking out. She crossed the room and went around the counter, opening the back door and stepping out. All the Wells Fargo people were in the fight and no one challenged her as she walked along behind the houses. She did not know if Brarsand's idea would work but she did know one thing. It was time she changed her affections again. When she'd sent off this message she meant to go back to the office and when the stage came in get on it.

She was walking between the livery barn and the corrals now and would cut between the houses, then to the post office. There she would either bribe or threaten the owner into sending the telegraph message to the sheriff. It was then she was aware that someone was running after her and swung around. Sudden hate welled up inside her. It was that damned Catlan girl.

Mary Anne Catlan and the other girls, Molly and the two O'Dea's were watching the fight from a safe place. The girls wanted to do something to help but none of them had any idea what. They might be able to fetch ammunition if any was needed but that was about all. It was then that Mary Anne saw Della leaving the Wells Fargo office by the back door. Turning without a word to her friends Mary Anne set after the blonde woman for she knew that Della was up to no good. Mary Anne ran along the back street and at the livery barn saw Della turn. There was no time to say anything now. The blonde was opening her bag and Mary Anne knew it was not to look for face powder.

Diving forward Mary Anne locked her arms round Della's waist and staggered her backwards. Della lost her hold of the Derringer and the bag. Her hands drove down, digging into Mary Anne's hair, pulling hard at it. Mary Anne gave a howl, let loose of Della's wrist and was pulled erect. Then Della let loose of the hair and swung a punch which smashed into the girl's cheek. It was a hard punch, harder than Mary Anne had ever felt. She crashed into the corral fence and saw Della, face contorted with hate, hurling at her.

They met like two enraged wildcats, tearing at hair, kicking, swing wild punches, oblivious of everything but their hate for each other. Della fought with the savage skill gained in many a bar-room brawl and Mary Anne fought back with the strength of a wild tomboy. They tripped and went rolling on the floor. Neither could gain the upper hand for long enough to make use of it. Della's dress, not meant to stand up to this kind of treatment, split at the seams and was torn off as they thrashed over and over but she gave it no thought. Mary Anne was luckier; she was still wearing her shirtwaist and jeans, and high-heeled riding boots on her feet.

Rolling apart, gasping for breath, they came to their feet. Mary Anne's shirtwaist was torn open, blood trickled from her nose and her left eye was swelling but she flung herself at Della without any hesitation. They tangled again in a wild, kicking mêlée and reeled back. Mary Anne yelled as she was pushed into the water-trough, her head forced under the water. Della leaned on the girl, holding her head down, feeling her struggles.

Mary Anne fought for breath. She brought her legs up around Della's waist and crossed her ankles, then tightened. The girl's legs were powerful, toughened by hours of riding, even in her eastern school. Della gasped as the crushing clamped on her. She fought to hold Mary Anne's head under the water but the power of those legs made her relax. Mary Anne forced herself up slightly then was pushed down, her hands trying desperately to tear away Della's grip. It was then she remembered that the water-trough had a plug in the bottom to allow it to drain. Letting loose of Della's hands, lungs bursting, Mary Anne felt for the plug and finally got it in her hand. She pulled hard, the plug came free and the water started to rush out. Mary Anne gasped in the air. Della screamed as the spur on Mary Anne's boot caught her. Her grip relaxed on the girl's throat and Mary Anne got both feet under Della's body, then shoved.

Staggering back Della tripped and sat down. Weakly, Mary Anne rolled herself from the water-trough and clung to it gasping for breath. For a moment they stayed like it, then Della rolled over and grabbed for her bag. Mary Anne did not hesitate. She flung herself forward, landing on the other woman and grabbing her wrist, holding the hand from the bag. Della fought back. Neither was screaming now; they were too short of breath for that. Coming up they staggered dazedly then Mary Anne caught Della a haymaker which rocked the blonde backwards. Della hit the corral rail and slid down to her knees, the bag just under her head. She looked down, then realised what it was. Weakly she reached inside, the Derringer came out and she started to lift it.

Mary Anne was almost exhausted but her pain-drugged mind was still working well enough to warn her of her danger. She staggered forward even as the sobbing Della started to raise her weapon. In a desperate move Mary Anne lashed up with her foot, the toe of the riding boot catching Della under the chin. Back snapped her head. She rocked over and hit the corral rail, the Derringer falling from her hand. She hung there for an instant then slid sideways. Mary Anne dropped forward and gripped Della's tangled, dirty blonde hair to smash her head into the corral rail. She did not know what she was doing. It meant nothing to Mary Anne that Della was unconscious.

'Rusty, stop it!' The voice seemed to be coming from a long way off. 'Rusty, stop it. You'll kill her.'

Hands were gripping Mary Anne. She tried to strain against them but she was too exhausted and allowed her three friends to pull her away from the limp, unconscious woman. She slumped down sobbing as the reaction set in. Molly snapped an order to the O'Dea girls to get a bucket of water.

It was some minutes before Mary Anne was able to take notice of what was happening. Then she sat on the water-trough and gasped in air while the other three worked on Della. The blonde was conscious and sat with her back to the corral. There was fear in her eyes. Mary Anne forced her aching body up and went forward.

'Don't let her touch me!' Della screamed. 'Keep her away from me.'

'All right,' Mary Anne looked down at the sobbing blonde. 'I want some answers and I want them now. What is it all about?'

The scared Della talked; told how Brarsand learned of the branch line of the railroad. She'd met him in a Kansas cattle-town and they'd come down here. It was Brarsand who'd killed Mary Anne's father, then found out too late about Mary Anne being in school. He'd been to Chicago to sound out the chances of Molly selling her place out. When he learned she would not he'd located Della's old boy friend, Doc Pilsener, who'd forged the letter telling Colonel O'Dea to sell. The idea was just as Waco figured it, to cut off the headwater of the Ranse River and break the nesters. When this failed he sent his men to stir up trouble between the S.S.C. and the nesters.

Mary Anne, aching in every fibre of her body, could still feel admiration for her little brother and the way he'd worked all this out himself. Then she looked down at Della. 'What were you doing back here?'

Della licked her bloody lips and gasped, 'Running out. I've done with Carl.'

'Running out, huh?' Mary Anne looked around and realised the direction Della had been headed. It was then she proved that not only her little brother could think things out. 'All right, girlie. What did you want at the post office?'

Della tried desperately to bluff. 'Post office?'

Mary Anne clenched her fists and snapped, 'Stand her up, girls.'

Molly and the O'Dea girls started to drag Della to her feet

but the blonde had taken enough punishment for one day. 'Don't hit me! I'll tell you. I was sending for the sheriff. Carl's willing to give himself up to the sheriff.'

'Why?' Mary Anne relaxed, bent and picked up the bag, opening it wide and removing the money, then the key which was underneath.

'His men want to quit. They'll hang on until the sheriff comes, but no longer.'

'Where's this key belong?'

'The back door of the saloon,' Della whimpered. 'Do not hurt me any more. Leave me alone!'

This last came in a scream as Mary Anne reached for Della. 'Get back down there.' Pulling the ripped shirtwaist into some semblance of order and modesty Mary Anne gave Della a shove. 'The boy'll want to know what you just told me.'

CHAPTER FOURTEEN

WACO PAYS HIS DEBT

'HEY, boy!'

Waco twisted around at the words, his eyes taking in Mary Anne's dirty, bruised and dishevelled appearance. 'What're you doing here?' he asked grimly. 'I thought I told you to stay at the ranch.'

'Yeah?' Mary Anne answered, bristling. 'Well, it's a good thing we didn't.' She jerked a thumb over her shoulder and indicated the even more bruised, battered and half-naked Della. 'She was going to send a telegraph message for the sheriff. I caught her.'

'Sure looks like you did, Rusty gal.' Waco grinned at the girl. 'I should have known better then try and stop you coming in. What's it all about?'

'Brarsand's the one we want. Della told us all about it.'

'Looks that way. What'd she say?' Waco asked.

'Brarsand's men want out. They're only sticking because they think the sheriff'll be coming to get them out.' Mary Anne glanced at the saloon. 'Reckon they'll not be sticking at all if they know Della didn't make it.'

Waco agreed with this. The men in the saloon, faced with a long drawn battle with the townspeople, would want to be out of it. Some of them just might stick but the majority would come out of Della's Tavern like weasel-chased rabbits. He did not know what the girl was thinking of doing and would have stopped her if he'd guessed. Before he could say or do anything Mary Anne pushed Della out into the street in front of her. 'Walk!' she snapped. 'Right in front of the saloon.'

Della staggered forward at Mary Anne's push, stumbling

blindly along. The firing died down for the men would not risk shooting a woman. Waco drew in his breath; he watched Mary Anne shoving Della along, making for the jail. Red Blaze also saw and darted across the street, around the back of the Wells Fargo office and came up to Waco. 'What the hell?' he asked.

'They'll be coming out any time now,' Waco answered. 'Get set.'

The two girls were just past the saloon when the batwing doors were flung open and a man erupted, gun out. He raced forward but went down under a hail of lead. Then more men came out, some came shooting and were cut down by the attackers, others threw aside their weapons and ran across the street to be taken in charge by the men who gathered.

Time dragged by slowly and the saloon was silent. Waco called, 'Brarsand, come out!'

If Brarsand expected to make Waco rush blindly in he failed badly for the youngster was no fool. Turning to one of the men who'd come out he asked, 'How many stayed on with him?'

'Talbot and one more, they're in the front.'

Waco handed Keith his rifle and checked over his Colts. Red and Doc were watching him and Molly took the key Mary Anne relieved Della of. 'This's the key to the back door. Rusty gave it to me.'

'Give me your hat, boy,' Red ordered. 'I'll move out so he can see it and keep them watching the front. You go around the back. We'll give you five minutes.'

Waco handed Red his stetson and Red laid his own on the sidewalk and pulled the black hat on. He stepped forward and Waco called, 'I'll give you five minutes, Brarsand, then I'm coming in after you.'

Saying this he turned and moved back, then bending low so that he could not be seen he darted across the street and between the two buildings. There were no windows on the bar side here and only one door which Waco guessed would be locked. He wondered where Brarsand's two remaining men were. One would be upstairs most likely, probably on this side and covering the street. By hugging the wall Waco should be able to keep out of sight. He reached the end of the building and moved along keeping flat. The back room was empty except for a man who lay still on the floor. Waco saw that through the broken window as he went by to the door. He inserted the key, standing to one side and turning it slowly. The gun came into his right hand as the lock clicked and he gently eased the door open. There was no sound from the room, no shot, no alarm. Drawing his second gun Waco went in fast but in silence and halted just inside with guns ready.

The man on the floor was dead, shot by a heavy rifle. Waco turned and waved back the men who came from the houses behind the saloon and ran forward to help him. This was a personal matter now. Brarsand was the man who killed Sunshine Sam Catlan and tried to ruin the S.S.C. or scare Mary Anne from her home. Brarsand was Waco's meat, the man he'd ridden from the O.D. Connected to find.

Crossing the room on silent feet Waco holstered his left-hand gun once more and gripped the knob of the door leading into the bar-room. This was the time of danger. If the door was locked he would be forced to kick it open and alert them, but it would do no good to hesitate now. He twisted the knob and pushed the door slowly.

Brarsand was standing with his back to Waco, looking at the batwing doors and lining his revolver ready to shoot down the first man through. Waco was about to lunge forward when he saw the bar mirror's reflected view of the room. Apart from a man who lay by a broken window he could see no one. The stairs leading to the first floor and the balcony were deserted, yet at least one man should be there.

It was then Waco detected a movement, caught it reflected in the mirror. Talbot was crouching behind the bar, ten-gauge shotgun in his hands, ready to turn loose the murderous charge when the batwing doors burst open. Then Waco saw the black hat moving, accompanied by another, white hat. Red and Doc were moving in and he must take a hand.

'Brarsand!'

Waco yelled the word and flung himself forward. The big

man started to turn, his gun coming up. Waco's right-hand Colt crashed, throwing lead into the bar, shooting as fast as he could thumb the hammer. There was a roar from the shotgun as Talbot stiffened up into view then went down again.

Brarsand came round. He was fast but not fast enough. The revolver in his hand roared, flame licking at Waco as the young man flung himself to one side. Even as he went down Waco was shooting, his left-hand Colt thundering. Brarsand rocked on his heels, his gun crashed once more tearing a furrow in the floor by Waco, then the youngster rolled right over and fired as he landed on his stomach. A hole appeared between Brarsand's eyes, the big man going backwards, his gun flying from his hand. The thud of his body hitting the floor was echoed by the crash as Red and Doc burst through the batwing doors.

A man came into view, leaping from a side room to the balcony at the head of the stairs, his gun slanting down. Doc Leroy brought up his Colt fast, firing almost without aiming it seemed. The man was flung backwards by the impact of the shot. He crashed into the wall and slid down, the gun dropping from his hand.

Silence fell and the smoke of the burnt powder slowly dispersed. Waco got to his feet, walking to the man who'd killed his adopted father. He bent down and picked up the revolver, noting the awkward-looking butt and the cylinder which was slightly shorter than that of a Colt. He turned to hand the gun to Red. 'Take this for Ole Devil. He doesn't have a Webley R.I.C. in his collection.'

'He's the one, is he?' Red asked.

'Sure's he's the one. We'll let Ed Ballinger know we got the man who killed Doc Pilsener.'

'How about you, boy?' Doc inquired, for their business here was done now and the O.D. Connected might need them again.

'Reckon old Rusty gal can handle things here herself. Her and Larry between them,' Waco replied and grinned. 'Sure be good to see Dusty, Mark and Lon again.'

The three young men walked towards the door of the saloon

as men came crowding in. Waco stepped out and looked to where Larry Beaumont was talking to Mary Anne and hanging a blanket around her shoulders. The youngster smiled. Mary Anne would be all right. She wouldn't need him here now. He'd paid his debt to Sunshine Sam Catlan.

THE END